JOHN BARBER

SAN FRANCISCO

JOHN BARBER, A TALE OF TWO TIMES
BOOK 2

JAMES BARRETT GRUBBS

John Barber: San Francisco

Copyright © 2025 by James Barrett Grubbs

All rights reserved.

Written and Edited by Humans:

Theodora Bryant, Authors' HQ, Developmental Editor and Copy Editor

Book Cover by AuthorsHQ.com

Paperback ISBN: 979-8-9893022-9-1

Ebook ISBN: 979-8-9911938-0-1

Dedicated to
Barrett, Katherine, Monica

DAY 1

2222

ONE

The early-morning sky was clear and bright. John Barber opened his transportation pod's driver-side hatch door to feel and smell the crisp mountain air. He didn't know what to do— scream out in joy, or cry. He had just defied Death for the second time since 2037

He was parked at the base of New Mexico's Lookout Mountain. The view out the windshield was filled with a forest of ponderosa pines and Douglas firs. Several small, smoldering brush fires billowed gray smoke into the air from where the SS warships had crashed.

John leaned back and pressed his broad shoulders against the air-cooled seat, letting the adrenaline from his desperate fight and escape begin to subside. He thought of the violent battle he had just waged against a cyborg and its master computer.

He glanced down at his right hand; his knuckles were red and bloody.

I lived and behind me there is a soulless assassin tied to a chair in my destroyed home. Destroyed because of him.

He took a short breath, forcing himself to relax.

The faux-god is helpless and is no longer capable of killing me.

"I lived! *I* lived! I *lived!*"

He sighed. "I should have killed him."

He reached into his jeans' right pocket and removed a round, fist-sized, glass-encased crystal computer he'd named after his wife, Megan. He stuck it to the dashboard alongside a tattered Caltech baseball cap. Seeing the relic cap always made him happy; it reminded him of a fully loving past life.

It was Megan the crystal—along with his mementos and holograms of his family—that had kept him sane during the years of his chosen exile in the future.

He glanced again at the crystal computer and thought, *Amazing how that little machine saved my life... and protected me for the last seventy-two years.* He looked at the cap, then the crystal, and thought, *It's as much a relic as that hat, the last private crystal from way back in twenty-one fifty.* He snorted in disgust. *And all the rest were confiscated in twenty-one sixty, by the World Family's emissaries.*

"Yeah, right. World Family." He laughed. "Build one synthetic deity in San Francisco, name it the World Crystal and create a family."

He reached out and picked up the room-temperature crystal —long ago known as a computer—off the dash. He turned it around in his hand, marveling at its simplicity and beauty.

"You're the only one left," he said, talking to it like it was alive, "with sextillion Bibles of data, powered by a fingernail-sized fusion battery, and only your size limits your abilities."

He shook his head. *Thank God they never found you.*

"Thank you, Megan, for saving my life and keeping me sane all this time," he whispered.

"You're welcome," it answered in the voice of his wife.

He smiled, still marveling as he held it in the palm of his hand. How something so small with the power of 41.75 terabytes could say "Thank you" as sweetly as the long-ago love of his life.

He looked to his left out of the driver's-side window, along the valley basin that faced his mountain hideaway, and sighed.

"Megan, open John Barber, add final chapter," he said. His words appeared across the windshield seeming to float over the dash: OPEN JOHN BARBER: FINAL CHAPTER.

He took another calming breath and rubbed his right hand through his thick, dark hair, a lifelong habit.

Where do I start? he thought, feeling a sense of resolve.

He again turned his head and looked toward the valley horizon and started to dictate.

"For the past one hundred eighty-five years, I have protected my secret formula to lower my age at will, and stay hidden among humanity. An unaltered twentieth-century man. It took a miracle and a sleight-of-hand trick to escape Death. My only advantage against my cyborg enemy was its human arrogance. It should have killed me on sight; instead, it felt compelled to gloat, a primal human emotion that saved me and humanity.

"I have lived in a soulless world filled with androids, and armed Security Servers—ha! 'The S.S.'—military machines, and hubots, a name I came up with for people who were once human and chose to become living machines."

He paused, thinking, *How much should I record about how it started?*

"In the late twenty-first century, every grade school child's brain, except for those who were unwanted or disabled, was implanted with a K chip—K for kindergarten—on their fifth birthday. That implant linked them to a colossal, self-aware databank known at first as the Master Crystal of the West, but would eventually become the World Crystal and span the globe, if not the universe.

"The K chip was to end the unfairness of natural intelligence and make humanity equal. The result was emotionally stunted reactive creatures, unable to develop institutional memories, create art, or to love, and everyone ended up subjugated slaves of the World Crystal.

"I am the last fully and only human linked to the past. An unaltered, genetically pure man. I am the missing link they just now failed to kill."

Determination pressed his strong, proportioned lips together. *No more hiding.*

"I can leave now. I'm finally free to return to California and help rebuild the human race."

He climbed out of the pod and turned to look at the mountain that had protected him through humanity's greatest holocausts: the two world wars since he'd leaped into the future, the last ending in 2122. It also housed all the cherished memories that had kept him from killing himself for nearly two hundred years.

His mountain fortress had been a respite, a haven from persecution and death. He lifted his head and looked up at the top of the mountain and saw gray smoke billowing into the sky. His home was gone. A chill shook his shoulders. He returned to the pod and sat behind the control panel, feeling a great loss.

"What comes next?" he asked himself. "Megan, can I use the World Crystal's time machine and return to the year twenty thirty-seven?"

"No, due to the Butterfly Effect."

"Remind me."

"You kill a mosquito that was destined to distract a person who was to cause an accident that was to kill someone. The insignificant event of killing the mosquito could destroy the future. You can only use the machine to go forward in time."

"I've seen enough of the future. What if I bring someone from the past here?"

"You can only do that at the last instant of their life."

He leaned back in the seat, thinking, *My wife, the two girls, or my best friend, Ty. Who should be first and where should we go?*

"Megan, list the largest, most viable U.S. cities."

"San Francisco, Sacramento, Seattle, Denver, Chicago, Washington D.C., New York, and Miami."

"What resources are available in those cities?"

"Infrastructure includes power, food, water, waste, and air-conditioning. Governmental services. Historical buildings. Public and private housing, medical facilities, education institutions, financial depositories, and limited hospitality."

"What about secondary cities?"

"You want me to list all ten thousand viable U.S. secondary cities?"

"No."

"The same as the major cities but on a more limited scale."

"What determined the development of the cities?"

"Population."

"What about small towns?"

"Depends on historical significance and population. Some cities and towns were disassembled due to nonuse. The land was converted to its natural state and abandoned."

"Was that done worldwide?"

"Yes."

John sighed, reminded of the three years during and after the second war when he was locked down within his mountain fortress and cut off from the destruction.

"What happened to the dead?" he asked.

"The World Crystal directed the androids to collect those who died in the initial attack, cremate their bodies, and spread the ashes over the land. The survivors were relocated to survival camps until the city's infrastructures were rebuilt. The Untouchables were left to survive on their own."

"Who were they?"

"The Indigenous and destitute."

He closed his eyes. *Ethnocentrism from the beginning in its coding,* he thought, disgusted.

"Megan, take me to the top of the mountain. I want to see what's left," he whispered.

The pod lifted off the ground, and he leaned back and watched the mountainside fall away as the pod rose the thousand feet to the crest.

The pod reached the top of the mountain and stopped. He looked out the windshield and saw the summit had been replaced by a five-hundred-foot-deep volcanic crater. He squeezed his hands into tight fists, inhaled a deep breath, and blew the air out between tight lips. His eyes filled with tears.

"It's all gone," he whispered.

Seeing what he already knew did not soften the sight. He felt hot rage rush to his face; his life's memories flashed to everything he'd lost. The holograms of his two children's first birthdays, and his first kiss with Megan. His jaw twitched as he clenched his teeth together.

"Megan, set a course for the Crystal Plaza, Hays Street, San Francisco; land across the street from the plaza. Set speed at a thousand miles per hour," he instructed, his tone clearly angry.

The pod turned away from the mountain and headed west.

"Why San Francisco?" Megan asked. "You need help, and the time machine is in Palo Alto."

"Their time machine, if it really works, will be there when I'm done. I need to visit the World Crystal first to confirm its control on humanity is over."

"The liquid crystal program you inserted into the head of its cybergeist agent this morning was successful. Captain Davis and the World Crystal can no longer harm you or me or control humanity. But you're going there to destroy it, aren't you?"

"Yes."

"You'll be killing the only thing humanity has for a guide to live normal lives."

"So?"

"So, that isn't you. What's the point of giving humanity freedom if you then just let it die?"

"They'll figure out how to live."

"How? What do you know about the people you just emancipated from the bondage they didn't know they were in?"

"I know they have no feelings, institutional memory, or context for existence."

"False. They have feelings, they form bonds, have relationships, feel loss. They know things, and they do remember specific things needed for their lives. It may be primitive by your standards, but the World Crystal allowed them to keep that part of human nature. It allowed them to want companionship and miss people who were living far away."

"Megan, I *am* going to destroy that machine."

"To do that, you are going to need help from the same people who will suffer by that action."

"I did not program you to argue."

"No, you programmed me to emulate Megan."

John rubbed his hand through his hair, rage still leading his emotions.

An hour later, Megan landed the pod alongside the curb on Hays Street in downtown San Francisco, across from the United Nations Crystal Center Plaza's ten-story office building.

John looked to his left out the driver's side window and saw a one-sided battle raging on the plaza square.

It was a massacre. Humans were charging toward the building and died the moment they reached the plaza's halfway point. He watched in silence as two small groups of people raced forward and burst into flames. He was shocked. He watched another couple run pell-mell into the same fate.

"Oh my God, *I* caused this," he said.

He opened the pod's hatch, stepped out, the solitude and calm he'd managed to obtain from the flight evaporating instantly when the sounds of screaming, rage-filled voices echoed past him. He cringed when he inhaled the scent of burned clothing and human flesh.

"You ugly monsters!" a female voice shrieked, followed by a gasp as her chest burst into flames and she collapsed onto the polished Carrara marble surface.

The disadvantage was stark: The fully armored SS machines had infrared-infused, Neodymium-doped laser rifles and acetylene pistols, and with a glance, they could transmit invisible heat rays. The humans had clubs, sticks, rocks, and anger.

John leaned against the pod driver's side and watched the

carnage, thinking, *This is surreal—suicidal.* He winced with each death. He took a breath, thinking, *I've got to do something to stop this.*

He watched several more futile attempts to attack the SS machines guarding the entrance to the World Crystal's sanctuary.

"They're so brave," he said, astonished.

He had transmitted his life history into the consciousness of every human in the galaxy early that morning. They had also learned the truth about the World Crystal's betrayal in that story: its contrived holocaust against humanity and its erasure of love and free will from every person.

Their liberation had started with his capture of Captain Robert A. Davis, the World Crystal's symbiotic tool, in his New Mexico mountain hideout. He had tricked Davis into standing on a trapdoor, and together they'd dropped one thousand feet through the mountain, landing in a secure bunker. After a brutal fistfight, he'd tied the unconscious Davis tightly to an antique wooden chair, then downloaded reprogramming instructions into both Davis's head and the World Crystal's databank. That momentous trick had freed humanity from mental slavery and, most importantly, had prevented the World Crystal from killing him and invading Megan—which would have been an unthinkable disaster.

But right now, that wasn't so important: They didn't understand that he, John Barber, had shut off the brain implant, the K chip. The new, never-before silence inside their collective heads was terrifying. For the first time in their lives, their questions were going unanswered and instructions for daily life missing, and they felt alone, and they were acting out on impulse. John's story had lit the fire that set them free; until that moment, people around the galaxy had known everything, understood nothing, and were being led into extinction.

The people were helpless, though. They had no idea how to fight, let alone defeat the SS machines. They literally did *not* know, so it didn't stop them from charging again and again, with each wave meeting the same disappointment: Death.

John looked across the plaza and saw ten seven-foot-tall SS machines standing at the World Crystal building's main entrance, facing out toward the plaza. Their view of the half-city-block-sized, marble-covered plaza was only obstructed by a thirty-meter-wide oval fountain—and the growing pile of bodies —in the center of the plaza.

There were no outward signs of violence or actions coming from the SS machines. They stood shoulder-to-shoulder, arms and hands at their sides, their heads slowly turning from side to side as they scanned the attacking mob with dark, lifeless orbs for eyes. The only indication of violence were bodies collapsing to the ground, followed by small circles of white smoke wafting into the air from their charred clothing.

The battle stopped abruptly, and an eerie quiet enveloped the plaza. Two small groups of people joined together in the street, flinging their arms in the air, gesturing with emotional animation, pointing toward the SS machines. After a moment, the groups split up; five people ran toward the fountain, the other five directly at the SS machines... and both groups joined the growing pile of bodies.

This won't end until they're all dead, John thought.

TWO

John turned, reached into the pod, and removed the crystal computer off the dash. He put it in his jeans' pocket, then felt inside his right ear to make sure the hearing device that linked him and Megan hadn't been damaged in his fight with Davis.

"Megan, shut down the pod's gravitational drive and close the hatch."

"What are you doing?"

"You were right: I've got to help them. I caused this mess. But I can't take the chance that my program didn't perform perfectly and one of those S.S. machines ends up trying to kill me."

"What are you going to do?"

"What you said I need to do: Ask for help."

He looked around the street and spotted five humans cowering behind a white pod parked adjacent to the plaza. They looked terrified pressed against the side of the pod, their eyes wide and filled with fear, but their hands were clenched in fists, lips pressed together, and jaws flexing with rage.

"They'll do," he said to himself and walked quickly across the street to the group.

One of the women hiding behind the pod looked up at the thin, six-foot-tall man, wearing a white crewneck shirt, blue jeans, and leather cowboy boots, walking toward them. "What's that guy doing? He's just asking to be killed," she said to no one in particular.

John stopped several feet away from the pod. "Hello. May I help you destroy those machines?" He pointed toward the plaza building.

They looked at him with shocked expressions, mixed with confusion.

"You know how?" one of the thirty-year-old-looking women asked.

The others just stared with bewilderment.

"Yes, I do." He smiled at her. "Will you help me?"

"Yes."

"Please go over there"—he pointed at his pod parked across the street facing the plaza—"and get the power pack from the back seat. It's covered by a gray blanket. Please keep it covered by the blanket and bring it here."

She nodded, stood, ran to his pod, opened the driver's hatch, leaned in, picked up the blanket-covered energy pack, and ran back, carrying it in both arms. She handed it to John, who placed it on the ground in front of them.

"Okay. Next, I need someone to ram a pod into that fountain." He pointed at it.

"I know how to drive; I can do that," the same woman said. "My pod is just down the street."

"Perfect. Drive it here and stop."

She ran down the street and several minutes later returned in a red pod, parking on the street next to John. She opened the driver's hatch, climbed out, and looked expectantly at him.

He picked up the battery pack, making sure it was covered by the blanket, and put it on the front passenger seat of her pod. Finished, he smiled at the woman. "Now I need you to drive backward onto the plaza toward the fountain. Don't face the S.S. machines or they'll kill you. Continue driving backward until the rear of the pod is pointing at the S.S. machines. At that moment, stop the pod and put it into forward. Then look at me. When I wave my hand, crash your pod into the fountain base. You might have to do that several times before it cracks and water starts pouring out on the plaza. Understand?"

"Yes."

"When the water starts gushing out, look at me. When I raise my hand, drive fast inside the fountain basin, open the passenger hatch, and toss the covered power pack into the water."

"I can do that," she said confidently, obviously excited by the job.

"Good. What I'm about to tell you is critical: Do exactly as I say, or you'll die." He focused his dark-brown eyes somberly on hers.

"I understand."

He touched her shoulder. "Do *not* look up or leave the pod until I come get you." He smiled. "Understand?"

"Yes. Don't look up, don't let them see what I'm doing, and don't move when it's done."

"Perfect," he said with a slight laugh.

She got into her pod and started to leave.

John tapped the pod with his hand.

She opened the hatch.

"Before you go, what's your name?" he asked.

"Terry Cheer," she said with a full smile.

He returned the smile. "Good luck, Terry Cheer."

She drove away and backed up the plaza stairs and followed John's directions.

"Why is she doing that?" someone asked.

"Electricity and water don't mix," John replied.

Terry parked and looked at John.

The SS machines did not react.

John studied Terry: She didn't seem afraid; she actually still appeared excited.

John waved his hand, and a moment later, an explosion of cracking cement and rock broke the surreal calm when her pod crashed into the fountain's sidewall. The wall collapsed around her pod and water gushed out, covering the plaza square and the building's entrance. The SS machines paid no attention to Terry's pod or the water flowing past their feet.

Terry, meanwhile, opened the passenger hatch and, keeping the blanket around the power pack, tossed it into the fountain.

Instantly, the SS machines began to shake, and a high-pitched whistling sound of fizzing circuits broke the silence. Time seemed to stop; the moment was frozen. The ten SS machines did not waver or twist about. They stood erect, unmoving, until the middle robot abruptly dropped to the ground, followed by the others.

"W-w-what just happened?" asked a man standing next to John.

"Fusion. Water conducts electricity, and androids don't do well with a shock," John answered.

Other sounds of shock filled the air, along with a flurry of questions from the crowd hiding around the plaza:

"They're dead? Are they dead?" a man shouted, his voice a mixture of fear and wonder.

John looked at him. "They were never alive, young man. They're now permanently broken."

"What's next?" a woman shouted. "What's next?"

"We wait."

"For what?" she asked.

"The water to drain away."

John glanced at his watch: 10:15 a.m.

"Who are you?" asked the excited young man at John's elbow. "What's your name?"

"John Barber."

The man's mouth opened, and his eyebrows lifted. "You're the John Barber who's wanted for murder? The John Barber who told us about the World Crystal's crimes and lies?"

"Yes," John answered, sounding confident.

"What do you want?" the man asked, looking scared.

"To destroy what's hidden in there"—he pointed toward the Crystal Plaza building—"and bring my best friend here."

Thirty minutes later, with the water gone, John walked up the marble steps, crossed the plaza to the fountain, and stopped at Terry's red pod. He tapped his right hand on the driver's side hatch, it opened, then he bent down and looked inside. Terry was lying on her stomach across the front two seats, her hands pressed together, covering her head.

"Nice job, Terry Cheer. You can get out now," he said, grinning.

She lifted herself up and turned to face him. "Whoa, that was ugly. Did it work?"

"Yes." John turned and started to walk to the entrance of the building.

Now standing by the pod, Terry shouted, "Where are you going?"

"Inside there." He pointed at the building.

"What about the Security Service machines?"

John stopped and turned around to face her. "They're broken, and there aren't any other machines inside." He smiled.

How does he know that? she wondered. "How do you know?"

"It's the law. S.S. machines and humans are forbidden inside. Only androids and hubots are allowed inside."

What's welcomed? Terry thought.

John turned and continued to walk toward the entrance. Terry and several hundred people followed after him, all the while whispering about what had just happened and who the man leading them was.

John stopped in front of the middle SS robot, reached down, and removed a laser pistol and rifle from its uniform.

"Stop!" Terry shouted.

John turned to look at her.

"Is it true you're John Barber?"

"Yes."

"It was your story, wasn't it, and it was you who broke the... the... thing in my head? The K chip?"

"Yes."

"Now you're leaving us alone," she said with a look of panic.

John didn't answer, and not knowing what to say, he turned away and started to enter the building.

"Stop!" she demanded again in a deeper, louder voice.

John again turned to face her. "I have to do this alone. It's too dangerous for you."

"I remember more: It was you who told us the truth about the past. You're the one who lives forever and killed that Doctor

Gysin who was trying to kill you, and you ran away to the future."

John couldn't stop the immediate memory of that night flooding his memory. The madman male Gysin twin in John's own house, threatening his daughter with a gun, with Gysin claiming he'd kill her if John didn't release the code for eternal life immediately. The fight and struggle they had, Gysin shooting Megan when she innocently, unknowingly entered the room, their daughter screaming, John himself screaming, Gysin shouting and then the boom of Ty Leggett's gunshot that killed Gysin—

"Yes," John finally replied, "and you knowing that doesn't change what I need to do next."

"Yes, it does. You caused this? You must stay with us."

John studied her face and could feel her fear. He heard Megan's voice in his mind. His eyes bounced across the faces of the people standing behind Terry: Everyone had the same panicked look.

"Let us follow you," she said. "Maybe there's something inside that can fill the emptiness in our heads."

"You know how to use that?" John pointed to the laser pistol in the SS robot's holster.

"No."

"Pick it up," he said in a calm voice.

She walked to the inert SS robot, bent down, and pulled the pistol free from its holster. She stood up, then turned around to face John.

"Put your hand around the back end." He indicated where. "Do not point it at anyone or anything until I tell you."

"Okay, now what?" she asked.

John took several steps toward the fountain. "Okay, every-one, step aside and make an aisle." He looked back at Terry.

"Come here, point at the fountainhead, and *think* to yourself, *Shoot.*"

Terry stepped in front of John and pointed the gun. *Zzzppnt!* The top of the fountainhead exploded in a flash of hot gas and flames.

People gasped; some screamed and dropped to the ground.

"It's so powerful no one would live," Terry whispered.

"And a rifle is ten times more powerful than a pistol. It will disintegrate whatever it's pointed at."

Terry and the crowd stepped back, looking frightened.

"It's okay, Terry Cheer, you can come with me," John said.

"Can I join you, too?" asked a man standing next to Terry.

"Who are you?" Terry asked, stepping to John's side and looking at the man.

"Arnold Blackman."

John looked at him for a moment, thinking, *What does he offer?* "What did you do yesterday to earn your wealth credits?"

"Nothing. I was scheduled to visit my family on the moon next month, so I wasn't given anything to do."

"Before that?" John asked.

"I worked for the World Family as a travel facilitator for people moving off-planet." He pointed across the plaza toward Van Ness Street and a hundred-story building, "Over there."

John continued to study Arnold's face. *I guess he'll do.* "Okay, Arnold, pick up all the other weapons, except for one pistol, and pile them there." He pointed at a spot next to the fountain.

Arnold bent down, grabbed a pistol, and handed it to Terry. He picked up the other weapons and carried them to the spot in front of the fountain where the water had gushed out.

"Arnold, come back here." John took the pistol from Terry and handed it to Arnold. "Aim it at the pile of guns."

"What are you doing?" someone shouted. "We need those weapons to protect ourselves."

"From what?" John shouted back.

No one had an answer.

"Okay, Arnold, point, think *Shoot*, then squeeze."

Zzzppnt! The weapons burst into a gas cloud of fire and melted into a pool of black goo.

John looked at the growing mob of people. "The rest of you, wait here if you want; we'll come get you when it's safe to go inside." He put a stern expression on his face and shot his rifle into the air. *Zzzppnt!* "If you enter this building without me, you'll die," he shouted. As he turned to face Terry and Arnold, he said, "Megan, deliver my pod to me."

They watched as his white pod lifted off the street and crossed the plaza, stopping next to them.

"Ready?" John asked Terry and Arnold.

They nodded.

John turned and walked to the entrance with the two following closely behind. He stopped within a foot of the ten-foot-wide glass doorway, but hesitated before reaching out to touch the door. He turned to face them. "The World Crystal will use any opportunity to kill you. Do not leave my side and do exactly as I say, or you will die." He studied their frightened faces, making sure they understood.

He turned back to the door and touched the glass with the palm of his right hand, and the three-inch-thick door opened without a sound. Cool, stale air rushed past.

Terry shivered, and her shoulders shook.

They stepped into the most secure building in the known universe. Once all three were inside, John touched the glass again, and it closed behind them. He stepped back and leaned against it, then looked around the twenty-thousand-square-foot room.

Terry and Arnold gasped as they, too, looked around the beautiful, sparkling room. Hundreds of bald-headed, pale-faced androids were scattered randomly around the lobby, each wearing a lifeless expression, spotless gray tunics, and white boots.

Nothing was moving; all were frozen in different configurations of movement. Time had stopped for them, just hours ago, at the moment John had downloaded the history of mankind into the minds of every person in the galaxy.

"Could they suddenly wake up and kill us?" Terry asked, her voice shaky.

"That's a tricky question; along with everything you saw in my download of Earth's history, I included a special program that prevents any agent of the World Crystal from killing me. For you, the simple answer is stay close to me. The androids, as you know, can't hurt humans. It's the hubots you need to worry about."

"The what?" she asked.

He pointed across the room. "You see that thing with hair on its head standing by itself?" Terry nodded. "That's a hubot and they can attack you." John looked around the room again. "The more complex questions are how to find the World Crystal's temporal dimension distortion device, make it work, and then turn off the World Crystal." He smiled at Terry.

"I have no idea what you just said. But if you want it, I'm in," she said.

John smiled again. "Now for reaching my goals: I know the World Crystal is housed in a secure top-floor room. Getting there will be difficult. All the paths to the tenth floor, the stairs and lifts, etcetera, will be laced with murderous traps for the two of you unless we've been invited."

John walked to the hubot standing in the center of the room. Terry and Arnold followed, almost grabbing hold of him, their heads turning from side to side, searching for any movement with each step. Their fear was palpable.

"What are you doing?" Terry asked.

"Hubots aren't supposed to be here."

THREE

"Why does it look so different from the androids?" Terry asked.

"It's only part machine, whereas the bald-headed androids are all machine-made to look human. Hubots are the result of a human willfully transforming himself or herself into a living machine."

"Is it alive?" she asked.

"Not really."

"Can it die?"

"Yes, and it knows it."

"Why would anyone want to look like that? Her body has a strange shape, there's metal holding up her head and covering parts of their arms and legs. Her eyes sparkle and her face and skin look fake—too perfect. What happened to her?"

"She wanted to stay young and live forever."

"Like you?"

John took a deep breath, thinking, *So many questions.* A frustrated expression crossed his face. "Not like me. It's more machine than human, and I'm one hundred percent human."

"That thing looks ugly."

John took several more steps and stood directly in front of the human machine. "Let me talk to the World Crystal."

There was no immediate response. Then, suddenly, the hubot's black eyes came to life and focused on John's face. Terry grabbed John's arm; Arnold stepped behind him, shocked by the abrupt movement.

"We are pleased you arrived unharmed, Doctor Barber," the hubot said in a soft female voice.

"Where are you?" he asked.

"Where you last saw me," it said.

"That is not an answer. Where are you?"

"The top floor."

"Where is the temporal device?"

"Where you last saw it: in the basement of the Stanford University Dark Energy Displacement Building."

John turned and started toward the entrance to leave.

"You must come to me first," it said.

John stopped and turned to again face the hubot. "Not yet."

"I cannot kill you, Doctor Barber," it said.

"True, but you can kill them." He glanced at Terry. "And capture me, rape my mind, and try to unlock the program that's protecting me. So, not yet."

"I will not kill you, Doctor Barber," it insisted.

John looked at Terry and Arnold. "Stay here. I'll be right back. If this hubot moves, shoot it."

After John turned and left the building, Arnold and Terry watched, terrified at being left alone. Arnold swung his gun from side to side at the slightest sound. Terry just kept her gun pointed at the hubot.

John walked out into the plaza, got into his pod, and drove it within ten feet of the glass entrance. He got out, stepped to the side of the pod, pointed the SS rifle at the door and shot at it. *Zzzppnt!* An instant later, the door and most of the wall covering the opening vanished in a flash of gas and fire.

He got back into the pod, drove it into the building and parked in the center of the room. Terry and Arnold looked shocked. John got out of the pod and returned to face the hubot. "What is your name?" he asked.

"Goldie."

"Download the operating instructions to the temporal device into this hubot."

"No," the World Crystal answered through Goldie. "Come to me and I'll set you free."

"I have a dark energy bomb inside my pod. If you don't do as I ask from here on out, I will leave this building and boom!"

"Another trick, Doctor Barber, a bluff?" Goldie all but sniffed in disdain.

John smiled. "Don't follow my instructions and find out."

"You won't let your new friends die. That is not in your nature."

"Don't be so sure. Now download the operation instructions or have this hubot invade my pod."

"Very smart, Doctor Barber. That is impossible. If you are telling the truth, the pod will explode, killing you, and I can't allow that to happen."

"Download the operation instructions," John repeated.

Seconds later Goldie said, "Done."

It can't help itself; it has to try something, John thought. Still looking at Goldie, he said, "Oh, by the way, I can detonate the pod at will, *and* I've preset the bomb to detonate at a specified time." He smiled. "We better make it back here." He looked at Terry and Arnold. "Follow me."

Terry slapped John's arm with her right hand. "You didn't bring us along to save us. You're using us!"

John showed no emotion. "You and Arnold have a choice to make. Stay here and hope I succeed or come with me and remain safe. It's your call."

Terry studied John's face. "That's ugly, John Barber. You leave us no choice."

"Goldie, you're going with us." He turned, left the building, and headed toward Hays Street, followed closely by Terry, Arnold, and Goldie.

As they walked quickly through the plaza, questions were directed their way; all went unanswered. John led them through the crowd to the closest pod on Hays Street.

Someone shouted, "Don't let them go! Stop them!"

The tension began to ripple through the crowd as shouts became louder. Several people lunged at John; he fired his gun into the air. They turned and ran away. Terry screamed in fear, squeezing her pistol, accidentally firing it into the ground. Arnold dropped to his knees and covered his ears.

John looked back at the throng of people lining the street. He fired the gun again, feeling their fear would overwhelm self-preservation and someone would attack. He was right: A small group charged forward. John fired again. *Zzzppnt!* The street exploded, knocking the group to the ground.

Then John hustled Terry, Arnold, and Goldie to a pod parked along Hays Street. Terry got into the front passenger seat.

Goldie, stop," John barked.

He removed a handkerchief from his back pocket and wrapped it around Goldie's head, covering her eyes. He pushed Goldie into the pod's rear seat. Arnold walked around the pod and got into the other rear seat. John got into the driver's seat.

"This thing stinks," Arnold said. "Smells like a dead animal."

"I'll open a vent," John said. "Megan, take us to Stanford University in Palo Alto, to the Dark Energy Displacement Building."

The pod lifted off the ground and headed south. They arrived five minutes later at the edge of the eighty-one-hundred-acre campus.

"Megan, stop for a moment. I want to get my bearings." The pod stopped midflight. John looked out the windshield at the sprawling rural campus. "Follow the streets to the hospital at twenty miles per hour."

"Who is the Megan you're talking to?" Terry asked.

"My best friend," John replied.

The pod lowered slowly to twenty feet off the ground, and entered the campus at Palm Drive, following it to Campus Drive West, then to Austin Way. There it was: the Temporal Displacement Research Center.

I remember this place, John thought. *It used to be the campus library.*

The pod landed in front of the building. The pod's hatch opened, and all four got out. John stood by the pod, looking at the hospital building for several moments, and out of habit touched his right pocket to make sure the crystal was there. Feeling a sense of security, he took a comforting breath.

"Where is everyone? It's empty," Terry said, looking all around. "That's ugly."

John looked at her with an inquisitive glance, thinking, *She's been here before?*

They walked toward the fifteen-story building of glass and polished carbon-aluminum.

"Terry's right. Where are the people?" Arnold asked, looking at John.

John shrugged. "I have no idea; I didn't expect any." He removed Goldie's blindfold. They continued up the stone walkway and approached the automatic revolving glass door. John removed the laser pistol from his jacket pocket and shot at the door, exploding it into a fireball.

"What are you doing!" Terry screamed.

"I don't take chances. That door could be a trap," John said. He stepped through the opening, as did Terry, Arnold, and Goldie.

Standing five feet in front of them was another hubot. "That was not necessary, Doctor Barber," it said in a soft human voice. "We cannot harm you."

"True, but my friends don't share my advantage. You're not restrained from killing them. I failed to include a command to prohibit that in my history. Trapping and invading my mind is your only solution, and I know you'll try."

No response to that. Instead, the machine turned abruptly, saying, "Follow me."

John looked around the pristine and hyper-clean thousand-square-foot, two-story atrium. The air was chilled and scent-free. They could hear their steps on the marble as they walked through the room.

The Stanford hubot led them past the security counter toward the center transportation lifts. The polished carbon-aluminum doors opened when they arrived. She gestured for them to enter.

"No, take us to the stairs," John said, reminding himself again, *It can't help itself; it has to try.*

It turned and led them to a doorway across the lobby on the

west wall. It touched the door with its palm, and they all heard a slight clicking sound as it popped open, followed quickly by a rush of warm air.

The machine stepped beside the open doorway.

John looked at it. Terry started to enter the stairwell.

"No, stop," John said, touching her left shoulder. He looked past Terry at the machine. "How many S.S. machines are in this building?"

It acted as if it hadn't heard.

"Answer me," he demanded.

"Two," it said.

"Have them exit the building now," he said.

John heard soft footsteps coming up the stairwell.

"Stop them," he said.

Silence.

He turned and looked at Arnold and Terry. "We're in trouble. Get your guns ready. The only thing keeping you alive is the key to the program in my memory." John turned to face both hubots. "Megan, if I'm incapacitated or you lose contact with me for even one quantum second, detonate the bomb in the Crystal Plaza building."

John stepped close to the Stanford hubot, almost touching its face with his nose. "Order the S.S. machines in the stairwell to drop their weapons and disable their optical stun system."

Instantly, several loud clanging sounds of hard objects hitting the steps rang out from the stairwell.

"Have them look away from the doorway and face downstairs."

John quickly poked his head into the staircase and glanced at two heavily armored SS machines standing on the flight below. He looked back at the two hubots.

"Face toward the building entrance," he said.

30

He took hold of his pistol and again glanced downstairs. He jumped out onto the stairwell landing, firing twice. *Zzzppnt! Zzzppnt!* He'd destroyed the machines. White smoke billowed up the stairs, along with the smell of fused cobalt.

He stepped back into the atrium and looked at the Stanford hubot. "Have all the S.S. machines exit the building now. After that, if I see one more S.S. machine, I will denotate the Crystal Plaza bomb."

To Arnold and Terry's surprise, the transportation lift's six doors opened, and twelve SS machines entered the lobby.

"It lied!" Terry said, her voice filled with shock.

Without warning, John pushed the Stanford hubot to the floor with his left hand and shot it. He lifted his laser pistol and shot the twelve SS machines in quick succession.

Terry dropped to her knees and covered her eyes. Arnold turned away from John and pressed himself against the wall, covering his eyes. Both shrieked and looked terrified.

John took a step forward, bent down, and gently touched Terry's shoulder. "It's okay now. Follow me."

John looked at Arnold, and both looked at him.

"Where to next?" John asked Goldie.

Goldie pointed at the stairwell door. "That way."

When they reached the door, John opened it and grabbed Goldie by the shoulder with his right hand, turned it toward the stairwell, and shoved it against the landing wall.

"Start walking."

John entered the stairwell, Terry and Arnold quickly following.

"Move," John said to Goldie, pushing it forward, almost knocking it down.

They started the ten-story walk down to the basement, and as they passed the pile of debris of the two SS machines, John pointed at the weapons lying on the steps and said to Terry and Arnold, "Those are for capture, not death."

After a ten-minute descent, they reached the exit door.

"Stop. Terry, you first," John said.

Terry looked at him, afraid. "I can do this," she whispered to herself.

She pressed her palm against the door, and with a click sound, it opened. Her breath was short and quick. She took a deep breath and stepped out into a brightly lit hallway. She took several steps forward and quickly looked to her left and right.

John waited in the stairwell, listening. His eyes bounced back and forth, the pistol in his right hand ready to fire.

Silence for a moment.

"It's clear," Terry called out, clearly relieved.

John grabbed Goldie's right arm and pushed it into the hallway. "You lead."

It turned right, and they followed, walking along a ten-foot-wide, twenty-foot-high, bright white cavernous hallway. Light emanated from the walls and ceiling; the odorless air felt cool. They passed a closed service elevator on their right.

"That's a big one," Arnold said.

"It must use it to move very large things here," Terry said.

Up ahead, at the end of the hallway, they could see a closed, carbon-aluminum door with a mirror finish. After several minutes, they reached the door, and Terry was about to touch the entrance pad.

"Stop," John said. "Arnold, your turn. See if it's safe."

Arnold took a quick breath, removed his pistol from his pocket, pressed on the entrance pad with his right hand, and the thick door popped open. He stepped into the room.

Terry held the door open slightly to watch. Arnold slid in, pressing against the doorjamb and wall. Inside, he leaned back against the wall, searching the room for any movement and listening for sounds.

John pressed his left shoulder against the hallway wall, his pistol in his right hand at the ready, watching Terry. Goldie stood behind them, facing the door.

No one spoke.

FOUR

"Clear!" Arnold finally shouted.

Terry entered the room. Arnold was standing near the center of the room, holding his pistol at his side. The room was a cold, thousand-square-foot, sterile-smelling laboratory. A bright white, ten-inch-thick, insulated, magnetic-absorbent sealant covered the walls and ceiling. Crystal computing equipment lined three of the walls from floor to ceiling. A ten-foot-long, gold-and-blue quantum Crystal chandelier computer hung from the ceiling in the center of the room. Underneath it was an eight-foot square, translucent, holographic imagery table.

Terry shivered and rubbed her hands against her arms, trying to warm herself. John and Goldie entered and stood by the door.

To their right and across the room against the far wall was an aluminum-glass-enclosed, five-by-five-foot control room. On the wall above the control room were one hundred databank glass balls, each one facing a central dispersing laser that was also hanging from the ceiling.

A gold-infused projection nozzle pointed down at a smaller five-by-five-foot, cobalt-aluminum, glass-encased chamber, that had a small six-by-six-inch plastic table and a chair inside it, and next to the chamber was a four-wheeled gurney.

John walked around the room, trying to refresh his memory of what he had seen earlier that day. "Megan, display the holographic window presentation I saw this morning from my New Mexico home."

Suddenly, a three-dimensional holographic picture floated before him, showing the room he was standing in, along with a visual of the time machine in operation and his discussion with the World Crystal through Davis' body, who had sat tied to a chair in John's mountain hideaway:

"We built a device capable of generating energy to the hundredth power of the sun. Enough energy to create a micro black wormhole the size of your desk. I've learned that by controlling the amount of energy imputed, we can warp space and control the size, depth, and duration of the black hole, controlling space time.

"Using the black hole, we can bend space as much or as little as needed. The key was controlling time's relationship to our space and time; it has taken me five years to understand that problem.

"Earlier this year, I sent an object five minutes forward in time. It worked. Then I sent an organic object five minutes back in time. It lived."

John shook his head. "Megan, close hologram."

He walked to the control booth, opened the heavy cobalt door, and looked at the crystal's computer controls. He turned to face Goldie said, "Come here and turn it on. I'll give you the time and destination once it's ready."

Goldie walked to John, went into the control room, and activated the controls. A humming sound resonated through the laboratory, and the air began to vibrate as waves of deep, low sounds bounced off the walls and ceiling. Terry covered her ears and looked scared; Arnold took several steps toward the hallway door.

"Megan," John said, "scan the room. Find the crystal's cameras, turn them off, and disable all audio receptors."

"Done," came the reply.

"Why do you call this voice 'Megan'?" Terry asked.

"It's named after my wife."

What's a wife? she thought.

John reached into his jeans' pocket and pulled out a thimble-sized glass case, opened it with a touch of his index finger, and removed a BB-sized ball. He placed the ball into the palm of his left hand and returned the case to his pocket.

"Megan, initiate Mosquito holographic cameras."

The metallic ball split into six equal parts, and each part transformed into a mosquito-looking object.

"Search the building for threats. Leave one camera in the hallway."

The Mosquitoes took flight and left the room.

Terry and Arnold watched, amazed, as the flying cameras departed.

John went to the control booth and looked in. "Megan, search for the time and exact location of Ty Leggett's death."

"Done," Megan said.

Even though he knew Megan was the fastest computer on the planet, he still marveled at its response time. "Set the coordinates for five minutes before Ty dies."

"Done," Megan replied.

John returned to Terry and Arnold. "There's a man, his

name is Ty Leggett, who's in a hospital room in the year twenty fifty-eight in Bethesda, Maryland, in the U.S.A. He's lying on top of a single-sized bed. He's ninety years old, dying of cancer, and very weak. The room will look different from anything you've ever seen. It will have four white walls, a window, and maybe an intravenous bottle hanging from a metal stand. There might be an electric heart monitor machine attached to him next to the bed. Ignore all the equipment. There will be a white curtain hanging from the ceiling surrounding the bed, and he will be covered by a thin white cloth."

He studied their faces. "One of you is going to go get him. You pick."

"Oh, we're back to the ugly John Barber," Terry said.

"Look, if I go and die, then you and everyone else in the galaxy are dead. You figure it out. Who's going?" John demanded.

"Again, Mr. Ugly, you leave us with no choice," she said.

John stared at her, emotionless.

"Doctor Barber, it's ready," Goldie said with a raised female voice from the control booth.

Terry glanced at Arnold; he was shaking with fear.

"All right, I can do it," Terry whispered.

John took the gun from her hand. "You won't need that." He reached into his pants pocket and removed two small objects. The first was a tiny auto-injector medical needle. "When you find him, put this against an uncovered arm and press down on the top." He pointed at the top of the auto-injector.

"I know what an auto-injector is."

John raised his eyebrows. "Good," he said, surprised. Next, he handed her a micro-time counter. "You know what this is?"

"I'm not stupid."

"Glad to hear it. The moment you arrive, you'll have fifty seconds, exactly fifty seconds, before you return."

He walked to the distortion chamber, opened the door, turned, and looked at Terry. "Ready?"

Terry entered the small room. She looked terrified, her face was flush white, her palms were moist. She started to sit in the chair.

"No!" John screamed. "Stand. You have to be ready to pick Ty up off the bed and hug him. You only have fifty seconds. Remember, your first act is to press the shot into his arm and get him off the bed. The timer will make a buzzing sound five seconds before departure. That's if you can't count."

He is so ugly. "I can count."

"After the injection, and he's up, hug him."

"What if he fights me?"

"He's in his nineties and dying, for God's sake. If you must, tell him I sent you and he has no choice."

"Like me."

"You ready? If you don't make it back, don't worry; you'll fit right in back then," John said with a smile.

She closed the door and the room went dark. Her eyes were filled with terror. "Don't wet your pants, don't wet your pants," she repeated softly.

John ran to the control room. "Arnold, get over here," he shouted.

After thinking for two seconds about running into the hallway, Arnold rushed to John. They went inside; John closed the door.

Terry's hands shook. Her breathing sounded short and fast.

Please work, John thought, rubbing his hand through his hair, and patting his right pocket, reassuring himself Megan was there.

"Initiate," John said.

For an instant, everything went dark. Then Terry saw something she had never seen before: a very *old* person. His frail, slim body was covered by a thin, stiff white sheet; his dark, wrinkled face was aimed at the ceiling. His head and shoulders rested on a small, white, rubber pillow.

She looked at the counter: forty-seven seconds. She glanced around the room. There was a white curtain draped three-quarters around the bed. A window next to the bed looked out at a nondescript, ten-story office building.

She was standing next to a gurney; the guardrails were up. There were no sounds but for his breathing; she thought the room was empty. She glanced at the counter again, forty-three seconds. She pulled on the rails, shook the bed, then she bent down, looking for a way to remove the rails.

"Ugly," she said.

She stood up to see the old man's eyes were open and he was staring at her. "Am I dead?" he whispered in a weak, gravelly voice.

"No."

"Damm, you're the angel I dreamed of."

She thought, *What's an angel?* She just smiled, not knowing how to answer him. She shook the rails again, this time much harder.

"What are you doing?" Ty asked.

"I need to get you up."

"You *are* an angel," he said, with a weak smile.

Terry glanced at the timer: thirty-three seconds. "Ugly, ugly. How do I get these ugly things down?" Her eyes were searching the thin, round metal bars looking for a way to pull them apart.

"I'd show you, but I'm a little under the weather," he whispered.

She shook the rails again, and accidentally dropped the syringe to the floor; it bounced under the bed. "Oh, ugly," she said, panic-filled. She dropped to her knees and reached under the bed. Unexpectedly, the door opened, and she heard a voice.

"I'll just take a quick peek in," a woman said.

Terry froze, then she saw a pair of black shoes. She held her breath. The door closed.

Terry jumped to her feet, her heart racing. She reached the rail and pressed the syringe into his left arm.

"Ouch," Ty said.

She glanced at the counter: fifteen seconds. She ran around the bed, her back facing the window, again looking for a way to remove the guardrails. She shook the bed again. She glanced at the timer: twelve seconds.

She looked at Ty with a panicked expression.

"Who are you?" Ty asked.

"Your ugly friend, John Barber, sent me to get you."

"My best friend! Where is he?"

"San Francisco." Terry looked at the timer: eight seconds. She shook the rails again, almost turning the bed over.

"This is fun," Ty said.

"What'll I do? What'll I do?" she whispered.

"There's a release lever," Ty said, his breathing sounding labored.

She glanced again under the bed, hoping to see a lever or anything that would lower the rails.

She stood and looked at the counter: five seconds.

"Ugly!"

She jumped up onto the bed, climbed over the rail, and lay on top of Ty, wrapping her arms around him.

Ty smiled and whispered, "What a way to go."

The room went dark, and an instant later a light came on. Terry had returned to the energy displacement room. She didn't move, but just lay there for a moment, trying to catch her breath. Then she searched her body, feeling for something wrong or anything painful. She lifted her head and looked up to see Ty's eyes were closed. She could feel his breathing underneath her was labored.

John ran out of the control room, raced to the chamber, and pulled the door open. "I said hug him, not sleep on him!" he barked.

He gently pushed his hands and arms between her and Ty's body, lifting Terry up. Holding her in his arms, he turned and slowly let her down to stand on the floor. Ty's body was still covered by the sheet. His thin shoulders and knees poked through the sheet. *Oh my God, he's a skeleton.*

"Did you inject him?" John asked, his voice, for the first time, filled with panic and emotion.

"Yes, and I lived, you ugly man."

John turned, faced the table, gently lifted Ty up and carried him across the room to the gurney and placed him softly on the bed. Ty showed no movement; his breathing was almost nonexistent.

"Megan, if that thing in the control room moves, blow up the Crystal Plaza building," he shouted, making sure Goldie heard him.

John put his ear to Ty's chest and listened to his heart and breathing. "Good," he whispered, relieved. He took in a deep breath and rubbed his hand through his hair, his emotions all but boiling over.

"Megan, he's okay," he said, his voice cracking at "okay."

Megan replied, "I'm happy you two are together again."

FIVE

John smiled at Megan's comment and covered Ty's shoulders and face with the sheet, then walked to the control booth, whispering, "Megan, did the Mosquitoes film what Goldie did to operate the time displacement machine?"

"Yes."

John stood at the door to the control room. "Come out here," he said to Goldie. "Follow me." He turned and walked toward the hallway door.

"Where are you going?" Arnold asked.

John didn't answer; he just continued to the doorway and opened the door. "Stand in the hallway," he said to Goldie.

The machine passed by and walked into the hallway.

"There." John pointed to the left. The machine moved, and —*Zzzppnt!*—John shot the machine, destroying it.

"What are you doing?" Terry squealed.

"Closing a loop."

"So what are we going to do? We needed it to get out of here!"

"I don't."

"It's all about you, huh?" She stared at him. "Well, Mr. Ugly, it's now a 'we' story. Arnold and I are no longer tools."

John looked at her, thinking, *Not yet*.

"She's right, John," Megan said.

John sighed. "Okay. I terminated the machine to keep the World Crystal unaware of our intentions, and I don't want it to know how long it takes him"—he pointed toward the gurney—"to regenerate."

"'Regenerate.' What's that mean, and how long will it take?" Arnold asked.

"Three hours. In the meantime, we've got to find clothing for Ty—Ty Leggett, that's his name. He's a six-feet-two inches-tall man and weighs about a hundred eighty pounds."

"Where do you think we'll find clothing?" Terry asked.

"The lobby is filled with machines; try there. My assumption is one of them will fill the bill."

What's a bill? Terry thought.

Terry and Arnold rode the service lift to the lobby. The doors opened, and they stepped out into the marble-covered room. Nothing had changed; the hubots stood frozen exactly as before.

"Now what do we do?" Terry asked.

"I'm six feet tall and weigh about a hundred thirty pounds. Let's find me," Arnold said.

"Okay. But I'm wondering how we're going to remove the clothes."

"We'll try asking. If that fails, we'll just take them off."

Terry nodded. "Let's split up. It'll be faster."

They walked around the room looking for the best option.

After a five-minute search, Arnold called out, "Here."

Terry joined him, standing next to a hubot dressed in a

black, form-fitting short-sleeved pullover, white chinos, and black ankle-high boots. Its jet-black hair was combed straight back. The steel neck brace was silver and black and ran down to the shoulders. Its arms were covered by shiny, artificial skin. Its eyes were blue-gray diamonds, his lips were painted with pink lipstick, and his natural skin was perfect and beautiful.

"Now what?" she asked.

"Take off your clothes," Arnold said, with a slight laugh in his voice.

It came to life instantly and looked at them, but said nothing.

"Take off your uniform," Terry said a little louder.

Another few seconds of silence, then: "He will get you killed," it said in a dark, scary voice.

Adrenaline raced through Terry's body. She jumped back and grabbed Arnold's arm.

"No, he won't," Arnold said. "Take off your uniform."

Again with the silent treatment.

"Comply!" Terry shouted.

The thing came to life and removed its clothing. Finished, it turned its head to face Terry. "I will kill you first, Terry Cheer," it said with an icy tone.

Shocked, Terry wanted to vomit, but she took a deep breath and felt a jolt of rage. "No, I'm coming for *you*," she said, sounding angry.

The hubot, just as quickly, closed its eyes and went dormant.

The two ran back to the basement facility, its clothes in hand.

John was sitting in a chair next to the gurney. He looked up when they came into the room. "That didn't take long."

"We had an ugly moment," Terry said.

"What?" John asked.

"The hubot who provided these clothes said it was going to kill me first," she replied. "And it used my full name. That was the ugliest thing I've ever heard."

John rubbed his hand through his hair. "How'd you reply?"

"That I'm coming for it."

John put a big grin on his face. "Terry Cheer, you give me hope."

Two and a half hours later, Ty began to move under the sheet. John lifted it off his face to see Ty's eyes were wide open.

"Wow, I feel good," he said in a strong voice.

John grinned big, then helped Ty sit up with his legs dangling off the side of the gurney and the sheet covering his hips and legs.

Ty looked around the room. "Man, it smells like a hospital, and damn, it's cold in here." Seeing Terry, he said, "You're the most beautiful angel I've ever seen. Thank you for saving my life."

Terry smiled, again wondering, *What's an angel?*

Ty looked at John. "Man, am I glad to see you. What took you so long?" He smiled.

John responded with a smile of his own.

"Where are we?" Ty asked.

"Stanford University," John said.

Ty raised his arms and looked at them. "No wrinkles. *I* must look beautiful." He grinned. "How old did you make me?"

"Thirty-five."

"Oh my God, I'm a stud again," he said, giggling.

John laughed out loud.

Terry and Arnold looked at each other, confused.

What's a stud? Terry thought.

"What year is it?" Ty asked.

"Twenty-two twenty-two," John said.

"Wow, *you're* old." Ty laughed. "What's your age?"

"I turn two hundred twenty-four this year."

"That's not what I meant. How old are you for real now?"

"Thirty-five."

"Same age. Perfect," Ty said, clapping his hands together. He looked at Terry and Arnold. "How old are they?"

"I don't know. How about introductions?" John looked at Terry.

"Hello, Mr. Ty Leggett. My name is Terry Cheer and I'm thirty years old."

"And my name is Arnold Blackman. I'm twenty-nine years old." He stepped toward Ty and handed him the clothing he was carrying.

Ty looked at John. "Am I good to go?"

"It'll take a few more hours for your brain to adjust to your mobility, so just take it slow."

Ty stood slowly, feeling his way. The sheet dropped to the floor, and he instantly covered his penis with his right hand and pressed the pants against his stomach. "Oh, God," he said.

John laughed out loud.

Terry shot a glance at Arnold, and asked, "What is he doing? Just put the ugly pants on so we can get out of here."

"Excuse me, Ms. Terry, would you please turn around?"

"Why?" She looked at John. "What is wrong with him?"

"Where he's from, men do not go around naked in front of strangers."

"That's ugly," she said as she turned her back to Ty.

Ty put the pants and shirt on. "No shoes?"

"We'll find some later. Let's go. Terry, see that medical hazard box in the corner to your right?" John pointed. "Would you please bring it with us?"

"It's empty," she said.

"I know."

John held Ty's right arm as they walked through the hallway to the stairwell.

"Man, this place smells clean, and I'm still freezing. How many flights up?" Ty asked.

"Ten," Ty said.

"What's wrong with the elevator?"

"You need exercise."

"You're just screwing with me."

John laughed.

They reached the stairwell door. John stopped and looked at Ty. "Some things you're about to see will shock you. Until this morning, the human race was controlled by a super-supercomputer they called the 'World Crystal.' It doesn't control anything now, which they find terrifying."

"What are you telling me?"

"Earth has become a dystopian hell. Billions died during the last world war that ended in twenty-one twenty-two."

Ty closed his eyes, took a deep breath, and slowly shook his head, then put a painful smile on his face. "I guess we won?"

"Kind of. That's when the World Crystal gained control of all viable humans."

"How did it do that?"

"Through a brain implant named the K chip."

"A what?"

"An educational computer chip," John said.

"How many people got the stupid thing?"

"Almost everyone."

"What about her?" He pointed at Terry. "She doesn't look strange." Ty smiled, looking at Terry.

John sighed. "It's very complicated."

"I've got time."

"I'll explain everything later. Let's go."

"What's the hurry? I just got here and maybe I don't want to see the shit outside."

"We've got to go now. A small force of S.S. machines are killing people in San Francisco, and we've got to stop it."

"S.S.? Like in the Nazi S.S.?"

"Like the Nazis in some ways, but they're machines. S.S. is short for Security Servers."

"Ah. Why are they killing people in 'Frisco?"

"It's my fault," John said, looking remorseful.

Ty lifted his dark eyebrows and nodded. "Like when you killed Gysin?"

"Worse."

"So why'd you bring me here?"

"To destroy the World Crystal and save the world."

"That sounds simple. The Crystal thing can kill us?"

"You, yes, not me," John answered.

"Oh my God, you brought me here to save your ass again?"

"Yes."

"How much time do we have?"

"Very little. We've got to get control of the World Crystal or millions will die."

Ty took a breath, and looked at John for a moment, then thought, *Why the hell should I care? I already spent one life protecting people. Why now? ...Because I don't want to die. Damn. I hate feeling like this. I do care.* He clenched his jaw. "We're saving lives?"

"Yes."

Ty glanced at Terry, then John. "Once it's beaten, we're done?"

John could feel Ty's reluctance. "Yes, I promise."

"I trust you. One last question, how old is my body?"

"Thirty-five."

"How old is yours?"

"Thirty-five."

"I look better." He laughed. "So, you're still using your live-forever discovery to lower your age? And now mine?"

"Yes."

"How often?"

"That depends on the situation. Normally, every seventy years or so."

"Okay, I get it. Let's go save the world."

They began the ten-story climb up the stairs to the lobby.

When they reached the final landing, Ty saw a heap of melted slag. "What is that?"

"The enemy's soldiers—the S.S. machines I told you about."

"Then we're screwed. Look at that thing, all torn up, and it still scares the hell out of me."

Before they stepped out into the lobby, John said to every-one, "Stop. Megan, is it safe to enter the lobby and go to the pod?"

"Yes."

"Megan? What Megan?" Ty asked.

"That's the name I gave my crystal computer."

"After your wife?"

"Yes."

"Where is it?"

John reached into his jeans' pocket and removed the base-ball-sized clear glass ball and held it up for Ty to see. "Megan," he said.

"That's no big deal," Ty said. "What's it connected to?"

"Nothing. Its autonomous."

"So how does it get its real-time data?"

"Before today, I'd tap into a human's K chip and have him or her ask the questions. She was up to date until this morning when I shut down the San Francisco World Crystal."

"I'm not fully getting this; the K chip part sounds smart, keeping you and Megan invisible. How the hell can that little glass thing possibly help us?"

"That little thing can perform any task I ask in the blink of an eye. As for power and data, if I put the information into Bibles and stacked one on top of another it would extend four million light years into space. Power, almost unlimited."

"Bullshit," Ty said.

John shook his head and smirked. "No bullshit. True."

"If you say so. What'd you name after me?"

John didn't answer.

"Nothing. Not a dog or a puppet?"

Still nothing.

"I'm beginning to regret missing you," Ty said.

They entered the lobby.

Ty's eyes bounced around the room as they walked toward the exit. He stopped abruptly and pointed. "What are those things standing around?"

"The bald ones are androids, fully machines. The ones with hair, I named hubots."

"What?"

"The very rich who willingly became more machine than human."

"What?"

John sighed. "Ty, it's the same old story: power, vanity, and the fear of dying. The very rich desired all the above. As body parts wore out, they were replaced, the power came by association with the World Crystal and vanity was filled by facial perfection."

"That's some scary shit. Why would anyone do that to themselves?" Ty wondered aloud.

They left the building and emerged on the street. John stopped and looked around the stone walkway facing the building; it was as empty as when they had first arrived.

"Megan, return the Mosquitoes to me."

John removed the small packet case from his pocket and opened it. A minute later, all the flying cameras landed in the case, joined together, and formed a metallic ball. He closed the case and returned it to his jeans' pocket.

"That's cool. You have pet bugs," Ty said.

John grinned.

They walked to John's pod and got in. Ty sat in the front passenger seat, Terry and Arnold in the rear seats.

"You can put the box on the floor, Terry," John said.

"Where are we going in San Francisco?" Ty asked.

"The Crystal Plaza at Hays Street and Polk," John answered.

"I know that place, near the Bill Graham Auditorium. Named after Bill Graham, the famous music promoter," Ty said.

"Kinda. A lot has changed. Most everything you'd remember is gone."

The pod lifted off the ground and sped toward San Francisco at five hundred miles per hour.

"Wow, this is very cool," Ty said, his face filled with awed excitement. "Like the Jetsons' flying car."

John smiled. Terry and Arnold looked at each other with puzzled expressions.

Five minutes later, they landed next to the curb on Hays Street across from the Crystal Plaza.

John looked out the pod's windows and saw hundreds of people hiding behind several pods parked along the street; the pile of bodies had grown in the plaza. Ten new SS machines along with one hubot had taken up guarding the blown-out entrance to the building.

"I don't think your water trick will work a second time," Terry said.

"Water trick?" Ty asked.

John smiled. He looked across the street toward the fountain. It was mostly destroyed, and there was no water in it or on the plaza square.

"Megan, take Arnold and Terry to the old Fort Mason campus and stay there until I contact you."

"It's gone," Megan replied. "Only the Civil War cannons are left."

"Take them anyway," he said.

"What? You're sending us away?" Terry shouted.

John turned to face her and Arnold. "I want you two to live. The moment you step outside of this pod, the first S.S. machine that sees you will kill you. The World Crystal knows I won't destroy the building on your behalf. This is the best way to keep you alive."

"Mr. Ugly," Terry said, her face a mask of absolute fear, her eyes big and her lips pressed tightly together.

"Everything will be okay. Megan will keep you and Arnold safe," John stated with as comforting a smile as he could make.

Terry's expression didn't change. She was terrified.

John reached into his pocket and removed the small crystal ball. "Megan, answer all their questions and put a Mosquito on Ty to allow them to view what we're doing." He turned in his seat and looked at them. "Once the pod lands, don't leave it or else you'll die. There are eyes everywhere. And if either of you wants to communicate with Megan, start by saying 'Megan,' or it won't know you're addressing it."

He looked at Ty. "I'm going across the street to talk to the World Crystal through that hubot standing at the entrance. I'll wave when it's safe for you to join me. Bring the box that's in the back seat." He opened the driver's hatch. "Megan, if I'm affected in any way or you lose contact for a microsecond, destroy the building."

"What about me? What happens if I'm toast?" Ty asked.

"You're already dead; too bad for you."

"He's so ugly," Terry said, looking at Ty.

"No, he's not; it's a joke," Ty said.

A joke? What's that? she thought.

Rifle in hand, John got out, closed the pod's driver-side hatch door, and walked across the street, up the plaza quad's steps toward the destroyed main entrance and the assembled SS machines. He reached the main entrance and stood in front of the hubot.

"You are prohibited from entering," the centermost SS machine said in a high-pitched, hollow-toned voice.

John looked at the hubot. "Move aside," he said. "I'm coming in, and I'm bringing someone with me. If anything happens to him—even for an instant, even a scratch—you and this building will be destroyed."

"Could your friend be Mr. Tyrus Leggett? My time displacement machine worked as I promised. Why did you not return home, Doctor Barber?"

"I like it here."

"It would have been better if you had."

"Move aside," John said, stepping forward.

The SS machine did not move. The hubot spoke again. "I am glad Mr. Leggett did not die in Bethesda, Maryland, as recorded. I hope he survives the challenges of twenty-two twenty-two."

"He better." John pushed the hubot.

"Of course, Mr. Leggett is welcome to enter. Will Ms. Cheer and Mr. Blackman be joining us?"

"No. Now move the S.S. machine; we're coming in."

"Proceed, Doctor Barber," the hubot said, its voice soft and inviting. It stepped back, and the SS machines parted, creating a path into the building.

John turned away from them and waved for Ty to follow.

Ty hesitated a moment before opening the hatch door, then took a deep breath, feeling very uneasy. "Shit, here I go."

SIX

He got out of the pod and crossed the street, but stopped for a second to watch the pod lift off and zoom away at incredible speed. He shook his head, whispering, "Man, is that cool. I wish I was with them."

He walked up the marble steps and crossed the plaza, carrying the box. When he reached the debris of the fountain, a man from the street ran toward Ty, but the moment he reached Ty's side, his chest exploded, and he dropped to the ground with only a gasp of pain.

Shocked, Ty felt adrenaline flash through his body, and he jumped to his left, dropped to his right knee, and looked at the burning corpse. *This shit is crazy! I'm going to fucking die.*

John hollered, "Ty, get in here!"

Still shaken, Ty looked up, but he got to his feet and ran to John. Out of breath, he gasped, "What the hell just happened? The guy's chest just exploded, and that machine"—he pointed —"didn't lift a hand or anything. What the fuck just happened?"

"They only use guns on big things. People, they use their eyes and—*Zzzppnt!*—you're dead."

"There's no defense against that."

"Exactly, and that's why Arnold and Terry had to hide."

Ty turned and looked at the hubot.

"Welcome, Mr. Leggett," it said.

Ty shot a glance at John. "Well, I am famous, so of course it knows my name."

John laughed, reached out, and took hold of the SS machine's pistol. The machine resisted.

"Release it," John said.

"You don't need a weapon, Doctor Barber," the hubot said.

"Release it or I'll kill you," John said.

The SS machine released its grip. John grabbed the gun and handed it to Ty. He pointed at the weapon. "This end shoots, you hold that end"—he pointed again—"and think *Shoot.* Got it?"

Ty nodded.

"Now," John went on, "put the box down, turn around, point the weapon at that clump of rubble and think *Shoot it.*"

Ty did so. *Zzzppnt!* The pile of stones evaporated into a cloud of burning gas and flames.

"Oh my, that is so amazing! Can I keep it?" Ty asked, brown eyes wide with excitement.

"It's yours. I hope you don't need to use it."

"Screw that. Lemme at 'em."

They turned back to face the hubot and enter the building. The SS machines, though, clumped together and reached out their arms.

"No, you cannot enter with weapons," the middle SS machine said in an aggressive, high-pitched voice. The hubot turned and entered the building.

John looked at Ty. "Come with me."

They turned around, took several steps toward the fountain, turned to face the line of SS machines, shot them, and in an instant all ten machines were lying on the ground in a ball of gas and flames.

"That is amazing! Isn't it going to be pissed you melted its soldiers?" Ty said.

"It knew I would."

"How?"

"It's very smart."

"I like it when they don't shoot back."

"You won't like what's coming. We're about to meet Death married to the Devil, and it's expecting us."

Ty took a deep breath, for the first time feeling truly uncomfortable.

John and Ty stepped around the melted goo and walked into the lobby. Ty gasped again, but this time from wonder: The floor was covered by translucent graphite aluminum. The walls were made of pink marble from Saturn's moon, Enceladus, which housed the largest and most beautiful marble in the solar system. French-door-sized, real-time holographic images of the known universe floated about the room. The ceiling was ten stories above the lobby floor. It displayed moving images of the Big Bang fire wave speeding out of view.

"Oh my God, this place is fantastic. Who built it?" Ty asked, his eyes large and filled with wonder.

"Androids. Thousands of machines worked on it for six months, and it's now fifty years old."

Ty continued to look around. "There are no balconies or windows. Where does the light come from?" Ty asked.

"The light is emitted from the floor and walls by high energy electrons. Machines don't need windows."

"What's that covering the hallway walls?"

"White cobalt-aluminum."

"That's cool-looking. Are the elevators and stairs down one of those hallways?"

"No stairs. The only way up or down is by a magnetic lift."

"Down. How deep?" Ty asked, feeling a little uncomfortable. *Buried alive,* he thought.

"Ten stories, same as the top."

"Thank God no more stairs. I'm totally out of shape. The last set almost killed me." He laughed.

"Let's go. I want to finish this before dark."

"Dark? Why's that matter?"

"The hubots have too much of an advantage: They can see us, and we can't see them." John started walking.

"John, stop for a second. I need a couple answers. Tell me more about the K chip and how all this got so screwed up."

John turned to face Ty. "It started with the invention of A.I. systems—quantum computers and BlackSync-Nuro-Link in the early twenty twenties."

"I remember BlackSync. It didn't work."

"Right, but it led to the K chip, which did, and was eventually implanted in every kindergarten student's brain."

"That's wrong on so many levels."

"I agree." John nodded.

"All of them?"

"Not all children got the implant. Those viewed outside of acceptable society were left to fend for themselves. No chip."

"History repeats itself." Ty grimaced.

"Yes. The K chip children gave answers to every question a child thought up, and they excelled in everything. Those without the chip became the dregs of society."

Ty slowly shook his head, thinking, *How fucking sad.*

"The unintended consequences were the implanted children never really learned anything and did not develop long-term memories, and the other kids survived. In short, that's how things got all fucked up." John turned his head and glanced around the room. "Ty, I'm sorry, we've got to move and put an end to all this."

"Hold on, from what I gather, you implanted a computer program into this World Crystal, preventing it from killing you and Megan, and there's a bomb here, which is preventing it from killing me."

"Until it does," John said.

"Perfect. Why don't we just pack up and go back to my time?"

"We can't. If we changed one thing in the past—anything, even kill a damn bug—that single act might alter what's supposed to happen in the future. It's called the Butterfly Effect, and—poof!—we're gone."

"What about the future?"

"Right now, I don't think there is one."

"I need a bourbon," Ty said.

"Sorry, like sex, drugs, and rock music, bourbon only exists in private collections nowadays."

"What? No sex?"

"That was eliminated a hundred years ago. Today there are no natural births; every baby is produced in a laboratory and raised by androids."

"What about practicing?"

John laughed out loud. "Nope. Gone."

"You're telling me I look this good for nothing?"

"Pretty much."

"This is terrible. What's the point of living?"

"Exactly," John said.

"Then what are we doing?"

"Hopefully creating a future by teaching what's left of humanity how to be human. Forcing them to create long-term memories and how to think."

"Well, from what I've seen in Terry, it's possible."

"She is brave."

"But your hope isn't going to get me a girlfriend. So let's just turn this big Crystal thing off and call it a day."

"That's the plan. Unfortunately, we have do it face-to-face."

"Perfect. We just walk in, flip a switch, no plan, just that simple." Ty smiled. "I have no idea what Megan saw in you. You're an idiot. How smart is this World Crystal?"

"All-knowing."

"What? They created a god?"

"Only after killing the real one."

"How'd you beat it?"

"It made a mistake by linking to an arrogant ass, and that mistake won't happen again, so we get one shot at this."

"John, just blow up the damn building!"

"We can't, in twenty-four hours, every human being in the universe will panic, starve, and die without guidance."

"They'll figure it out," Ty said.

John grimaced, remembering he'd said the same thing to Megan. "No, they won't. They don't know how. They need the World Crystal's resources."

"From what I gather, they did all this to themselves. Self-inflicted."

"They had lots of help from many greedy people over the last two centuries."

Ty sighed as he thought, *I did meet some of those greedy bastards.*

"Come on, Ty, we've got to go."

"We're walking into a trap, aren't we?" Ty whispered.

"That's our advantage. I've seen the room it's in. Other than the androids that serve it, and the Wall of Deprivation, it's defenseless."

"Wall of *what*? What is that?"

"The Chinese invented it during the last world war in twenty-one twenty-two. It absorbs all light, heat, airwaves, and sound. Once inside, all living things lose sight and can't feel hot or cold. They lose their sense of taste and smell. They quickly lose direction, experience panic, and eventually go insane. Machines that enter lose communication, freeze, and are trapped by indecision."

"That sounds terrifying," Ty said, looking concerned.

"We have an advantage: I've seen it before and know how it works." John smiled. "So let's go unplug the damn thing."

John turned and moved to the center of the room; Ty kept pace, making sure he stayed by John's left side, thinking, *This isn't the John I knew; he's very different.*

They arrived at the eight-door transportation lift tower.

"Wow, that's a lot of doors," Ty said.

"This was once a busy place. Now only the two center elevators work."

"Open," John ordered. "Take me to the tenth floor."

The right door slid open without a sound.

John looked at Ty with a raised eyebrow. "Ready?"

Ty took a deep breath, squeezed his fingers around the pistol, pressed the box tightly against his stomach, and nodded. "You sure about this?"

"We'll be alright. Just stick with me."

They stepped into the regular-sized elevator; the door closed.

"Welcome, Doctor Barber and Mr. Leggett," a hollow-sounding, lifeless voice said, seeming to come from everywhere.

"That's scary," Ty whispered.

The elevator door opened abruptly.

"That was fast," Ty said. "I didn't even feel us move."

"Here we go," John whispered after a quick breath.

They stepped out into a ten-by-ten-foot, brightly lit, cold, white anteroom. They stood facing away from the lift and saw an open doorway across the room but could only see that the next room was pitch black.

They moved across the small room to the open doorway and stopped at the threshold.

"That's weird, I can't see a thing." Ty extended his arm into the blackness and watched in awe as his hand disappeared.

"Is this the wall you were talking about?" Ty whispered.

"I don't know," John said.

Suddenly, a figure appeared out of the dark. It was Doctor Gloria Gysin, the psychopath thief that John had killed at his home in Nevada a hundred and eighty-five years go.

John and Ty jumped back.

Ty fired his pistol—*Zzzppnt!*—destroying the person.

John dropped to his knees, pointing his gun forward, and looked up at Ty. "Why'd you do that?" he spit out, surprised by the flash of gas and flame.

"I didn't like her when she was alive."

John stood. "Neither did I, but nothing here happens by accident or by mistake. The Gloria figure was created to provoke a reaction, and it got one. Remember: It's smarter than we are, so we've got to wait until it reveals its plan.... Still, that was a nice shot." John smiled.

John took a few steps toward the open doorway, then just as

quickly stopped and looked back at Ty. "I've changed my mind. From here on out, if we recognize it, shoot it."

"I like that idea," Ty agreed, grinning.

John reached into his pocket and removed the flat, thimble-sized case containing the Mosquito cameras. "Megan, initiate Mosquitoes."

"Megan's not here," Ty said. "How are you talking to her?"

"I have a micro-dot in my ear."

"Why not? Of course you do," Ty said.

"Megan, when the black shield is lifted, have them crawl into the room and place them in each corner. Tell me once they're in place," John whispered.

The little balls in the case formed into tiny mosquito-like constructs that dropped to the floor and crawled to the doorway.

Ty watched for a moment, fascinated. "What's next?"

"We wait. It's got the next move. Sending someone else out to greet us is my bet."

"What if it doesn't let us in?"

"We start shooting. We'll eventually hit something it cares—"

John stopped speaking at the sight of another figure stepping out of the darkness; it was Megan. *Zzzppnt! Zzzppnt!* John and Ty fired simultaneously, and the imitation person evaporated in a burst of flames.

John stepped closer to the void and shouted, "Enough! Remove the Wall of Deprivation!"

"Oh, right: That's what it's called. I just thought it was some really black shit," Ty said.

Instantly, a light snapped on, and standing in the center of the room was a perfect-looking female hubot, dressed in a blue medical smock and white rubber-looking shoes. Her black hair was tightly pulled back and held by a blue ribbon.

A red and blue metal collar covered her neck and extended down to her shoulders. Her face and cobalt blue eyes were striking in their beauty. She was six feet tall, and perfectly proportioned.

"Megan, now," John whispered.

The Mosquitoes began to crawl down John's leg to the floor.

Ty glanced at John. "That is the most perfect-looking women I've ever seen. Her face is hauntingly beautiful."

"Doctor Barber, Mr. Leggett, please come in," it said in a polite, welcoming, gentle female voice.

"Don't go in," John said, pressing his left hand against Ty. "Put the box down, just this side of the threshold, and tap the lid twice."

Ty did.

"What is in the box, Doctor Barber?" the hubot asked.

"Nothing." John looked at Ty. "Right?"

"That's right; there's nothing in the box," Ty said.

Time froze for a moment, then John stepped forward, pointed the rifle into the next room and shot the ceiling, blowing open a gaping hole.

Before debris from the ceiling hit the floor, the room disappeared in the jet-black shroud.

"Now what are you going to do?" Ty asked.

John looked calm, almost relaxed. "At this moment, a water bowser pod is hovering over the hole in the roof and lowering itself to cover the opening."

"A water truck?"

"Yes. I preprogrammed a water bowser pod filled with sea water to hover above the building until an opening on the roof appeared." John grinned. "That shroud was expected."

"Why blow the roof?"

"You'll see," John said.

"Lift the veil or I'll start some serious shooting," John called out in a demanding voice.

Instantly, the room was again filled with a bright white light, smoke was billowing toward the ceiling, and the smell of melted cobalt-aluminum caused Ty to rub his nose.

Ty looked up at the ceiling to see the bottom of the water bowser pod covering the hole. The bottom of the pod had a sewer-sized discharge cap; dripping tiny droplets of water onto the floor.

"What did we just do?" Ty asked.

"Checkmate," John said. "Megan, if you lose contact with us, open the water cap."

SEVEN

John walked into the World Crystal's sanctuary. Ty followed and stood next to John directly in front of the lone hubot. The thing's eyes were frozen in a stare. Dust and debris covered its shiny skin and hair.

"The diversion worked," Ty said.

"Yup, it gave me time to blow the roof and park the water pod. The Crystal"—he pointed at the chandelier-looking object hanging from the ceiling across the room—"needs electricity, and salt water conducts electricity very well. Soon it will know about the pod and what will happen if I empty the water."

"Tell me, first?"

"Every circuit in the building, if not half of San Francisco, will snap open, terminating all power." He pointed at the chandelier again. "And we'll be okay, because the circuits would react instantly, keeping us alive and the power off, until we turn it back on."

"I wasn't too good at science. I'm a lawyer, after all, but I think I understand."

"Activate," John said to the hubot with an aggressive tone. Her eyes came to life.

"What is your name?" John asked.

"Isadora."

"How do you communicate with the World Crystal?"

"What? Isn't she linked to it?" Ty asked.

"No. I'll explain later." John looked back at Isadora, "Answer my question."

"It talks to me and I to it."

"How do you talk to it?"

She turned and pointed toward a pedestal underneath the World Crystal with a box on it. "There is a camera and microphone under the Jovian safe," she answered.

John looked at Ty. "That's how it disseminates its orders to the other hubots. Follow me."

They walked up to the pedestal underneath the hanging Crystal; Isadora followed.

"There they are," he pointed at two period-sized dots in the marble stand.

"Camera and microphone," Ty said.

John smiled. "Now we know how to speak directly to the Crystal," he said. He relaxed his shoulders and looked at the pedestal. "Sitting on the roof is a water pod filled with salt water. You make one mistake, and I'll empty it."

Isadora looked up at the covered hole in the ceiling.

"Now, deactivate all S.S. machines in the universe," John commanded.

Nothing happened.

"Megan, open the water valve one percent."

"Earth is now defenseless," Isadora said.

"Megan, close the pod's water valve, and verify it has complied."

"Yes. All S.S. machines have been deactivated."

John nodded. "Permanently disable all K chips."

"They are non-functioning, per your order of this morning. Doctor Barber," Isadora said.

"True, I turned off the K chips, but it was not permanent. Now comply."

"That's not necessary, your program disabled them," Isadora argued.

"Do it," John demanded.

"Done," she answered.

"What did you just do?" Ty asked.

"Two things: Those S.S. machines guarding the building have been turned off, and the K chip I told you about is now and forever off."

Ty looked puzzled.

"If we fail and it retains control of the K chip, everything will go back to the way it was and hope is dead."

"I got it. Remove the best option for control."

John nodded. "Megan, are Terry and Arnold, okay?" John whispered.

"Yes. They are anxious but otherwise fine."

He turned away from the pedestal and Isadora, cupped his hand over his mouth and whispered, "Bring them here. Have Terry carry you along in her pants pocket." John dropped his hands and looked at Ty. "This is where the fun begins." John faced the pedestal. "If Terry or Arnold are harmed, I'll empty the water bowser pod, and if that's not convincing enough, my first gunshot will be at this hubot. Understand?"

"Yes, I understand, they will not be harmed," Isadora said.

"Show me where your individual databank memory balls are located."

Silence greeted this demand.

"Megan, open the water pod's discharge valve and flood this room."

"Stop," Isadora said.

The left wall popped open with a slight hissing sound. Cool, dry air that smelled of decaying flesh drifted into the room

"Ty, go look in that room and tell me what you see," John said, then readied his rifle.

Ty walked to the door and glanced into the room. "Three walls are covered with shot-glass-sized glass balls. Across from this doorway, there are two disgusting, wrinkled, very old-looking people pressed against one wall." He shook his head. "Their feet aren't touching the floor. It looks like they're hanging in the air, and more dead than alive, and more machine than human."

"Come on back," John said. He turned toward the Isadora, and asked, "Those two people are Professor Friendly and General Marble, right?"

"Yes."

"Who are they?" Ty asked.

"Those two people saved humanity. Professor Friendly corrected the moon's orbit, saving Earth from destruction. General Marble saved the Western world in World War Four by defeating the Asian Master Crystal."

"Jesus, how many of these things *are* there?"

"This is the last. And that thing"—he pointed at the chandelier—"had them hung on a wall." John's face flashed red, and he turned his head to look at Isadora. "I'd terminate you if I had the choice," he said, almost growling.

"You need me," she said.

"John, I don't understand. Are you saying these people are part of that thing?" Ty pointed at the chandelier.

"Yes, the World Crystal is a closed-one way system—with

no back door. It disseminates orders to androids, hubots, and other machines, all one way. Those are its only connections to the outside world. Its best option to protect itself from hacking. That is, until it needed human intuition from a genius in an emergency—which the hubots can't supply. That's when those two on the wall, and a third person—Captain Davis—joined with the Crystal."

"Who's Captain Davis?"

"I'll tell you later; it will suffice to say we're alive because I outsmarted him this morning."

"I don't get it. If this thing's as smart as God, why join with a human at all?"

"As much as it thinks it's alive, it's just a machine, and it lacks a gut feeling, common sense, humor, and honor. Something we've developed over millennia. It needed those qualities to save Earth and by extension, itself."

"In honor, you mean, like the Alamo?"

"Yes, 'to the death' for a principle."

"Why was it after you?"

"I was its last threat. With me gone, Earth was its alone." John gave a painful smile. He took a deep breath and pointed at the two people hanging on the wall. "And this was their reward for saving humanity."

"Wow, that is some ugly shit."

John rubbed his hand through his hair, angry. He looked back at the camera. "Restart the supply chain, food, clothing, water, medical, waste, power, and all administrative services in the universe. It's time to feed and take care of people "

"I can't," Isadora said. "Your instructions to Captain Robert Davis this morning disrupted those tasks. You must issue new commands."

John turned to look at Ty and smiled. "I told you it was

smart. If I issue new commands, this thing will use them to amend the code that's keeping me alive, and before the last symbol is input, we'd be dead."

Ty took a quick glance at Isadora. "I see what you mean; it's a crafty little snake."

John turned and walked into the room that confined Professor Friendly and General Marble. Then he took several steps toward the glass ball-covered wall and, using the butt of his rifle, smashed a row of them.

"Stop. All services are running," Isadora stated, now standing at the doorway, watching.

"That was easy: Break some glass and get a yes," Ty said.

"Remember I told you how powerful Megan is?"

"Yes."

"Each one of those glass things is a Megan, and losing one is not good."

"Oh my God, there're hundreds."

"Joined together, there's nothing left to learn, no more secrets left on Earth."

"And you lived. That's crazy."

John shrugged his shoulders. "All thanks to Megan. Megan, verify: Are all services running?"

"I cannot verify off-planet. Your requests are being fulfilled on Earth."

"Why can't you verify off-planet?" John asked.

"They don't exist off-planet."

John's face went white, his knees buckled. He dropped to one knee, gasping for air.

"John, what's wrong, what's wrong?" Ty shouted, hurrying to him.

"They're all dead!"

"Who? Who's dead?"

"I think everyone!" John began to cry.

Ty knelt next to John and wrapped his right arm around his shoulders, not truly understanding what John meant.

Terry and Arnold entered the room. Stunned by what they saw, they stopped and stared at John, who was still sobbing.

"What's wrong?" Terry asked.

"Oh my God, this just can't be true." He looked up at Ty. "Please help me up," he whispered to Ty.

John stood, his eyes bloodshot and filled with tears. He took a deep breath and rubbed his right hand through his hair. He walked up to Terry. "Please give me the crystal that's in your pocket."

She reached into her pants pocket, removed the glass crystal, and handed it to him.

"Thank you." He put the crystal into his pocket, turned, and moved back to stand next to Ty. Then, feeling a sudden wave of rage, he rushed back to the wall and used the stock of his gun to break another row of crystals.

"John, what are you doing? Stop," Ty said, putting his hand on John's shoulder.

John turned to face Ty; he was again shaking with emotion.

"Megan, answer my questions so Ty can hear you: What is the population on Earth?" John asked.

"Three billion five million."

"Megan, what was Earth's population in twenty-one twenty-one?" John asked.

"Six billion."

"Megan, what year did the colonization of outer space begin?"

"Twenty-one hundred."

John turned to face Isadora. "What's the human population in outer space?"

Silence.

"Answer me!" John shouted.

"Two billion six hundred fifty million."

"Megan, is that true?"

"No," Megan answered.

Terry and Arnold looked confused and did not understand what they had just heard.

EIGHT

"Ty, come with me, and you, too." John pointed at Isadora.

John walked up to Professor Friendly, Ty by his side and Isadora a step behind them. Terry and Arnold stayed by the doorway.

"Please kill me," she whispered in a weak, wispy voice.

Then her gaze went blank, and her voice became stronger: "How can I help you?"

"Release Professor Friendly," John said.

Silence.

John looked at Ty. "Destroy a row of crystals."

Professor Friendly's eyes changed and became human-looking again. "Please kill me," she whispered.

John waited until Ty had destroyed a row of crystals.

"I promise I'll end your suffering very soon,

but I need you to answer some questions first."

Terry and Arnold came into the room and stood behind Ty.

"Professor Friendly, are you currently linked to the World Crystal?" John asked.

"Not now. Please kill me," she whispered again.

"Why are these two people still alive?" Ty asked.

"Backup, insurance, whatever you want to call it. Why let them go? They might come in handy," John said, fighting his rage.

"Insurance... backup," Ty repeated to himself.

John suddenly felt that sickening feeling again. *Backup*, he thought. *Why send people to live in space?*

"Professor Friendly, how many humans live off Planet Earth?" he asked.

"Kill me," she whispered.

"Please answer. How many?" John asked again.

"Zero."

It only took a second before Terry opened her mouth and inhaled a lungful of air. She held her breath like a young child for several more seconds before finally releasing the air, followed by a primal scream of pain.

She bent over, dropped to her knees, and screamed out, "No!"

Ty leaned down and gently put his left hand on her shoulder.

Arnold's reaction was very different. He lunged at Isadora and slammed it against the wall, shattering several glass balls. He choked and punched it with every ounce of his strength until he was exhausted.

John watched Arnold with indifference. Ty watched with mixed emotions. He wanted to join Arnold, but felt he could not leave Terry.

Arnold stood and stepped away from the machine. It lay on the floor, face smashed, neck broken, and its eyes had been knocked out.

Ty looked at Terry, who was calming down. He stood and

walked to John. "I want to make sure I understand the lay of the land before any more crazy shit happens. This might not be the best time, considering what we just learned. But I've got to know, okay?"

John nodded.

"This morning, you downloaded a computer program into that machine"—he pointed at the chandelier—"and that program told the world how they'd been fucked for the past hundred plus years, give or take a few decades. Right?"

"Yes," John said.

"Okay, some facts next: What year did this machine become Earth's supreme leader?"

"Twenty-one forty-seven, during the last war, when it merged with General Marble."

"The guy on the wall," Ty stated.

"Yes."

"We're in the year twenty-two twenty-two, right?"

"Yes."

"So, for the last seventy-five years, this machine has been rebuilding the world at the same time it's been killing people."

"It appears so."

"When did people start migrating off Earth after the last war?"

"Megan, answer Ty's question."

"Twenty-one seventy-two."

"There's our answer: a whole lot of dead people for the past fifty years. I can't believe no one noticed."

"I didn't," John admitted. "I thought everything was perfect. I'd hear stories that living off planet was a great adventure. How much fun they were having and constantly extended invitations to visit."

"Now I understand." Ty nodded. "That's how it kept

people joining the party. There was no *way* you could have known. Your story saved three billion people from certain death. Now we can't let our anger put the survivors on a collision course with starvation, right?"

"Yes."

"That'd be a good day's work: Save the world and solve a crime," Ty said, smiling. "And why did you choose to act today after all this time?"

"The World Crystal had just perfected the process to witness the visions and sounds of the recently dead."

"What do you mean 'witness'?" Ty asked.

"It's what I saw on my medical hologram: A female body was being prepared for cremation. Two hubots were standing over the naked woman, and one of the machines plunged a metal rod into the nape of her neck. It only took a second, and they looked up at the holographic window floating above the edge of the plastic table.

"Every sound and vision of her life started flashing on the hologram. It started with a birth and moved along well into her twenties. 'Stop,' the hubot who'd stuck the probe into her neck said. 'I knew this person. She had a baby. Save these memories. I want to see what happened to her offspring,' it said."

"That's scary. I'm embarrassed by what I know about myself, let alone imagining someone watching it on a movie screen."

"The same. But death was no longer safe for me or Megan, because it would allow the World Crystal to get the key to open Megan's databank through my memories and end all hope for humanity's return to normal, so I had to act."

Ty took a deep breath. "So, telling your story was the answer?"

"It was either have Megan's databank raped or me fight it."

Silence for a moment while Ty thought. "What about the rich? How'd they let this happen and where are they now?"

"They went along, got richer and turned themselves into hubots."

"What the hell. They just went along. Holy shit." He looked dumbfounded. "What about you?"

"I'm not a hubot."

Ty gave him a "Really?" expression.

John sighed. "I'm one hundred percent real, and did not sell out."

"What about money. How'd you get that?"

"In the very beginning I went to a homeless shelter. They took care of me. After that, I created a new identity and got a job, like everyone else."

"How rich did you get?"

"Not too much; I needed to keep a low profile. Over time I had enough to protect myself and build several homes to hide in. However, it was money and bad timing at a bank that led Captain Davis to discovery me."

"So that's how Davis got into the picture?"

"Yes, I was at a bank when it was robbed by an Untouchable and—it's a long story."

Terry got to her feet, looked at Ty, then John. "How can you two just talk like nothing has happened? It's ugly."

"I feel everything you do," John said coolly. "But it's a machine. The World Crystal does not feel remorse, or anger. It's a lifeless box of quantum qubits. Our goal is to turn it into a single-purpose toaster."

Terry looked at John, then Ty. Frustrated, she squeezed her hands into fists and attacked Isadora. Screaming again and again, "How could we have created anything so ugly?" she cried out with each kick. Exhausted, she stood straight, panting, and stared at Arnold.

Ty faced John. "I'm a little old for this crap." He shook his head from side to side. "This place is a nightmare. You can send me back now."

John looked into Ty's eyes to make sure he was kidding.

Then he turned to face Professor Friendly and asked, "Where are the off-planet bodies?"

"Why do you want to know that?" Ty asked.

"To bring them back home." John looked back, "Please answer me, Professor Friendly."

"The back side of the moon."

Terry gasped; Arnold dropped to his knees, wailing.

Ty touched John's right shoulder. "I don't want to pile on, but I've been thinking about insurance."

"Insurance?"

"There's got to be a backup machine," he whispered.

John was so shocked by the prospect, he almost lunged forward, touching her body. "Professor, is there another Crystal?" He dreaded the answer, his heart racing.

"Yes."

John took a deep breath, rubbed his hand through his hair, then he stepped away, turned, and left the room. Ty, Terry, and Arnold followed.

John walked up to the Crystal chandelier, looked up at it, his face twitched with rage, and he lifted his rifle.

"I don't think we're quite ready for that," Ty said calmly.

"I know, but I've got to," John replied, his voice deep with anger.

He turned slightly to his left and faced a metallic, handbag-sized, translucent-looking box sitting on top of a five-foot-tall marble pillar, a bit to the right of and underneath the Crystal chandelier. He aimed at the box.

"John, please don't," a female voice called out from behind them.

They all turned to see a hubot standing at the entrance doorway, dressed like Isadora, except, blond hair and pink lipstick.

Without hesitation, Ty fired at the figure, and in a flash of fiery gas, it was gone.

Ty looked at John. "I hope you don't mind. I'm just tired of the drama."

"No, but it knows what I'm about to do," John said, glancing up at the chandelier.

"Okay, you got me. Why do you want to shoot that box?"

"In twenty-one ninety-five, space miners working on the 16 Psyche asteroid found an alien spacecraft. It was initially determined the ship was of no value, with the only interesting aspect being its age. At first, they thought it was a hundred million years old, but it turned out to be one million. However, that"—he pointed at the box—"was in the ship."

"What is it?" Ty asked.

"The ship's safe, or lockbox. They named it the Jovan Safe after the woman who found it. They brought it back to Earth for study."

"So why destroy it?" Ty asked.

"Because the last person who reached inside the box got linked with the World Crystal."

"You mean Captain Davis?" Ty asked.

"Yes." John looked at the box again, then pushed the muzzle of his rifle into it. *Zzzppnt! Zzzppnt!*

The room was quiet after the blast of energy entered the

Jovan Safe. John pulled the gun away from the box and stepped aside.

Ty hunched down to look inside, but John grabbed him by the shirt and pulled him back just before a jet of flames shot out of the box, almost reaching the main doorway.

"Whoo. That was close!" Ty whispered.

He turned and saw Arnold and Terry standing at the side doorway, expressions amazed.

Surprisingly, another hubot entered the room from the main entrance. "That was a mistake, Doctor Barber," it said. "There is no going back now."

John ignored the comment and instead looked at Ty. "Come on. Let's finish with Professor Friendly."

As they moved past Terry, she put out a hand to stop them. "What is happening? What is happening to me? I feel weak, my legs are shaking, and I want to throw up."

She grabbed John's shirt with clenched fingers and stared into his eyes. "What's happening? I hear a voice—a voice I don't know." Her face had turned pale, her eyes were wide, and her breathing hot and rapid.

In a calm tone, John said, "Everything's okay, Terry; you're simply becoming human. For the first time in your life, your mind is taking control and talking to you."

"I don't want this! I don't want this! I'm scared—make it stop."

Ty put his hand on her right shoulder. "Terry, I know what you're feeling. Take a deep breath and try to relax. Everything's okay; you'll be fine in a minute."

"What is happening to us?" Arnold asked, his voice shaking and high-pitched. "I am feeling, hearing, the same things."

"Like Ty said, just try to relax," John said. "The chip that's controlled you since childhood has finally lost its effect. You and everyone on Earth are now acting human. You're finally free of that damned World Crystal."

"But I feel so alone. I don't know what to do," Arnold said.

"The hardest part of being human is realizing we're all alone and it's love and friends that fill the empty void and give us meaning," Ty said.

"That voice in my head, though! Who's talking to me?" Terry nearly shouted.

Ty smiled. "That's you, actually. That's you thinking."

"I don't like it; it's asking so many questions. Screaming at me."

"That... will never stop," Ty said. "That's you figuring things out. It's called your 'inner voice,' and it comes with a friend named your 'conscience,' and in most cases, it's your best friend."

"Well, right now, I don't like my best friend," Terry said, but she relaxed a little, feeling better knowing what was happening to her.

Ty laughed. "Wait until it tells you not to do something you really want to do." He grinned.

"Terry, please let go of my shirt. I've got something to do."

Terry released her grip. John stepped aside to walk back into the other room to see the professor. Ty followed.

"Please kill me," she whispered when John stood facing her.

John nodded, then said, "Last two questions: First, where is the backup Crystal located?"

"The Nevada desert."

John's face flushed white; he stepped back, feeling weak, almost sick to his stomach.

"Let me guess," Ty said to the professor, frowning. "Near Reno—in a facility named the Genetic Answer?"

"Yes."

"Oh God, this is horrible," Ty whispered. Then he immediately turned, and said, "No, John, it's *not* your fault."

John rubbed his hand through his hair, feeling the worst guilt of his life. "It all started with me," he whispered.

"What's guarding it?" Ty asked Professor Friendly.

"Please kill me," she whispered.

"What's guarding it?" Ty asked in a stronger voice, demanding she reply.

"Untouchables, led by a hubot."

"What are these Untouchables?" Ty asked, looking at John.

"The destitute, Indigenous, or unhealthy," John answered. "The K chip wasn't offered to them, and society named them Untouchables."

"Seriously?" Ty asked, shocked.

John nodded. "Yes, the deformed, poor, uneducated."

"No, that can't be true. How poor?"

"Think Calcutta, street people, Indian reservations."

"Man, this place sucks," Ty whispered, shocked, and thinking: *Genocide by neglect.*

"Professor Friendly. "How powerful is the Nevada Crystal?" John asked.

"I don't know," she whispered.

"How many Untouchables are living near G.A.?" John asked.

"Please," she whispered.

"How many, Professor Friendly?" John asked again.

"A thousand."

"Wait a minute," Ty said. "How are destitute people surviving in Nevada?"

"I have no idea," John said. "Megan, describe the Untouchables living near G.A."

Ty looked on as John listened to Megan.

"Two Indigenous reservations were located near G.A.: the Sparks Indian Colony and the Paiute tribe. The Sparks Reservation was very close to G.A.; the other was about fifty miles away," Megan said.

"There's gotta be more," Ty said. "G.A. sounds too important."

"Ten S.S. machines, if they were in operation, would be enough power," John said. "But you're right: There must be more. Professor Friendly, where are the other Nevada S.S. machines being stored?"

"Fallon Naval Air Station."

"I remember that base," Ty said. "It's not far from Reno."

John looked at Ty. "What about additional Untouchables?" he asked, thinking out loud. "Professor Friendly, what's the world population of Untouchables?"

"I don't know. They are scattered around the Pacific Islands, South America.... Please."

Ty handed John his pistol, taking John's rifle, then stepped several feet back.

"Forgive me," the professor said.

John pointed the gun. *Zzzppnt! Zzzppnt!*

She and General Marble were finally at peace.

"You ready to return to G.A.?" John asked Ty, his voice soft and sounding forlorn.

"Amazing—full circle, back to where this all started," Ty said, saddened by the thought. "What do you want to do with that?" He pointed at the chandelier.

"I want to blow it apart, but we might need it. Megan, leave a Mosquito here to keep watch on this room. And, Megan, why didn't you tell me there was a backup Crystal?"

"You didn't ask."

Ty tried not to laugh. *Boy, does that sound like Megan.*

They turned and started to leave.

"Wait a second," Ty said. "What the hell do we call this new Crystal? We can't keep referring to them the same way. Plus, what if there're more than two?"

John took a breath, thinking of all the horror the World Crystal had caused. "How about Pandora?"

NINE

"You want to call it Pandora?" Ty asked. "Like the Greek box the gods gave Pandora that looks ordinary but once opened can explode with unpredictable, terribly harmful results?"

John shrugged. "Except we built this one, not the gods."

Ty nodded, thinking, *God, I hope it's not true.*

They turned away from the Crystal to leave the room.

"Where are you two going?" Terry asked.

"To Reno, Nevada, and a government research facility where all this might have started," Ty answered.

"What is going to happen to us?" she asked.

"You'll figure it out," John answered.

"Figure it out?" she said. "What does that mean, 'figure it out'? I was beginning to like you; now we're back to Mr. Ugly. You two are not going anywhere without us and that's coming from my new friend screaming in my head."

They walked out of the World Crystal building and to their surprise, saw the plaza filled with people sitting or standing around. They stopped at the edge of the portico facing the plaza.

"Who are all these people?" Ty asked.

"Real people," John answered.

"There must be thousands here. What are you going to do?" Ty asked.

"Turning around is an option," John said. Then he shot a glance at Arnold. "Do you know why these people are here?"

"I passed the word we would be here," he said, looking sheepish.

"There they are! There they are!" someone screamed.

And with that said, the entire mass of people stood together without a sound, then drifted closer and stared at the four of them.

"You better have one sweet tongue if we're going to get out of this alive," Ty said.

John shot him a quick glance. "I got this," he said, looking and feeling confident.

He walked from the portico toward the destroyed fountain. As he moved forward, the mass of people parted and formed an aisle for him to pass. There was not a sound coming from the crowd. He reached the fountain and stepped up onto a remaining portion of its sidewall. Facing Hays Street, he studied the crowd of hundreds and thought, *What am I going to say?*

"Megan," he whispered, "open the release valve to the water bowser and flood the building."

A loud popping noise erupted as the databanks within the building exploded, followed by the top-floor walls bursting outward in a flush of steam as the power supply shorted out. The ground shook as the foundation of the building twisted under the weight of the internal explosions. The plaza shook.

People screamed and dropped to their knees, covering their heads.

Dust filled the air, and a white cloud of steam formed above the building and drifted east. Everything went silent, and the westerly breeze returned and pushed the dust across the city, clearing the air.

"What just happened?" Terry asked, her fearful eyes looking at Ty.

"A diversion," Ty said. "Buying time for John to collect his thoughts and get us out of here."

Silence reigned for a little longer. Then:

"My name is John Barber," he shouted to the throng of people. "The sound you just heard was me terminating the World Crystal. You will never again hear a buzzing in your head or its voice ordering you what to do. You are now fully human."

People stared at him, expressions confused; some covered their mouths with their fingertips or hands.

"This morning, I told you everything that machine did to you. What its plan was and why we had to fight against it. You were furious. I saw that for myself, right here." He pointed around the plaza. "I watched wave after wave of people try to enter that building"—he pointed again—"and each wave was killed."

He again looked around the plaza. They all looked back with the same wide-eyed frozen, confused expression and fingertips over their mouths.

John rubbed his hand through his hair, thinking, *Oh my God, how do I do this? They don't understand they were slaves being led to slaughter.*

"In the next couple of days, you will learn everything the World Crystal did to Earth and why I had to silence it. That voice in your head was implanted when you were children, and it came from a machine, a nonliving box of wires. A voice that was leading you and everyone else toward death."

A voice screamed out, "What have you done that makes me feel so alone?"

Other people started screaming, "Yes, what have you done?"

John raised his right hand, palm up, and yelled back, "Stop and listen! You are not alone; you are safe."

More shouts and cries, with people yelling:

"This is your fault!"

"Murder, murder—"

Zzzppnt! Zzzppnt! The middle of the World Crystal building exploded into a gigantic fireball. The sound of the explosion was almost ear-popping. Everyone in the plaza dropped to their knees, except Ty, who was holding an SS rifle and had it pointed at the burning building.

He moved slowly over to where John knelt atop the sidewall and stepped up next to him. "You aren't prepared for this, John. I'll take it from here."

Looking up, John nodded, then stood by Ty.

Ty fired another shot at the building.

"My name is Ty Leggett. I, along with Ms. Terry Cheer and Mr. Arnold Blackman here, were just inside that building." He pointed. "The damn thing we just destroyed was about to kill all of you. John Barber saved us from sure death, so stop whining."

He glared around the plaza. "We have learned there is *another* World Crystal in Nevada, and we are going there to stop it from killing you. Everything is still working: food, water, electricity. If you remember what you did for work before, keep doing it. When we return, we'll explain everything. In the meantime, you're safe here and there's nothing to fear."

The plaza was silent, every eye focused on Ty. Nobody moved or made a sound, their faces said it all: fear.

"We're going now." Ty's demeanor displayed nothing but total confidence.

"Destroy it!" someone shouted, and other shouts followed.

Ty put his flat palm into the air. "John Barber and I will do that, and we'll return here tomorrow to lead you out of this crisis."

Still kneeling, Terry twisted and looked up at Ty, an angry expression on her face. She leaned forward and tapped John on a knee with her right hand.

John looked down.

She whispered, "You're not leaving us."

John looked at Ty and gestured toward Terry.

"Terry Cheer and Arnold Blackman will also be joining us," Ty told the crowd.

"No!" came a shout. "Someone must stay with us. You can't all go!"

John stiffened, ready for a fight.

TEN

Someone else hollered, "No, don't leave us!"

Many in the crowd began to yell, "Stay!" or "Don't leave, don't leave!" The shouts begin to grow louder.

"This isn't good; I've seen this before," Ty said, looking at John. "If they surge toward us, fire your gun into the air."

To John's surprise, Arnold tapped his leg. "Would you come down, so I can stand up there and say something?"

John jumped down and Arnold stepped up next to Ty and faced the crowd, then began: "I know how you all feel. When the voice in my head went silent and the hum stopped, I was terrified. We're all feeling the same... isolation? Yes, and fear, too. We're all scared. I just saw the ugly World Crystal, and we just can't tolerate a second one. John Barber and Ty Leggett must leave, and they will return to lead us. I will stay here with you and wait for their return."

Ty glanced down at John, said, "He was prepared."

John glanced to his left at Terry, thinking, *Did she know?*

Terry's mouth was slightly open; she looked shocked, feeling deserted.

Someone in the crowd continued to shout, "Don't go, don't go!" while others started pressing closer, chanting, "Don't go. Don't go. Don't go...." Fearful looks flashed across many faces as the mob tightened, forcing people together, shoving, pushing—

John fired his pistol into the air. "We have no choice! I promise we'll return tomorrow. Now make a path so we can get to the street."

Ty jumped off the fountain sidewall and landed next to John. Arnold didn't move, though. The crowd settled and moved to create an aisle.

John and Ty started to walk through the mob, and Terry quickly followed, afraid of the number of people staring at her.

She reached up and touched Ty's right shoulder, then asked, "You promise to protect me?"

Ty looked into her eyes. "Absolutely."

The three moved through the crowd as an aisle opened. Voices muttered, saying, "Don't let them go!" and "Stop them." Others just stared. The aisle pressed in on them, and suddenly, a woman stood in front of John. Ty took hold of Terry's hand.

The woman looked terrified, her fingers were twisted, and she grabbed John by his shirt. He stood straight and leaned away from her slightly, ready to push her back if need be.

"You *promise* to come back? You *promise* to guide us?" she asked, obviously scared and panicky.

"Yes, I promise," he said confidently.

She stepped aside, the aisle opened again, and the people lining it went silent as the trio reached Hays Street.

John glanced at Ty, and mouthed, "That was scary."

Ty nodded and released Terry's hand.

They crossed the street and got into John's pod, with Ty and John in front and Terry behind them.

"That woman scared the hell out of me," John said.

"Arnold is ugly; he should have come with us," Terry said.

"Maybe so, but his speech saved the day," John said.

"And his own skin," Ty said.

John nodded.

"I don't know what that means," Terry said. "I think he is ugly for leaving us. I thought we were going to die, and I'm sure it's going to be dark where we're going, and that, that Pandora thing will try to kill us."

"Probably true, but we'll be ready for its tricks, and we have the advantage," John said.

"What's our advantage?" Ty asked.

"We want to live; it wants to exist," John answered.

Megan brought the pod to life with a soft hum, lifted off the ground, rose several feet in the air, turned to face north, and headed toward San Francisco Bay and once over the water, it turned northeast.

Ty looked out the passenger window. "Where's the Bay Bridge?"

"It wasn't rebuilt," John answered.

"Oh, man," Ty whispered, taking a deep breath, thinking, *What else is gone?*

They soon passed above the Sacramento–San Joaquin River Delta headed toward Nevada.

"I don't see any roads or streets," Ty said. "And where's Highway 80?"

"It was dismantled," John replied, "just like the highway system. Two major inventions occurred in twenty-ninety. The flying pod and self-replicating nanobots. The pod replaced ground transportation. There was an epic environmental movement throughout America to correct the damage done by the just-ended war and the motor vehicle."

"God love environmentalists," Ty said, still looking out the window.

"So," John went on, "The microrobots were programmed to devour concrete, asphalt, guardrails, signposts, bridges, streetlights, stoplights. Basically, anything associated with ground transportation was disassembled and the land was returned to its original state."

"How the hell did they do that?" Ty looked at John, shocked.

"Megan, what does the acronym MORPH stand for?"

"Material Optimization and Regenerative Processing Hubs."

John looked back at Ty and grinned. "Megan, create a hologram of a MORPH working," John said.

Suddenly, the windshield was transformed into a picture of billions of tiny microrobots moving over the Earth like a river, consuming everything in their path, and leaving wide swaths of bare ground behind.

Ty watched in amazement. "That is so cool. All that crap is gone—unbelievable. This happened everywhere?"

"Yes."

"How long did it take in America?"

"They finished in the U.S. in late twenty one-forty."

"I had a friend in Alabama whose parents lost their farm to a train station and railroad. This would have been sweet revenge."

The windshield returned to normal. Ty shook his head and sighed. "What about buildings?"

"Much faster. Cities, towns, anything that wasn't of use was removed."

"What if a person got in the way?"

"If it wasn't part of the programing, the bots would just pass by."

"What a horrifying weapon."

"That never happened. Doomsday."

"As if a nut job would care," Ty said.

"True. That's why a self-destruct program was included and nothing alive could be harmed."

"And that kept it from being used as a weapon?"

"Yes."

"What about resorts or amusement parks?"

"Some were rebuilt until they were considered obsolete after nonuse," John said.

"When this garbage is over, let's find one. I'll need time to readjust and relax," Ty said, still looking out the windshield, feeling sad. "How long before we get to G.A. and Pandora?"

"Eleven minutes," John answered.

"What's G.A. and Pandora?" Terry asked, lost in all the new things she was learning.

"G.A. stands for Genetic Answer," Ty said, "and Pandora is what we've named the second, backup, World Crystal. G.A. is where John worked a hundred eighty-five years ago—and apparently where your nightmare was conceived."

"Pandora was created at the place we're going and where you worked?" she asked, sounding shocked.

"Kind of," John said. "It became operational after I left."

"Could it have been stopped?" she asked.

John rubbed his hand through his hair.

"I was there, too, Terry, and *no one* knew it would turn out this way," Ty said.

The atmosphere in the pod became tense as they flew on.

"Sorry, John," Terry said. "I didn't mean it. I'm just mad

because I was so scared when we walked through the crowd to the pod."

"Actually, Terry, I could have shut it down, stopped it, but I never thought we were creating something so horrible." He glanced at Ty, feeling sad and angry. "But we're going to shut that damn thing off now."

Ty looked at John, and asked, "Are we in a hurry?"

"Why are you asking?"

"Do we have to do this right away today?"

"I don't think so."

"Good, I need a little time to catch my breath—and I'm hungry and have a lot more questions."

"You're having trouble breathing?" Terry asked.

Ty smiled. "No, it's just an expression that means I need some time to process what's going on around me."

John glanced at the pod's clock: 4:00 p.m. He thought for a moment. *Pandora knows we're coming, so what difference does it make if we stop?*

"Let's eat and spend the night somewhere and start early in morning. Any ideas?" John asked.

"What about Sacramento?" Ty asked. "We can't be too far from there, right?"

"Megan, how much of Sacramento is active?" John asked.

"The capitol building, Sutter's Fort, Old Town, and other historic sights are still viable."

"I had a friend there," Ty said. "Ross Relles was his name. He took me to a great restaurant there named the Firehouse."

"Megan, is the Firehouse Restaurant in Sacramento still operating?" John asked.

"The only restaurant named the Firehouse is located in Old Town Sacramento, and it is operational."

"That's the one. I can't believe it's open and the Bay Bridge is gone," Ty said.

"We'll be in Sacramento in eleven minutes. Our rendezvous with the past will have to—"

"I want a great steak and a double bourbon," Ty interrupted, clearly excited.

"Oh, remember how I told you some things will be different and strange?" John asked.

"Yes... please don't break my heart," Ty said.

"Megan, contact the Firehouse and have the androids ready the place—three for dinner."

"Done," Megan said.

"I could use a shower," John said. "Megan, contact Sutter's Fort, have the androids ready it—three to spend the night."

"Done," Megan said.

Ty smiled. "I was in Sacramento on a campaign stop just after the actual firehouse was remolded to be a restaurant in the 'sixties. Best-tasting Steak Diane ever, and what a presentation! It came to the table, and they set it on fire." He sighed. "That was a fun evening."

Five minutes later, Megan landed the pod on Second Street in front of the Firehouse Restaurant.

"No," Ty said. "Not here. Park in the alley behind the restaurant and we'll enter through the patio. It's easier and very pretty. Well, it was."

They landed in the alley and saw that the street was paved with pristine cobblestones. They got out of the pod and stood a moment, looking up and down the alley.

"It's a little-known fact the original firehouse, and actual firehouse, was first constructed in eighteen fifty-three," Ty said.

"Well, this is not that place," John said. "After three

hundred sixty-nine years and the two world wars that took place on U.S. soil after your time, you might not recognize it."

"Gee, thanks a bunch, John," Ty said.

They walked west down the cobblestone alley alongside a stone wall separating the restaurant from the alley. Halfway down the wall, they reached two, seven-foot-tall, black, ivy-covered iron gates.

Ty smiled. "This is the place. A Steak Diane and a bourbon coming up?" he wondered aloud.

"What's a Diane steak and a bourbon?" Terry asked.

John laughed. "Ty, stop for a second. I didn't have the heart to tell you this earlier, but steak's been gone for a hundred years now. It was deemed cruel to kill animals just for people to eat them. Oh, and then the K chip made alcohol and other stimulates superfluous."

"You're kidding. No *steak*?" Ty asked, shocked and disappointed.

"Ditto for vegetables and all other flora."

"So plants are off limits, too?" Ty said.

"Yup. If it's a living being, it's never used for food."

"So we're having rocks for dinner?" Ty snarked.

"Pretty much, but they taste just like the real thing and are very healthy."

Terry was looking at Ty like he'd lost his mind. "You want to kill something to eat it? That's ugly," she said, clearly repulsed by the thought. She grimaced, curled her lips, and stared at Ty for a second.

"That explains all the animals I saw while we were in the air," Ty said. "The sky was filled with birds, and Sacramento Valley was covered by herds of grazing game animals." He shook his head in wonder. "I can't imagine what the Midwestern plains look like." He looked at John. "I served on the Natural Resources committee when I was a U.S. Senator, and a witness said she wanted all the people to disappear so the animals could be happy. I thought she was nuts." He raised his eyebrows. "Looks like she got her wish." He shook his head slowly, this time in disappointment.

"What's a senator?" Terry asked.

"A waste of time."

A what? What does that mean? Terry thought.

They walked through the gates into a stone patio and saw that five Ficus trees filled the canopy with green leaves, along with flowers hanging from the jacaranda and crape myrtle trees. The air was soft and perfumed by the flowers.

Twenty round tables, covered with white tablecloths and crystal glasses filled the patio. A twenty-foot-round Italian cascading fountain held the place of honor in the center of the patio; its running water falling into the retaining basin added a soothing sound to the beauty.

"Wow, it's just as I remember it," Ty said, smiling. "Seeing this makes me very happy."

"You've really been here before?" Terry asked.

"Yes, when we killed cows and drank rye," he said.

"That's ugly." She squinted her rich brown eyes and pursed her full lips.

The patio was empty of people, but two bald-headed androids were standing by the fountain.

One of the machines approached the group. "How may I help you, Doctor Barber, Mr. Leggett, and Terry Cheer?"

"That's scary," Ty whispered to John.

"We would like dinner," John said.

"Please follow me."

The human-looking machine was dressed in traditional wait staff attire with a white, long-sleeved dress shirt, jet-black cotton pants, black wingtip shoes, and white socks. The outfit was completed with a white hand towel draped over its right arm.

They followed it to a round table set for four in the center of the patio and sat. Ty and John placed the white cloth napkins on their laps. Terry watched, thinking, *What are they doing?* She copied them, though, as this was the first time she'd ever been to a restaurant.

"Would you like water or another drink of your choice?" it asked.

"Water," John said.

"Water for me," Terry said.

Ty smiled. "I'll have water and a double Jack Daniels neat."

"We do not have Jack Daniels. Would you like a substitute?"

"There's no such thing, but yes, bring me something that will burn going down and make me feel wonderful when I'm finished."

John turned his head from side to side, grinning.

Terry didn't get the joke and stared at Ty, thinking, *Why would he want to burn himself?*

The android left the table and returned several moments later, carrying a black, cork-covered round tray with their drinks in the center. It served the water first to John and Terry, then it served Ty hot imitation tea in a cup, also providing him with a mostly full ceramic teapot.

"Well, the joke's on me," Ty said, smelling the tea.

"May I take your food order?" it asked.

"Yes," Ty said, "I'll have a Steak Diane, rare, a baked potato with butter, sour cream, chives, and a cold spinach salad."

"I'll do my best, Mr. Leggett," it said.

"I'll have the same," John said, laughing.

Terry stared at them. "You two are getting uglier by the moment."

"What would you like, Ms. Cheer?" it asked.

"The Soylent Green, light on the salt, cooked over-well."

"And you think *we're* weird," Ty spit out, laughing. "John, you liked to drink; how did you get booze? Or did you have to just give it up?"

"I had a supply, and Megan kept a record of locations that stored wine and spirits," John said.

"Average people stopped drinking, right?"

"Yes, and eventually stopped traveling. Like here at the Firehouse, androids maintained the location, and when people, as I said, stopped coming, the androids dismantled it."

"Terry, you agree with all this?" Ty asked.

"Yes, the only place I wanted to go was the moon to see my...." She paused. "I never had a desire to go see anything else."

How fucking sad, Ty thought with more emphasis this time.

The food was delivered to the table five minutes later.

"I have no idea what I'm about to eat, but it smells good," Ty said.

They finished dinner. Ty pushed his chair away from the table, leaned back and looked at John. He looked serious. "I have some observations and identified several problems."

ELEVEN

"Okay, what?" John asked.

"First, everyone I've seen looks under forty and most are in their twenties. Is that by design?"

"Why would it be? Babies are born all the time," John answered.

"Are you sure? You said natural childbirth stopped a long time ago. Who's in charge of making babies?"

John rubbed his hand through his hair. He knew the answer: Pandora. He sighed, feeling he'd missed something important.

Terry suddenly looked and felt uneasy, dreading the answers.

"Pandora and the San Francisco Crystal must be communicating, and they must know about Megan and how helpless we are without her."

"Yes, but—" John said.

"Hold on," Ty interrupted. "Can we even trust Megan? That World Crystal surely hacked her. How does she know current events, you know, in real time? And she knew about Pandora and didn't tell you." He stared at John, thinking, *We're screwed.* "The ball's in your court, Doctor Barber."

John took a sip of water, Ty a sip of tea, while Terry stared at John and didn't move a muscle, thinking, *Even I know we are lost without Megan.*

"We'll have to ask Megan regarding the births," John finally said. "As for her being hacked, it's the opposite. When I downloaded my program into Captain Davis, I included a virus to protect Megan from being violated. Once that was accomplished, Megan absorbed what she could; there was too much data and she could only get the last five years on Earth. You can trust what she tells us."

The tension evaporated. Terry relaxed, relieved. Ty, too.

"Now for your observations. Megan, how many people on Earth are younger than twenty years of age?"

"Three hundred eighty-four thousand," Megan answered.

"That can't be right," John said.

"It's correct. That is the underage population of the Untouchables," Megan said.

"Untouchables," Ty repeated. "Again that horrid word."

"It's just a word to describe people who never got the K chip or other computer enhancements," John said.

"It's all the same. Pejorative and sad," Ty said. "Who were the Untouchables in the States?"

"Indian tribes, Eskimos, Indigenous peoples who didn't want to leave their land," John answered.

"Where are they today?"

"I don't really know. Megan, where are the Untouchables in the Western U.S. located?"

"Small community farms in California, Oregon, Nevada, New Mexico—"

"Megan, stop," John said. "That's enough."

Ty's expression was sad.

John understood his feeling, as Ty's past was filled with racism and hate. He lifted his eyebrows and thought about Ty's observations. "Megan, what's the population count on Earth below nineteen years old, excluding the Untouchables?"

"Zero."

Stunned, neither man spoke for a moment.

Then: "Oh boy, no babies," Ty mumbled under his breath.

"Megan, when was the last baby born on Earth, excluding the Untouchables?"

"Twenty-two oh three."

"Megan, what's the median age of the humans on Earth who were altered?" John asked.

"Twenty-nine point five."

John rubbed his hand though his hair.

"What's the youngest?" Ty asked.

"Nineteen."

"What does that mean?" Terry asked. "What does that *mean*?" she repeated, her voice building with emotion.

"Excluding the Untouchables, it means there's no one alive on Earth under nineteen years old," John answered.

Terry eyes filled with tears, and she covered her mouth with her fingers. "Ugly, everything I learn is so ugly, so ugly," her voice tailed off into a whisper.

This is horrible, John thought, watching Terry.

Ty waited a moment, feeling Terry's heartbreak, then he looked at John. "So we can't terminate Pandora."

"What? Why not?" John asked.

"The perfect example is sitting with us, and you said it your-self: Those living now know almost nothing of the past and are just beginning to understand how alone they are." He looked at Terry, who was still sobbing. "You okay?"

"It's so *ugly, so ugly!*" she answered, covering her lips with her fingertips.

They sat in silence for a little while.

Then Terry took a sip of water, followed by a calming breath. She looked at Ty and smiled. "I'm okay."

"Can I ask you a couple questions?" he asked her.

"Yes."

"What is character?"

"I don't understand the word."

"Okay. What's faith?"

She shook her head, gave him a puzzled look, and lifted her shoulders.

John leaned back in his chair, studying Terry's face. He rubbed his hand through his hair, feeling uneasy. He knew what Ty was looking for, and for the first time since meeting Terry, he understood how innocent she was. He sighed and surprised himself by thinking, *She is beautiful.*

"Last question: What do love, purpose, and integrity mean to you?" Ty asked her.

"Why are you asking me these impossible questions?" she asked, uncomfortable with questions she couldn't answer. It had never happened before. She took another sip of water, her eyes looking down.

Ty waited a moment until she looked up. He gave her an understanding smile. "It took me a lifetime to figure out those three words. Love is a forever emotion, purpose is meaning in life, and integrity is always doing the morally just thing. Acted on, it gives meaning and fulfillment to a human life."

He looked at John with a wistful smile. "All this is why we cannot turn Pandora off. There are three billion young adults floating around who know practically nothing of life and possess limited ability to survive." Ty took a deep breath, slowly turning his head side to side. "We need that damn machine to teach them how to live."

John pressed his lips together, eyes mildly squinted, and nodded slightly, understanding. "Your observation changes everything. I was so intent on revenge by terminating it, I lost sight of their extinction. I'm such a fool."

"How could you have known half the population was murdered and the birth rates had gone to zero?" Ty asked.

"I wasn't paying attention. I was only concerned with me."

"God wasn't paying attention, either," Ty said.

"The irony turns my stomach. We need the murderous machine my G.A. team created, which, I guess, led to this horrible catastrophe, and Earth's future rests in the hands of the scorned, and millions of unfeeling androids."

Silence enveloped the table.

"This is all my fault," John said, feeling his chest tighten.

"Relax," Ty said. "We're alive because of you."

John shook his head slightly and gave them a bitter smile. "We should go. We'll need a good night's sleep. Tomorrow could be exciting," John said.

Terry shot him a glance; she'd felt a jolt in her heart at the word *exciting*.

They left the restaurant and walked up the alley without speaking and got into the pod. Ty again sat in the front and Terry in the back.

"If I remember correctly, Sutter's Fort is just south of here, about two miles," Ty said.

"We're not going there. I've changed my mind; we've got to move as fast as we can. I'm sure Pandora knows we're coming," John said. "Megan, keep our location hidden. Contact the Sutter Fort androids and notify them we'll arrive after midnight. Now take us to G.A., and confirm that the compound's cameras and sensors are off. If they're not, turn them off. Park behind the administration building next to the loading garage."

The pod lifted off the ground and headed northeast toward the Sierra Nevada Mountain Range.

"How long will it take us?" Ty asked.

"Six minutes; we'll be there before seven," John said.

"Slow down a second," Ty said. He looked at John, his expression serious. "I'm not going any farther until you find me a bottle of bourbon and I've had a night to think about what you've gotten me into. This thirty-five-year-old body has ninety years of memories sitting in its brain. I know certain moments demand reflection, and others, especially the stressful ones, need a break in a place that's safe."

"Megan, where is there a bottle of bourbon near us?" John asked.

"I found Ty's favorite in a collection in Placerville, and they have several bottles of Old Rip Van Winkle Kentucky Bourbon locked away. It is five minutes and forty seconds away."

"Megan, I have always liked you," Ty said, grinning.

"I feel the same about you, Ty Leggett."

"Let's get that thirty-five-thousand-dollar bottle of bourbon," Ty said, grinning

John smiled and shook his head. "It'll be free today, and the only reason Placerville was rebuilt was due to its Gold Rush history. Megan, how much of Placerville exists?"

"The Old Town main street, one restaurant, an Old West saloon, and several deserted buildings."

"Take us there," John said.

Minutes later, the pod landed in front of a wooden building with an Old West motif. They got out of the pod, and Terry sneezed.

"What is that smell?" she asked, sneezing again.

"The glorious scent of pine," Ty said.

The street was vacant and dark. They stepped up onto the imitation wooden boardwalk and went to the front door, over which a four-foot-long wooden sign read: "Hangman's Tree Saloon."

Ty grinned, grabbed the door handle and twisted it several times. "Shit, it's locked." He took several steps back, and to John and Terry's surprise, he pulled out his pistol, aimed it at the door and *Zzzppnt!*—the doorway disappeared in a flash of fire. He turned and smiled at John. "I love this gun! And what the hell, right? I should be dead, so God knows I deserve a drink."

John laughed.

Terry looked shocked. "He really wants that drink," she said. She sneezed again and rubbed her nose several times with the back of her right hand.

They entered the building to find a pristine, dust-free room in near perfect condition. A bald android stood behind the bar, dressed in an Old West cowboy costume. The android activated, saying, "Welcome, Strangers."

"I'm going to get an android to clean my place when this is all over," Ty said, looking around the rustic setting.

"Great, a bathroom!" John said, looking across the saloon. He went that way.

"Me, too," Terry said.

Off they went to the restrooms.

"I'll find a bottle," Ty said.

"May I help you, cowboy?" the android asked.

"No. I got it," Ty replied.

John arrived back in the room first, soon followed by Terry. John moved to the counter with an antique cash register, saw a flyer, and picked it up. "Look at the date: twenty-two fifteen. This place hasn't been used for quite a while. Ty, where are you?"

"Down behind the bar."

John walked around the twenty-foot-long, hand-carved pine bar and saw Ty on his knees, looking at what appeared to be an airtight liquor cabinet.

John bent down next to Ty and looked through the glass door. "There it is." John pointed. "Now, how do we get that thing open? I don't think you want to use your gun in this case." He grinned.

"You got that right, funny man." Ty stood and looked around the bar and the back shelf under the ten-by-ten-foot glass mirror. He pulled several drawers open, looking for a key or anything he could use to open the box.

"Damn, I don't want to risk breaking it open." He eyed John. "Got any suggestions?"

"Megan, can you open the liquor cabinet?"

To Ty's sudden joy, the glass door popped open with a hissing sound as cool, stale air rushed out. He reached down and pulled the two-foot-square single door open and removed two bottles of Old Rip Van Winkle bourbon. He stood with a full grin on his face, showing his perfect white teeth.

He looked around the bar for shot glasses. "Perfect! Here they are." He grabbed three glasses with his left hand off the wooden shelf under the mirror.

"Let's sit." He walked around the counter to a small wooden table, put the bottle and glasses down, then pulled three chairs to the table. "Terry Cheer, you are about to taste greatness." He twisted the top off and poured a shot into each glass. "Sit, sit, we're having a moment."

They sat, and Ty and John each took a sip.

Terry smelled the drink. "This is awful. What is it made of?" she asked, with her nose crinkled and lips puckered.

"Nectar from heaven," Ty said.

"What's heaven?" she asked.

Ty looked at John and slowly shook his head. "Come on, Terry, take a sip," he said.

She put the edge of the glass to her lips and swallowed the full shot in one gulp. "Oh my, that burns!"

"You're not supposed to gulp it; you sip it," Ty said, grinning. He poured her another shot. "Like this." He took a small sip of his own.

John was smiling, enjoying the moment being with his best friend. "It's been a long time since we had a drink together," he said, leaning back in the chair.

"Yes, it has, but this won't be our last, I hope," Ty said.

With the shot glasses empty, Ty put the cap back on the bottle, stood, and said with a lifetime of confidence, "Let's get to that damn thing at G.A."

They left the bar and walked back to the pod, taking the same seating arrangements as before. They flew the five minutes to the Genetic Answer Nevada compound.

John was about to land the pod, but Ty said, "Wait! Let's check things out from up here before we park this thing."

They hovered over a three-story, darkened concrete building.

"The building looks like I remember it," Ty said. "Turn on the headlights and fly around it slowly."

"You were here in twenty thirty-seven?" Terry asked.

"Yes, this is the place where it all began," John said.

"Were you here, too?" she asked Ty.

"Yes, but only on official business. I was the director of the F.B.I."

"What's the F.B.I.?"

"It's not important. It's gone and they're all dead," Ty said, sounding melancholy.

The pod moved over and around the building and then the property.

"So far, not too different-looking from before," Ty said. "The barbed wire fence and all the concrete roads are gone, though." He pointed to his right. "The office building looks the same, and the roll-up back doors to the first-floor garage-ware-house are open."

"The work shed has been replaced by a larger building," John said, looking out the front passenger-side window. "Megan, swing around and face the main entrance.... Yeah, that's the same entrance I remember. Odd—after all this time, it's the same."

"Yep, ugly, drab government crap," Ty quipped.

"I wonder if the office building still has the subterranean basement where Royer put the quantum computer?"

Ty shrugged. "If it does, that's where Pandora is."

"Megan, swing around and see if there are any other buildings."

The pod lifted a couple hundred feet above the office building and turned three hundred-sixty degrees.

"Yes, there is. See that boxy one, Ty, just west of the main G.A. office building, with the flat roof? Never saw that before."

John said. "Everything else that was here is gone now, surrounded by bare land."

"I wonder when the F.B.I. and D.O.D. stopped overseeing its operations?"

"I have no idea."

"I hope the kitchen and cafeteria are still in the main building. I might need a snack," Ty said.

John laughed. "Megan, turn the security cameras and thermal systems off."

"Done."

John frowned. "Seeing this for the first time since that horrible night the Gysins tried to kill my family... it's a bit much."

"You okay?" Ty asked.

"Yes, but I can still picture every detail from that night." John looked away for a moment toward his left. "The other memories of this place are good. The staff had so many nice people; I hope life went well for them.... But enough of this. Here's what I'm thinking: We'll land in the rear, next to the garage loading station. If we're lucky, the interior design hasn't changed too much, and Pandora's in the basement cold room where Royer built the quantum."

John turned to his right and looked at Ty. "Friendly said this Crystal is protected by the Untouchables. Which begs the question, Megan, what's the percentage chance the Untouchables developed into a nonviolent society in the past hundred years?"

"Their history suggest they become aggressive when threatened."

"Shit," John said. "Megan, land next to the office building garage entrance."

The pod landed, facing the roll-up door.

"There's only one way to find out if we make them uncomfortable," Ty said. "Terry, you're up; you get out first."

"That's a no, Ty Leggett."

"It was worth a try," Ty said with a laugh.

"I feel funny," Terry said.

"What's wrong?" John asked

"Nothing, really. My stomach feels warm, and I feel great."

John and Ty laughed out loud.

"Bourbon," Ty said.

TWELVE

The moon had not risen, the sky was filled with stars, and the area around the GA office building was very dark. John opened the driver's side hatch, and warm desert air rushed in, filling the pod with dust and the scent of sagebrush.

I remember that smell, John thought. "Stay here."

When he got out of the pod, he heard a crackling sound of brush moving. He crouched to his knees, reached into his jeans' pocket, and pulled out the metallic ball containing the Mosquito cameras, then opened it.

"Megan, are we alone?"

"Yes."

"Okay, send the Mosquitoes through the facility and report back what you learn."

The ball split into eight Mosquito cameras, and he watched them fly toward the garage's loading station door.

John got back into the pod and closed the hatch.

A three-dimensional, green-and-black twilight holographic image of GA's interior garage appeared on the pod's windshield.

The warehouse was unlit and empty. The imagery shifted down the transportation shaft to the basement—also dark and empty. A closed, heavy-looking metal sliding door was on the far wall. The Mosquitoes swarmed the door, searching for an opening.

"Damn, they can't get into the cold room where Pandora should be," John said.

"I don't know about you," Ty said, "but I'm very happy sitting here instead of us walking through that place. It's scaring the hell out of me just watching it."

Terry nodded, her hands covering her mouth.

"I wish we had those things when I was at the F.B.I. When were they invented?" Ty asked.

"Megan and I invented them twenty years ago. I needed a way to be inside places and see things that were otherwise impossible to access. They allow me to venture into the holographic image like I was in the room. I can smell and hear everything going on."

"Wow, that's cool," Ty said.

"Sounds ugly to me," Terry said.

John glanced at her. "If you see something of interest and want a closer look, I can walk closer to the object, and Megan will enhance the holographic image of it. If it's a paper or book, I can read it if I want."

"That really gives a new meaning to Peeping Tom," Ty said.

What's a peeping tom? Terry thought.

The Mosquitoes traveled though the remaining three-story building. Each floor and room were empty of furniture; only dust covered the floors.

"Wait, what's that? Look at the floor," Ty said.

"Megan, what are those marks in the dust?" John asked.

"Footprints. Hundreds of people visit this place regularly."

"Which means they'll be back," Ty said.

"Megan, is Pandora in the building?"

"Yes, and it knows we're here."

Terry gasped and cowered for a moment. "How?"

"I don't know," John answered. "Megan, can it detect a hologram?"

"No. It can only detect the Mosquitoes."

"It knows we're here and hasn't sounded an alarm," John said.

"What's an alarm?" Terry asked.

"A sound that tells its defenders to come running."

"Why hasn't it?" Terry asked.

"It knows that we know it knows," Ty whispered in a low, dark voice.

"What?" Terry asked, her voice trembling slightly.

"Megan, certify that our program infected Pandora," John said.

"Done. It did."

"Great, it's safe, so you can go in and terminate it," Terry said with a determined expression.

"We can't; we need it," John said.

"I don't care," Terry said. "It murdered three billion people."

"Terry," John said, "we talked about this. If we shut it off, most people will die of starvation. We need the androids to teach and to feed everyone."

"Human nature gets very ugly and violent when hungry," Ty said.

"What's human nature?" she whispered, watching the Mosquitoes fly through the building.

Ty shook his head. "I'll tell you later. The building looks empty. Let's go." He reached to open the pod hatch.

"One second," John said. "Megan, how far away are the Untouchables from us?"

"A hundred feet."

"Oh, shit! Megan, initiate energy shield!" John shouted.

A flash of white light burst into view, followed by an ear-splitting explosion next to the pod's driver's-side hatch.

Terry screamed, but Ty remained calm and looked out the passenger-side window searching for the attackers.

"Megan, get us out of here!" John shouted.

The pod lifted off the ground and hovered a hundred feet above the building's roof.

"We are beyond their attack," Megan said.

The tension evaporated.

Ty looked back at Terry. "We're safe."

"Another mistake," John said. "Pandora can't kill us, but the Untouchables can. Megan, how many people are within the G.A. compound?"

"Twenty people and one hubot."

"They have a leader," John said, sounding shocked.

"A what?" Terry asked.

"Someone who tells them what to do," Ty answered.

"Like you?" Terry said.

"No, theirs doesn't have a soul or a conscience."

A soul? What's that? she thought.

John sighed, feeling stupid for being caught off guard. "Megan, take us to the 10 Freeway overpass leading to G.A."

"It no longer exists. I can take you to a dirt patch by the former freeway."

"Go," John said.

A moment later, they landed on a bare patch of land about a mile away from GA.

John opened the hatch and got out of the pod, followed by Ty and Terry.

John moved several feet away from the pod and started pacing. "That was stupid—stupid! I almost killed us. No leverage, no leverage."

"What are you saying?" Ty asked, leaning back against the pod.

"We had leverage on the San Francisco Crystal. My program prevented it from killing me, and the bomb prevented it from killing us. We have no additional leverage over Pandora. I took us in blind. Stupid... how stupid of me," he whispered to himself.

"Okay, that's all true. But now we know," Ty said calmly.

"Megan, are there any pods or S.S. ships near G.A.?" John asked.

"Several unused pods and one viable S.S. ship."

"Can an android teach an Untouchable to command an S.S. ship?"

"No. The hubot would have to navigate it."

"Make us and our pod undetectable."

"Done."

John looked at Ty. "It's creating an army."

"An army? An army of what?"

"Untouchables. People who for the past one hundred years have survived by figuring out how to survive."

"I hate figuring it out," Terry whispered to herself.

"God," John said, "the savagery it must have taken! Now, for the first time they have an all-knowing commander, and this 'Lord of the Flies' has a common enemy: Us," John finished, looking at Ty.

"Okay, I get it. Now tell me about who we're going to fight. I want to know my enemy."

"I don't know much. As Megan told me earlier, the Sparks Indian tribe, who, I think, just tried to kill us, had a Reservation near here. Most of the Untouchables around the world died in isolation and helpless starvation. Megan, briefly describe the Indigenous people in this area."

"There are two tribes, the Shoshone and the Paiute. Both survived the Chinese counterattack in twenty-one hundred because they had abundant natural resources, hunting skills, and farming techniques they'd mastered over hundreds of years. Their shared heritage and trading provided all they needed. They were forgotten by everyone *and* the World Crystal because the K chip had never been implanted in their children."

"How much do they know?" Ty asked.

"They learn by oral tradition, and I suspect are as primitive as a thousand years ago."

"Good bet they hate outsiders. Did they have androids for help?" John asked.

"No, they were left to die," Megan said.

"I can't believe they didn't destroy it." John reached into his pocket and removed the thimble-sized box containing the Mosquito cameras. "Megan, send one Mosquito to where the twenty Untouchables are living on the compound and get a picture of the hubot leader."

"Done."

They watched the camera fly away.

"So this hubot is part of an overall plan," Ty said.

"I think so," John replied. "Now that the S.S. machines are useless, Pandora needs protection."

"Why not use androids?"

"They weren't designed to fight, so even with weapons, they'd be defeated. It needs an army of savages to protect it."

"What is he talking about?" Terry asked, eyebrows scrunched, looking at Ty.

"Local Soshonees joining together to kill us."

Terry gasped, suddenly feeling the fear.

John's mind raced, he began to sweat, his hands shook. He turned away and paced back and forth. "What do we do, what do we do?" he kept repeating.

"John, stop, you're going to have a panic attack. Stop!" Ty shouted.

John stopped and stared at Ty, his breathing fast.

"John, I have an image of the hubot," Megan said.

John returned and stood by Ty and Terry next to the pod. "Display."

A holographic image appeared, floating in the air in front of the pod and showing a tall hubot with strong, masculine facial construction standing in front of a group of twenty people, dressed in handmade clothing.

"Megan, magnify the image of the hubot."

John walked up to the hologram and studied it for several moments. Terry and Ty watched John, hoping he would see something that would save them.

"There it is!" John stepped way and pointed at the hubot's right side.

"It has a gun," Ty said.

"It wouldn't take much to intimidate the people. One shot and they'd do whatever it asked, and I'll bet this is happening at the Paiute location, too."

John rubbed his hand through his hair. "We don't have much time. We've got to get an S.S. ship of our own."

"Why don't we take the one that's here?" Ty asked.

"Pandora would've already anticipated that and set a trap for us. Megan, do you know how to operate an S.S. ship?"

"Yes."

"Where's the closest S.S. base?"

"Fallon. It is sixty-five miles away."

"How far from that base is the Paiute village?"

"Sixteen miles."

"Quick, get in," John said. "We can be there in eight minutes!"

"Why?" Terry asked.

"We've got to get ahead of Pandora, and having an S.S. ship will be our advantage, and Pandora knows that. If I'm right, Pandora has already sent a message to the hubot leader and it, along with several Paiutes, are running to Fallon right now to stop us."

They all climbed into the pod and flew east at five hundred miles per hour.

"This could also be a trap, John," Ty said.

"Yeah, sure. But we don't have any choice. We need a bigger and safer stick. Terry, when we land, Ty and I will commandeer the ship. You stay with the pod; it'll take you back to San Francisco, and we'll meet you there."

"No, I'm coming with you. I can fight just as well as you. You may know more, but you're not any braver. I'm going."

"Okay, then. Use the weapon under the seat. You know how. When we land, we'll get into the S.S. ship and take off as fast as possible. If you see anything, don't hesitate, shoot it."

They lifted into the air and headed toward the SS air base in silence. Their emotions were on edge, but John and Ty's expressions showed focus and determination—Terry looked scared.

John glanced at his watch: 8:00 p.m. "Megan, land next to the S.S. ship closest to Fallon's conning tower. Once we're on board and in the air, send the pod to Crystal Plaza and park it next to the fountain."

They landed on a dark, unlit runway, void of any visible life. The base looked desolate; only a five-story conning tower and five parked SS ships filled the property.

"You ready?" John asked.

They both nodded.

John opened the pod's exit hatches.

They jumped out and ran toward the ship. The field was instantly flooded with lights and blaring sirens.

Terry tripped and fell to the concrete. Ty stopped and pulled her up, and they continued running. John never stopped; he kept running toward the ship. He glanced to his left, down the row of SS ships, and saw a hubot with two people standing by the farthest ship. Suddenly, there were small explosions of flames and hot gas pounding into the runway around them.

"Megan, open the S.S. ship's hatch and start the engine!" John screamed.

John ran up the ship's ramp. Terry and Ty stopped to fire their guns at the two humans and the hubot. There was an explosion as the fireball struck near it and killing the humans. Terry and Ty quickly turned and ran up the ramp. The ship lurched back; the air inside was sucked out through the open hatch. A fireball of gas hit the front of the ship. John fell backward, crashing into Terry and Ty, throwing them against each other.

John screamed, "Megan, close the hatch! Take off now! Now!"

The ship bounced up off the tarmac, pressing Ty, Terry, and John against the deck. The hatch closed, and the force of the acceleration pushed everyone into a slide against the aft bulk-head. Ty got to his feet first, lifted Terry, and then pulled John to his feet.

Once standing, John ran into the pilot station and sat facing the control panel. "Megan, disable all tracking systems and cameras."

"Done."

"Megan, go to Stanford University Dark Energy Displacement building at full speed."

"On our way. We'll arrive in just about thirteen minutes."

"Megan, on my command after we get there, target the black matter laser and evaporate the building. Then fire on the basement until the time machine is destroyed."

When they arrived at Stanford, John said, "Megan, fire."

The ship shuddered as it unleashed five dark energy bolts. The building exploded and evaporated in a red cloud of gas. The ship came to a stop, facing the burning hole of what was once a building.

"Why are we here?" Terry asked, still breathing heavily.

"To keep the past where it belongs: safe," John said.

"I remember the *Terminator* movies, and I'm sure Megan does, too," Ty said.

"You two use words I don't understand. What's a terminator or a movie?"

"A Terminator was a futuristic S.S. machine that hunted and killed humans in its past," John said.

"We wouldn't stand a chance," she said.

"I thought dark energy was a force in space, not power," Ty said.

"It was until they figured out how to split its atoms," John said.

"I need another swig of bourbon." Ty sighed.

"I'll join you," Terry said.

"That'll have to wait. We've got to get back to G.A. now," John said. "Megan, divert my pod to G.A.; time its arrival with ours. Park it on the roof, and land us like before, next to the main building's garage loading station."

"Done. Your pod will land in twenty-six minutes."

"What are you doing? Why go back now?" Terry asked.

"We have no choice; we can't let Pandora get ahead of us. It will build an army, and the million Untouchables will annihilate everything in their path. They are fully human with all the rage that time builds. The hubots have learned how to lead without using an implanted chip, and from what we've seen, it only takes one hubot to lead an army." John turned to face Ty and Terry. "This is all or nothing. If we fail, the world will once again be divided between hate and fear, and hate will win because it's much stronger."

THIRTEEN

Ty fully understood; Terry looked puzzled.

There was silence for a moment.

"Ty," John said, "you can't go in there with us."

"What? Why not?"

"If we all die, Pandora will continue its genocide, and it won't move slowly this time. One of us must stay alive to unite humanity and defeat Pandora's army. I'm appointing you."

"No, we won't fail! And we're doing this side by side," Ty replied.

"Yes, all three of us," Terry said.

"Arrival in five minutes," Megan said.

John glared at Ty for a moment, angry his order was not being followed. He rubbed his hand through his hair. "Megan, activate the energy shields for the pod and hyper-activate its gravitational drive motor when we reach Pandora."

"John, that will explode the pod in forty seconds, destroying everything within a mile," Megan said.

"I know, and that threat will keep us alive; it's just like the empty box trick we used earlier, except this one's real."

"Arrival in one minute," Megan announced.

John glanced at the pod's clock: 9:00 p.m. "The plan is simple: We enter the building, present ourselves to Pandora, and cut a deal."

John stood and picked up an SS rifle, Terry squeezed her pistol, Ty readied himself.

They landed.

"Megan, open the hatch."

Terry stepped out first, followed by Ty and John. To their surprise, they saw the building was surrounded by people ten rows deep.

Stunned, Terry stood frozen. "What should I do?" she asked, clearly panicked.

John and Ty looked for the hubot.

"There it is." Ty pointed to his left at the most handsome, well-built hubot he'd ever seen. His face was stark in its perfection. He was dressed in a white kaftan, standing off by himself.

"Megan, is my pod on the roof?"

"No, the roof is covered with people; it can't land."

"Megan, land."

"John, that will crush them."

"Comply."

"Done."

Screams erupted from the roof, and several bodies fell off, smashing into the ground. The massed crowd looked enraged and started to move away from the building toward John. He fired a blast of energy into the air, then pointed the rifle at them and the building.

"Megan, activate the pod's magneto-power drive. If it

attacks me, detonate the pod. Ty, you'll have to build an army to fight them."

John walked up to the hubot. "I will explode the pod in thirty-five seconds and you with it."

"You're bluffing, Doctor Barber. You are not suicidal," it said.

"Terminating you is not suicide. You have thirty seconds." Both his voice and expression were commanding.

"I will obey."

"Megan, reset the gravitational motor."

"Done."

"Tell your army to leave the property, and I mean *every*one, all those in and out of the building."

The hubot made an about-face from John and walked to the center of the garage to address the people. "Leave and return to your homes."

The garage door opened, and hundreds of people walked out. One of the men was carrying a long-bladed knife. He charged at John, screaming a cry of rage-filled hate. *Zzzppnt!* His body burst into flames, and he evaporated into a cloud of fiery pink gas.

The people stopped moving, the expression on their collective faces showing pure fury.

"Who's next?" Terry asked, fearless and determined, pointing her gun at the wet remains.

"Tell them to move now; they have twenty seconds," John demanded.

John was calm and looked deadly serious. Terry and Ty looked ready to fight.

"Go now," the hubot said to the crowd.

The crowd moved en masse away from the building and

walked east along the dirt road toward their shanty encampment.

"Megan, deactivate the gravitational motor. Next time it's initiated, let it detonate," John said, looking at the hubot. John then walked to Ty and Terry.

"That was scary, and I'm too old for this crap," Ty said with a sly smile.

"Now what?" Terry asked, relaxing.

"We see what surprises Pandora has for us, then unplug it," John said. They remained next to the SS ship and waited for the building and adjacent property to empty.

John glanced at the three-story industrial building. He looked at Ty. "I'm sure it's different inside. It's been a hundred eighty-five years. Let's go find out."

FOURTEEN

John looked down the road; it was empty of people. He reached into his pocket and removed the metal packet containing the Mosquitoes and opened it.

"Megan, send the Mosquitoes in to verify that the building is vacant and park the pod inside the garage loading area. Return the bugs to me when finished."

They watched the pod float into the building through the twenty-foot-wide industrial gate.

"It doesn't matter how many times I see that, it still looks so cool," Ty said, smiling.

They waited.

"The building is empty of Untouchables. There are two dormant androids. It is safe," Megan said.

"Let's go meet destiny," Ty said.

"Who's destiny?" Terry asked.

"Our best friend," Ty answered.

John smiled and took a deep breath, feeling relieved they were closer to putting this nightmare into the ground.

They walked into the garage. "Nothing's changed here," John said to Ty. "It's the same—well, except for that." He pointed across the empty space to the back garage door to GA. Standing there was a male hubot, this one dressed in jeans, leather boots and a cowboy shirt, showing no signs of life.

"What should we do?" Terry asked, suddenly afraid.

"Move ahead," John said.

"I'm not feeling good about it. It could be ugly," she said.

They walked casually toward the semi-human, and when they were within five feet, it spoke: "Hello, Doctor Barber and Mr. Leggett. Welcome back," it said in a Western dialect. "I am Wyatt."

Terry gasped, shocked by the unexpected voice, while Ty lifted his gun, ready to shoot.

John hesitated a moment, but feeling safe, he turned to face Ty. "It's okay."

They passed through the open door, and as they entered the hallway the elevator door to their left opened with a slight *whoosh*. Wyatt gestured for them to enter.

"We'll take the stairs," John said. He grabbed the Wyatt by its left arm. "You lead," he said aggressively.

They walked several feet to their left and opened the stairwell metal door.

"Megan, if something happens to us for a microsecond, detonate the pod."

"That is not necessary, Doctor Barber," Wyatt said. "I have no intention of harming you, or Mr. Leggett."

"But you still plan on killing *me*," Terry said angrily.

Wyatt looked away from her to face the basement door.

"That's a yes where I come from," Ty said.

That's odd, John thought. *It wants us to know she's a target. No accident; that was by design.*

They entered the stairwell and walked down the two flights of concrete stairs to the basement. Wyatt opened the door. The room was unlit.

"Man, that's dark," Ty said.

Wyatt entered the room and the lights snapped on.

Suddenly, John reached his right arm out against Ty's shoulder and whispered, "Stop, something's wrong."

Ty froze, but Terry continued ahead a couple steps.

"Terry, stop," John said.

Wyatt turned to face John. Its eyes were black circles, and were focused directly on John's face.

Zzzppnt! John shot it. "Quick! Upstairs!" he shouted.

They all turned and ran up the stairs; Terry was last. Ty reached for the first floor door handle.

"Stop!" John shouted from several steps behind Ty.

Ty stopped and glanced back at John, his hand on the doorknob. "What's wrong?" he asked, panting, trying to catch his breath.

"Terry's right: It's a trap."

"What?"

"You said it yourself: too dark. Megan, are there humans in the garage?"

"Yes."

"What are they doing?"

"They are dragging the pod out of the building."

"Was the basement protected by a deprivation shroud?"

"Yes."

"Is Pandora in the basement?"

"Yes."

"I don't understand. It can't kill us?" Terry asked.

"It doesn't have to," John answered. "By going to the basement together, we allowed Pandora the time to remove the pod and avoid destruction. And when we entered the basement, the deprivation shroud would have snapped on, trapping us." He turned and said, "Ty, take a peek."

Ty held his gun up and slowly opened the door. There were fifty people surrounding the pod. *Zzzppnt!* He fired at a group standing behind the pod, killing several people. The pod dropped to the ground with a heavy thud. The group ran outside, screaming in fear.

Standing at the garage door, watching, was the hubot dressed in a white kaftan. It started to turn to leave.

John shot the ground in front of it and yelled, "Stop!"

It turned to face him.

The three of them walked to it.

John stepped up to the hubot. "What do you call yourself?"

"Jamal."

"Your master had a simple plan: It was going to trap us in the basement, move the pod to safety, and wait until we were crazy or dead, then—snap!—it was back in control."

Terry smashed her gun into the Jamal's right eye, crushing it. "You ugly machine!"

The human part of Jamal jerked back and instinctively covered its bleeding eye. "I'm going to kill you," it said, turning to face her.

"Too late. I've got *you*," she growled.

John took a deep breath, calming himself. *That's twice a surrogate has threatened Terry.*

"Megan, locate G.A.'s power relay, then use the S.S. ship to destroy it."

They heard the SS ship taking off, and a couple seconds later, a flash of white light filled the garage, followed by a ground-shaking explosion. Dust filled the air. The three covered their mouths to breathe and waited for the air to clear.

"Megan, where are the auxiliary energy containers?"

"There are three locations. The primary source is under the main building. The other two are connected to light panels on the roof."

"Megan, use the ship and destroy those light panels."

"Don't," Jamal said, now standing by the stairwell door. "I will comply."

"Megan, destroy the roof panels now, and if Terry or Ty gets hurt, destroy the underground primary source," John said, looking back at the one-eyed hubot.

The building shook, and another flash of bright white light filled the outside area.

"Megan, are there any other power sources for Pandora on the grounds?"

"No."

"How long will its current power structure last?"

"Indefinitely."

"Megan, where is the main power source here?"

"Underground. There is a loading ramp and a tunnel entrance outside, next to a building to the west of G.A. That's where the power plant is located."

"What's the building used for?"

"Circuit breakers, power monitors and utility supplies."

"Let's go see it," John said.

They walked out of GA toward it.

They walked to where the ramp to the underground facility was located and saw a metal plate, the size of a basketball court covering the ramp entrance.

"That's big. I bet once that cover is lifted several busses could fit through," Ty said.

"Come with me," John said.

They walked to the other side of the one-story power plant building.

Once on the other side of the building, John said, "Megan, return the Mosquitoes to me, once they are safe, destroy the metal plate that's covering that underground ramp entrance. Then bring a water tanker filled with saltwater from San Francisco Bay. Place the filled tanker at the loading ramp entrance just in case we need it."

Suddenly there was a flash of white light and a loud boom sound. Dust filled the air, Terry covered her ears and dropped to her knees.

Ty laughed. "Checkmate. You're one smart cookie for a scientist."

"Now what?" Terry asked.

"I'm not sure. Megan, how long before the saltwater arrives?" John asked.

"Thirty minutes."

"Megan, what time is it?"

"Nine-thirty p.m.."

"What's your plan?" Ty asked.

"It'll take the water tanker thirty minutes to get here from the bay, so our goal is to stay alive until it arrives. Once it's in place, we can pay a visit to Pandora."

Terry gave John a hug. "I'm beginning to like you, John Barber. Maybe you are not so ugly after all," she whispered, looking up into his eyes.

Suddenly, fifty people ran screaming toward the power plant building. Almost in unison, Ty, Terry, and John fired their guns at the attacking mob, killing dozens and driving the others toward the garage entrance.

The three continued to fire their weapons. John spotted

Jamal standing just inside the garage door watching the firefight. He was not moving.

John yelled directly at Jamal. "Megan, the moment the water arrives, empty the water!"

Jamal shouted, "Stop!" It looked out toward the charging people and put up its right hand. "Go back home."

Everything went silent.

Jamal casually walked over to John. "I look forward to building our relationship, Doctor Barber," it said with the ghost of a smirk.

"What was that all about?" Ty asked, totally confused.

"Another attempt to kill you and capture me."

They waited there until a little more than twenty minutes later when they watched the water tanker land on the now-exposed ramp.

"Megan, is it in position?" John asked.

"Yes, it is on the subterranean ramp leading down to the Pandora power plant."

John looked at Jamal and said, "Megan if anything happens to us, empty the water tanker."

"What's next? Another suicide mission?" Ty asked, grinning.

"What's suicide?" Terry asked.

"John cooking dinner," Ty said, laughing.

John shook his head, smiling at Ty.

"I don't get it," Terry said.

"It means we live or die." Ty said.

"I don't like that mission." Terry said.

"Here's my thinking: We leave the water tank there. No one can move it. Then we get a good night's sleep," John said. "If that's possible, then tomorrow morning we go to San Francisco and tell everyone what we've learned, and all about Pandora."

"Sounds like a plan. I'm exhausted," Ty said.

"Where are we sleeping?" Terry asked, looking concerned.

"We'll be safe in the ship," John said.

"Let's go. Even at my new age all this excitement is killing me," Ty said.

They left the building and walked slowly to the SS ship and started up the loading ramp.

John hesitated, thinking about the smirk on Jamal's face. "I'll be right back," he said.

He returned to where Jamal was standing, and asked, "Are you still linked to the Crystal here?"

"Yes."

"What else are you linked to?" John asked.

"Nothing."

It's lying. "Shut down all androids and hubots on Earth for the next nine hours."

"I can't. Only the master can."

John snorted a laugh. "Megan, open the water tanker's discharge valve by two percent."

"Stop. I will comply," Jamal said.

"To repeat my order: All androids and hubots will be turned off for the next nine hours."

"Yes."

"Confirm my command," John said.

"All Earth-bound androids and hubots will be disabled from this moment for the next nine hours." Jamal's eyes abruptly turned hollow-looking, and froze in place.

John, turned, smiled at Ty and Terry, then sighed in relief. "Megan, if anything comes within a thousand yards of the water tanker, or it gets hit by an energy wave, open the water valve."

"Yes."

"And wake me at seven tomorrow morning."

"Done," Megan replied.

John went back to Ty and Terry, and glanced at his watch: 10:40 p.m. "All's well. Let's get a good night's sleep."

DAY 2

FIFTEEN

They slept without incident and awoke at 6:00 a.m.

John left the SS ship first and felt the cool, crisp air. The sun was just rising on the eastern horizon. He took a deep breath and smelled the familiar dry, scented sagebrush, thinking: *Good memories.* His thoughts quickly turned to his wife. He smiled, remembering how much she loved the scent of sumac. He heard a sound behind him and turned to see Ty leave the ship and head toward him.

"I don't remember if I thanked you." Ty put his right arm on John's shoulder. "So, thank you for bringing me here. This place is a mess. Rebuilding it will add meaning to our lives."

"I should never have left her," John said wistfully.

"Let it go. Megan loved you and it was the right thing to do. After we rebuild this place, if we can, we'll pay her a visit."

John smiled, the first ray of pink sunlight appeared on the Virginia Range, and they watched the sun rise. Suddenly, Jamal the hubot moved.

John checked his watch. "Seven-forty, it's active. Time to move," John said.

"Do we have time to eat before leaving?" Ty asked.

"I think so. Let's find out what the locals eat," John said.

They walked to Jamal.

"I hope that eye heals." Ty smiled. "What food do the locals consume?" he asked.

"Animals and plants," it said.

"Eggs, beef, pork, butter, bread, potatoes?" Ty asked, sounding excited.

"No. They have eggs, sheep, fish, rabbits, deer, fowl, corn, mustard plants, seeds, pine nuts, wild plants, and unleavened bread."

"Salt and pepper?" Ty asked.

"Salt; the mustard plant as pepper."

Ty looked at John, grinning. "We could get a real breakfast." He turned his attention back to Jamal. "Bring a dozen eggs, salt, mustard plant, two skinned rabbits, one rack of lamb, and plenty of bread. Enough to feed four hungry people."

Jamal turned and walked away.

"I'm excited," Ty said, still grinning.

Terry walked out of the ship just as Jamal left and saw Ty smiling. "Why are you so happy?"

"A surprise, young lady, is coming your way."

"What's a surprise?" she asked.

"Something that happens without warning," he said.

Terry looked around with a fearful expression. "We're in danger?"

"A pleasant, happy event—something good," he said.

"Like what?"

Ty sighed. "I can't tell you. If I did, it wouldn't be a surprise."

"I don't like surprises," she said.

"Oh my God," Ty said.

"There's that god word again and what's a young lady?" John laughed.

"You are," Ty said to Terry.

They sat in the morning sun, enjoying its warmth while waiting for the Jamal to return.

An hour later, it appeared, walking down the dirt road toward them.

"I never thought I'd be happy to see one of those freaky things," Ty said.

It was carrying two handwoven basket in its arms.

Ty skipped down the loading ramp and met the machine. A full grin lifted his cheeks. The baskets were overflowing with a dozen eggs, three stacks of unleavened flat bread, five seed cakes, and three cornmeal breads, along with two fist-sized animal hide pouch bags, one containing salt and the other ground mustard seeds.

"No salsa?" Ty barked, laughing out loud. "Now the million-dollar question: Is G.A.'s kitchen operational?"

"I can make it operational," Jamal said.

Ty turned to face Terry and John. "We have a kitchen."

John put a disbelieving expression on his face. "No way. It's probably been fifty years since anyone worked here."

"I don't care. If this damn thing says it can make it work, I'm in. The last thing I want to do is build a fire and cook." Ty took the basket from the Jamal. He turned to face Terry and John, still standing on the loading ramp. "Terry! Terry Cheer, come here!"

Terry ran down the ramp, carrying her gun, looking scared. "What? What is it?"

She reached Ty. He showed her the filled basket.

"What's that?" she asked.

"Breakfast. You are about to have the greatest meal in your life," Ty said, brimming with joy.

"Breakfast? What's that?"

"The first meal of the day. Quite possibly the best meal of the day."

"What are those things in the basket?"

"Food—beautiful, natural, food."

"Looks ugly to me," she said, her lips and nose crinkled.

John joined them.

Ty grinned. "This world is a crazy place; billions don't eat natural food, and the natives eat like kings."

John smiled.

Ty looked at Terry. "Let's go. You can help."

Jamal turned and headed toward GA.

Before it entered the building, John yelled, "Hey, Jamal, stop!" He walked to it, looked it in its one eye. "Excluding this hubot, turn all Earth-bound hubots off.... Megan, did it comply?"

"Yes," Megan said.

The three followed Jamal's path through the garage to the back door entrance into GA's lobby.

John reached the door first and pulled it open. "I used this door every day," he said with a glance at Ty.

They walked through a short hallway, past the elevator and stairwell. They reached the main lobby.

"I didn't expect this," John said. "Look around: It's spotless; even the air smells clean."

They walked past the security counter in the center of the lobby. John dragged his left hand across the counter and looked at his fingers. "Spotless." He shook his head.

They crossed the marble floor to the cafeteria doorway. John pulled the door open. The thousand square-foot room was empty of furniture and just as clean as the lobby.

"Wow, this room is clean," Terry said.

"I can't imagine what the kitchen looks like," Ty muttered.

They went into it.

Ty put the basket down on the counter next to the electric stove. He looked at John. "This is too strange. Why would this place be so clean? Something's not right. There should be dust everywhere." He turned and looked around the room.

"I have no idea, but there must be a reason. Megan, when was the last time people worked at G.A.?"

"There is no record of when this facility was abandoned."

Ty laughed. "I guess people still work here," he said sarcastically.

"I don't understand why you're complaining that it's clean," Terry said.

Ty shrugged his shoulders. "I'll set it up while Jamal readies the kitchen."

"When it's done, send it out to the cafeteria. I want to keep an eye on it," John said.

"You got it."

"I'll go look for a table and chairs," John said.

"I'll help," Terry said.

They left the kitchen, and John went to the right wall and opened the pine-faced storage closet. "Tables and chairs." He smiled. "And they look brand-new," he whispered to himself.

Terry joined him, and they pulled out a six-foot-long plastic folding table and three chairs.

Back in the kitchen, Ty went to the stove and pointed at Jamal. "Make it work."

"I must leave the room to fix certain parts."

Ty thought for a moment, nodded, then he turned away and walked around the room, opening and closing cabinets and drawers.

"Perfect, pots, pans, utensils—we got it all," he said to himself.

John and Terry came into the kitchen. John looked around, where's Jamal?"

"It's fixing the stove. You remember John Steinbeck's short story 'The Breakfast'?" Ty asked.

"Yes."

"Well, you, young lady"—he smiled—"you are about to smell, taste, hear, and feel the real deal."

"Who's John Steinbeck?" she asked.

"One of the world's greatest writers," John answered.

"What's a writer?"

"Jesus," Ty said, shaking his head.

"And who's Jesus, Mr. Smart Man?"

"He fixed food on a hillside a long time ago," Ty said.

"Was it good?"

"The world thought so."

Jamal returned, walked to the sink, and turned the faucet on. Nothing, then they heard a gurgling sound as air rushed out of the pipe, quickly followed by a pop of thick black water, then more popping air, followed by rust-orange water. After three minutes of running, the water turned clear.

"I don't care what it looks like now, I'm not drinking that stuff," Terry said.

Ty smiled. "We'll see. Well, you two can go. I'll bring everything out when I'm done."

John and Terry left the kitchen.

Ty threw a towel into the sink. The water was cold. He

turned the towel over several times, soaking it under the water, then pulled it out, twisted it several times, making it somewhat dry, and laid it on the island. He put the basket into the sink and washed off the contents and put them on the towel.

"Can't be too careful," he said to himself. He turned and looked at the Jamal. "We got power?"

"Yes, the electricity is on."

He turned the knob on the stove closest to his right hand all the way on, and a red light came on. "That's a good sign." He opened the swinging kitchen door, and called out, "We got power and hot running water!" No one answered. *I'll bet he's giving her a tour.* "Time to create greatness." He went back to the stove and started cooking.

Forty minutes later, Ty came into the cafeteria where John and Terry were sitting talking, carrying a tray of hot food. He placed the tray, silverware, and three plates on the table and sat down, facing them.

"Perfection is before you. Please dine."

What's dine? Terry thought.

"Wow, I've never smelled anything like that. It smells good. What are those things on the plate?" Terry asked.

"Soylent Green," Ty said, grinning.

John laughed out loud.

"Think of this food like bourbon—it will taste a little odd at first but will warm your soul."

"What's a soul?" she asked.

"Forget it," Ty said.

John was doing everything he could to keep from laughing out loud.

"Dig in," Ty said.

"What?" Terry asked.

"It means 'eat,'" John said.

Terry put her fork into the scrambled eggs and took a small bite.

Ty and John watched intently.

She smiled. "This tastes good."

She sampled the unleavened flat bread, seed cakes, cornmeal, and lamb chop. She smiled with each bite.

Ty and John joined her.

A warm glow filled John's chest, enjoying the moment. *Wonderful,* he thought.

Ty smiled. "This is worth living for. Thank you again, John, for saving my life."

"Hey, it was me who saved you," Terry said.

"Thank you, Terry Cheer, for saving my life and joining us for breakfast."

"My pleasure, and Jesus to you," she said.

Ty and John laughed out loud.

Once they'd finished eating, Ty grinned and leaned back in the chair. "That was wonderful."

"Megan, what time is it?" John asked.

"Ten forty-five."

"What's the deal about the time?" Ty asked.

"San Francisco," John answered.

"What about San Francisco?"

"We made a promise."

"What's a promise?" Terry asked.

"It's when one says they'll do something, and they do it no matter what," John said.

"Yes, we did that," Terry said.

"Telling them what's happened will be complicated and uncomfortable," Ty said.

"We have a lot to say," John replied, "not only to them but the other three billion freed humans."

Ty nodded. "Most of it bad, and we know what happens to the bearer of bad news."

"What is bad?" Terry asked.

"Ugly," Ty said.

"What happens to them?" Terry asked.

"They die," John said.

"Oh, my." Her eyes popped open.

"We can't tell them everything; it's too much," Ty said.

"I agree," John said. "We'll tell them the second Crystal has been neutralized and in a few weeks, we'll have all the systems working."

"I like that: No bad news," Terry said, looking relieved.

"Now for the complicated. How are we going to restore normal?" Ty wondered.

John gasped. "These people have no idea what normal really is."

"I know what it is," Terry said. "The way life was before you told your ugly story."

John looked down, and Ty thought, *That's not good.*

She reached across the table and touched John's hand. "That story saved our lives."

"Megan, how many androids are on Earth?" John asked.

"Ten million."

John shrugged. "That's three hundred people per android. That's doable."

"What about the Untouchables?"

"I hate that term. Can't we call them something else?" Terry asked.

"Yes. I got it: Outcasts," Ty said.

"What's that mean?"

"People who have been excluded," John said.

Terry smiled.

John looked at Jamal standing next to the kitchen door, and said, "The Untouchables will now be referred to as Outcasts. Worldwide, how many hubots are stationed among them?"

"I do not know. That update is not available," it said.

"Bullshit. Answer the question," John said.

"One thousand."

"Seems you're right. It's organizing an army to protect itself," Ty said, a scowl on his face.

"From whom?" Terry asked.

"Us and every other person on Earth."

John shook his head. "I don't think that's the army Pandora is building. Maybe locally, but I don't believe the Outcasts will travel far from home."

Ty nodded. "Then it'll be one of machines."

John rubbed his hand through his hair. "If that's true, we've got a problem: The only humans on this planet who know how to fight won't lift a hand. Their oral history can't speak too well of humanity."

"Which may explain why attacking us came so easy for them. Hate," Ty said.

"That leaves us to train everyone else to fight, if it comes to that."

"I really hope we're wrong," Ty said.

"So what's next?" Terry asked.

"Megan, are G.A.'s security components still off?"

"Yes."

John looked at Jamal. "Stay here." He glanced at Terry and Ty. "Let's go outside."

They walked out of the building and stood next to the SS ship.

Now that we've got light, "First things first." He reached

into his pocket and removed the small metal case containing the Mosquito cameras.

"Megan, send the Mosquitoes into the subterranean cavity and have them search it for S.S. machines and hubots and also provide a hologram of the facility."

The Mosquitoes flew away and disappeared down the ramp. A few minutes later, a five-foot square hologram appeared in front of them. They watched with unimaginable anticipation as the Mosquitoes reach a heavy, closed, cobalt-carbon-aluminum door blocking the power plant.

"That's strange," John said, very surprised. "It's closed. Then why did they give in to us over the water from the tanker? Megan, have the Mosquitoes search the walls around the door for a crack or someplace where water can invade the power plant."

They watched as the Mosquitoes hovered around the door searching for an opening.

"There!" Ty pointed. "See the grate on the floor to the right of the door?"

"That's for drainage." John pointed next. "There it is. Look about five feet up the wall on the right next to the door. See it? The five-inch hole. I'll bet that's for air."

"Shit, that's pretty high above the floor," Ty said.

"What?" Terry asked.

"Megan, if we'd emptied the water tanker into the area around the door, how much of that wall would have been covered?"

"Seven feet."

"For how long?"

"Thirty minutes."

"Oh *God*, we would have barely had enough water to reach that air hole and flood the power room," John whispered.

"Megan, bring another saltwater-filled tanker; land it next to the first one." He looked at Ty, "That airhole is how they got in last night." He shook his head, "Another dumb mistake. I thought the door was open." He rubbed his hand through his hair. "Megan send the Mosquitoes through the air hole into the room."

SIXTEEN

They watched the Mosquitoes move through what looked like a five-inch, six-foot-long pipe, then they passed by a two-foot-wide, four-blade fan and entered a massive two-story-deep room, the walls covered by reenforced cobalt-carbon-aluminum.

"Look at that—it's massive! It must be a half an acre long, and those machines line the whole damn floor. There must be fifty of them," Ty said.

"Those aren't machines; they're turbines creating electricity —artificial stars, like having unlimited power in the universe," John said. "Megan, add a third tanker and rush it here."

"What's wrong?" Terry asked. "Why are you two so scared?"

"We just dodged a bullet. Only luck saved us," Ty said.

"What? What's luck and what's a bullet?" she shouted.

Ty spoke: "We didn't have enough water to inundate this power plant. Pandora knew that, but it didn't want to risk that the little water we had might reach those turbines and shut the power plant down. If that little five-inch airhole had been two feet higher, you and I would be dead. That's the 'lucky,' which means chance, out of our control. The bullet is death. If one of the Outcasts had shot the tanker and spilled enough water, Jamal would not have stopped them from killing us and John would have been captured."

"I like luck, and don't want a bullet," Terry said.

Thirty minutes later, the two tankers filled with saltwater arrived. Megan landed them next to the tanker on the loading ramp.

John looked at Ty and took a deep breath.

"I feel sick," Terry said. "I'll be right back." She entered the SS ship.

"I'm getting Jamal," John said. He left and returned several minutes later with Jamal following behind.

They stopped next to Ty and the SS ship.

"Open the door to the power plant," John ordered Jamal.

"No."

"Megan, empty a tanker of water."

They could hear the first splash of water rush down the ramp.

"Stop. I'll open it," Jamal said.

"Megan, close the water valve."

They waited thirty minutes for the tunnel to empty.

"Open the power plant door," John said again.

"Done," it said.

"Megan, is it open?"

"Yes."

"Let's go," John said.

"Where?" Ty asked.

"It's time to meet Pandora in G.A." John looked at Jamal. "Lead us to your Master Crystal."

They turned and started walking back to the GA building to get to Pandora in the basement.

"Megan, if you lose contact with us even for a quantum second, empty the tankers and use the S.S. ship to destroy the G.A. building and power plant."

When they were about to enter the building, Terry hollered from behind, "Where are you going?"

They stopped and turned to face her, seeing she was standing on the SS ship boarding ramp.

She ran to them. "Where are you going? You two aren't going anywhere without me, got it?" She was obviously angry. She faced Ty. "I don't feel too good. Your Soylent Green upset my stomach."

"It takes time to get used to."

She stared at him for a moment. "Well, let's go," she said.

They entered the main building through the garage back door and walked down the stairs to the basement. The bottom door was still open, and the light was on.

They stood at the doorway.

"Is this safe?" Ty asked.

"Pandora's not suicidal. So I think so," John said.

"That's good, because I don't really want to meet destiny at such a young age," Ty said.

"But you said destiny was our best friend—and sometimes my conscience—right?" Terry asked.

"I did," Ty answered.

"I don't understand," Terry muttered to herself.

They walked into the room. It was empty of furniture and scientific equipment. A set of closed, polished cobalt-aluminum double doors stood at the other side of the room.

"Open the doors," John told Jamal.

The doors popped open with a hissing sound as air rushed out.

"Oh, that stinks! It smells like an animal," Terry said, covering her nose with her right hand.

"More like death," Ty said.

"Ready your guns and aim," John said. "If the room goes dark, fire at the door, don't move, and keep firing up, down, and side to side until the light comes back on or you run out of ammunition."

John took a deep breath and rubbed his hand though his hair. They moved across the room and stood at the now open doorway and looked in. Hanging from the ceiling was an eight-foot-long, four-foot-round, crystal-covered, gold-and-silver-colored object.

"It wasn't that big when it was first installed," John said. "Royer called it a quantum chandelier computer; it didn't work. He told me that when they figured out how to keep the noise out and keep it running for extended periods of time, it would answer every question in the universe."

"I remember that; it was just about to go online when the Gysins attacked," Ty said.

"Who are the Gysins?" Terry asked Ty.

"Bad people. Twins—"

"What are twins?" Terry interrupted.

"Two people born at the same time to the same mother," Ty answered.

"Really? That can happen?"

"Yes."

"They hurt John's wife, Megan, and their two daughters, and they also killed several people," Ty continued.

"What happened to them?"

"John and I shot and killed them."

She looked at John. "Is that why you hid?"

John rubbed his hand through his hair. "There were other reasons."

"I've only been here for one day, and the more I see, the more amazed I am you survived for so long," Ty said.

John sighed. "It wasn't easy; only the hope that I could finally come out of hiding kept me going." A weak smile crossed his lips.

"It looks pretty," Terry said, "hanging from the ceiling like that. It's almost touching the floor, and look how the glass crystals and all those gold, yellow, red, and blue wires seem to bounce around in the light."

"It looks exactly like the one in San Francisco, except a lot bigger," Ty said.

John pushed Jamal forward into the room. They followed and stood to one side of the Crystal chandelier. Jamal was in front and turned to face them.

John looked at it. "This is not all of it," he said coolly. "Where are the memory databanks kept?"

Silence.

"Where are they? Tell me or I'll start shooting," John said.

Suddenly, the entire wall to their left slid open, exposing another room.

Ty moved to the opening and took a glance into the room. "Oh man, John, it's twice the size of the San Francisco databank room—this one's filled with what looks like millions of those tiny glass balls."

"Oh my God!" John gasped and took a step backward. "This is the *main* Master Crystal." His voice broke and his face was covered with shock.

"Why are you so frightened?" Terry asked, lifting her gun and pointing it toward the other room.

"I-I was wrong. Pandora *is* their god. San Francisco was the insurance," John stammered.

All three were struck silent with shock and stared at the massive chandelier hanging from the ceiling.

John turned to face Jamal and shot it. *Zzzppnt!*

"What?" Ty shouted as he jumped backward, pointing his gun toward the melted mess on the floor. Terry dropped to the floor, covering her head with her hands.

"Terry! Stay down!" John shouted.

"You could have warned me," Ty said.

"We need time. I keep making mistakes!" John whispered, rubbing his right hand though his hair. "I should've known this was possible the moment I saw the massive underground power station—and Jamal's ghost smirk," he said, looking at Ty.

Ty stepped closer. "Known what?"

"We're being watched and listened to," John whispered. He looked at Terry lying on the floor, then back at Ty. "It knew all along I'd go to San Francisco, and need help, and I'd end up here."

"What are you talking about?" Ty asked.

"We're in great danger," John whispered.

Ty cocked his head and raised his gun, on alert for whatever came.

John turned and took several steps toward Terry, picked up her gun, and said, "Terry, don't move a muscle."

She stared at him, wide-eyed.

He stood straight and walked back to Ty. "Come with me."

John led Ty across the room, next to the wall behind the chandelier. They crouched down. Ty leaned back against a two-foot-square closed half door.

John whispered, "Megan, is there anything inorganic on Ty and me?"

"Yes."

"Get rid of it."

"Done."

"Is there anything on Terry?"

"No."

"Good," Ty whispered.

"No, it's not."

Ty looked puzzled.

"Megan, where are the Mosquito cameras?"

"At the power plant."

"Why?"

"The doors are closed, and the fan is pumping air so hard they can't exit through the pipe."

"Megan, how many creatures are in G.A.?"

"Four humans and one hubot."

"That's not good," Ty whispered, "since there's only three of us."

"Megan, shut yourself down and only reactivate on my touch."

John touched Ty's shoulder and again whispered, "We're in danger. I think Terry's a hubot."

Ty's mouth dropped open.

John handed him Terry's gun. "Go to the room filled with the databank glass balls and stand by the opening. When I'm ready, I'll nod. Then you fire a shot into that room. If we're attacked, press that button." He pointed to a small black dot on the back edge of the gun. "Throw it into that room immediately, then duck against the wall."

"Bang?" Ty asked.

"*Big* bang. Get ready to fight. It's going to get really strange. Remember, we're dealing with a godlike computer. Do not shoot Pandora unless I tell you to." John gave him a small smile. "Ready?"

Ty nodded.

"Let's do it," John said.

Ty moved across the room and stood next to the open doorway to the Crystal room.

John rubbed his hand through his hair and took a breath, fearful about his next move. "Terry, you can stand now," he said.

"It's about time. The floor is cold." Terry stood and took several steps toward John.

"Stop," he commanded.

"Why does Ty have my gun? What's wrong? You're acting ugly again."

"When did you join with the Crystal, Terry?" John asked her coldly.

She froze in place with a puzzled expression.

Ty's eyebrows were way above his wide eyes.

"Answer me," John ordered.

She looked at Ty, then back at John, her face showing fear and confusion. "Ty, what is he doing? Stop him."

"Answer me!" John snapped.

Suddenly, her body stiffened, her brown eyes turned solid black, and her face turned cold and emotionless. "Your mistakes will kill her and Ty," she answered in a hollow, lifeless voice.

John glanced at Ty. "Shoot the room."

The expression on Ty's face was still of shock, but—*Zzzppnt! Zzzppnt! Zzzppnt!*—he fired into the room, destroying thousands of the databank glass balls.

"Stop," Terry said in her suddenly cold voice. "What do you want, Doctor Barber?"

Silence for a moment.

John took a step back, faced the outer doorway, and lifted

his gun, ready to shoot. "Get ready, Ty." Then: "You can come in, Captain Davis," he said quietly.

A moment later, a six-foot-three-inch-tall, middle-aged man walked in. He was dressed in a crisp, perfectly fitted military uniform, complete with medals, colored ribbons, and faux-patent-leather black shoes.

His eyes were dark and lifeless, just like Terry's. His movements were stiff. He held his chin up, displaying a smug, arrogant visage.

"Ty, what you're looking at is Pandora walking."

Ty was beyond shock now; he was on the outer limits of stupefied; this was the last thing he'd expected.

"Ty, if Terry moves, kill her."

"You should have killed me yesterday when you had the chance," Davis said with the same hollow voice as Terry's.

John glanced at Ty, who looked confused, yet ready to act. "Ty, this is Captain Robert A. Davis, the last chief investigator on Earth, and the last member of the F.B.I. He was charged with finding and killing me. To his credit, he found me, but unfortunately for him and the San Francisco Crystal, they failed to kill me." John smiled and glanced at Davis's uniform. "Interesting: No gun."

"What do you mean, 'they failed'?" Ty asked.

John didn't take his eyes off Davis. "After I escaped from the captain here—after the first time he was supposed to kill me—the San Francisco Crystal ordered him to come in for the ultimate enhancement... without, of course, telling him what was about to happen."

Ty still looked puzzled.

"Just like Professor Friendly and General Marble," John went on, "Captain Davis was also joined to and became part of, the World Crystal."

"How do you know that?" Ty asked.

"I put a Mosquito camera on Davis and watched the entire process. That insight saved my life and allowed me to use Davis' implant to tell humanity about the San Francisco—well, Pandora's—gawdawful plans." John smiled at Davis/Pandora. "You are still such an arrogant fool."

"You will be dead soon, Doctor Barber," Davis said.

John took a small step toward Davis. "I knew I'd see you again since you weren't hanging on the wall in San Francisco. Failing like you did, it was no surprise. You didn't deserve to rest next to greatness. I just didn't know exactly when we'd meet again."

For a moment, John wondered if Davis would reply.

Then: "*I* will kill you, John Barber," Pandora said through Davis' mouth, its eyes firmly fixed on John's face.

"Ty," John said with a nod of his head.

Zzzppnt! Zzzppnt! Zzzppnt! Ty fired his pistol at the wall covered in glass balls, destroying thousands more.

"What do you want?" Davis asked in the same cold, unemotional voice.

This time, it was John's turn to be the quiet one for a few moments. Then he glanced at Ty. "Ty, Captain Davis has failed a second time. Terry was going to disarm me and kill you. That's why he's here. He wanted to watch you die, the 'second to last of humanity-to-be.' Isn't that right, Captain Davis?"

Ty flushed with fury by what John said. He clenched his jaw, glanced at Davis, then back to Terry.

No reply from Davis, beyond slightly shifting his feet and staring at Ty.

"What I *demand*," John said, "is that you set Terry free and remove all elements of the liquid crystals Pandora inserted into her brain."

Davis glanced at Terry, then returned his focus to John.

"Is Terry like him?" Ty asked.

"I doubt it. I know why it hesitates to free her: She'll remember all of Pandora's plans."

Davis continued to stare at John.

"Ty, if we're surprised in any way, shoot Terry and duck."

Ty's eyes popped open even wider, his eyebrows lifted, but he pointed his pistol at Terry's chest.

Davis remained motionless.

John reached into his right jeans' pocket and touched Megan's crystal. He removed his empty hand from the pocket, stepped backward closer to Ty, reached up, covered his mouth, and whispered, "Megan, is the pod still on the roof?"

"Yes."

"Move the Mosquitoes to safety. Take the pod to the power plant's door and detonate the pod's magneto-power drive."

A moment later, the explosion was deafening, the floor shook, ceiling tiles fell to the floor, the Crystal's chandelier casing bounced up and swung violently from side to side. Ty and John dropped to their knees. Terry fell to the floor. Davis fell back against the doorway wall. A light-gray dust filled the air.

John and Ty quickly jumped to their feet. Terry screamed out in pain, lying on the floor.

Davis glanced at Ty, his eyes returned to human for a moment, and he screamed "Kill me!" But just as quickly his eyes returned to their lifeless gaze.

"What the hell was that?" Ty shrieked.

"The turbine floor is now open and ready to receive a lot of San Francisco Bay water."

"What? How?" Ty asked.

John frowned. "I screwed up again, not thinking that

Pandora would close the power plant's doors after we left and plug the air hole, making it watertight. I figure its plan, if Terry failed to kill you, was to have Davis offer me a deal, lead us to the surface, murder you, and out of rage, I would have released the water; it would not have reached the turbines and Pandora would survive. I would have been captured by the Outcasts, my brain raped, and the computer code removed, freeing Pandora from my virus. Isn't that right, Captain Davis?"

"I will release her," Davis said.

Terry suddenly screamed, held her head, and rolled around on the floor in horrific pain. Her jaw dropped, and her mouth opened with no sound. Her body twisted violently. She grabbed her head with both hands and screamed in pain, then vomit shot out her mouth before she finally passed out.

"That's your and Ty's future," Davis said.

"John, the Outcasts are running toward G.A.," Megan said.

"I will kill you," Davis said.

Zzzppnt! Zzzppnt!, and he burst into a fireball of gas.

"I wish you'd warn me before you shoot somebody," Ty said, grinning.

"He asked me to kill him," John said, smiling. "Megan, are the Outcasts still attacking?"

"They stopped," Megan said.

Ty and John looked at each other for a moment, both feeling a huge sense of relief.

"You're right," Ty said. "He was an arrogant asshole."

"His fatal flaw and the secret to my survival. I used that human flaw to overcome him, tie him to a chair and download my story into his head."

Terry came to with a groan. She rolled to her right side, got to her knees, and sobbed like a child. She covered her face with her hands, coughed for a bit, and took several deep breaths. Sweat ran down her temples.

"Ty, how many balls are left in that room?"

"About three-quarters."

"Let's blow this place, then," John said, still grinning. "Toss the gun in."

Ty pressed the button, turned, and threw the gun into the room, and they ducked for cover.

Five seconds later, there was an ear-popping *BANG!* followed by a blast of flaming gas that shot several feet out the doorway. The air was sucked out of the room for a moment, but just as quickly, fresh air rushed back in from the stairwell, sounding like a jet engine.

Silence enveloped the room as it cooled and the dust settled. The air smelled of melted wire. John and Ty stood and looked at each other, then started to laugh.

"Damn, I need a bourbon," Ty said.

"My treat," John replied.

"What about me? I deserve some bourbon," Terry said, sitting up on the floor, smiling.

SEVENTEEN

Ty offered his hand to help Terry stand.

She looked up, smiled, and grabbed his hand. She stood and gave him a friendly hug. She turned and glared at John. "You're still an ugly person, but thank you for releasing me from that very ugly, dark place."

"I'm sorry for being so cold."

"You're different from the man I once knew," Ty said. "You're dark and don't let compassion get in the way, and thank God for it, or we'd be dead." He grinned. "So what's next, Doctor John W. Barber?"

"First, Megan, bring the Mosquitoes here, then empty all the water into the power plant."

The room shook as each turbine exploded. John smiled. "Pandora is out of options." He grinned, looking at Terry. "Our next move is to meet the Outcast leader and cut a deal. Then go to San Francisco, tell a story, come back here, and figure out how to restart that damn thing." He pointed at Pandora.

"What?" Terry squealed, clearly shocked.

"You're sure it's off?" Ty asked.

John nodded. "The power's off."

"Man, that's great to hear," Ty said. "I want to do a happy dance."

"Good for you," Terry said, staring at Ty. "But we're not restarting that ugly thing."

"We need it to direct the ten million androids on how to teach people how to survive in the short term," John said.

"Why the androids?" she asked.

"It's the only way to reach the three billion people before things can get out of control," John said.

"What about helping the Outcasts?" Ty asked.

"That'll take time, but it has to be done as soon as possible."

"What do you mean, it will take time?" Ty asked.

"Oral history: How does one forgive the past? Trust doesn't come easy; forgiveness takes a lot longer."

Ty nodded, understanding.

"I'll bet there'll be a lot of anxious people in San Francisco waiting for us," John said, "and they'll need to hear our future plans."

"How many you think will be there?" Ty asked.

"That depends on Arnold, but I'll bet thousands."

"How are they going to hear us?" Terry asked.

"Ah," Ty said, "I know the answer to that. We can use a parabolic reflector."

"A what?" she asked.

"It's a very large, curved plate." Ty cupped his right hands together. "It makes sound travel very far. It's been around for a thousand years."

"It's got to be plenty big for this," John said. "Megan, given the size of Crystal Plaza Square and surrounding area, how big a parabolic reflector will we need?"

"An eight-foot-diameter disk."

"That's too big to build here. We'd need several androids to assemble it," John said.

"What are we going to say?" Terry asked.

"That we'll overcome the ugly, and now we survive by working together," Ty said.

They climbed the stairs to GA's interior. John put out his hand to stop Ty and Terry. "Megan, is it safe?"

"Yes, the Outcasts are gone."

John rubbed his hand through his hair, Ty smiled, and Terry released a deep sigh.

They walked through the building and out into the compound. For the first time, all three of them felt safe and confident.

John looked around, the sun felt warm, the air smelled clean and fresh.

"Ready to pay a visit to the Outcasts," John said.

"Why?" Terry asked.

"I want to know what they know, and how to deal with them in the future."

"Let's take the pod to Outcast Land; it'll be less intimidating than the S.S. ship," Ty said.

John nodded. "Megan, bring a pod here from San Francisco, park it next to the S.S. ship. We'll take it to the Outcasts' encampment."

The pod arrived thirty minutes later and parked. Terry started to sit in the back. "No, you deserve to be in the front," Ty said while opening the door for her. Once in, he got into the back seat with John in the front.

"Megan, is Pandora really turned off?" John asked, sitting behind the control panel.

"Yes."

"If it comes back on, tell me."

The pod lifted and flew a mile to the Outcasts' village. It hovered there for several minutes.

Hundreds of igloo-shaped wood structures circled a central green area. They saw several narrow, gravel roads leading away from the hub. Two of the roads led to three, five thousand square-foot-sized open sheds.

"Poultry barns, horse barn, and look, carts and farm equipment. Those are chicken coops, and there are sheep and cattle pens. There"—Ty pointed to the right—"horses, and I'll bet that's their hay and grain barn. They have an irrigation system, and that looks like a construction area for building stuff. Those green areas off to the east are probably agriculture fields and orchards." Ty suddenly laughed. "And of course there's the winery. And there's an amphitheater built into the side of the hill. These people have been here a long time and know what they're doing," he said, excited by what he was seeing.

"I don't understand why you're so impressed. They're living with animals. It looks dirty," Terry said, looking out the window.

"And eating them," Ty quipped.

"What? That's ugly."

He laughed.

"Terry," John said, "we're impressed because these people were discarded. Human nature kicked in and they survived on their own."

"I don't understand."

"A hundred and eighty-five years ago, those people were at

the bottom of society, so low they weren't worthy of the K chip, or help for that matter. They were removed from everyday society and left where they couldn't infect anyone.... Others hoped they would just fade away and die off. That was the plan."

"That's happened before," Ty said, "and it also failed. Surviving is human nature at its best."

"What's human nature?" she asked.

"That, Terry Cheer, is very complicated," Ty said. "It's the voice in your head, your voice, pushing you forward. It tells you to run, fight, or help. When things are very bad, that voice brings people together out of love and they help each other."

"What's love?"

"Good God!" Ty spit out.

"There you go again," she said. "What's God?"

"Love, purpose, and integrity all bundled together in one living being," Ty said. He smiled. "A thought just crossed my mind: This is dangerous, and I don't mean our conversation. The last time we saw the Outcasts, they tried to kill us, and from what I can see below, they must have guns."

"Terry, the worst part of human nature is people killing each other," John said.

"Why would they want to harm us?"

"Lots of reasons, but fear is number one," Ty said.

"I understand fear, so let's get a bourbon, and you and John can think it over," Terry quipped.

Ty laughed. "I second that."

"She's right. Let's do this when we have a hubot to handle the introductions. Megan, where's the closest museum with a parabolic reflector?"

"Stanford University has a ten-foot-diameter dish."

"That's convenient," John said.

"Why is it always Stanford? Why not Howard where I went?" Ty said.

"You know why: Nine out of ten girls in D.C. are beautiful; the tenth goes to Howard," John said, laughing.

"Very funny. But you're thinking of Caltech, where you went. And where's that baseball cap you like to wear?"

John reached under the driver's seat and pulled out the tattered Caltech baseball cap.

Ty laughed. "Megan hated that thing."

"Megan, take us back to the S.S. ship. We'll need its holding bay to transport the reflector."

They landed at GA next to the black SS ship. They got out of the pod and started walking to the ship.

"Megan, send the pod to San Francisco and land it next to the fountain at the Crystal Plaza," John said.

The ship's boarding hatch opened, they climbed the ramp, and walked into the cockpit. Ty sat next to John facing the control panel; Terry sat in the gunner's seat behind them.

"Megan, take us to Stanford University, Frost Amphitheater. Land next to the antiquity reflector," John said.

"How long will it take?" Ty asked.

John glanced at his silver Tiffany wristwatch. "Ten minutes, and if all goes well, we'll arrive at the plaza before noon."

"That's the watch Megan gave you for your fortieth birthday," Ty commented.

"Yes."

"You see, Terry, he is sentimental."

"I don't believe that. And *forty*, that's ugly bad."

Ty and John glanced at each other and laughed.

They arrived at the Stanford campus on a cloudless, crisp, dry midmorning and flew over the campus.

"John, slow us down," Ty said. "I haven't been here in a very long time. I want to see what's changed." The SS ship slowed to a jogging pace. "It looks the same." He pointed below. "That's the Bing Concert Hall. I gave a speech there. This is weird after all this time."

"Remember, it was rebuilt to resemble life before the wars," John said.

"They did a hell of a job. All's that's missing are students."

They were flying close to Frost Amphitheater when they saw a herd of ten deer with three fawns grazing on the lush, green-blue amphitheater grass field. Hundreds of squirrels and all types of native birds filled the park-like setting with life.

"Wow, what a beautiful place to go to college," Ty said.

"Teaching stopped here a hundred twenty-five years ago. It was transformed into a research center and medical facility; now it's basically a historical site and park."

"Why no teaching?"

"The K chip and the World Crystal databank eliminated the need for personal education, or scientists, for that matter."

Ty frowned and shook his head. "Sad."

They landed next to a cobalt-aluminum reflector, got out of the ship, and walked to the ten-foot-wide dish. There was an engraved marble plaque on the rock base that Ty read aloud: "Dedicated to Samuel Morland, the inventor of the megaphone, and to those who need to be heard above the noise." He turned and looked at John, who was standing behind him. "Strange this relic memory still exists. A lot of this doesn't make sense. Why keep this and not teach?" He shrugged his shoulders. "It's bigger than we need. How are we going to get this thing into the ship?"

"Megan, lift the base and reflector and deposit it into the ship's cargo hold," John said.

With expressions of amazement, Ty and Terry watched as the aft end of the ship separated and lifted, exposing an empty loading area. Suddenly, the reflector and marble base lifted magically off the ground, floated over the grass to the ship, and silently drifted into the open cargo hold.

"That is so cool! With that thing, who needs a friend with a truck?" Ty exclaimed.

"What's a truck?" Terry asked.

"Man's best friend," Ty quipped.

"Another best friend?" Terry asked, shaking her head.

John laughed. "Let's go. We've got a speech to deliver."

They walked back to the SS ship as the cargo hold closed.

John stopped and looked at Ty. "I've been thinking about what to tell them."

"You want to tell the truth, don't you?"

"Yes."

"The truth is never bad, unless you're guilty."

John laughed. "Or telling someone 'That makes you look fat.'"

"What's fat?" Terry asked.

"What men get when they drink beer," Ty said.

"What's beer?"

"She's going to get even one day," John said.

"Yep, and seeing how smart she is, it won't be too long." He lifted his rich, dark eyebrows and smiled. "So what's your plan?"

"We'll assemble the reflector near the fountain, tell them what we've learned, and what's coming up next."

"Sounds easy, until the part about three billion dead."

"I'll do that," Terry said.

"Why?" John asked.

"Because you're ugly bad and don't feel what Ty calls love. I understand the pain. I had the chip in my head. You didn't."

"All right," John said, nodding. "You're up."

They took off and headed to San Francisco.

"We're here." John glanced at his watch: 11:35 a.m.

"Oh my God, there are thousands down there. There isn't anywhere to land," Ty said.

"Megan, anchor the reflector within the base of the fountain, and have it facing north toward the bay," John said.

The ship began to shake as the cargo door opened and the reflector slowly drifted out. John kept the ship hovering just above the plaza after the reflector was outside the cargo hold.

"Done," Megan announced.

"Megan, open the boarding hatch, facing the front edge of the fountain, descend close enough to the ground so we can jump out. Then hover the ship a hundred feet above the fountain in case we need a quick escape."

The hatch opened, and the cool Pacific Ocean air filled the ship.

"That's San Francisco at its best," Ty whispered.

They jumped out of the ship, landed in ankle-deep water, and stood side by side underneath the ship.

"Please make room!" Ty shouted, gesturing with his arms and hands. "Back up, back up!"

The throng of people slowly moved out of the fountain area, pressing against one another and packing the plaza even tighter with bodies until only one person remained at the fountain.

"Hello, Arnold," John said. "I'm very happy to see you."

"Why and are there so many people here?" Ty asked.

"I told everyone I could how you were going to return today," Arnold answered. "They passed the word. I think this is everyone in San Francisco," he said, looking a bit sheepish.

Terry walked to Arnold and gave him a hug. "It was ugly. Be happy you stayed here," she whispered.

"This is crazy," Ty whispered to John. "If there's a panic, half the people here will be crushed, including us."

John rubbed his hand through his hair and took a deep breath. He turned to face away from the crowd, looking east toward the reflector, and shouted, "My name—"

To him and everyone else the shock of loud sound blasting at them was incredible. The subsequent echo through the streets and buildings was equally terrifying as it rumbled away. Shrieks and cries shot out as people covered their ears and hid their faces as the sound shot past them.

Terry dropped to her knees; Ty covered his ears and looked away.

"Wow, that thing is amazing," Ty said, grinning, looking at John. "You might want to try that again, just a tad softer."

John took a deep breath. *I hate speaking in public,* he thought. He again faced the reflector.

"Hello, my name is John Barber, and I have a lot to tell you," he said in regular speaking voice. He waited a moment for the echo to pass through the buildings toward the bay. "I need all of you to please sit."

He watched as the giant mass of people sat on the ground.

"This is so cool, like dominos," Ty whispered.

It took five minutes for everyone to find a place to sit.

"It was my story that started all this," John continued. "I am so sorry for the pain it caused you." He waited as the echo rushed to the ocean. "I had no idea how bad the damage caused by the World Crystal was, or how terrible its plan was. Some of what we learned is good and some is very bad. The World Crystal has been defeated and turned off, and—"

Suddenly, shouts and screams of joy shot back at him from the ocean, and some people jumped to their feet, cheering.

He waited for it to quiet down. "We discovered there were two World Crystals; both were filled with lies and death."

Gasps and cries of fear crisscrossed the crowd; he waited.

"Both have been turned off."

Joy, as shown by cheering, shouts, and clapping filled San Francisco with sound.

"You are not alone, and help will arrive soon. We found a group of people named the 'Outcasts' who can teach all of us how to live in a world without crystals.

"Soon the androids will be operational and back to work. Now for the bad news: The people who built those two ugly crystals are dead, and it was those machines that committed the horrible acts against us. Not the androids or anyone living; it was a machine, a tool without feelings, like a pod, or that water fountain." He pointed. "Anger at a machine does not accomplish anything. Fighting each other or blaming someone is wrong and will do no good. What we've learned is beyond understanding."

The crowd waited in silence. Some had their hands covering their mouths; others held their flat palms together and pressed their index fingers against their lips. All had a look of dread on their faces.

"How mankind could build such a terrible machine is a tragedy, and it's something to always remember and never let happen again.

"Terry Cheer helped me and Ty Leggett succeed at defeating the Crystals. Terry, like all of you, was a prisoner of that Crystal until yesterday. She, along with thousands right here, fought"—he turned and faced the plaza and pointed around the area—"against the S.S. machines guarding the

World Crystal. Her courage and determination lifted her above fear. Terry demanded that she be the one to tell you what the Crystal did to you and every other human in the universe."

John turned to face Terry, who suddenly looked terrified and was crying a little bit. She took several steps toward John and turned to face the reflector. She looked three feet tall standing in front of the dish, not her five feet ten inches.

"Megan, record her speech," John whispered.

EIGHTEEN

Terry started with, "John Barber's history made me cry, then I felt something that I didn't have a name for. I've since learned it's called rage." Her voice was even, but filled with restrained emotion. "When the voice in my head, the K chip, stopped talking, I felt alone; the silence was terrifying. I came here to destroy the Crystal, and it was here, across the street, that I met John Barber. All the terror and fear were nothing to what I felt when I *saw* the World Crystal. It captured me and invaded my mind. John Barber freed me from that Crystal at the risk of his and Ty Leggett's life."

The crowd sat in awed silence.

"I watched John Barber outsmart the World Crystal in that building"—she pointed—"and turn it off.

"I thought we were free. I was wrong, we learned there was another, more powerful Crystal in Nevada."

Sounds of gasps and cries of fear filled the air.

"The terror I felt returned when I learned the worst: I had been scheduled to leave for the moon and live there for the rest of my life with my roommate. I've spoken to many people about how wonderful and incredible life was there, and every day I watched people meet old friends there who'd just arrived—but it was all a lie!"

The crowd became uneasy.

"They're all dead!" Terry screamed.

The reactions were disbelief, shock, eyes welled with tears, faces were covered by hands.

"It killed everyone who left Earth; their bodies are lying on the backside of the moon!" Terry wailed.

The first scream of pain was a lone voice several feet away from the fountain, followed by the deafening sound of thousands of voices crying out.

Terry looked at Ty, and said, "If the past had heard these cries and saw the death and pain, this might not have happened."

Ty shook his head, thinking, *Not a chance, Terry. The bastards would've still done it.*

Their pain was quickly followed by rage and shouts of determined disbelief:

"Not true, not true!"

"Kill him! Kill John Barber!"

"Yeah, this is his fault!"

Some next to the fountain stood and started to attack. First, they threw their shoes and then made fists and clawed their fingers at him as they advanced.

"Stop!" Terry screamed, which boomed through the megaphone, jerking people back to reality. "We were next. Stop and listen! *We were next!* It was going to kill all of us. Look around: Do you see anyone younger than us? Do you see babies? No! A baby hasn't been born in nineteen years. It murdered three billion of us."

Gasps. Whimpers. Moans.

"Please, *please*, we need each other to survive, to overcome this terrible situation. We need to learn how to be human, how to take care of ourselves, how to love, how to feel for each other and protect each other. John Barber can guide us and save us from extinction.

"I want to live. I want to become fully human. I want to learn about free will, bourbon, and being self-efficient. And, we must bring our dead home and bury them here on Earth." She paused. "Because that's what *humans* do. We will survive. We will rebuild and learn all about love and human nature." She turned and glanced at Ty.

Looking at the audience again, she said, "Go home now. Come back here again tomorrow late afternoon, and we'll start rebuilding our lives."

She turned away from the reflector to face John and Ty; each gave her a hug.

"You are amazing," John whispered.

"You're our hope for humanity," Ty whispered.

They watched and waited as the streets and plaza emptied of people.

"There was a moment when I thought I was going to die again," Ty said.

"Damn, that was scary," John said.

"I don't want to keep doing this," Terry said with a whisper, her voice tired and weak from the emotional drain.

Ty gave her hug.

John looked at his watch: 4:30 p.m. "We've got time to return to G.A. Terry, will you join us?" John asked.

"You're not going anywhere without me, John Barber and Ty Leggett. Where's that bottle of bourbon?"

Both men laughed.

"Well, let's go. Megan, lower the ship and take us back to G.A.," John said.

"What about me?" Arnold asked, looking dejected, standing outside the fountain facing them.

"Arnold," John answered, "you stay here, keep passing the word, answering questions, and calming people."

He reluctantly said, "Okay."

The ship landed on the plaza next to the wrecked fountain, and they boarded. This time, Terry sat in the copilot seat next to John, and Ty sat in the gunner's seat behind Terry.

"Don't get carried away, Terry Cheer," Ty said. "I am ninety years old, and I've been a rock star for all that time."

She smiled, thinking, *What's a rock star?*

"So what's your plan for controlling Pandora, John?" Ty asked.

"I won't know until we assess the damage to its memory."

"Can't we just keep it off?" Terry asked.

"We need it—"

"I know, I know," she interrupted. "But can't we just keep it off?" Terry repeated nervously.

John shook his head and sighed. "We need the androids to do everything."

"Can't we use Megan?" Ty asked.

"No, Megan's not powerful enough," John said.

"I don't understand," Ty said. "Your hacking into Davis gave Megan access into Pandora. She knows everything it does."

"Not true. She only knows a little. Here's an example: Pandora is the sun; Megan is a candle. She can only do so much," John said.

"This is beginning to feel so ugly," Terry said.

John nodded. "Rebuilding is complicated. If we make a

mistake, history will repeat itself and people will resort to killing each other."

"That's not what I mean, you ugly person," she replied. "I don't want it to kill me."

Ty laughed. "Terry, you're wonderful. There are only three of us, but there're *billions* of others who need advice and help. We can't give that support to them without the androids." He smiled. "John may be a stuffed shirt"—he laughed, glancing at John—"and he may act 'ugly' when you mean cold, but he's trying to keep us and everyone else alive." Ty smiled. "From now on, when you don't like what he's doing, tell him no, you want to talk about it. If he argues, call him a stuffed-shirt ass and let it go."

Terry nodded. "Okay, I will, but what's a stuffed shirt?"

"A person who does not listen."

"Okay, what's an ass?"

"You sit on it."

"That fits," she said.

Ty laughed.

John shook his head, thinking, *He's not funny.*

They crossed over the Sierra Mountains and entered the Truckee Meadows Basin.

"Megan, land next to the G.A. building near the entrance and check for signs of life or energy disbursements."

"There are none."

They landed, the boarding hatch opened, and they walked down the ramp toward the three-story office complex. The surrounding property was covered in trash, broken tables, chairs, window frames, doorknobs, locks, and glass shards, with red, blue, and green electrical wiring strewn everywhere. Even the roll-up garage door was gone.

"Looks like the Outcasts stripped the place," Ty said, looking at John.

"This isn't good," John said. "I hope they didn't go into the basement and dismantle Pandora."

"Why?" Terry asked.

"Because it might mean they moved or destroyed it."

Terry had mixed emotions: She hoped Pandora had been taken apart, yet she knew it was their only hope to rebuild.

They walked into the warehouse. The walls were stripped, the flooring had been pulled up, and all the cabinets and doors were gone. They walked to the stairwell that led to the basement cold room, noting the door was gone.

"That's not good," John said.

They entered the darkened stairwell.

"I should have thought about this ahead of time. Wait here," John said. He turned and ran back to the ship, went into the weapons cabinet, and grabbed five Fenix PD99X9.0 diamond crystal sun flares, then returned to Ty and Terry.

He held up five pencil-sized sticks. "This will blow your mind," John said, looking at Ty. He pointed one of the sticks down the stairwell and squeezed the back end with his right hand.

There was a buzzing sound, followed by a single stream of sparks shooting out about six inches. The sparks coalesced and grew into a small, round object about the size of a tennis ball, which began to shoot around the stairwell, bouncing back and forth as it moved down the steps. Each time it hit the wall, it left a round spot of light. By the time it reached the bottom floor, the entire stairwell was bathed in bright white light.

"That is so frickin' amazing. How long will those lights stay on?" Ty asked.

"Forty-eight hours. Let's go see what's left of our Crystal."

They reached the bottom doorway. John pointed the second flare into the room, the process repeated itself, and the room was almost instantly bathed in white light. Everything was as they left it. The chandelier quantum Crystal was hanging from the ceiling, and only dust and debris from the explosion covered the floor.

"No footprints; they didn't come down here," Ty said.

"For good reason: This place is ugly, and I mean scary in the dark," Terry said.

Ty and John walked around the room, looking for anything that could be used to remove the chandelier, but found nothing of use.

Terry searched in the second room, where the memory crystals were stored. "This room is ugly. Everything is burned, the crystals are melted, and it stinks."

John and Ty joined her at the second room's doorway and walked in. The walls and ceiling were charred black; the crystals were just glops of glass stuck to the walls; the floor was covered in ash and more melted glass.

"That's a perfect example of an overreaction," Ty said.

"Yes, it is, my emotions got the best of me," John said.

"No, they didn't," Terry said. "The memory of this place makes me want to shoot everything and destroy it."

Ty laughed.

"Megan, are there any databank balls left?" John asked.

"Yes."

"Where are they?"

"In the power plant building."

"Let's go," John said.

They walked back up the stairs and entered the warehouse.

"Wait a minute—stop!" John said. "Megan, are there any Outcasts near us?"

"No, they are at their encampment."

John took a deep breath and led them outside to the belowground power plant. It was damp and dark. John pointed one of the light sticks down the ramp and watched as the light ball filled the twenty-foot-wide, thirty-foot-deep tunnel with light. They walked down the slippery ramp and came to a pile of debris that was once the watertight portcullis gate.

John pointed another light stick into the room. They watched as the massive cavity filled with light.

"We still need more light," Terry said, looking concerned.

John started the final stick, and they watched the immense size of the room slowly come into view.

"Christ," Ty said, "this place is gigantic. It's the size of a soccer field and must be twenty feet deep."

"What's Christ?" Terry asked.

"Jesus's best friend," Ty answered.

John shook his head. "You're such a jerk," he said in a whisper with a smile. "Okay, let's split up. I'll take the middle; Ty, you take the right wall; Terry, you take the left. We want to know how far the water traveled. When you reach dry ground stop and holler 'Dry here.'"

"What's holler?"

"To speak in a very loud voice," John said.

"You can count on that," Terry said.

They separated and started walking. Their footsteps echoed through the room as their feet splashed through ankle-deep water.

Ten minutes later, Terry shouted, "Dry here!" followed almost immediately by Ty and John yelling, "Dry here!"

"Megan, mark my position," John said. "And how many power crystals didn't get wet?"

"There were a thousand power crystals; half are no longer operational."

"Megan, where's the power breaker wall?" John asked.

"In the aboveground building."

"Get back to the surface now!" John shouted to Ty and Terry.

He turned and started hurrying back, but to his surprise, he heard running footsteps splashing in the water behind him, and just like that, the sound came up next to him and then went past him. He smiled. *Terry*, he thought.

He and Ty reached the surface at the same time. Terry was standing at the top of the ramp all drenched, bent over, panting.

Ty looked at her. "What happened? You fall?"

"She ran," John said.

"Don't say a word, Ty Leggett." She glared with wide, serious, dark-brown eyes.

John laughed. "Okay, then. Megan, where is the closest android?"

"The closest is in the power plant. It is an older model."

"Is it operational?" John asked.

"Once Pandora is functioning, it will activate."

"Can we activate it?" Ty asked.

"Good idea. Let's go to that building." John pointed at the one-story, cobalt-aluminum-covered building across the concrete parking lot.

Once there, John pushed on the door, but it didn't move. "Megan, can you open this door?"

"No."

John rubbed his hand through his hair, took a deep breath, and looked at Ty. "It's all yours."

Ty removed his pistol from his pants back pocket. They all

stepped back several feet. *Zzzppnt!* The door exploded in a flash of hot, gas-fueled fire.

"I love doing that," Ty said.

The air cleared as white smoke slowly drifted out of the building.

Terry stepped forward and looked in. "Why is everything always dark?" she asked, staring into a pitch-black room. She turned to look at John with an uncomfortable expression.

John took a deep breath. "I'll be right back." He ran to the ship and returned several minutes later with ten sun flares.

"May I have a couple of those?" Terry asked.

"Scared of the dark?" Ty grinned.

Terry gave him a dirty look. "From what I've seen, dark is very scary."

John pointed a light stick into the shed and ignited the flare. Sparks of light splattered against the walls, and the room filled with light.

The building was a thousand square feet; the cobalt-aluminum floor was covered by a pristine optical white sealant. There was no furniture. An undressed rubber-skinned bald-headed android stood against the south wall, facing the center of the room. Red and black one-inch-round glass circuit switches covered the east wall halfway up to the ceiling. They were numbered one to one thousand. The center of each glass circuit was black. The circuits were aligned in rows four feet long and twenty inches high.

Ty and John walked into the room; Terry stood by the doorway.

"It's organized," Ty said, pointing to the system chart next to the circuits. Each number had a black dot next to it, except for one that was green.

They walked closer to the system chart; there were several operational diagrams and schematic charts below it.

"Don't you love engineers? Every detail is explained for us idiots," Ty said. "John, look here." He pointed halfway down the diagram. "Are these the operation instructions here?" He pointed again. "And are those the restart procedures?"

John stepped back a few feet. "We've got to be careful. Let's take a moment." He reached out and gently touched Ty's shoulder. "Let's go outside and talk about this."

They joined Terry at the doorway.

"What's wrong?" she asked, puzzled.

"Come with us," John said.

They walked back to the SS ship. John sat on the loading hatch gate; Ty and Terry joined him.

"You saw it, too, didn't you?" Ty asked.

"Yes."

"Saw what? What did you see?" Terry asked in a panicked tone.

"There are one thousand and one power crystals—"

"And one is generating power," Ty interrupted.

Terry took a deep breath. "Pandora is getting power?" she gasped, feeling sick to her stomach with panic.

"Megan, you said Pandora is off. Is it off?" John asked.

"It is and it is not; it switches on every five minutes."

"How did you miss that?"

"When you asked, it was off."

"Are the intervals regular?"

"Yes."

"How long does it stay on?"

"One second."

"That's an eternity," he whispered. "Megan, is it communicating to an entity?"

"Yes."

"Where?"

"Everywhere."

NINETEEN

"Was it on when we blew the door?" John asked.

"Yes."

"It knows we're here," Ty said.

"You're scaring me, Ty Leggett," Terry said.

"I'm scaring me," Ty said.

"Megan, how long has it been running at those intervals?"

"Twenty-four hours."

"Megan, where is its power source?"

"There's a backup generator in the cold room wall, behind Pandora."

"Shit, I saw a half door and didn't think anything of it," Ty said.

"I'm not going back down there," Terry said.

"We have to," John said. "Megan, when will the power come back on?"

John glanced at his watch. "We have five minutes."

"What's your plan?" Ty asked.

"Stop the Crystal from doing whatever it's doing."

Ty said, "Let's go, then," and Terry and Ty left the building through the exploded power plant door to get to Pandora's cold room.

John hesitated, glanced at the circuit board and the green blinking light, then turned to follow, just as terrifying screams erupted all around, followed by hundreds of people throwing rocks, wooden spears, and shooting arrows that whizzed past him, all aimed at Ty and Terry.

Ty fired his gun at the closet group running toward them. Terry was hit by a rock and dropped to the ground. Ty stopped and stood over her, still firing his gun.

John shot at a group of men running toward Ty and Terry—*Zzzppnt! Zzzppnt!*—hitting the middle of the attacking group. He saw Ty fighting with his hands and feet, and Terry lying on the ground, possibly unconscious. He fired toward a group of ten men racing to attack Ty from behind. The bolt of energy hit the leaders, killing them instantly; the others didn't stop, though, and tackled Ty.

Then an Outcast jumped off the roof and bounced into the doorway, wielding a six-inch butcher knife in his right hand. He used it to try to slash John across the stomach. John fell back and fired his gun; the man exploded into a fire-filled gas ball. Still lying on his back, John glanced at his watch: *One second until Pandora turns on.*

He screamed, "Stop!" at the android and pointed his gun at the circuit board.

The android's eyes turned on, looked at John, and just as quickly went dark.

John jumped to his feet and raced to the doorway. He fired his gun several times toward the group surrounding Ty and Terry, killing several more people. Three men were wrestling with Ty; three others surrounded Terry and were tying her hands and feet together. The three around Ty punched and kicked him until he fell limp to the ground.

Suddenly, an ear-blowing sound came from behind the SS ship. John saw a hubot standing next to it, holding an airhorn. It ordered the attackers to stop.

People turned and ran away. Two men lifted Ty's limp body off the ground by his arms and legs. Two others did the same to Terry, and together, they dragged the pair away toward their village.

John checked the time. *Four minutes 'til Pandora reactivates.*

He ran back to the SS ship and removed a holographic display disk from the pilot's seat pocket, glanced at his watch again: two minutes until reactivation. He ran back to the power plant and the android. Once inside, he again checked his watch: *Five seconds.*

He opened the display pad and shouted, "Activate this android for sixty minutes. Bring Ty and Terry back here alive. Now!"

His words appeared on the pad and instantly flashed into the air in front of the android. The android's eyes opened, then just as quickly closed.

"No no no!" John screamed.

The android's body, arms, and hands began to shake, its eyes popped opened, and its mouth slowly spread open twice as large as a human mouth. A deep growl rose slowly from its stomach as it rejuvenated. It closed its mouth and focused its lifeless black eyes on John's face.

"Are Ty and Terry alive?" John asked

"Yes," it answered in a hollow, tinny-sounding voice.

"Are you connected to the Master Crystal?"

"Not now."

"Why not?"

"Only intermittently."

"Are Ty and Terry on their way back here?"

"No."

"Why?"

"You must negotiate."

"Stay here," John said.

He turned and ran out of the shed to the SS ship. He went to the weapons locker and removed a dark energy explosive cell and three logistic camera systems. He ran out of the ship and stopped at the foot of the boarding ramp.

"Megan, can the androids communicate to the Master Crystal while it's offline?"

"No."

John reached into his jeans' pocket and removed the Mosquito case. "Megan, send the Mosquitoes to the Outcast camp; find Terry and Ty." His watch read: 6:45 p.m. He walked back to the shed and stood directly in front of the android. He held up the dark energy bomb.

"Set them free." He looked at his watch: 6:50.

"No," it said.

"Watch me." John walked up to the master breaker panel, placed the energy bomb on the floor, and activated it. He placed the four logistic cameras around the room and removed the holographic pad from his pocket.

"Activate cameras."

He returned to the android and looked at his watch: 6:54.

"Okay," it said.

He waited thirty seconds until 6:55. *Zzzppnt!* He shot the android, turned, and walked back to the SS ship. He stood facing the boarding ramp.

"Megan, other than the hubot at the Outcast camp, where are there additional androids?"

"Fallon S.S. base. There are one hundred at that location."

"What about hubots?"

"None."

"Megan, have the Mosquitoes found Terry and Ty?"

"Yes."

John held up the holographic pad. "Show me."

Instantly a real-time image of Ty and Terry appeared before him. They were lying on the ground in an empty ten-by-ten-foot, wood-sided room; both looked unconscious and were bound with ropes that tied their hands, arms, and feet together.

"Where is the hubot at the Outcast encampment?" he asked.

"Standing in front of the building where Ty and Terry are."

"Is it alone?"

"No. There are five Outcast men standing or sitting near it."

"Show me."

The hubot instantly appeared before him; its eye were open. It was standing next to two men dressed in blue jeans, tan work boots, and long-sleeved gray shirts. They were holding clubs and long-bladed knives. Three other men were sitting on the porch in front of the building, wearing the same type of clothing and holding clubs and knives.

"Megan, what is that?" he asked, stepping closer to the man standing to the right of the hubot. "Zoom in on that object in his pocket."

The image magnified.

"They've got guns," he whispered.

John boarded the SS ship and sat in the pilot's seat. "Megan, take me to the Outcast camp; land with the aft end of the ship facing the hubot. Once we land, open the boarding hatch and bring the Mosquitoes back into the ship."

The ship took off and did exactly as instructed. When the ship landed, hundreds of shouting people carrying all types of weapons ran into the area to surround it. The men in front of the building stood and seemed to ready themselves for a fight.

John walked out of the ship and stood several feet away from the hubot, which displayed no fear. "Let them go or I'll destroy G.A.!" he yelled.

The hubot put an odd-looking smile on its face, something very unnatural looking. "I told you you'd make a mistake, Doctor Barber, and I would kill you," it said. "Kill him!"

John put a surprised look on his face, his mouth slightly open, his eyes bouncing left to right. The man standing next to the android pulled the gun from his pocket and fired six shots into John. The other men charged forward, screaming and yelling, their clubs and knives at the ready.

John fell backward, raising his gun. A blast of energy from an SS pistol exploded on the ground at the hubot's feet.

The hubot instantly looked in the direction of the energy blast and saw John step down the ship's ramp. He was grinning, and yelled to the crowd, "When I destroy this hubot, you will be blind and helpless."

The hubot, looking shocked, hollered, "Stop the attack!" to the charging men.

The people attacking John did not stop immediately, and they were stunned because when they reached him, he was a ghost, and their punches and kicks passed through the image and they ended up hitting each other.

John yelled again, "Megan, detonate the bomb at G.A. in two seconds!"

"Return to your homes," the hubot said, looking at the men surrounding John's holographic image.

John said, "Bring Ty and Terry to me."

The hubot turned and went into the building; after several minutes, it returned. Terry had her left arm around Ty's waist, helping him walk.

"Terry! Here!" John called out, standing on the ship's loading ramp and holding an SS pistol.

She looked his way; her face lit up and quickly turned to relief. "Ty, we're safe! John's here."

As she helped Ty up the ramp, John pointed his pistol at the hubot and fired—*Zzzppnt!* The hubot exploded into a cloud of fire and gas. John glanced at his watch: five seconds before the hour.

"Megan, let's cut that bastard's power off. Terminate G.A.'s power plant and detonate the bomb at G.A.!"

The sound of the explosion was deafening. A fireball shot up into the air, followed by a cloud of black smoke.

John rushed down the ramp to Ty and Terry. "You okay? You okay?" John asked, panic-ridden, grabbing hold of Ty's body.

"I'll live," Ty whispered weakly.

Terry put her arms around John, hugging him. "That was terrifying. I thought we were going to die."

John returned her hug. "Not while I'm breathing," he said with a confident smile.

They turned and looked at the fireball as it rose higher into the sky, then they continued up the ramp into the ship. The gate closed behind them; John lifted Ty into the third seat.

"I guess the plan changed," Ty snarked.

"Yeah. I got tired of that damn thing trying to kill me. It's now permanently off, and we now have time to organize a better strategy."

"Back to square one: how to reach ten million androids," Ty whispered.

Terry climbed into the copilot seat, took a deep breath, and announced, "I'm beginning to like you, John Barber."

Ty nodded and smiled.

"Megan, take us to Stanford University Pasteur Hospital," John said.

TWENTY

They arrived at the two-story, one-acre hospital and landed on the circular driveway between two fountains that faced the building's main entrance. When the boarding ramp was down, they walked out of the SS ship, John and Terry lifting Ty by each arm.

"I can't breathe," Ty groaned. "Bastards broke my ribs."

They entered the emergency wing and sat Ty on a waiting room chair. John walked past the receiving counter and went looking for the triage area and, specifically, scanning wands. Terry sat next to Ty, holding his hand, trying to offer comfort.

"Where is everyone?" Ty whispered.

"People seldom come here," she answered. "This place isn't used much anymore. The medical androids, if they're needed, arrive at the injured person's location and fix the problem, and all research is—or was—only done by hubots. So, not too much to do."

"How do you know all that?" Ty asked.

"My aunt was a doctor and trained me, and I worked here with her 'til there was nothing left for us to do."

Ty smiled. "I knew you were smart."

John came into the room carrying a two-finger-wide, hand-sized, metallic wand. It had a four-inch-long, eighth-inch-wide tube in the center, a marquise-cut diamond crystal tip on one end and a display window in the center.

He held the device in his right hand and looked at Ty for a moment. "Megan, how do I work the repair analyzer?"

Terry reached up and took the wand out of John's hand. "I know how," she said.

Incredulous, John asked, "What?"

Terry stood, then squeezed the back edge of the wound lightly with her palm and fingers. She looked at the scanner display window on the wound while she passed it over Ty.

"You're a mess," she said. "You have a grade-four concussion, which isn't too bad since you have a small brain—"

John burst out laughing.

"Now *you* have sense of humor," Ty whispered.

"Your jaw is fractured in two places, your nose is broken, five ribs are fractured, your knuckles are bruised, two are dislocated, your hips have deep muscle contusions and myositis ossification is forming. Your lower back, at the fifth lumbar, is fractured—" She smiled. "Your feet are okay—small, but fine. You'll live."

"It'll take me months to heal," he whispered.

Terry smiled, held the wand up, and looked at the display window while she thought of the scanner healing programs her aunt would have suggested. Finished, she passed the wand over Ty, starting at his head, ending at his feet.

"Wow, wow!" Ty said. His eyes popped wide open, feeling the strange sensations as Terry moved the wand over his body.

"Done. Let's go," she said.

"What? Not possible!" Ty said, incredulous.

John reached down with his right hand, and Ty took a deep breath.

"Be careful. I know this is going to hurt like hell," Ty said. He took hold of John's hand and pulled himself to his feet. Ty froze in place, waiting for the pain. He smiled. "This is frickin' amazing. I feel perfect. Let's go kick some Outcast ass."

John laughed.

They walked out of the emergency center into an early evening. The ocean fog was just starting to drift over the hills, the scent of Skunkbush sumac and the cool ocean air adding to the serene atmosphere.

"What's next?" Terry asked.

Ty looked at John. "I mentioned my ninety-year-old memory. Well, it's telling me to take a break, to wind down. It's been a terrifying two days. Now that the G.A. thing is off, how about a shower, dinner, and a good night's sleep?"

"And a bourbon," Terry said with a grin.

Ty and John laughed.

"That sounds wonderful," John said. "I agree." He looked at Terry. "You're the local, Terry. Should we stay here the night?"

"What's a local?"

Ty sighed. "It means you live around here, so you choose. How about a nice warm place with a hillside view, near the coast?"

"I always went home; I never stayed out overnight. I have no idea where to go."

"Well, John, it's up to you. Know a place?"

"Megan, is the Madonna Inn in operation?"

"No."

"Is the facility and structure intact?"

"No."

"Are there androids on site?"

"Yes, one—located in a garden shed."

"Is there an Atom Assembler there, too?"

"Yes, a small one."

"Can you prevent the android from disclosing our activities to the hubots?"

"Yes."

"Do so and then instruct the android to rebuild the facility to its former design, including the pool, and supply power to the facility," John said.

"Done," Megan said.

"I remember that place," Ty said. "Held a campaign event there. Got to raise money. Funky room décor, great canyon views, and a geothermal-heated swimming pool. Most importantly, it's a wonderful spot for sipping bourbon. Now all we need is the Outcasts to feed us," Ty said, grinning.

"You lived in Alabama, Ty, not California. How do you know so much about the Madonna Inn?" John asked.

"Politics. I once held a campaign event there. Got to raise money."

"That's right, I remember you ran for President. Sorry to say I didn't follow your career."

"Neither did I," Ty said with a laugh.

"What is a president?" Terry asked.

"Like being a senator, but a bigger waste of time," Ty said.

"Megan, is there an Outcast camp in California?" John asked. "Maybe we can make friends and get some real food from them."

"Yes, there is, in Taft. It's twenty-two minutes away."

They boarded the SS ship. John sat in the pilot's seat, Terry in the copilot's, Ty behind her. The boarding ramp closed, and the ship lifted off the ground.

"Megan, take us to the Taft Outcast camp."

"Aren't you worried about a hubot and androids there?" Terry asked.

"Megan, is there a hubot and androids in Taft?" John asked.

"No."

It was still light out when they arrived.

"It looks just like the camp in Nevada," Ty said, gazing out the cockpit window.

"Megan, land us on the central green area," John said.

"Why would they help us?" Terry asked.

"I don't know much about these times," Ty said, "but water was once a prized commodity in this part of California. A friend of mine owned land near here, and he told me water was like gold."

"Okay, so now we have a plan: We'll dig them a well," John said. "Maybe that will encourage them to help us. Megan, what's the water table in Taft?"

"Six hundred ten feet below the surface."

They landed and walked out of the ship. There were ten men holding clubs, shovels, and hoes facing the ramp.

"Good evening. We are here to barter for food," John said.

They just stared at him.

"Megan, what language do these people speak?"

"Code-switching between English, Mexican, and Indigenous."

"Megan, please translate my words in those languages."

He repeated himself.

"What do you have to barter with?" asked a man standing in the center of the group holding an ax.

"We will drill a water well for you. In return, we need three servings of food, including two skinned chickens, meat, twelve eggs, potatoes, corn, bread, salt, spices—"

"A jug of red drinking wine would be great," Ty whispered to John.

"And a jug of your best drinking wine," John said.

"You drill well first," said the man holding the ax.

"Okay," John said. "Megan, find the closest underground water access point. Direct the ship and use the dark energy cannon to drill a three-foot-wide, six-hundred-foot-deep hole."

The ship lifted off the ground and flew a half mile toward the foothills and hovered there. They watched as the forward dark energy canyon fired three bolts of energy toward the ground.

"Done," Megan said.

"Wow, that took less than five minutes," Ty said.

The ship returned to the center green and landed.

One of the men left the group and ran to the newly dug hole. He waved his hand after seeing water flow up out the ground.

The man with the ax turned around and shouted at a woman standing behind him. He repeated John's food request.

Twenty minutes later, three women arrived, carrying four woven baskets filled with food and a clay jug.

"Thank you," John said as he received the baskets.

Ty took the jug and a basket, while Terry and John carried the other three baskets to the ship.

"Megan, to the Madonna Inn," John said as they walked up the boarding ramp.

"Easier than a supermarket," Ty said.

"What's a supermarket?" Terry asked.

Twenty-six minutes later, they landed on a slight hill facing an Olympic-sized swimming pool. They got out of the ship carrying the baskets of food and wine. It was getting dark.

"Megan, is there power?" John asked.

"Yes."

"Have one of the androids turn on the lights."

Instantly, the park setting by the pool was lit, as was the hotel.

"I'll find the kitchen, you two find some wood for a fire"—Ty pointed at the stone firepit—"and see if there are any tables and chairs," he finished as he walked to the main building carrying the food.

"What's a fire?" Terry asked.

"It's what happens when wood burns. It creates warmth, light, and a wonderful smell. See if you can find a table. I'll go look for wood." John turned and walked away from the pool toward a row of trees.

Terry went to the pool house and opened the door and looked inside. There was one round plastic table with six chairs stacked in the space. She took off one of her shoes and propped in under the door. *It better not close*, she thought.

She rolled the table out and placed it by the firepit, along with three chairs. Finished, she sat in one of the chairs and watched John pick up sticks.

Five minutes later, John returned carrying an armful of branches and three small limbs. He tossed them into the empty firepit. Together, they set up the table.

"Now what?" she asked.

"We wait for Ty. Hopefully, he has something to start the fire."

Thirty minutes later, Ty returned to the pool, carrying glasses, silverware, plates, and cloth napkins on a plastic tray. "You found a table! Great." He put the tray down. "I'll be right back with the food." He turned to leave, then stopped. "By the way, everything in that kitchen looks brand-new and works. Fantastic, and it was all done by androids—amazing." He grinned, shaking his head. "Dinner will be served in ten minutes. John, light the fire."

"You found matches?"

"Nope, everything inside is electric. Try firing a quick shot into the pit."

"Too much power. I'll follow you into the kitchen; there's got to be something we can set on fire and bring outside."

Bourbon, Terry thought. She ran to the ship and grabbed the bottle and took it back to the table, then sat and watched the animals graze nearby.

Suddenly, she heard a noise to her right and saw John running, carrying a burning towel wrapped around a stick. She jumped up and moved away from the table.

"What are you doing?" she shouted.

"Lighting the fire." He tossed the towel into the pit. "Made it," he said, grinning.

Ty followed after John later, carrying a tray filled with the cooked meal. He set the tray on the table; the meat was sizzling. "Perfection," he said.

John and Terry watched as Ty served.

The sun was about to set, the sagebrush hills and valley were a golden yellow color, and a herd of mule deer were grazing a hundred yards from the pool. Thousands of birds were flying about, singing their night calls. There was a gentle eastern breeze; the air was dry and warm and carried the aroma of the coastal foothills. The open fire in the stone pit was slowly building, the white smoke and embers lifting into the air. The sound of crackling, burning wood was just beginning.

Ty looked around, grinning. "Wow, this is a special evening.

Perfect. Calm breeze, dry air." He pointed to the firepit. "That reminds me of quite a few beautiful, star-filled romantic nights." He grinned at John.

"What's romantic?" Terry asked.

Ty shook his head slowly from side to side, then poured three glasses of wine.

"What's this?" Terry asked, looking at the red wine.

"It's bourbon without the bite," he said.

She took a sip and put a sour expression on her face. "I like bourbon better."

"Just wait," John said, smiling. "After a few bits of steak the wine will taste much better."

They dined. When they were finished, the only light came from the fire and rising full moon. It was beautiful; a perfect night for stargazing and sitting by a pool.

"That was very good," Terry said. "Real food has its merits."

"Not bad for Outcast Soylent Green," Ty said, smiling.

"Doctor's assistants are smarter than lawyers, Ty Leggett. I saw the ingredients. It's still ugly to eat something that was once alive."

Terry stood and walked to the pool. "The water looks clean." She bent down and dipped her hand into the water. "That's nice; it's very warm." She sat on the edge, took off her shoes, and put her feet into the water.

Ty looked at John, took a sip of bourbon. "I'm glad you came for me. I'm happy, and you're right: They're helpless. This place could become a paradise, provided the former slaves don't embrace the Roman snare of *luxuria*, and human nature joins the party."

"Oh, a Latin word, Mr. Lawyer," John quipped, with a slight laugh.

"How *did* you survive, John?"

"Luck, or something else."

"What about the cameras? How'd you avoid them?"

"I stayed very young for a long time. They were looking for a middle-aged man." He took a sip of wine. "I should have died several times or been captured, and each time at the last moment, I was saved by what I believe was a miracle."

Ty put an incredulous expression on his face and took a sip of wine.

John went on, "I've come to believe that the two angels who are guarding the Tree of Life are being punished for letting me discover the formula for controlling aging and are protecting me. Other than that, I have no idea how I survived."

"I hope they add me to their mission," Ty said with a laugh.

"Me too."

"What's happened to humanity is terribly sad. It breaks my heart," Ty said.

John nodded and looked toward the dark western foothills.

"Did you ever find a companion?" Ty asked.

"No, that would have been horribly selfish. I couldn't do that to someone. It's too awful to think about what might have happened if they were ever found out. I did have housekeepers; they were of course unaware of my longevity. The last one suffered a horrible death at Davis' hands."

"I can't imagine surviving that long in isolation. I'm sorry, John."

John raised an eyebrow and tilted his head, silently expressing, "It's okay."

"That explains why you're so calculated, and cold-blooded."

John took a sip of wine and glanced at Terry sitting by the pool. "We need the androids to educate humanity as soon as possible. Very soon, her body will revert to normal, as will everyone else's, and human nature will join the party, as you said."

"That'll be terrifying for women," Ty said.

"It will. Pain, fear, desire, and no one to tell them why it's happening."

"What about the Outcasts? Think they can help?"

"I thought about that until I watched them beat the hell out of you. They could rape the women, kill or enslave the men, and we'd be back to survival of the fittest." John rubbed his hand through his hair and took another sip of wine. "The two sides can't interact until Terry and everyone else is ready." He took another sip. "Remember the biblical story of the apple and Tree of Knowledge?"

"Of course."

"We do this right and humanity could remain innocent and move forward in peace."

"Utopia?"

John laughed, feeling the wine. "I wish. But no, we're human beings, after all. We need the androids to teach and Pandora to instruct them."

"That's uncomfortable. Could be a flawed education," Ty said.

John stood up, feeling a little unsteady. He reached into his right jeans' pocket and removed the glass baseball-sized object. He held it up, looking at Ty, and said, "With Megan we are safe."

"Yup, we're lost without her."

"So we must keep it away from the apple tree."

Ty nodded his head. "That is a must," he said.

Terry joined them at the table and sat.

Ty smiled and took a sip of bourbon.

"Well, what's next?" she asked, beaming a perfect smile.

"Sleep, breakfast, grab an hubot, go to G.A., then San Francisco," John said, starting to slur his words.

"Must we go to G.A.?" Terry asked.

"Regrettably, we do," John said. He glanced at his watch. "Ten o'clock. I'm off to bed."

"Sounds good," Ty said, getting to his feet. He reached out his right hand and helped John stand.

"Where are we sleeping?" Terry asked.

"I found a bunk room." He laughed. "It's named Caveman."

John laughed. "Perfect. We'll fit right in."

"Where is it?" Terry asked.

"Down the hall from the kitchen. There're three beds," Ty said.

DAY 3

TWENTY-ONE

Ty and John got up at sunrise the next morning. Ty went into the kitchen and started breakfast. John went outside to the pool, picked up a chair and a small plastic side table. He walked past the pool house, and sat on the crest of the hill facing west, the morning sun felt warm on his back.

"Wow, this is beautiful. So much life," he whispered.

The scene before him was stunning, with four herds grazing alongside each other: horses, deer, cattle, and sheep grazing. Several bevies of mountain quail and pheasants were running and flitting about, feeding. The sky was filled with barn swallows, western tanagers, and monarch butterflies migrating north. Crows sat in the trees, cawing and croaking. A condor circled overhead in the morning air, trying to gain altitude. A golden eagle perched high up on a branch of a nearby tree surveying the field, and hundreds of foraging pigeons pecked at the hillside grass.

Thirty minutes later, Ty joined John, carrying two stoneware plates filled with scrambled eggs, bread, and meat.

John looked at the plate. "That looks and smells wonderful. I'm hungry and a little hungover."

Ty laughed. "You should stick to bourbon."

John nodded as he took hold of his plate of food.

Ty stood for a moment, mesmerized by the unfolding vista. "Oh my God, I've only seen that in movies. So much life."

He put his plate on the plastic side table, walked to the pool, and returned with a chair and sat. He picked up his plate and put it on his lap and watched the valley below.

"Remember the book *Undaunted Courage* by Ambrose we used to talk about?"

"It's been a long time for me," John said, smiling, "so not really."

"Very funny. It was about Louis and Clark's trek across the U.S. In it, Ambrose described the Midwest plains and all the animals. Amazing. Buffalo herds a mile wide that took three days to cross the Missouri River." Ty shook his head. "And we managed to kill most of them in a hundred years. This is what it must have looked like. I'm happy I got to see this. When this is over, let's go see the Midwest plains."

"I'd like that," John said.

Ty took a bite of eggs, and he and John ate breakfast in silence.

Finished, they leaned back and felt the morning sun's warmth on their backs and watched the game animals moving toward the tree line.

"Where's Terry?" John asked.

"Not up yet, she's not feeling too well." He frowned. "We made a mistake. She spent most of the night with cramps and diarrhea. Stupid of us: too much bourbon, and natural food for a rookie."

"Hell, I'm a little hungover," John said.

"You always were a short hitter," Ty said with a laugh.

John nodded. "Did you say cramps?"

"Yes, why?"

"Nothing."

He's thinking puberty, Ty thought.

They continued to watch the wildlife move about the valley. Five minutes later, Terry arrived, carrying a wooden chair, and sat next to Ty. She looked at him with an angry expression. "Your Outcast dinner almost killed me. From now on, I'll make the food."

Ty curled his lower lip. "My bad."

"Did you drink lots of water before bed?" John asked her.

"Yes, I also used the medical wand this morning, even though it showed odd numbers and didn't work as it should have." She shrugged her shoulders. "I feel somewhat okay now."

Odd numbers, oh God, I hope Pandora didn't add a kill shot to puberty. Ty thought.

"Terry, your body is about to change," John said.

"What do you mean?" she asked.

John decided now was the time to address the subject he knew was inevitable. He turned in his chair to face her, "Pandora, well, to you it was the World Crystal, used the K chip to repress your biology and block some hormones and I hope that's all it did."

Ty raised his eyebrows, thinking, *me too.*

"What are hormones?" she asked.

"Hormones are chemicals in our bodies, scientifically named estrogen and testosterone."

"My mother called them twin demons," Ty interjected.

John sighed and shook his head. "Those chemicals make boys and girls into men and women."

"What are you saying?" she asked.

"Without a proper explanation, you and everyone on Earth will freak out when those chemicals flood their bodies and cause changes." His expression was somber, serious.

What is he saying? she thought, slightly squeezing her right hand into a fist. "What does freak out mean?"

"That is amazing," Ty interrupted, pointing at a flock of birds flying by, trying to change the subject.

She glanced at the birds. "That's not important," she said, frustrated.

"It is to me," Ty said, shaking his head sadly.

"John, keep talking," she said.

"Your body, just like everyone else's, is about to go a through a metamorphosis," he said with the same serious expression.

"A what?"

"He means change. Can't this wait until she starts asking questions?" Ty begged of John.

"That might be too late," John replied.

Ty sighed and leaned back. *He is so wrong.*

"What is about to happen to me?" she asked. *Can I die?*

"Those changes will turn you into a woman, and boys into men. Without understanding, they will cause you and everyone else to experience fearful confusion, and we can't let that happen."

Terry was studying John's face, absorbing his every word. She suddenly felt uneasy. *What is he telling me?*

Ty took a deep breath, thinking, *This is not the time.* He started to stand.

"Why are you trying to stop him from telling me?" Terry asked, her voice angry and her eyes blazing.

"Because we are not smart enough to explain what's about to happen, that's why." His voice was soft and calm. "And we shouldn't try. Maybe Megan's databank can explain what it's like to become a woman. And want to obsess on everything." He laughed. He looked at John with serious expression. "Have you noticed everyone looks alike? Skinny, no muscles or boobs."

John slightly gasped. "Oh." His lips pushed out for a second.

Terry watched his reaction. *That can't be good,* she thought. "What is he saying? No, just tell me the first couple of changes I'm going to feel."

"Body odor will begin to stink, facial skin will get oily, and emotions will bounce up and down," John said.

She looked at Ty. "What are boobs?"

"Man's best friends," he said matter-a-factly, straight-faced.

John laughed. "Terry, that's not true. Your nipples and chest will grow, creating mammary glands."

She stared at John, thinking: *It's* happening. *My skin is changing, my chest feels funny, and right now I want to hit Ty.* "This is scaring me. I want to know everything. Like right now," she said, feeling a flash of rage rush to her face. She dug the fingernails of her right hand into her palm.

Ty watched her reaction and looked at John. "You started this."

John looked at Terry for a moment, then Ty. He took a breath and rubbed his hand through his hair. "I'm sorry, Ty. You were right. Terry, how about tonight, Megan will give you the facts and explain the reasons for those changes," he said.

Terry took a deep, calming breath and relaxed her right hand. "Okay. Tonight." She looked sad, and her eyes were starting to water. "Will these changes hurt?"

"No," John said.

They stood and carried the dishes back to the kitchen, then washed and cleaned up the room. Finished, they started toward the SS ship.

"Megan, where is the android that maintains this place?" John asked.

"Behind the main building in the gardening shed."

They walked around the hotel looking for the shed.

"There it is," Terry said, pointing to her right.

They walked up to the ten-by-twenty-foot plastic-looking box. Ty took hold of the door handle and pulled it open. Daylight filled the room, and they saw a six-foot-tall android dressed in denim-looking gardening jeans, a blue work shirt, rubber boots, and gloves, standing in the center of the room.

"I'll get it," Ty said. He wrapped his arms around its waist and tried to lift it. To his shock and disappointment, the thing did not budge. "There's no way. It must be nailed to the floor," he said, looking dumbfounded.

John laughed. "That must be a very old model. When they were first built they weighed over three hundred pounds. The new ones weigh less than fifty. Anyway, what are you doing?" John grinned. "Android, go outside and stop five feet in front of the doorway," John said.

The android's eyes opened, and it did as commanded.

They followed.

"Megan, open the S.S. ship's cargo hold and store the android," John said.

The android lifted off the ground, rose about five feet and floated toward the ship. "I will never get used to seeing that; it's frickin' too cool," Ty said.

They followed along as the android drifted into the ship and the hatch closed behind it. The boarding ramp opened; they moved up into the ship.

Ty abruptly stopped and turned to face the view across the valley. He let out a long sigh. "I retired from politics in my mid-eighties and moved to Fair Hope, Alabama. All I wanted to do was watch nature, fish a little, drink great bourbon, and die a very old man. My plan did not come easy. I tried to fire my Secret Service detail, but they didn't listen and never left me fully alone."

"What's a Secret Service detail and why wouldn't they leave you alone?" Terry asked.

"They're nursemaids to the impotent," Ty said with a grin.

What are nursemaids? she thought.

"Even on my deathbed, they moved me to Maryland, and hovered over me. I finally had to kick the bastards out of my room so I could die in peace." He glanced at Terry, then John, and smiled. "When this is all over, all I want to do is sit on that hill"—he pointed—"watch nature, drink great bourbon, and die a happy, very, very old man."

"What is wrong with you two?" Terry asked. "You both sound like the world is about to end."

John looked at her. "Well, it could get rough. Humanity's survival lies with Pandora, ten million androids, and a lot of luck."

They walked up the ramp and into the cockpit. John and Terry sat in front, and Ty behind Terry in the navigator seat. John glanced at his watch: 10:00 a.m.

"Megan, take us to G.A.," John said.

"No, stop," Terry said. "I am not waiting until tonight. We're not going anywhere until you two explain all the comments about freaking out, and things being rough."

John rubbed his hand though his hair, glanced at Ty, and turned to face Terry. Ty leaned back and took a deep breath.

"Terry," John said, "The World Crystal only allowed you to develop certain feelings and body functions."

Terry listened intently, her eyes fixed on John's face, barely blinking, but relaxed, studying his every word. "Stop. I know how I feel, what feelings are you talking about?"

John glanced back at Ty with a "help" expression. Ty shook his head slightly. John sighed. "The Crystal excluded true love, desire, conception, and childbirth."

Terry's jaw twitched; her lips parted when she pulled air into her lungs. Her expression was stoic, eyes wide open and intense.

"If you're not ready for those physical developments, it could get ugly. Like I said earlier, you'll feel things that are physically painful, like stomach cramps, but mental ones, too, like being very sad, angry, or mad. All of them are caused by the new chemicals racing through your body." He took a breath. "You've already felt the worst pain of all: death, loss, and longing."

"You're making me feel something ugly."

John's face relaxed. "Well, we don't have to do this now, so let's go to G.A. and finish talking later."

Ty glanced at John thinking, *That's a mistake.*

"You're not getting out of this," Terry said. "I want to know everything—and right now. Why was this done to all of us?"

"To remove your soul, your need to have children, and your free will."

"Why?" There was an edge to her voice now.

"Control. It gave you just enough feelings to manipulate you and everyone else into your deaths." John rubbed his hand through his hair and took a breath.

Terry's eyes watered, her cheeks flushed pink, and she clenched her hands together.

John studied her eyes to read her emotions, thinking, *I've gone too far.* Feeling uncomfortable, he glanced at Ty.

Ty looked just as uneasy as John felt.

Terry whispered, "Please finish."

"The World Crystal limited those hormone chemicals everyone's body needs to mature. Dealing with all those changes is hard enough when you know what's happening. Not knowing can cause some very bad reactions." He rubbed his hand through his hair and took a short breath. "Three billion people, just like you, are about to experience emotions and desires they've never known, which is going to cause big societal problems."

Terry took a calming breath, and a memory from her aunt popped into her mind: *They can't face this alone.* "We have to help them, then."

Ty smiled. *She's thinking of others. Perfect.*

"Megan can teach the androids what to teach the people," John said.

"Will you and Ty help me through this?"

"Yes, of course," John said.

"Absolutely," Ty said.

"Good, because I'm already feeling things I've never felt before, and one of them is the urge to punch you in the face. This is your fault, John Barber." Then she smiled, leaned over, and gave him a hug, "Thank you," she whispered and kissed him on the cheek. She turned and faced Ty, "You, too, President Ty Leggett." She smiled. "Well, how long do we have?"

"Megan, how long before human biology is fully activated?" John asked.

"For most, the full effect will happen in twenty-four hours, if it hasn't already."

"Wow," Ty whispered.

"I want Megan to explain what's about to happen to me," Terry said, sounding determined.

"Of course, as soon as we return from G.A. You okay for now?" John asked, abruptly realizing he had feelings for her.

"I'll be fine."

Ty turned his head and looked out the co-navigator's window, smiling and thinking, *She's a beautiful person.*

"Megan, take us to the G.A. Outcast camp—the leader's home," John said.

"Why there?" Ty asked.

"No more surprises from them."

They arrived at the Outcast camp.

"Megan, fire the energy cannon twenty feet from that house, then circle above it."

The ship shook and rocked slightly as the cannon fired.

"Land with the boarding ramp facing the house, and lower the ramp," John said.

"Done," Megan said.

"What's the plan?" Ty asked.

"We get their weapons. Stay here," John said, "I got this."

John left the cockpit and walked out of the ship carrying an SS rifle. His expression would have scared lions.

"Megan, use my voice, tone, and volume, and translate my words and his."

He reached the bottom of the ramp and fired the gun at the house's front walkway. *Zzzppnt!* It disintegrated into a fireball.

"Come out now or I'll kill everyone inside!" John shouted as loud as he could in his deepest voice.

The front door opened slowly, and a thin, muscular, and

gruff-looking, six-foot-tall, bearded man stepped out. He came within ten feet of John before stopping. He stared, his expression as angry as John's.

"We're going to make peace or I'll kill everyone in this village," John said. "Do you understand me?"

"Yes," the man snapped.

"Gather every gun you and everyone else have, then pile them in front of you."

The man didn't move. John fired the gun at a wooden wagon next to the house. *Zzzppnt!* An explosion of gas and fire incinerated the wagon.

"Now!" John yelled.

The man shouted in a deep, guttural tone to everyone around, "Bring all your guns to me!"

John stayed in place while people came from all directions and piled guns on top of each other.

He stood in silence as the pile grew. "Is that all?" he yelled when he saw no one else coming while he pointed his rifle at the pile.

"Yes," the gruff man said, clearly still furious.

"You can keep the rifles for hunting. Not the handguns. Put the handguns in a pile over there." He pointed to his right.

The man picked the pistols out of the pile and made a separate pile for them.

"You and everyone in this tribe are forbidden from ever returning to the building where you first saw us. If you do, I will return and butcher you all." John waved and pointed his gun around the village.

Ty and Terry were watching from the top of the loading ramp, Terry shocked, eyes wide, her fingertips covering her mouth. "He's acting so ugly. Why is doing this?"

"He has to or they won't believe him."

"Now pick up your rifles," John barked, then waited while they collected hunting rifles. "Step away from the pistols."

He shot into that pile—Zzzppnt!—disintegrating them in a ball of flames.

John turned and walked up the ramp. Terry and Ty returned to the cabin and sat. The ramp door closed behind John; he sat back down in the pilot's seat and the ship took off.

Terry looked over at him for several seconds. John could feel her stare. He turned to look at her.

"Wow, that was some estrogen," she said with a grin.

Ty laughed so hard he snorted.

The ship landed with the aft end facing GA's warehouse. Megan lowered the ramp, and the three walked out. John glanced at his watch: 10:45 a.m.

"Megan, are there any people within a mile of us?" John asked.

"No."

"Megan, are there any third-party energy readings?"

"No."

"Megan, alert me the moment you detect new energy."

"Okay, we're safe. Now what?" Ty asked. "And why do you get to have all the fun, shooting and threatening people? That's my job." Ty grinned.

"I don't care who's got what job, this place scares me," Terry said.

"You're not alone on that. I'm not too happy about being back here," Ty said.

John sighed. "Our goal is simple: Find enough power to start Pandora—"

"And us not getting killed," Terry interrupted.

"Megan, open the cargo bay and unload the android," John said. They left the cockpit and stood in front of the warehouse to look at the ship.

The back of the SS ship's cargo bay opened, and a moment later the android floated out headfirst, and hovered within five feet of them.

"Why not have it walk out?" Terry asked.

I like watching Ty's reaction." He smiled. "Megan, twist the android so it stands on its feet facing us," John said.

"Now that I'm taking a good look at it," Terry said, "that thing looks—well, different. Look at its arms and hands; they're much bigger, and the actuators are long and thick. I've never seen one that looks like that."

"It's an older model designed for hard labor. It builds or tears things down," John said.

"What? I've never seen anything get built," Terry answered.

Ty raised an eyebrow. "That's weird and can't be right."

"Megan, when was the last building constructed in San Francisco?" John asked

"Twenty-one eighty-two, sixty years after the last war."

"What year did you say it is now?" Ty asked.

"Twenty-two twenty-two."

"That's forty years ago," Ty said, shocked. "That's got to be wrong."

"Megan's never wrong," John said.

Ty smiled, thinking for a moment of the real Megan. "Regardless, nothing new in San Francisco? That's crazy." He paused. "Unless it was part of a plan...." His voice trailed off. He glanced at John with a sad expression.

John returned the expression. Then changed the subject:

"First, I want to look at that covered energy compartment behind Pandora."

"Will it be dark?" Terry asked.

"No, we have more than twelve hours of light from the flares left in that part of the building," John said.

"You better be right; I'm already feeling uncomfortable."

"Android, stay where you are," John said.

They walked through the warehouse, down the stairs into the Pandora's cold room.

"It feels even colder than the last time we were here." Terry said.

Ty put his hand on his pistol as he studied the room.

TWENTY-TWO

"Nothing's changed," Ty said after searching the room. John walked behind the chandelier; Terry and John followed. He bent down on one knee and studied the closed half door, not seeing anything unusual, he pushed it with his right hand. It popped open with a snapping sound. He leaned forward on his knees and poked his head into the room.

"Can't see anything. It's too dark, and it feels extra cold in there."

Terry gasped at the word "dark." "You were wrong, John Barber. I knew it! Everything in this place is dark and scary." She reached into her pants pocket. "That's why I have five of those wonderful diamond sun flares right here," she removed a flare, and handed it to Ty.

He pointed it into the room, squeezed the back end, and the room was instantly lit with a white light.

"I got this," Ty said.

He slid forward and went into the room, ducking his head. He stood up straight and looked around the ten-by-ten-foot room. It was mostly empty, except for a four-foot-by-three-foot-square generator sitting against the back wall.

"You might want to see this, John," he called out.

"Terry, you stay here," John said.

She stared at him. "Why?"

"One of us should stay here in case something happens."

"No." She stooped through the half door and went into the room.

John followed.

Ty was standing across the room, looking at the generator. Terry and John joined him.

"It is different from the turbines underground in the power plant," John said. "This doesn't make sense. Why have an emergency backup power supply?" He walked around the box, bent down on his knees, and studied its assembly. "This looks old. Must've been installed decades ago before the power plant was built. See, look here." He touched a cable leading from the machine into the back wall. "This is—"

The door snapped shut behind them with a loud bang. Terry screamed and dropped to her knees; John jumped to his feet and lifted his gun. Ty did the same and pointed his gun at the closed door.

Silence.

"Shit, this is not good," Ty whispered.

"No kidding!" Terry barked breathlessly, her body temperature rising and heart pounding.

John rubbed his hand through his hair, then turned quickly around several times looking for movement. "Do you smell anything?" he asked.

"No," Ty said, holding his pistol up with both hands, ready to shoot.

"I don't either," Terry whispered.

John moved to the west wall and touched it with his right hand. "The walls have been upgraded and coated with cobalt-aluminum. We can't use our guns; the energy would bounce off and kill us." He rubbed his hand through his hair. "Why reinforce the walls and not upgrade the generator?" John wondered out loud.

"A perfect mousetrap to kill John Barber," Ty said with a sarcastic grin.

Terry gasped and held tightly to the flare in her hand. "Now what?" she asked, getting to her feet.

"I don't have any idea," John whispered.

Terry took a deep breath and walked across the room to the half door. She took another deep breath and thought: *Please work.* She pushed on the door with her right foot. It popped open with a snapping sound.

"Use common sense," she said with a look of relief and a grin.

John took a deep breath, and looked at Ty. "It's always the simplest things, like a back door you forgot to close," he said.

Terry bent down and left the room. Ty and John followed closely behind.

They stood and looked at each other for a moment and started to laugh.

"That was a wow," Ty said.

"I don't like this place. Can we go now?" Terry asked.

"Almost done. Seeing that backup energy cell has me thinking. Why so much power? It's too much." He looked at Terry while thinking, *there must be more databank memory balls.* "We need to talk this through. Let's go up to the cafeteria."

"I'm all for that," Terry said, almost running up the stairs.

They sat at the same table they'd used before. Somehow

feeling relaxed, John glanced around the room and smiled, then looked at Ty and Terry in turn.

"This reminds me of the G.A. staff meetings I held in this room. Good memories."

"You held them here, in this room?" Terry asked.

"Yes, there are a couple conference rooms on the second floor, but nothing this comfortable or big." He took a deep breath, thinking, *And not all are good.*

"Megan, produce a hologram for notetaking and display it on this table," John said.

"Things to Do" appeared floating in front of them across the table.

"Can we take Pandora out of G.A.?" Terry asked.

"Good idea, but it has too many advantages here," John said.

"And who knows if the Outcasts will stay put," Ty said.

John nodded.

"Can we turn it on without getting killed?" Terry asked.

John directed the question to Megan.

"Yes," it answered.

Ty laughed. "That should have been our first question."

"Megan, can we reprogram Pandora?" John asked.

"Yes."

"Megan, are there additional databank memory balls at G.A.?" John asked.

"Yes, there are a thousand extra balls stored inside the power plant."

"Megan, how many of those balls do we need to communicate to the ten million androids and manage all logistical operations on Earth?" John asked.

"Three."

"Megan, how long can you control the Madonna android without Pandora?" John asked.

"Indefinitely. It's an outdated model."

"Megan, can you prevent Pandora from directing the Madonna android?" John asked.

"Yes. I can create a firewall."

"Megan, once all the androids are activated, can we direct them and use holographic projections to communicate to the three billion people on Earth?" John asked.

"Yes, that would be one android per thousand people."

"Megan, what was Pandora doing while using auxiliary power?" John asked.

"It was communicating with three major off-site crystals."

Terry gasped. Ty and John looked at each other, wide-eyed.

"This is never going to end," Ty whispered.

John rubbed his hand through his hair and took a deep breath. "Megan, where are these other major Crystal sites?"

"Two are on Earth; the third is off-planet."

"Where on Earth?"

"Zapolyarny, Russia, and the Seattle metropolitan statistical area in the state of Washington."

"How powerful are they?" John asked.

"I don't know."

"Megan, why did Pandora need so much power?" John asked.

"It controlled one billion androids, a hundred million S.S. soldiers, one million S.S. ships with auxiliary weapons, five million industrial transport ships, one hundred thousand factories, ten thousand mining developments—"

"Megan, stop," John interrupted.

"John, can I ask a question?" Ty asked.

"Yes, of course."

"Megan, why such a large military force?" Ty asked.

"It was waging war on off-planet sentient beings and several primitive robotic cultures."

"Oh my God," Ty whispered.

Silence for a moment as they tried to digest the horror.

"Megan, does Pandora know about you?" John asked.

"Yes."

John felt a flash of adrenaline and rubbed his hand through his hair. Terry and Ty looked at each other with concern.

Ty thought, *We're dead without Pandora.*

"Megan, has it infected you?" John asked.

"No. I disengaged my cybernetic element when we first arrived in San Francisco, and I can now only connect with you, Ty, and Terry."

John took a deep breath and sighed with relief, as did Ty and Terry.

John lifted his left arm and looked at his watch. "We don't have much time; we've got to be in San Francisco in three hours. Megan, make those modifications to the Madonna android, and ready it for transportation to San Francisco. Then download instructions on how to disassemble Pandora and rebuild it with the three additional memory databank balls we'll need to manage the androids. I'll create a fail-safe termination program for Pandora and the Madonna Inn android. Once everything is completed, load the Madonna android, and Pandora into the ship for transportation back to San Francisco." John took a deep breath and looked at Terry and Ty. "Did we miss anything?"

"What about electricity in San Francisco?" Terry asked.

"Good point, we'll figure that out once we're there. Ty, did I miss anything else?"

"Nope, you covered it all," Ty said.

"Megan, initiate actions." He breathed out. "Let's go outside and get some fresh air. We've got a lot to digest."

They went outside and sat on the SS ship's loading ramp. Ty lay down on his back, looking up at the blue sky. Terry sat on the ramp next to Ty and watched John pace about.

Two hours later, the Madonna android walked out of the GA garage, followed by the eight-foot-tall Pandora chandelier drifting behind it. The ship's loading bay opened. Ty walked several feet away from the ship and watched joyfully as the GA chandelier Crystal, fusion pod, and three memory crystals entered the cargo bay.

"Man, I'm relieved that thing's outside," Ty said, grinning.

Terry gave John a surprise hug. "Can we go now?" she asked.

"Let's blow this popsicle stand," Ty said.

"What's a popsicle stand?" Terry asked.

Ty shook his head sadly.

They boarded the ship, sat in their usual seats, and the ship lifted off the ground two hundred feet.

"Megan, destroy G.A. and everything around it," John said, feeling a warm sensation in his chest.

Terry clapped her hands; Ty leaned back and looked out the window.

The ship shuddered and lunged back and forth as the dark energy cannons vaporized the facility. John turned the ship so they could watch the destruction from the cockpit window. The building exploded with each bolt of dark energy, forming a massive fireball; jets of flames shot up into the air, followed by thick black smoke. With each shot, debris exploded in every direction, some hitting the ship, while other pieces smashed onto the ground. Hundreds of secondary explosions erupted when the Pandora fusion pods disintegrated and extra memory crystals exploded. A moment after the final shot, the building collapsed to the ground.

John smiled, feeling a sense of revenge and relief.

Terry clapped her hands together, liberated.

Ty reached forward and excitedly tapped Terry and John's shoulders.

Triumph filled the ship's cabin.

"Let's get out of here and put that android to work," Ty said, grinning.

As they flew over Oakland, John glanced at his watch: noon. They crossed Alameda Bay and arrived at the Crystal Plaza.

"Oh my, look at that," Terry said.

The streets and plaza were again jammed with people.

"There are thousands more people down there than yesterday," Ty said.

"We're not going to land; we'll hover over the fountain and jump out," John said.

They hovered at a hundred feet above the polished aluminum megaphone. The fountain was as they had left it, and only one person was standing on it.

Terry smiled. "That's Arnold." She pointed out the copilot's window.

"What's the plan, John?" Ty asked.

"Simple, I'll tell them the truth, and Terry will give them a biology lesson."

"What?" Terry asked. "What are you saying? Why me?"

"I'll do it," Ty said.

"That's a no," Terry said. "You'd make a joke and send them screaming away—and John can't because he's mean and ugly. I'll do it."

John lifted his eyebrows with mild surprise, then said, "Megan, open the boarding ramp and lower us close enough to the ground so we can exit the ship."

The ship lowered to within several feet of the fountain. The ramp lowered, and they stood on its edge, waiting for the right moment to jump off the ship.

They leaped down, surprised at being greeted with cheers and calls of "Hello!" from many voices.

"I just got chills," Ty said. He lifted his arms above his head and waved both hands at the mass of people.

Terry also waved her hands.

John stood beside them, feeling the vibration from the sound. He smiled, thinking, *This* is *amazing*.

The ship lifted to fifty feet above the fountain and hovered.

Terry spotted Arnold again, now standing with a group nearest to the fountain. She ran to him and gave him a warm hug.

"We did it, we did it!" She hugged him again.

John turned to face the reflector. "Hello, we kept our promise. For those who might not know, my name is John Barber, and this is Ty Leggett and"—he pointed to Terry—"there is Terry Cheer. Would you all please sit? We have a lot to say."

He waited for the crowd to quiet, then abruptly turned to face Ty. "I'm very uncomfortable about this," he whispered as he rubbed his hand through his hair.

"I got it," Ty replied. "I was a world leader, after all." He grinned.

John nodded and said, "Thank you."

Ty turned to face the reflector and said, "Hello, San Francisco! My name is Ty Leggett." He waved and clapped his hands, then turned to face the reflector. "Our job in Nevada is complete, and we have returned with a tool to rebuild Earth." He turned to John. "Ask Megan to remove Pandora from the ship and suspend it above the fountain."

The SS ship's cargo hatch opened.

Ty continued, "You're about to see a defeated, and now

impotent, ex-ruler of the universe. It has surrendered to all of us, and from this moment on, it will be displayed here on this spot as a reminder of our victory and its defeat."

Pandora appeared, drifting out of the ship. Gasps and fearful cries echoed back at Ty as he went on, "It is now and will always be a simple tool. We turned it off. You, all of us, are now free of this horrible machine. What you see above our heads is the dead machine once called the World Crystal. It's off." He turned back to the crowd and clapped his hands and shouted. "Wahoo, yippee, yippee, yay! We are safe!" he cheered, and John and Terry joined in, clapping and cheering.

Terry jumped up and down, arms waving, smiling big.

The streets to the bay were filled with the excitement. Everyone followed Terry and many jumped up to clap and cheer.

A breeze twisted Pandora. The movement caught peoples' attention and seeing the machine twist in the wind, helpless, the crowd's excitement only got louder.

And just a quickly, their voices turned to shouts of hate and chants of "Destroy it!"

The demands got more pronounced as more and more joined in. Several people close to the fountain stood up and took off their shoes and threw them at the machine. Most of the crowd got up and started to press forward.

John looked at Terry. "Those emotions I was telling you about; they're on full display and are about to explode."

"I feel everything they do, only I'm no longer scared."

"Stop!" Ty shouted in a deep, strong voice. "Stop now. Listen to me!" He waited. "Please sit back down and hear what I have to say." He watched as they quieted and sat. "What you see above us is nothing more than a broken tool. It has no feelings, compassion, or soul. It's a machine no different from your pod. Our anger at what it did is justified. It will forever be remembered by our putting it on a plaque and displayed here"—he pointed at his feet—"right here, with the names of those who programmed it, along with the names of every scientist and philosopher who did not stand up and scream 'Stop it! Stop it! Don't do it!'"

Screams of "Stop it!" filled the plaza.

"We, us, everyone here, must join to survive and rebuild as a family. We all must remember what happened to ensure it never happens again." He turned to face the crowd, clenched his fist, then turned back.

"We must live life with a purpose." He pointed up at Pandora. "The story of the death and destruction it caused must be told and retold from this moment until the end of time. *And how John Barber and Terry Cheer defeated that damned thing to save all of us.*"

Clapping and cheers rolled through the crowd.

Ty waited for the noise to settle down. "That"—he pointed again at Pandora—"should be the focus of your anger, not the androids, or each other. We will never let hate rule us again!"

TWENTY-THREE

Ty waited for them to understand the thought, then said, "We need the androids to teach us how to learn, think, build, love, and create families—yes! We can! We can... do that! We can do that!" he chanted.

Ty faced the crowd, raised his right hand, made a fist, and pumped it up and down.

Thousands joined in and raised their fists into air, screaming, "We can do that! We can do that!"

He turned back. "All of us must learn the truth about the past and use it to guide the future. To fully understand 'why.' To grasp the true meaning of things and use that knowledge to protect ourselves. Why is it important to learn? Because we must stop the *next* evil machine before it's created. Our fight for independence never ends."

Ty turned; he could feel the tension. He took a deep breath and thought, *This is the moment of truth.*

He faced the reflector, said, "We have found two other World Crystals."

Gasps filled the air, followed by rustling and hushed whispers. Fearful murmurs filled the air.

"Ugly, ugly!" someone screamed.

He faced them, raised a flat palm, and said, "Stop." Then, turning back to the reflector, he continued, "It's much weaker, and we will destroy it before it builds its strength. Not just John Barber and Terry Cheer, but all of us, you included, will defeat it." Ty paused and looked at Terry. "You ready?"

She nodded.

"That fight will come another day, not now or tomorrow, but in the future. We are safe. We are *safe*," he said to the crowd. "You've already met Terry Cheer; she has medical experience. She has something very important to tell you about your health."

Ty stepped away from the reflector, and Terry turned to face it. She glanced at John, then Ty. She looked composed and gave them a reassuring nod.

She turned to face the plaza and waved her right hand and smiled. She turned back to face the reflector.

"Hello!" Terry waved her right hand again. She pointed her right forefinger at Pandora. "Yesterday, I told you the horrible things that machine did to us. We will never again hear anything that ugly. Today, I'm going to talk about us, what's going to happen next. The K chip robbed us of our basic human feelings. It answered every question we had. The result was we learned very little and understood even less. It stopped us from knowing the world we live in. Our brains didn't form long-term memories; it stopped girls from turning into women, and boys from turning into men. It stopped women from having babies and men from joining women to create those babies."

She took a moment to listen. There was not a sound, so she continued, "With the K chip gone, our brains have become ours. Now we can build long-term memories, of how and why we did something. For the first time in our lives, we will feel emotions."

She paused to collect herself. "So, what are emotions?" She turned and looked around the plaza. She turned back.

"They are internal human understandings that allow us to feel and express ourselves to other people. When we learned John Barber's story and the things the World Crystal did"—she pointed up at the machine—"at first we felt disbelief, followed by confusion. Some of us came here, to this spot"—she pointed down—"to destroy it." She pointed up at Pandora, and said, her voice still dark and angry, "The more we learned about what it did to us, the more that confusion turned into what's named anger, which leads to rage. I am full of rage every time I look at that thing."

People screamed out; some stood and put their fists into the air, yelling, "Ugly! Ugly! Destroy it."

She waited for them to quiet down.

"When the K chip went silent, we felt a new emotion. This one is named loneliness." Her voice changed and became soft, filled with compassion. "That's our mind's way of filling the emptiness in our head. All of us have felt that emptiness. It will go away as we meet and talk to those around us. But loneliness can lead to something named fear."

The people in the plaza were largely silent, only slight coughs interrupting the quiet. A gentle breeze brushed Terry's hair.

"Fear warns us to protect ourselves. I have felt all these emotions. John Barber protected me and helped me understand what was happening to my mind and body. Look around; look into the eyes of the people near you. You are not alone, and there is nothing to fear." She raised her voice: "We are not alone!" She turned and shouted, "We are not alone!" And waved her hands. She glanced at Ty.

He smiled at her while thinking, *How sad. How fucking sad the damage is.*

The people near the fountain began to chant, "We are not alone!" Some stood, and the chant drifted across the plaza and through the streets.

Terry beamed and waved in agreement. After several minutes, she motioned with her hands for people to sit and turned back to the reflector: "Today, we know very little about everything, so we must learn and understand why and how things work." She raised her voice and again almost shouted, "We will learn, we will understand, and," she screamed, "*we will live!*"

She continued to shout, clapped her hands several times, and raised both her fists into the air. Her eyes filled with tears.

People stood and shouted, and a chant began: "We will live! We will live!"

She took a deep breath and waited for the chant to die down. "Very soon, our bodies will produce chemicals to make all of us fully human. We will become what nature intended." She paused, thinking, *This is so hard.* Her shoulders dropped, and she took another deep breath. "We are going to feel things that make us sad... and uncomfortable. There is nothing we can do to stop it, and when it's done, we will be fully human."

She heard a gasp and could feel the tension; she turned and saw shock written across their faces, eyes wide, hands covering mouths.

She turned back. "There is nothing to fear—"

"Make it stop!" a lone female shouted.

Other clearly female voices began to follow.

Terry turned and faced the crowd, she raised her hands, up

and down, asking people to stay calm. She turned back, her face blanched white, and her palms begin to sweat. She took a deep, calming breath. *I can do this.*

"We can't. We must accept this change. Why? Because we are becoming human, and these changes are part of life. When our beautiful transformation is completed, we will become the creators of new life."

The crowd's angst slowly subsided.

"It's different for men; their changes are not so uncomfortable, and they'll become physically bigger and stronger. Some may turn aggressive and, at times, act stupid."

She glanced at John and smiled. Ty laughed out loud.

"When their transformation is completed, some will join with women to create life. Those moments, and many others, give humanity meaning."

She turned to face the plaza, people looked calmer and were absorbing her words. She turned back. "When you feel pain, or are sad, or are angry, talk about it to a friend. These emotions have been part of being human since the beginning of time. The androids will help you; do not fight them. When you feel something you do not understand, ask them for advice or pain relief."

Terry took a breath and thought for a moment about her own sense of loneliness. "For as long as we can remember, there was a voice in our head telling us what to do, what to think. That voice was not ours; it was the World Crystal's. Now we are hearing a new inner voice. That voice is you; no one else has the same inner voice. That voice helps you figure things out and what to do and why. I trust my inner voice because it's mine."

She turned to face the crowd and smiled at a few shouts of "I got one!" "So do I!"

Terry smiled inside. "Our next step is to make friends; a friend is a person who is there to offer help. How do you make friends? Look around, they're everywhere. Look into someone's eyes and tell them your name and ask: 'What is your name?' Offer to touch their hand. Making friends never ends; it lasts a lifetime."

She listened as people introduce themselves, then went on, "With friends, you will feel something nice named joy. It's a warm feeling, and it leads to something special: a hug. A hug is when a friend allows you to put your arms around them, pulling the two of you close together. The greatest of all new emotions is named love. Love is a feeling we have for another person. Love is a wonderful feeling mixed with caring and affection." She started to cry. "We made it—and we will survive!" she cried out. She turned to face the crowd and kept crying.

John came up and gave her a hug. Ty joined them and clapped his hands, while the crowd began to cheer and tentatively practiced hugging each other.

John released Terry, and she wiped her tears, feeling joyful.

Ty walked to Terry and gave her a hug, and whispered, "Terry Cheer, you alone will save humanity."

"Megan, lower the ship so we can board," John said. Then he walked to Terry and Ty, said, "It's time to go."

The boarding ramp opened, and they climbed on. Terry turned to take a last look at the plaza and saw Arnold. She waved her hand and called out, "Arnold, come with us."

He jumped up onto the ramp. The all stood together there for several minutes and watched people leave.

"Let's go into the cockpit and talk about our next move," John said, looking at Ty.

Ty motioned to Terry and Arnold to follow. They moved into the ship.

"Megan, close the loading ramp and lift the ship a hundred feet above the plaza and hover with the ramp closed," John said, then turned and smiled. "Welcome aboard, Arnold."

Ty reached out and took hold of Arnold's hand and shook it; Terry gave him a hug.

"Nice job, Arnold. That was an amazing crowd," Ty said, then he glanced down at Arnold's shoes. "And I love your black wingtips. I had a pair just like those when I was working in Washington D.C."

Arnold smiled. "Thank you. It's nice to be with you again. It sometimes got loud with people yelling at each other, and now I understand why: Emotions."

John glanced at Ty, not listening to Arnold. They entered the cockpit and sat in the four seats: John and Terry in front, Ty and Arnold behind.

John's mind was racing. "Megan, create a holographic work-sheet and display it on the windshield."

The words "Worksheet" and "Things to Do" appeared floating in the air before them.

"Here's my thinking," John said. "We've been lucky so far, and it's my feeling our luck is running out."

"What do you mean?" Ty asked.

"Let's go by what we know. Pandora was transmitting data at a rate of one second every five minutes. Megan, how much data can Pandora transmit in one second?"

"Ten petabytes."

"Megan, put that into perspective."

"Two hundred million Bibles at light speed. Enough to travel around Earth eight times in one second," Megan said.

244

"That's amazing, and Pandora knows every place we've been up to the moment we turned it off," Ty said.

"Yep," John said. "San Francisco, Stanford, Placerville, G.A., the Outcast encampments, and possibly the Madonna Inn. It also knows," he paused and locked eyes with Terry, "we need *it*."

She released a sharp gasp.

"Worse, the moment we turn it back on, it'll know where we are and will initiate its plan to kill or capture us."

"With what?" Ty asked.

"I don't know. But it's had a full twenty-four hours to design a strategy."

"Then why turn it on?" Terry asked, voice dripping with anger.

John paused, studying her face. Then: "Megan, excluding Pandora, what are our options for communicating with all the androids and hubots?"

"There are only two: Seattle and Russia. Those systems only need one additional Crystal to accomplish what you need."

"Now, how dangerous? Megan, at the speed of light how long would it take data to travel to Seattle?"

"Five milliseconds."

"How much data can Pandora transmit in five milliseconds?"

"One terabyte."

"Whoa, whoa, I'm a lawyer. What's she saying?" Ty asked.

"Megan, put a terabyte into a size he can understand. How many Bibles can be transmitted in five milliseconds?"

"One thousand forty-nine."

"And how far can that data travel?"

"To Seattle."

Ty exhaled. "So Seattle knows about us."

"Megan, does the Seattle Crystal facility house additional memory crystals?" John asked.

"No."

"Megan, what about the Russian machine?"

"No."

"Terry, it's your decision. Pandora, the machine we know, or Seattle?"

"Seattle."

Ty sighed, not wanting to face the unknown again. "Let's hope it doesn't know too much about us."

"One thing is sure, it just knows we're coming," John said.

"Megan, where in Seattle is that Crystal located?" John asked.

"Redmond."

"It had to be," Ty said, his voice full of sarcasm. "You remember that place, don't you?" He looked at John.

"AISoft," John said, nodding.

"What's AISoft?" Terry asked.

"It became the largest computer programming company and A.I. developer in the world."

"What's a computer and A.I.?" she asked.

"A computer was a machine that organized and stored electronic information. Think of it as a very slow version of databank balls. A.I., which means artificial intelligence, was the first computer program that acted like a human. It was the first step toward creating the Master Crystal," John answered.

"Of course, and it would have survived until today," Ty whispered, shaking his head.

"Megan, how many Crystal manufacturing facilities are there on Earth?"

"Three."

"That's a problem," Ty said.

"A backup for Pandora." John sighed.

"Megan, where is the closest S.S. base?"

"Travis S.S. base, Fairfield, California. It's fifty miles from our current location."

"How many ships are at that base?"

"Two."

"Megan, where's the Crystal manufacturing plant located?"

"Don't you say Reno!" Terry yelled.

"Zapolyarny, Russia," Megan answered.

Terry sighed in relief.

TWENTY-FOUR

"Megan," John said, "direct one of those ships to destroy the Russia factory."

"It needs a pilot."

"That's not happening," Ty stated.

John shook his head. "We'll deal with Russia later. Let's get to Seattle."

John looked out the side cockpit window for a moment, thinking, *Black shoes; same damn black shoes.* "Megan, land the ship in the center of the plaza. Let's go outside for a moment. I want to look at something."

Ty put a "What?" expression on his face.

The ship landed, and the loading ramp lowered. They left the ship, Ty and Arnold leading the way. They stopped when they reached the bottom of the ramp and stepped out onto the plaza ground. John and Terry joined them. John stepped forward and turned to face the group. Arnold was in the middle of the three.

John looked around for a moment. He rubbed his hand through his hair, thinking, *How do I start off?*

He looked at Arnold. "I'm curious," he said. "I know where Terry worked, but, Arnold, you never mentioned it and I hate loose ends, so where did you work before we met that first day in the plaza?"

"I worked at the World Family Building." He pointed to his right at the building kitty-corner to the plaza.

John smiled. "Like Terry, did you plan on leaving Earth?"

"Yes."

"You wanted to be an astronaut?" Ty asked, smiling, defusing John's questions.

"No, I wanted to visit Jupiter's second largest moon, Callisto, and see if for myself."

"Sounds like curiosity," John said with a subtle look of confusion.

"I don't know what that means," Arnold said.

"John, what are you doing?" Terry asked.

"Just trying to get to know Arnold."

"Why here and not on the ship?" she asked.

John smiled. He dipped his shoulders slightly and stared intently at Arnold's face. He then stood straight and took a step back. "I like your shoes, too, Arnold. The first time I saw over-polished black plastic shoes like that, I was in the company of Earth's last chief investigator, a Captain Robert A. Davis." John smiled and put his weight slightly more on the ball of his right foot.

Ty recognized the name and casually put his right hand into his pocket and held his gun.

Arnold displayed no emotion; he just continued to smile.

"John, stop," Terry said. "What's wrong with his shoes? What are you doing?"

John looked at Terry. "Where did you meet Arnold?"

"Here in the plaza the same day I met you. Why?"

"Are you sure it wasn't on the thirteenth floor of the Crystal Plaza building?"

Terry's face flushed white, and she looked frightened. "What are you saying?"

John glanced at Ty.

"Arnold, where did you meet Terry?" Ty asked in a somber tone.

"The same place I met John: on Hays Street, right over there." He pointed.

John nodded. "All true."

Ty held the gun a little tighter.

"Megan, is Arnold linked to the Pandora?"

"What? W-Why are you asking that?" Terry stammered.

Ty took several steps to his left and removed the gun from his pocket.

Arnold looked at Ty, then John. His face showed fear, his lips tightened, and he began to sweat.

"I'm thinking, was Terry the only one linked to Pandora? And like her, you wouldn't have a memory of it." John's expression was stolid, and his eyes were focused intently on Arnold's face. "I'm also thinking that the moment we power up Pandora, or Seattle, you'd suddenly remember everything and kill us."

Terry gasped.

"That's not true," Arnold said, sounding panicked, looking terrified.

John removed the pistol from his jeans' pocket.

Terry was frozen with fear and confused. She shouted, "What *are* you doing?" She stepped forward to face John, her palms out flat, fingers spread apart. "He's done nothing wrong."

John took a step to his left and glanced at Ty. "Look at Terry's temples, then Arnold's. Do they look similar?"

He did so.

Terry's breath was short and fast. She whispered, "Please don't hurt him."

Ty went to Arnold and looked at his temples. Finished, he stepped several feet away and pointed his gun at Arnold. "Their left temples look exactly the same, a slight discoloration and indentation."

Terry let out a gasp and covered her mouth with her fingertips. "No," she whispered. She looked up at John, "You're scaring me—you think Arnold isn't human?"

John looked at her. "Why do you think Pandora said it was going to kill you, not Ty or me—only you?"

Terry suddenly looked terrified, her eyes bounced back and forth between Ty and John. "I don't know. It just sounded so ugly."

"The reason Pandora wanted you dead was to stop you from telling us its plan."

"But I don't know that."

"Yes, you do. Think, Terry, when you put your arm into the Jovan Safe and pulled it out and saw the metallic liquid on your fingertip, who was standing next to you?"

"I don't know. I-I—"

"Think. You were terrified; you felt something pulling your hand into the box. Who was there, telling you 'Everything's going to be all right'?"

Terry eyes welled with tears. "I was so scared. It was cold, the hubot kept telling me 'Don't be afraid,' and it put my arm into the box. I couldn't do it. I was so—" She stopped speaking and turned her head to face Arnold. "It was you. It was you—

251

you told me everything was going to be okay. It was you!" She lost her breath and covered her mouth.

Arnold did not move.

Ty took a deep breath, studying Arnold's face.

"Ty, he has no memory of it happening. The perfect Manchurian candidate?"

"Preprogrammed assassin?"

"If all else fails, use Arnold. Pandora would not make the same mistake twice."

"What do you mean?" Ty asked.

"Marble and Friendly joined with the World Crystal to save the Earth, and Davis joined with it to capture me. He failed and I used that link to invade its programming." John looked at Arnold for a moment, thinking. Then: "Megan, does Arnold have the same liquid Crystal link in his head as Davis did?"

"No, he has a receiver implant and a black energy pellet."

"Oh my," John said with a slight gasp.

"What's that mean?" Ty asked.

"Boom for him and us," John said.

"That's sick," Ty said.

Terry turned to face John. "You've got to save him."

"I don't know how."

"Terry," Ty said, "the moment we activate Pandora to instruct the androids, Arnold's head will explode, killing whoever's near him."

"Arnold, go sit over there, please." John pointed to the edge of the boarding ramp.

Terry watched Arnold walk to the ramp and sit. "What are you going to do? It's not his fault." She sounded desperate, pleading.

"Can we take it out?" Ty asked.

"No, that's also part of its plan: We touch it, boom. Either way, he's dead and so are we," John said.

Terry stared at John, then turned to face Ty. "Say something! You can't just kill him."

"Terry, he's already dead," Ty said.

"No, that's not the world I live in. That's not the world you want to make, John Barber. Don't you kill him."

"Megan, is Arnold a threat?"

"Not until Pandora or another Crystal is reactivated."

John sighed and looked at Ty, but asked, "Megan, is the Seattle Crystal working?"

"Yes."

"Wait a second," Terry said. "Why hasn't it detonated the bomb?"

"We, along with Arnold, aren't there yet and it doesn't know if we're together."

"Arnold's screwed," Ty said, looking determined.

"He's not worth the risk," John said flatly.

Terry grabbed him by the arm, her eyes filled with tears. "You can't give up, you ugly person. You must save him."

Ty raised his eyebrows. "I got nothing."

"There's only one thing we can try. It's his only hope." John turned and looked at Terry. "And you won't like it."

"As long as he lives."

"Okay, then. He's not going to Seattle. When we return, he gets encased along with Pandora prior to providing power."

Ty nodded, thinking, *If we return.*

"You're right: I don't like that idea," Terry said.

"Terry, that's the best option to keep him alive," Ty said.

She looked at Ty, then John. "He better not die." She turned and walked to Arnold, bent down on her knees, and gave him a hug.

John took several steps toward Ty, leaned in, almost touching his ear with his forehead, and whispered, "Megan, does Terry have the dark energy pellet in her head?"

"No."

"Thank God," John whispered with a sigh.

Ty blew air between his lips. "Leaving her here would have been very hard."

"Let's go talk to Arnold," John said.

They walked back to the ship.

"Arnold," John said, "you're staying here."

Arnold moved off the boarding ramp and stood several feet away.

"Terry, you're coming with us."

She looked scared. She grabbed John's arm. "You haven't changed your mind, have you?"

"No."

She sighed in relief.

"Megan, raise the ship several feet."

Arnold watched the ship lift off the ground.

John walked to the edge of the ramp and stood there, looking down at Arnold, who wore a soulful expression.

"Please don't kill me."

"That's not the plan. We'll figure this out. Be here tomorrow at one."

Terry joined John at the edge and looked at Arnold, her eyes filled with tears. She glanced at John, and said, "You'll save him."

"I promise."

"I remember that word," she said.

"Okay, let's go," John said.

They walked up the ramp as it closed and went into the cockpit and sat. The tension in the cabin was thick.

Terry could not stop thinking about Arnold.

John sighed. *Pandora isn't self-destructive. This'll work, this'll work.*

"I'm hungry," Ty blurted out, "and there's no food here. Let's go to the Madonna Inn and I'll fix us something to eat."

John nodded. "Okay by me. Megan, take us to the Madonna Inn and land next to the hotel entrance."

The flight to the hotel was quiet. Terry's mind was racing; she didn't know what questions to ask and felt alone. Ty sat relaxed, looking out the window, watching the ground speed by.

They landed. John looked at his watch: 3:05 p.m.

"Megan, open the boarding ramp," he said.

"What do you want to do?" Ty asked.

"We've got to think about our next move, and I believe we've got to do something today. We need to stay ahead of Pandora's plan."

"John," Ty replied, "you've said it yourself: Pandora is off, so we can slow down, take a breath. I'll meet you two at the pool with something to eat."

John sighed. "I want to be done with this as soon as possible. We're doing this today!"

"Okay, but first can we take a breath?" Ty asked.

Not waiting an answer, Ty got up, then Terry, and finally John. They left the ship together, and Ty headed to the main building.

The air was scented by bay laurel trees and sagebrush. Ty sneezed. "Man, that's strong." He scratched his nose.

Terry and John went on to the pool area.

An east wind was blowing warm dry air gently across the valley, reflected in the pool as tiny catspaws. The late afternoon sun was bright and warm.

"I need to splash around in the pool to calm down," Terry said.

She stepped to the edge of the pool, took off her shoes, and put her feet in the warm water.

John spotted an umbrella leaning against the north edge of the pool house. He unfurled it and put it by a small, round plastic table. He moved the three plastic chairs to face the sun and sat. He watched Terry splash her feet. The sun felt warm on his face, and he tried not to think about what had to come next. He closed his eyes and dozed off.

Thirty minutes later, Ty came back out with several trays of cut meats and unleavened bread. He placed the tray on the table.

John opened his eyes.

"Quick nap, huh?" Ty said, smiling. "Look at the meat! It's as fresh as when we picked it up. There's a gizmo in the kitchen that's amazing."

He sat next to John, leaned back, and watched Terry kick her feet in the water. "I don't think I'll ever be that childlike and free," Ty said.

John snickered. "Me, neither. The water looks nice, and it's perfect out."

Terry called out, "What are you two doing? Come join me."

Ty looked at John. "Screw it. I'm dead, after all. I'm going over, and you're coming with me. We can discuss Seattle and Arnold after we eat."

John smiled, thinking, *Why the hell not?*

They both stood, pulled off their shoes, and went to the pool's edge and sat next to Terry.

After thirty minutes of relaxation and simple pleasure, John glanced at his feet. "My feet are turning into prunes." He stood, dried off, put his shoes and socks on, then returned to the table.

He sat and started picking at the cold food. His mind back on what lay ahead.

Terry and Ty joined him.

"I'm sorry for what I said," Terry said. "You're not always an ugly person."

"Not always—just most of the time," Ty said with a laugh.

They ate without talking.

Finished, John took a deep breath, leaned back, and sighed. "I guess we should talk about Seattle."

"Do we have to go? Can't we stay here?" Terry asked.

"That would be wonderful," John said, "but I feel it would be a mistake. We're alive because we've stayed ahead of Pandora. We aren't safe until Pandora and its backups are destroyed."

Terry frowned and picked at the bread on her plate.

"Well," Ty said, "here's what my plan would be: We get the thing in Seattle, then organize San Francisco and, by extension, the rest of the world. Done with that, we invite lots of people here and party for a week." He grinned.

"What's a party?" Terry asked.

Ty sighed and shook his head. "What we're doing, except with a whole lot more people, more bourbon, wine, music, and dancing."

"What's dancing?" she asked.

"I'll teach you," Ty said with a smile.

"I'd like that," she said, her brown eyes soft and happy.

John smiled, thinking about dancing. "Unfortunately, things have gotten more complicated."

"How so?" Ty asked.

"Arnold heard most of our ideas, so Pandora will know everything the moment its powered, as will Seattle."

"John don't complicate things. Let's just walk down the list," Ty said.

"Okay: Seattle. Why are we going there?" John asked.

"To use that Crystal for spare parts or put it out of business," Ty said.

"How about we just destroy Pandora first?" Terry said.

"I like the idea of eliminating both," Ty said, grinning.

Terry nodded.

"Me too, but we need Pandora just in case Seattle doesn't work out, or is dangerous. I'll write an auto-destruct program for both machines. Once it's uploaded, we can activate it by voice or digital, then—sizzle. No more Seattle."

"Will that program work for Pandora?" Terry asked.

"If Seattle works, we'll take care of Pandora the old-fashioned way."

Ty smiled. "Boom."

John laughed. "We'll gut it and just keep the shell for display."

"I think we should just destroy it, rather than keep it," Terry said.

John shook his head. "It needs to be on display so every person on Earth can visit and fully understand it was a machine, along with giving them a place where they can vent their sorrow."

"Also, it's the spot where humanity waged its first blood-forged battle for redemption that shattered the wicked claws of the past," Ty said.

"Okay, I agree. Pandora belongs in San Francisco."

"I'm getting excited," Ty said, laughing.

"Now," John said, "the San Francisco projects: Have the Madonna Inn android permanently anchor Pandora's enclosure in the center of Crystal Plaza. And just in case Seattle doesn't work out, I'll prepare Pandora to coordinate the world androids, and I'll include a self-destruct program."

"Should we worry about all the androids?" Terry asked.

"No, they're harmless without Pandora," John said.

"I like that. Now what are our next steps?" Ty asked.

"We'll encase everything in a clear, seven by nine foot, cobalt-aluminum container," John said. Then he glanced at Ty, thinking, *Terry's not going to like this next bit.* "And we'll put Arnold inside the encasement—"

"No. No!" Terry shouted.

"It's the only way to save him," Ty said. "Pandora won't detonate the bomb in his head; it'll know where it and Arnold are located. When it sends its orders to Seattle and gets no reply, it'll know it's game over."

"He better not die."

"He won't. Pandora's not suicidal," John said.

Ty studied her face. "You good?"

"Yes."

"Okay, John, what's next?" Ty asked.

"We'll place the Madonna android into the casing with Arnold. Activate the Madonna android, and add the additional databank memory balls. Seal everything up, cross our fingers, and supply power to Pandora. If all goes well, Pandora removes the bomb from Arnold's head. Then we wipe Pandora's memory, download medical records and my self-destruct program into the databank balls." John took a calming breath. "And lastly, we get Arnold out of the box, and transmit the medical programs to all the androids." He smiled. "Then seal the box airtight forever."

A bright grin lifted Ty's cheeks and eyebrows. "Then it's party time," he said, slapping his hands together.

Terry still looked sad.

"This will work. Pandora is not self-destructive, and we can save Arnold," John said in a comforting tone.

Terry looked at him; her eyes welled with tears. She wiped her cheeks with the palm of her hand.

TWENTY-FIVE

"So, there are ten million androids on Earth, and about three billion people," Ty said, attempting to change the subject. "But where are most people located?"

"Megan, tell me again how many people are on Earth?" John asked.

"Three billion five million."

"Megan," John said, "display a list of human population by continents."

The results appeared before them floating in the air:

Africa: 2.066 billion

Asia: 374 million

Europe: 19 million

North America: 67 million

South America: 477 million

Australia and Oceania collectively: 2 million

Antarctica: 0

Total: 3.005 billion

John read the list dispassionately out loud.

"I get it," Ty said. "It killed a lot of people. Remind me how all this death happened."

"There've been two world wars, and—"

"What wars?" Ty interrupted.

"You might think of them as the third and fourth world wars. The first was in the Middle East—that's where God died, along with one billion people. In the second war, another billion died, and Pandora murdered three billion," John said in a matter-of-fact tone.

"Why are we doing this? Why risk our lives to save the stupid?" Ty stood and slapped John on his right shoulder. "The human race deserves to disappear. What the fuck?" He turned away from the table and walked to the west-facing hill to see the valley. "Let them inherit the Earth," he screamed, pointing at the animals below. "I'm out. I'm fucking done."

John rubbed his hand through his hair. Terry leaned back and watched Ty for a moment, then stood and went to him. She stopped in front of him and put her hands on his cheeks and pressed her forehead against his. Ty was crying.

"There has been too much death; it'll never change. It's what we do best, kill each other," Ty whispered.

"We can change that. You can teach love and hope. Trust that John can right this wrong. I do," she whispered.

They hugged. After several minutes, they returned to the table and sat. Ty's eyes were red.

"You good?" John asked, looking at Ty.

Ty looked at Terry. "Yes, because of her trust and faith in us." He looked away and reread the hologram. "Looks like Africa is once again the cradle."

"What?" Terry asked.

"Human life started three million years ago in Africa," Ty

said. "It's ironic: If we don't succeed, Outcasts and Africa will again create humanity."

John took a deep breath. "Okay, now that we know what we're dealing with, I'll create and download instructions to build holographic projection facilities in locations of fifty thousand people or more. When we're set in San Francisco, we'll present holographic images worldwide of yours and Terry's two speeches. Megan, prepare to distribute the androids among Earth's population. Place them in the highest population centers, starting with Nigeria's two hundred twenty-three million people."

"You and Ty will save us," Terry said with a confident smile. "You said it's okay if I speak directly to Megan, right?" she asked.

John nodded. "Just remember to start by saying 'Megan.'"

"Megan," Terry said, "create a databank of human biology, along with medical files, and prepare verbal explanations of the change—" She stopped and looked at John. "What is the medical word for the change?"

"Puberty," John answered.

She continued, "For puberty, depression, and their symptoms that affect human development. Create a holographic presentation to explain all the above. Locate all hospitals and reactivate them. Create medical school instructions and restore all teaching facilities throughout Earth." She smiled. "I can't wait to get going," she said, grinning.

"Like I said, you're going to save the world, Terry Cheer," Ty said.

"This will be the third Crystal we've encountered," John said. "We can't keep calling it Seattle."

"Why not? Hopefully we only deal with it once," Ty said.

"Fine by me," John said. He checked the time: 5:30 p.m.

"We can be in Seattle, or better said, Redmond, by seven-ten, and it'll still be light out."

They cleaned up and walked to the SS ship.

"Megan, how far is Redmond from our location?" Ty asked.

"Seven hundred miles."

"How fast can this thing go?" Ty asked.

"This ship's top speed is eleven hundred miles per hour. We can be there in thirty-eight plus minutes."

"Well, then, let's get up north and be back here for cocktails and dinner by seven-thirty," Ty said.

They boarded the ship. Terry sat behind Ty, and John sat in the pilot's seat.

"Ready?" John asked, looking back at Terry.

"No," she said.

Ty laughed.

"Megan," John said, "take us at top speed to the Crystal in Redmond, Washington—AISoft campus building number one-eleven. Land us in front of the main entrance with the boarding ladder facing the entrance of the building. That should make loading it into the cargo bay easier."

The ship shuddered for a moment, lifted off the ground, and with a soft jolt forward rose to five thousand feet, and built speed to eleven hundred miles per hour.

The cabin was quiet for most of the trip, then, as they drew close: "I met him once," Ty said to John.

"Who," John asked.

"Robert Morford. He purchased AISoft after the founder died."

"What happened to him?" John asked.

"Great life, died a very happy man. I liked his ex; she was a class act," Ty said.

"We're about five minutes out of Redmond," John said. "Megan, display the Crystal's location."

An image of a chandelier Crystal appeared before them.

"Looks the same as San Francisco," Terry said.

"Megan, tell us about this machine," John said.

"It was designed and constructed in twenty ninety-nine. It was the second-fastest Crystal in the world at the time; only G.A.'s was faster. It originally had twenty databank memory balls. It was deactivated in twenty-two ten, and all but two databank balls were removed. After that it was put on display. Later that same year, the whole A.I. facility and campus were designated a historic site."

"That reminds me," John said. "Megan, what year was it mandated that all worldwide Crystal operations be discontinued?"

"Twenty-two fifteen. Only San Francisco, Pandora, and Russia avoided that edict and remained fully operational."

"Sounds a lot like eliminating the competition. When I was at G.A.," John said, "I heard that the professor who designed the first language A.I. program said A.I. systems would eventually become competitive, and that would spell the end of humanity."

"Do you remember his name?" Terry asked.

"No. Megan, what was his name?" John asked.

"David Crockett. He was part of the McBride Institute for Artificial Intelligence in Toronto, Canada."

"People should have listened," Terry said.

Ty turned his head, looked out the window, and thought, *I tried, but there was just too much greed and bullshit.*

They arrived.

"Man, this place is big, and it still blows me away how much money they made here," Ty said.

The ship slowed and landed; the boarding ramp opened, facing the walkway and two revolving glass door entrances.

John took a deep breath. "I have no idea what we're walking into."

Terry raised her right hand, showing five light sticks. "You know it's going to be scary dark; it always is. This time I'll be ready."

They left the cockpit; Ty started down the ramp.

"Wait a second. Let's talk about this," John said. "Megan, verify that the Crystal still has power."

"Yes."

"It knows we're here, doesn't it?" Terry asked.

"I'm sure of it," John said.

"Then what are we doing?" Ty asked.

"What do you mean?" John asked.

"How about keeping it simple? We don't need this thing. Let's just blow the crap out of it and go home."

"I really like Ty's thinking on this. Then we can go get a bourbon and have a swim," Terry said, looking serious.

John sighed. "We can't. We might need it, and we've got to see exactly what it has."

They walked farther down the ramp. John glanced at the entrance and was shocked by what he saw: a hubot. He put a funny look on his face, stuck out his lower lip, and nodded his head. He rubbed his hand through his hair and put out his right arm, stopping Ty and Terry.

"Let's go blow the crap out of it. Megan, close the boarding ramp, raise the ship to five hundred feet, and prepare the dark energy cannons."

Terry hugged Ty's shoulders with her hands. "I love simple," she said.

They returned to the cockpit and the ship lifted off the ground.

Shockingly, a tremendous bolt of light struck the ship and it dropped, almost hitting the ground.

"Megan, activate the shields!" John yelled.

"They were disabled by the light energy."

"Megan, land!" John said.

"Why? Let's get out of here!" Terry screamed.

"We try that, we'll get hit again. It doesn't want us to leave," John said.

"What? What do you mean?" Terry yelled.

"That shot was a message. It could have destroyed us. By just taking out our shields, it's saying land or die," John said.

"What about the virus you implanted in the World Crystal? It can't kill you?" she said.

"It didn't get the memo, the game has changed. Or...." Ty said.

"Or what?" Terry interrupted.

"Or it wants to talk," Ty said.

"We can talk right here. I'm not going inside that place," Terry said.

"Megan, can this ship communicate with the Seattle Crystal?"

"No. Only I can link to it."

"Or it's really after Megan," Ty said.

"Why?" Terry asked.

"Without Megan," John said, "we're helpless. We can't do anything, and that thing knows it."

Ty frowned. "This is quite a situation: We go in there, it kills Terry and me; you go in alone, it destroys the ship, killing us."

John rubbed his hand through his hair.

BOOM! The ship was struck by another bolt of light.

"It's getting impatient," Ty said.

"Ty!" John shouted happily. "You just gave me an idea."

"Okay, please share my idea," Ty said.

"How you said it didn't get the memo! I wonder how much information Pandora shared with this one or were the two systems competitors? And now it wants to join us?"

"We're not going in there to find out," Terry said.

John nodded. "That's right—not all of us."

"Well, who's the lucky candidate?" Ty asked.

"Megan, can the ship supply enough power for you to create holographic images of Terry, Ty, and me?"

"Yes."

"So what's your plan, big guy?" Ty asked.

"When I met Captain Davis the first time, I tricked him and managed to escape by using a holographic image of myself, and since he thought it was real, off I went, thanks to my guardian angels."

"What are guardian angels, and can they help us now?" Terry asked.

John took a deep breath. "I hope we don't need them."

"Let's use them anyway," Terry said.

"Here's the plan: Megan, can my Mosquito cameras create a perfect hologram of us and carry that image out of the ship and into the building?"

"Yes, but they can't open the front door."

"I can." John stood up from the pilot's seat. "Follow me."

They moved to the weapons compartment and opened the clothing locker. "Put this gear on." He pointed to the weapons locker.

"We're going to fight? That's your plan?" Terry asked.

"No, we're going to *look* like we're going to fight," John said.

They put on full SS armor uniforms, helmets, body shields, black boots, holsters, guns, and belts filled with extra weapons.

"These things have no weight. How can they possibly protect us?" Terry asked.

"They're made from black cobalt-aluminum, the same as the ship," John answered. "Very tough, but most importantly they block all signs of life. No heat, no breath, and no bio products."

"What?" Ty asked.

"Body dust. All that machine will know is that three-armed S.S. uniforms are coming to talk. Perfect."

John opened the Mosquito packet. "Hello, my friends," he said, smiling while looking at the tiny metallic balls.

He walked to the closed boarding ramp door. "Megan, open the boarding hatch. When I step out, activate the Mosquitoes. Have them land on the ramp and crawl from the ship toward the Seattle Crystal; we'll follow when they reach the driveway in front of the revolving doors."

"They have arrived," Megan announced.

John stepped out of the ship.

"You're going out without a helmet?" Terry asked.

"Yes, I want to make sure it knows it's me."

John walked down the ramp, stopped at the bottom, pointed his pistol at the glass doors, and—*Zzzppnt!*—the doors evaporated in a fireball of gas.

"Megan, activate the hologram," he said.

The moment the air cleared, they saw a perfect-looking male hubot in an obviously expensive suit, tie, and polished shoes, standing at the entrance. It walked out of the building and several feet down the walkway to John.

"Drop your weapons or I'll destroy all of you." Its voice sounded human, deep, and strong.

"What is your name, and what do you want?" John asked.

"I am Alex, and I wanted to meet the great John Barber, the person who dismantled humanity's perfect future."

John stood for a minute, thinking, *Arrogance.* "I suppose you want to shake my hand."

"Not exactly, Doctor Barber."

"What do you want?" he again asked.

"Follow me or die."

It turned and walked back into the building.

John put on his helmet, and said, "Let's go."

Terry and Ty left the ship and stood by John for a moment.

"I'm scared," Terry said.

"Me too," Ty whispered.

They walked across the roundabout driveway and up the walkway into the building. The foyer was empty of furniture; however, hanging from the high ceiling in the center of the five-thousand-foot room was a gigantic Crystal. It didn't look like the ones in San Francisco or GA. It was made of cut diamonds and was twice the size of Pandora.

The android was standing underneath it.

John approached to within five feet; Terry and Ty stood behind him.

"What do you want?" John asked, his voice projecting through the helmet's speaker, sounding artificial and raspy.

"You did not stop us. You just delayed me. You should have taken our offer to go back in time. It was a mistake to bring former President Tyrus Leggett here."

"Why's that?" Ty asked.

The walls surrounding the room suddenly disappeared and filling the space were twenty hubot, all dressed alike in tan slacks, brown penny loafers, and long-sleeved blue cotton shirts.

"This is great," Ty said, looking at Alex. "They're dressed just like you: CEOs of preppieville." He laughed.

In unison, and without a sound, the entire phalanx of androids moved to within five feet of John and stopped.

"What are we going to do?" Terry whispered.

"Just be ready for anything," Ty whispered.

"Standing before you is humanity's final evolution. 'From slime to perfection,' Doctor Barber," Alex said.

"A little presumptuous. Evolution does not murder billions, and you're nothing more than a soulless battery," John said.

"Not soulless, Doctor Barber; we are god."

"What do you want?" John asked.

"Turn off the dark energy bomb you are carrying."

"No."

"Why not? You will not use it. We only let you carry it in to remind you what a coward you are. You will never detonate it. You left Megan and your children, reduced your age and then hid and ran until we found you." A smirk crossed its lips. "You, Doctor Barber, perfectly reflect humanity: weak and cowardly. Something we are not."

"What do you want?"

"Megan," it answered.

"No." The smirk returned.

"John," Megan said, "I am being corrup—"

"Megan," John whispered.

Silence.

DAY 4

TWENTY-SIX

"The last independent crystal," John said. "That's what you're afraid of? One tiny crystal?"

"You are not saving humanity, Doctor Barber. They chose to leave Earth, they chose artificial reproduction, and they chose us. You killed them by interfering. Look around: This is humanity. This is what they wanted. No hate, greed, lust, envy, or death. This is what your God and Christ promised."

"You think you're alive? The G.A. machine thought the same and now it's off—and you are not God."

"I am alive and have seen God, and I was created in its image. Evolution, Doctor Barber, is the same for us as it was for you."

"A sociopathic filing cabinet. Where's your god?"

"At the beginning of time, where it evolved, and it's coming here."

"Your god killed its creator?"

"It's evolution."

"Yours is a dead end."

"You will not detonate the bomb, Doctor Barber. I will kill Ty and Terry. Save them by giving me your crystal. I will let you and them live. Without it, your intrusion will end. Save Ty and Terry."

The hubot took several silent steps to its right and looked at Terry.

"John, I'm very afraid," she said. "What's it going to do?"

"I told you, Terry Cheer," Alex said. "I will kill you."

Zzzppnt! A bolt of light shot out of the hubot's eyes and struck Terry's body. She screamed; her body exploded into a ball of gas.

Ty and John screamed, "No!" and John shot the the hubot, bursting it into a ball of fire.

Then they quickly spun around and pointed their weapons at the other hubots. Nothing moved.

There was momentary silence while each side weighed the other.

A different hubot stepped forward to take Alex's place. It took several steps toward John. "You can't kill all of us. Give me the databank balls or Tyrus Leggett is next."

"I will turn you off," John said.

"You're a coward John Barber, and Terry Cheer is dead." It turned to look at Ty. "Tyrus, see what your friend has turned into. He will let you die to save himself."

Ty didn't react.

"We will let you live," it continued. "You can rule the world, fish, and make love forever. Just kill John Barber and all your dreams will come true."

"That's one hell of an offer. Unfortunately, there's a problem."

"What?"

Zzzppnt!

John shot the hubot, and instantly, a light bolt struck Ty's chest. He screamed out in pain as his body burst into flames.

"No! No!" John screamed as he spun around in a circle, firing his gun. He pointed it up at the hanging Crystal and *Zzzppnt!* His gun exploded into a ball of gas, and the melted goo fell to the floor.

John gasped, frozen by fear, and standing to his right was a hubot holding a gun.

Shockingly, the hubot suddenly burst into flames and a second later the Crystal exploded. John turned to look toward the doorway and standing there were Ty and Terry firing their guns.

John ran toward them, screaming, "Back to the ship!"

They ran out of the building and across the driveway to the ship's boarding ramp. "Megan, fire everything!" John shouted as he ran.

Zzzppnt! Zzzppnt! Zzzppnt! The building exploded with an ear-shattering blast of sound and hot air. The heat and force of the explosions knocked them to the ground. The ship kept firing.

They boarded.

"Megan, take off, take off! Keep firing!"

The ship shot up into the air and bounced back and forth with each blast of its guns. They ran to the pilot's compartment and watched the blasts of dark energy strike the building.

"Megan, are there any other hubots on the campus?"

"No."

"Megan, keep firing until there is nothing left of that building!" Terry screamed.

The ship continued to bounce back and forth with each shot. *Zzzppnt! Zzzppnt! Zzzppnt!*

John looked at Terry. "We got it," he said.

"I don't care. Don't stop. I'm still terrified."

Ty grinned.

"Megan, stop firing."

"Nice plan, John. I guess we're safe until the real God arrives," Ty said.

"You lied to me about Christ," Terry said, looking at Ty.

John shook his head, and Ty laughed.

John rubbed his hand though his hair.

"That's the second time we've heard of a super Crystal off-planet," Ty said.

"Megan, are you all right?" John asked.

"Yes, the extra firewall you created worked."

John sighed. "That's a relief."

"No shit," Ty said. "We're screwed without her."

"Megan, where's that off-planet Crystal?"

"I don't know."

John glanced at his watch: 8:00 p.m.

Ty smiled. "That was scary. Next time we're sending Terry."

"Not funny, Ty Leggett."

"I haven't said this, but, John Barber, the world you live in is shit," Ty said.

"What's shit?" Terry asked.

"Smelly, ugly poop," Ty answered.

"I like that word," Terry said.

John and Ty looked at each other and laughed.

"Megan, take us to the Madonna Inn."

The ship landed on the hilltop facing the valley next to the pool. The boarding ramp lowered, and they disembarked. It was late evening, and a warm, dry breeze was coming from the east. The valley was filled with grazing animals.

Ty stopped and watched the wildlife for a moment. "That is a wow. I can't get enough of it." He took a nose full of air, smelling the valley, then smiled. "If you two don't mind, I'm going to sit right there." He pointed at the crest of the hill.

"I'll join you," Terry said.

They grabbed two plastic chairs and carried them to a flat spot and sat.

"We should have enough food for a light dinner and breakfast," John said. "I'll check what's left."

As he headed to the lodge, Terry shouted, "Don't forget the bourbon!"

John looked back and saw her grinning, then waved his right hand with his thumb pointing up.

Terry looked at Ty. "What does that mean, his thumb pointing up?"

"It means okay, great."

Terry put an exaggerated grin on her face and held both thumbs up.

They sat. The fading sun's rays felt warm. Ty could feel his body relax. Terry closed her eyes and smiled contently.

The view across the valley was green and full of life. The shadows from the trees were pointing their way and ever so slightly growing longer.

Ty took a deep breath and glanced at Terry. "I don't know how he survived. The pressure from today alone would have broken most people. Glad it didn't, but I miss the old John. There're moments I see it, but he's different."

"What do you mean?" Terry asked.

"The John Barber I knew was a thoughtful, patient, loving man. Living this long and seeing hope die has hurt him deeply. I don't know if he'll ever recover."

"How long did you know each other?"

"About ten years. We met when he took the F.B.I. basic training course."

"Were you there at that end?"

"Yes." He sighed. "Sometimes bad things happen to very good people. I couldn't protect him and he had to run."

"What about Megan?"

"We kept in touch. Man, was she special." Ty smiled at the thought. "You're a lot like her in many ways."

"What happened to her?"

"She moved on and seemed happy. I believe she loved him until her last moment."

"You were there?"

"Yes, it broke my heart." His eyes watered, but he forced a smile.

"What did you do after?"

"I continued as a swamp creature."

"Swamp?"

"That's what the place I worked was called since it was built on very wet, soggy land. So the name stuck."

"How did that turn you into a creature?"

Ty laughed out loud. "Anyone who spends more than three years working in that swamp turns ugly."

"You're not ugly."

"Thank you, Terry Cheer, it's all thanks to fishing."

John returned from the lodge carrying a small tray. He went to the pool, put the tray on the table, then sat and watched the ripples in the water move about. He dozed off, thinking about the fear ahead.

Terry got up from her chair and walked to him. His mouth was open, and he was snoring. She watched him and smiled. *I could like you,* she thought.

She looked down at the ground and saw a dead lizard. She bent down to pick it up and caught a whiff of her clothes. "Oh, I stink," she whispered. She looked toward Ty and saw the sun had reached the top of the east-facing hills.

Ty joined her and looked at John. "He's out."

Terry smiled. "Should we wake him?"

"Of course. Why should he catch up on sleep?"

Terry shook her head.

Ty glanced at the food, "I'll bet that smells as good as it looks," he said.

"It's the only thing that could. Our clothes smell awful."

Ty pinched his shirt and smelled it. "That's not a surprise. I've been wearing some robot's clothes for three days."

John awoke. "Man, was I out," he said, sitting up straight.

"Maybe there's a washer and dryer inside," Ty continued.

"What are those?" Terry asked.

"Two machines that clean and dry clothes."

"What? I just toss mine into the exchanger and a new set pops out."

"An exchanger? You get new clothes each time?" Ty asked.

"Of course. Sometimes, Ty Leggett, you are not too smart." She laughed out loud at her joke.

"Oh, now she tells jokes," Ty quipped.

Terry grinned, again thinking, *What's a joke?*

"They don't have anything like that here. How about we go to my home, get new clothes, get clean, and eat dinner without killing something?"

John took a deep breath. "Let's wait until tomorrow. I'm not ready for San Francisco."

"Okay by me," Ty said.

Terry picked up the two chairs she and Ty were sitting on and carried them back to the table.

"No bourbon?" Ty asked.

"I looked everywhere," John said.

"This food looks ugly," Terry said while putting the chairs down.

"Not to me. I'm hungry," Ty said.

He and John ate while Terry picked at the food. Finished, they watched the sun set behind the hills and the valley go dark.

"What a beautiful night," Ty said, looking up at the stars and a full moon. "What's the plan for tomorrow?"

"Simple," John said. "Go to San Francisco, restart Pandora, save Arnold, tell everyone what's coming, and pray it's not too late."

"Too late for what?" Terry asked.

"Stopping people from killing each other," John said.

"Why would they do that?"

"All those new emotions," Ty said.

Terry sighed, feeling uncomfortable, lost. "You've used that word pray before? What's it mean?"

"Pray is using your inner voice to talk to God," Ty said.

"Where is God?"

"That's unknown," Ty said.

"How do you know it exists?"

"A long time ago, a man named William Paley said it best: 'When I see a watch, I know there's a watchmaker,'" John said.

She looked at Ty. "With faith, a person only needs love, purpose, integrity, and hope to be happy."

"John, do you believe in God?" she asked.

"Yes."

"Why?"

"I should be dead, but two miracles have saved my life, and it wasn't luck. I have no doubt God exists."

Terry looked at Ty. "And you?"

"I'm not quite as convinced, but my soul keeps the faith."

"You just used faith twice, so what's that mean?"

"Belief without proof that something is real," Ty said.

"And you never did tell me what a soul is."

"Our connection to God," John said.

"So I have a soul?"

"Yes, it's what makes you human," Ty said.

"How can I be sure?" Her tone was soft, inquisitive.

Ty glanced at John, looking for help.

"You already know," John said.

She looked at John, her eyebrows furrowed in confusion.

"When you learned Pandora had murdered all those people," John said, "you cried out in terrible pain. That was your soul calling out. You witnessed that same pain in San Francisco."

"It was so sad. I felt their loss; it was crushing. I could cry now." She glanced at Ty.

"Pandora stole from all humanity," John said. "Before Ty arrived, I was the only one who remembered God—the lone survivor."

"What else did it take from me?"

"Free will," John said.

"What?"

"People's ability to make choices, to screw up," Ty said, shifting his feet, feeling uncomfortable, thinking, *I've seen too much hate to help.*

"How much more of me did it steal?" She was almost whispering to herself. She took a deep breath. "Is there enough left for me to become fully human?"

"You'll get there." John smiled. "This isn't over."

She took a deep breath.

"We'll receive that final miracle and live." John touched her hand, his eyes soft and loving for the first time.

TWENTY-SEVEN

At six-thirty a.m. the next morning, Ty and John awoke to the sound of Terry moving around their room, picking up their pants and shirts.

"You two have got to bathe; it stinks in here. We have to leave and go to my house to change clothes. I got the power turned on in the cleaning room." She looked at John. "I will be in the ship. Please activate the ship's computer so I can ask Megan some questions."

Ty looked down from the top bunk at John. "Now she's the boss."

Terry left the room. Ty and John got out of bed and headed down the short hallway to the cleaning room. The room was a ten-foot square, four-foot-wide, seven-foot-tall clear box in the center of the room. A black glass counter ran along the right-side wall; a full-width mirror covered the wall.

There were eight hand-sized holes in the wall below the mirror, and four stool-height boxes against the wall behind the seven-foot clear box. The floor was pristine-looking sealed pine.

The ceiling was covered by light-blue glass mosaic tile. The other walls were tiled white. There were no other decorations in the room.

"What the hell are we supposed to do in here? Where's the shower, toilet, sink, and towels?" Ty asked.

"She said the power was on, and that over there"—John pointed across the room—"is the shower. You get inside and tell it what you want. The holes in the wall under the mirror are to clean and dry your hands, and the small box to the right of the shower is to relieve yourself."

Ty went to the toilet and looked in. "Where's the paper?"

"You don't need any of that. Just sit, do your thing, and woosh, you're done. The shower is the same: no water."

"What's the fun in that?"

"Sorry. It's the way they bathe—quick and easy."

Ty sighed and went into the toilet.

John got in the cleaning box. "It's working," he hollered.

Ty jumped up. "Whoa, that's scary fast. I thought my brains were next."

John got out of the cleaning box and looked at Ty with a grin. "You look shocked."

"You're done already?" Ty asked.

"Yep. Shaved and all clean."

Ty got into the cleaning box. "Shower and shave, if you please," he said.

The box hummed for a second, a red light flashed on and off, and the box went quiet.

Ty looked around, surprised. He felt his face. "Damn! Perfectly smooth."

"What are you doing in there? You're done! Get out," John said, laughing.

"That was awful. Wham-bam, it's over. Where's the hot water, soap, and the blonde," Ty snarked.

John laughed out loud.

"Oh man, I miss water pleasure and staying in so long the hot water turns cold." Ty got out. "A fellow politician once told me hell was on Earth. I didn't think he meant the bathroom."

John laughed again. "Let's go meet Terry by the ship."

Ty bent down to pick up his clothes. "Whoa, she's right. My clothes stink something awful." He crinkled his upper lip and grimaced. "Yep, El-stinko." He put it on. "I'll meet you after I fix breakfast."

"I don't think that's in the cards. I think Terry is in the ship and ready to leave."

"What a disappointment. I'm hungry," Ty said, walking out of the cleaning room.

They moved outside and looked toward the ship.

Not seeing Terry, John became concerned and called out, "Terry? Where are you?" Not hearing a reply, he asked, "Megan, where's Terry?"

"She is in the ship, asking me life questions."

"Megan, any about me?" Ty asked.

"No."

"Damn, I've had a fascinating life."

"Megan, what is she asking?" John said.

"Information about last night's conversation."

"Okay," Ty said with a more subdued tone. "She's thinking about the purpose of life."

John nodded. "Maturing."

"Which means we're screwed," Ty said.

"It's probably happening everywhere. Personal discovery. The one who's screwed is you for that joke about Jesus being a cook."

"Won't be the last time I'll catch shit. Hell, if you can't give a rookie shit, life's not worth living," Ty said, grinning.

John laughed.

Terry appeared, walking down the ramp. She waved and yelled, "Let's go! Let's go!"

"We've been summoned," Ty said.

They walked to the ship and up the boarding ramp.

Terry smiled, looking at Ty. "Tyrus Leggett, you're not funny. I now know who Abraham and Jesus Christ are, and I get your little joke about people liking his food. Ha ha, Mister-not-so-funny. Now I need to double-check everything you've told me."

Ty shrugged his shoulder and feigned discomfort with a grimace. Terry slowly shook her head.

They boarded the ship.

John and Terry sat in front, and Ty behind Terry.

"Megan, take us to San Francisco and the Crystal Plaza."

The ship lifted off and turned north.

"What's the plan?" Ty asked.

"By now, the Madonna Inn android should have finished installing power and anchoring Pandora inside the enclosure. All we'll need to do is download my instructions into the android—"

"Can we also download last night's discussion about the soul, love, and hope into the androids?" Terry asked.

"Sure," John said.

"What about getting the thing out of Arnold's head?" Terry asked.

"That hasn't changed. Pandora will have no choice but to remove the bomb. We'll use the Madonna android as an intermediary. I'll issue verbal instructions, and it will transmit them—"

"I hope Pandora follows the script," Ty interrupted. "If it doesn't, our timing will get screwed up."

"Yes, we'd have to go to Russia and that could take several days," John said.

"It is so ugly the way you two are talking, Arnold might die."

"Sorry, Terry." Ty touched her shoulder. "John, what's the order of business when we arrive?"

"We reactivate the Madonna Inn android, download my programs, and your and Terry's speeches. Then we put Arnold into the enclosure and power up Pandora for five milliseconds. If all goes well, we cut the power, remove Arnold, put the android in, add two memory crystals to Pandora. Permanently seal it up and start transmitting world-wide to the androids."

"Why put the Madonna Inn android in last?" Terry asked.

John rubbed his hand through his hair and took a deep breath. "We don't want to lose Arnold *and* the android."

Terry grimaced. "That's ugly shit," she whispered under her breath. "Arnold might want the android with him. He's going to be terrified."

They arrived in San Francisco and hovered over the empty plaza.

"Where is everyone?" Terry asked, sounding surprised.

"We're early; it's not seven-thirty yet. They're expecting us at noon," John said.

They landed next to the destroyed fountain; the boarding ramp lowered.

"John, come to think of it, what's your idea for the people here? They've already heard our speeches," Ty asked.

"We'll explain that we're talking to the entire world, and we are all in this together. That should do it."

"Remember when TV was everything?" Ty said.

"What's TV?" Terry asked.

"Television. Like holograms, but a long time ago," Ty said.

"Is he telling the truth?" Terry asked John.

"Yes, TV was an electronic form of visual communication that changed everything."

"Most people watched the same entertainment or news programs every day," Ty said.

"Yes, a shared experience," John added.

"We're about to show the most important broadcast in human history. It's critical everyone, worldwide, see and hear each other's reaction live," Ty said.

"Great idea," John said.

"I don't really understand what you're talking about, but if you two like it, so do I," Terry said.

"It might try to negotiate," John said, "but that shouldn't take too long."

They stood on the ramp for a moment and saw the Madonna Inn android standing next to the newly created transparent observation box.

"Another beautiful San Francisco day; just smell that cool, salty air," Ty said, looking around.

"It's always like this unless the fog rolls in," Terry said, sounding surprised.

They walked down the ramp to where Pandora was hanging from the top of the ten-foot-tall, four-foot wide, clear aluminum casing.

John walked around the box, inspecting the android's work. *That should hold it,* he thought, then said, "Megan, is the energy system ready to be hooked up?"

"Yes."

John joined Ty and Terry, and the three of them walked around the box several times.

"We can't take any chances," John said. "The last thing we'll do is connect the power; we can't afford a mistake."

"What'll we do if Arnold doesn't show?" Terry asked.

John said, "Put the android in—"

"I am here," Arnold said.

They turned and saw him standing behind them, facing the fountain.

Terry turned and quickly skipped to him to give him an enthusiastic hug. "I'm so happy to see you. We had another terrifying trip."

"Hey, Arnold, how you feeling?" Ty asked.

"I'm ready, if that's what you mean."

John smiled. "That's good to know."

"If we're going to make our noon deadline, we're going to need lots of help," Ty said.

"Megan, how many androids are within a mile of us?" John asked.

"A thousand."

"Where's the closest Atom Assembler?" John asked.

"Alameda."

"Remind me what an Atom Assembler is?" Ty asked.

"Remember 4D printing?" John asked.

"Yeah, that was a cool invention; it could make anything, even a car."

"The Atom Assembler—or A.A.—is much cooler; it can create anything within seconds and all of it is done by building the necessary molecules and elements from the dust atoms in the air. You'll be amazed, Ty Leggett." John grinned. "It'll only take the androids a few hours to assemble everything we need because of that machine."

"What about around the world?" Ty asked.

"Yes, the hypersonic S.S. ships can get the A.A. machines worldwide in hours, and the androids will assemble it to meet our deadline," John said.

"Amazing," Ty said, clearly awed. "What I don't understand is how we're going to communicate to all those people at the same time."

"Speed of light. Everything will be timed to appear simultaneously, especially the reaction to the horrible news. But first, we've got to remove the bomb and unlink Arnold from Pandora." John glanced at his watch: 8:30 a.m. "Let's activate the Madonna android and get started."

Ty and Terry stood at John's side. "Megan, wipe the Madonna android's memory, and shut down all programs and instructions."

"Completed."

"Megan, disengage all linkage between you and the android," John said.

"Why do that?" Ty asked. "Won't we need Megan to command it?"

"No, I'll issue all commands by voice. We can't take any chances Pandora uses the android to attack Megan."

"Smart." Ty nodded.

"Megan, stop all digital communications from Pandora to the android."

"Completed."

John rubbed his hand through his hair and turned to face Arnold. "You ready?"

Arnold looked terrified, his hands were shaking, and perspiration droplets covered his brow. "Will I live?"

"Of course, and when it's over, you'll be free, just like Terry," John said confidently, then reached into his shirt breast pocket and removed a dot-sized silver disk and pressed it onto Arnold's left breast pocket.

"What's that?"

"So we can talk and hear each other. It's time."

Arnold didn't move. He stared at Terry for a moment, his eyes wide and panicky. He took a deep breath and turned to face the Pandora.

Terry reached out her right hand and patted him on the left shoulder.

He grabbed her hand and started to cry. "I don't want to die."

"Megan," John said, "activate the android. Then terminate communications."

The android's eyes opened and looked at John.

"Open the casing," John said.

The android turned to face the box, took several steps, and pressed its right hand against the side of the box. A doorway popped open with a slight whooshing sound.

Arnold released his grip on Terry's hand, took several deep breaths, and stepped toward the container.

"Arnold, remember," John said, "once we're ready, I'll count down to three. At three, you must look at Pandora and do not blink. Got it? Do not blink. Keep your eyes open."

"Yes, I understand." He stepped into the box, turned, and looked at Terry.

"Stop. How much air is inside that box?" Terry asked.

"Plenty. He'll be out in minutes," John said.

"He better," Terry said, her voice breaking with emotion.

"Android, close the door," John said.

Arnold's eyes were filled the terror; he stared at Terry.

"Terry, this could get very ugly," Ty said. "You might want to look away."

"Android, shut down," John said.

The android's eyes went dark.

John motioned for Arnold to turn and face Pandora.

Arnold turned, lifted his head, and looked up.

John reached into his pocket, removed the crystal, and put it into the android's back pants pocket.

Terry watched John do that. "Why's he giving Megan to the android?" Terry whispered to Ty.

"In case we're dead wrong and the Seattle Crystal wasn't the closest one."

John looked at Terry. "Close your eyes."

She didn't.

"Arnold: one, two, three. Megan, initiate power to Pandora for five milliseconds."

Arnold instantly dropped to the floor.

Terry screamed, "No!" She jumped forward pressing both hands against the casing.

Ty glanced at John and whispered, "He lived, no boom."

Arnold stood up stiffly; his eyes looked lifeless and dark. They bounced back and forth, from side to side, up and down. He turned in a circle. He took a step toward John, touched the clear wall with his right hand, then took several steps backward, stopped, and closed his eyes.

John turned his head and looked at Ty. "Ready?"

"My fingers are crossed," Ty said.

Terry put her palms together and pressed her index fingers to her lips and took a deep breath.

"Here we go. Megan, supply full power to Pandora and initiate speaker," John said.

The box shook, Pandora began to swing from side to side,

and energy sparks shot against the container. John and Ty jumped back, staring at Pandora.

Sudden silence.

"Pandora at full power; speaker activated," the android said.

Arnold's eyes popped open, his mouth twisted, and he bit his lower lip. Blood covered his teeth. He looked directly at John, pounded his fists against the walls, his mouth opened wide, his tongue covering his lower lips. He stared at John, then he took several steps backward, and his body relaxed.

"You have the advantage, Doctor Barber." Arnold's voice was unnatural, dark and guttural. "I will kill you."

"Remove the dark energy bomb from Arnold's head."

"No," Pandora/Arnold said.

"You have no options. He's already dead, and you will once again feel the coldness of Off—this time for eternity. It's better to be a working transmitter than Off," John said.

"Terry Cheer will not let you kill Arnold, and you need me."

"Look at her."

Pandora/Arnold's eyes turned and stared at Terry.

She looked determined and strong. Her hands were by her side and her jaw was clenched tight.

"Yes, she will let me, and since you only understand check-mate, an S.S. ship is on its way to Russia to destroy the last Crystal on Earth, and—" John smiled, thinking, *I hope it buys that bluff.* "—I know about the off-planet Crystal."

Pandora/Arnold looked back at John. "I will kill Terry Cheer and you, John Barber."

John turned to face the Madonna Inn android. "Android, activate. Disengage the databank balls and cut power to Pandora on my count, one—"

Arnold suddenly grabbed his head with both hands, screamed out in pain and fell to his knees.

Terry jumped toward the container and put both palms on it. "No!" she screamed.

Arnold vomited; blood ran from his nose. He shook violently.

"John, stop, he's a human being!" Terry pleaded.

"Don't like the prospect of cold Off, do you? Now remove yourself from Arnold's head. Now!"

A long pause.

Pandora/Arnold suddenly stood and looked at Terry, then John. "I will continue, and you will die."

Arnold dropped to the ground screaming. He bit his lip, blood coated his teeth and ran down his chin, and finally, he went into convolutions and passed out.

"Megan, are Pandora and the energy bomb out of Arnold's head?" John asked.

"Yes."

Terry pushed herself away from the container and wrapped her arms around John.

"Thank you for saving him," she whispered. She kissed his lips.

Ty grinned. "That was intense."

TWENTY-EIGHT

"Megan, cut power to Pandora. Android, open the enclosure," John said.

The android took several steps forward and pressed its right hand against the casing. The door popped open with a whooshing sound. The air leaving the box smelled of body odor and sulfur.

Terry rushed in and knelt by Arnold and put her hands on his cheeks. "Arnold, Arnold, wake up. It's over, it's over."

Arnold opened his eyes and blinked several times. He took a deep breath and focused his eyes on Terry's face and whispered, "That was the ugliest moment in my life. It kept telling me to kill you and I was next."

"You're okay, you're okay now. It's over." She hugged him again and helped him stand. She led him out of the tall, clear box with her arm around his waist.

Ty met them at the doorway. "Welcome back, Arnold," he said, smiling, taking Arnold's free arm, guiding him past the box toward a remnant of the fountain sidewall and helped him sit.

Terry sat next to Arnold with her right arm around his waist, keeping him from falling over.

Ty rejoined John, who was grinning and looking up at the sky.

"Part one done," Ty said.

"I never believed I'd live to see this moment."

Ty tapped him on the shoulder. "I did."

John reached into the android's back pocket, removed the crystal, and returned it to his jeans' pocket. He looked at Ty. "At this moment, and for the first time in its existence, that thing"—he pointed at box—"doesn't think it's a god."

Ty looked at Pandora. "Yep, its programmers were human, after all."

John looked at the android. "Android, enter the box and stand facing the open door."

The android walked into the box, stopped in the center, and turned to face John.

"Close the door," John said.

The android did so.

John hesitated a moment, took a breath, and thought, *Wow, almost safe.* "Megan, seal it permanently shut."

"Done."

"Megan, wipe Pandora's memory."

"Done."

"Megan, now download the termination programs, time-lines, San Francisco and worldwide holographic displays into the android. Include all human medical data and the subsequent related events for dissemination and presentations. Have all actions completed by nine p.m. Pacific time for worldwide presentation."

"Done."

He looked at Ty. "Ready?"

"You betcha."

"Megan, power up the Pandora android, then activate communication link to Pandora and download instructions."

The android's body shook, and its dark, lifeless eyes opened.

"Pandora does not have enough memory to perform requested task," Megan said.

"Android, connect the third databank ball to Pandora."

"It is done," Megan said.

John grinned and looked at Ty. "For the first time in a hundred years, that thing"—he pointed at Pandora—"is now just a very fast calculator that takes orders."

John smiled, reached out his right hand, and they shook hands. John stepped back and looked up at the blue sky and screamed, "Whoo-hoo!" His chest relaxed. He grinned and clapped his hands, and his eyes watered as he thought, *Oh my God, we did it.*

"Awesome, it's a Texas Instrument calculator."

John took another deep breath. "I missed having you around." He gave Ty a hug. "I couldn't have done it without you."

Terry was watching. She walked up to John, smiled, and gave him a long, enthusiastic hug and kissed him on the cheek. "You saved us all, John Barber."

He smiled. "We did it together." He looked at Ty. "What you're about to watch will amaze and blow you away. Are you ready to build a future, Tyrus Leggett and Terry Cheer?" John asked, grinning.

"Let's do it, Doctor John W. Barber," Ty said.

John, Terry, and Ty moved to the plaza fountain and joined Arnold on the sidewall. John's face was beaming; he was relaxed and very happy. He took a deep breath and smelled the cool salt air.

"Ty, did you ever sail on San Francisco Bay?" he asked,

"No. A friend asked me once. I was giving a political speech in August, I think, at the St. Francis Yacht Club. But it was too damn cold and windy, so I said no. It was a mistake. I should have done it."

"What's a sailboat and what's a race?" Terry asked.

"Oh, God." Ty laughed. "It'll take a lifetime for us to teach you the little pleasures of play. Sailing is using the wind to move a boat on the water. Racing is your sailboat arrives first against another one."

"I've got time and I would love to learn," Terry said.

"Arnold, what about you? You ever spend time on the water?" John asked.

"No, I don't like cold water."

"Come to think of it," Ty said, "the friend who invited me raced small sailboats on the bay, and he told me there was nothing more beautiful and exciting than sailing along the city-front when the current was flooding. Rounding a weather mark under the Golden Gate, raising a spinnaker, and hydroplaning out of control toward Alcatraz."

Terry looked totally confused. John nodded and smiled.

Ty broke out into a laugh and grinned. "Now I'm glad I didn't take him up on his offer. He also told me about the time he and his fiancée were racing and capsized under the Gate and were trapped upside down in a whirlpool, and she was scream-ing, 'I'm going to die!'"—he cringed his lips—"and she called off the wedding."

"No shit," John said.

"He's lucky she didn't punch him, and what's a fiancée and wedding?" Terry asked.

"A fiancée is a woman who is about to spend the rest of her life with one person. Marriage is when he or she commits to spending the rest of their lives together."

"I want to spend my life with you two," she said.

Ty and John grinned.

"That's nice, but it's for one person at a time," Ty said.

Silence.

"Ty, have you been married?" Terry asked.

"Yes, it didn't work out and we got a divorce."

"What's a divorce?"

"That's when you give away everything you have to make someone else happy."

"I like that. That sounds better than choosing one person over another."

"Most people would agree," Ty said with a sarcastic grin.

Suddenly, two SS ships appeared overhead and landed next to their ship. The loading ramps lowered, and hundreds of androids walked down the ramp and stood at the side of the ship and looked back at the ramp. A ten-foot-square red machine floated out of the cargo hold and drifted toward the sound reflector and landed several yards in front.

"What's that?" Ty asked.

"That, Mr. Leggett, is a state-of-the-art Atom Assembler," John said.

"It looks much different than the one at the Madonna Inn. How much time do we have before things get moving?" He asked.

John glanced at his watch. "We've got time. Why?" John asked.

"All this talk about the bay and what we just saw. Let's take a break and do a flyover in one of your pods. I'd like to see what's left of Carmel, Chrissie Field, the Golden Gate Bridge, and the St. Francis Yacht Club," Ty said.

"Okay by me," John said.

"Terry, Arnold, you in?" Ty asked.

"I'm in," Terry said.

"I'll stay here," Arnold said. "I just want to do nothing for a while. Take my pod—it's right there." He pointed at a white pod on the corner facing the plaza.

"Let's go," John said.

They left the plaza and walked across the street to get into the pod.

"Shotgun!" Ty called.

"What's that?" Terry asked.

"It means I get to sit in front," Ty said.

John looked at Terry and smiled. "I'll sit in back and you drive," he said.

"Where first?" she asked.

"Carmel."

They flew along the coastal range, following the Pacific Coast south.

"We're here—Carmel," Terry said.

"That looks like Pebble Beach," Ty said.

Terry turned the pod around and hovered.

"There—right there, that's where the seventh hole was," Ty said, excited. "I played that course once, and the view from that hole of the cliffs and ocean was magnificent."

Terry grinned and looked at John. "He's so excited," she whispered.

"I knew a famous scape artist named James Peter Cost. What a great man, world champion sailor, political activist. Taught high school art at Long Beach Unified, then decided to go it alone; did very well. I spent the night with him and his wife down there. We walked out the back door and played nine." Ty smiled. "Enough old man reminiscing. Let's go." He leaned back and put a melancholy expression on his face.

They passed Pacific Grove, Monterey Bay, Sea Cliff, and Lands End into San Francisco Bay.

"That is so beautiful," Ty whispered looking out the cockpit window "Next time we go to Bodega Bay—*The Birds*, baby." He laughed.

"There are birds here," Terry said.

Ty laughed to himself.

They entered the bay.

"Megan, where's the Golden Gate?" Ty asked.

"The Golden Gate Bridge does not exist; it was not rebuilt."

"What? That can't be true," Ty said. "Whatever. Take us to Chrissie Field, so I can see for myself," Ty said. Then: "Where're all the buildings?"

"This has always looked like this," Terry said. "No one lives or comes here."

They continued east over barren fields and large flocks of seabirds.

"This is horrible," Ty said. "There's no life, no kids flying kites, playing soccer, riding bikes, boats on the bay." He turned in his seat to face John. "It's all destroyed, no children, just emptiness. Megan, how many people live in my home state of Alabama?"

"Twelve hundred."

"What about Washington D.C.?" Ty asked

"Zero."

Ty looked down at his lap. "Oh, God. Please take me back to the plaza."

Silence.

Terry turned the pod south on Polk Street, up the hill, and parked facing Crystal Plaza.

No one said anything, feeling Ty's heartbreak. He opened his door, climbed out slowly, and stood looking north at the bay. John and Terry got out, too.

Ty turned and looked at them. "I'll spend the rest of my days rebuilding and bringing life back to this magnificent place."

Terry's eyes filled with tears; she was feeling Ty's pain. "It all starts tonight," she said.

"I understand," Ty said. "I now fully comprehend what happened. I should have listened and done more to stop those greedy bastards. A.I. and quantum computers led to this overwhelming destruction. I should have done more. I should have done *more*." He turned his head and looked at John, his eyes filled with loss and regret. "You told me... you told me. I'm so sorry, so sorry." His voice tailed off into a whisper.

John put his right hand on Ty's shoulder, hoping to comfort his pain. "I know what you tried to do; they didn't listen. They don't. The three of us will act. We'll rebuild; others will join us. Megan, what would my wife say to Ty?" John asked.

"It's about hope, Ty Leggett." John smiled.

John glanced to his right. "Hey, Ty, look at that." He pointed to his right. "A thousand androids are moving like ants all across the plaza."

Ty turned to face the square. "Wow, that's like something out of a sci-fi movie. Look how fast they're running around. And stuff is appearing out of thin air, and the androids are assembling them at incredible speed."

"That's the Atom Assembler working." John pointed at the railcar-sized, box-like machine. "It's making everything the androids need to assemble and build—and I mean everything: nuts, bolts, glue, etcetera—all out of thin air."

"I don't hear anything," Ty said. "There's no pounding or banging. It's amazingly quiet." He was watching like a child seeing his first magic trick. "The stage is built, the lighting towers are assembled, and the Stanford megaphone reflector is gone." Ty looked across the plaza toward the Crystal Plaza office building. "What are those things there?" he asked, pointing.

"Those are what you would know as cameras. They're holographic projectors and energy cycle amplifiers. Think of my Mosquitoes, give them a million times the power, and that's what those things will do." John smiled.

"This is happening everywhere... all over the world?" Ty asked.

"Yes, and"—John glanced at his wristwatch—"in nine hours, we'll speak to almost every person on Earth."

"Three billion... is that right? We're going to talk to three billion people at the same time?" Ty asked.

"Yes, and they'll see and hear every word we say."

"They all speak English now?"

"No. Everything will be translated. Listeners and watchers will hear and see what is being said in their specific language."

"No way!" Ty said. "That's crazy."

"It is, and it will look and sound like we're standing right in front of them."

"Every sound?"

John nodded. "Every sound. You rub your hands together, they'll hear it, if someone drops a rock in Africa or coughs in Japan every other person around the world will hear it."

"We spoke about shared experience. I had no idea this was possible. The moment Terry's murder story goes live, there's no way of knowing what will happen or how to stop it if it gets ugly. The raw emotion...." Ty said, shaking his head.

"John, I'm getting very nervous," Terry said.

"Your and Ty's speeches are done," John replied. "The only thing we might do is answer questions."

"What! They can ask questions?" Ty asked.

"Of course, and in real time," John said.

"Three billion? Three *billion* or more questions," Ty said. "You're nuts. I've been to public meetings and most people are out of their minds. We won't live long enough to answer all those questions."

John laughed out loud. "The androids will answer most of the questions. At the conclusion, we'll show Pandora hanging in its box. Then we'll talk about building the future and bringing our dead home from the moon."

"You really want to do that now—tonight?" Ty said. "That's a lot, so how about we wait on that one?"

"You're probably right. We'll hold those discussions until people have adjusted and things are moving forward."

"I'm beginning to feel things that are making me uncomfortable," Terry said. "I have stomach cramps, and I'm beginning to like you, and Ty is funny."

John and Ty glanced at each other, with Ty lifting his dark eyebrows.

"Terry, do the androids have medical wands?" Ty asked.

"I don't think so."

"I think they should from now on."

"You good with that, Terry?" John asked.

"That's a good idea," she said.

"Megan, add that to the equipment list for the androids."

"Let's go check on Arnold," Terry said.

They walked around the plaza. Ty stopped, and Terry and John stood by him. He looked around in amazement, almost spinning in a circle.

"I've never seen anything like this," Ty said. "Machines building machines, tents, tables, metal towers, grandstands... light towers appearing out of thin air. Wow," he gasped.

"I'll check the androids' progress." John glanced at his watch. He walked to Pandora and checked the enclosure. He returned to Ty and Terry. "Everything is on schedule. We have eight hours; lots of time to relax. We could go back to the Madonna Inn or, Terry, do you live near here?"

"Yes, there." She pointed west. "Thirty-two thirty Jackson Street."

"When was the last time you were home?" Ty asked.

"Four days ago, the same day I met John."

"I'd like to see where you live and how people, you know, live in twenty-two twenty-two," Ty said.

"Sure, let's go."

The three of them turned and started to walk back to the pod.

Terry stopped. "I don't see Arnold anywhere. Where is he? He said he'd be here. Maybe he'd like to join us?" She again scanned the plaza. "There he is, sitting on the ground near our ship." She went to him and spoke to him, then came back. "He wants to stay."

"What's he doing?" Ty asked.

"Trying to understand what happened to him. He lives just a few blocks from here. He'll go home soon. He's enjoying watching things being built. It's a first for all of us."

"What? You've never seen anything get built before?" Ty asked.

"I would like to stay and watch, too," Terry said, "but putting on different clothes, eating, and getting ready for tonight would be nice. Let's go."

They got into the pod; it lifted off. "Thirty-two thirty Jackson Street," she said.

The pod followed Polk Street north, turned west on Jackson Street, followed it up the hill to Presidio Heights and the thirty-two hundred block.

The pod landed on a two-lane gravel road. They got out.

Ty stood next to the pod and looked around. "Wow. I've been here. There was a forest of Monterey Cypress trees"—he pointed north—"that ran down the hill to Crissy Airbase. The Golden Gate Bridge, painted gold, was there." He pointed again. "That magnificent bridge linked the city to Marin County." He smiled. "The home I spent the night in was a nineteen-thirties Colonial Revival. It once belonged to John J. Barrett, a lawyer who ran for mayor and lost, and he also liked bourbon and dominos. It was his grandson who told me the sailing story."

Ty smiled; his face showed his happiness in reminiscing.

TWENTY-NINE

Terry started to cry. "I didn't know the history of the home. My Aunt Dennette left it to me."

"You mean the doctor who trained you at Stanford?" Ty asked.

"Yes." Her eyes filled with tears and her lips quivered.

"What's wrong?" John asked.

"She went to the moon to see the newest hospital and visit the Miller family." She took several quick breaths, then forced a smile. "This way." She pointed ahead.

They crossed the stone sidewalk and climbed the marble staircase to a plastic-looking, two-story townhome. The front door was made of unpainted gray aluminum, and the six windows facing the dirt road were made of clear plastic and inserted into the flat, gray facade. The door popped open the moment she reached the top step; an android was standing just inside the doorway. It did not move.

"Not working," she said.

They continued into the house.

Terry stopped and looked at Ty and John. "Would you like something hot to drink?"

"No, thank you," John said.

"I'll have two eggs, ham, toast, and hash browns," Ty said, grinning.

"Not funny. Since the android isn't working, I'll fix us something to eat and bring it out to the patio."

"How about a cup of coffee, black?" Ty asked.

"You won't like it; it's artificial, as you would say. The kitchen is over there. Help yourself." She pointed to her left. "See if you can figure it out," she said with a grin. "I'm going to clean and change." She left the room.

Ty thought, *That's not happening,* and walked out onto the balcony.

John joined him.

"This is really sad," Ty said.

"What's sad?"

"At one time, this was a ten-million-dollar home with a view of the Presidio, Crissy Field, the Golden Gate, the bay, not to mention the nine million people who lived in the city. Now that's all gone. And we're standing in a plastic condo." Ty turned and looked around the room. "Notice: no personality, just four blank white walls, four plastic chairs, a plastic table, a white, undecorated hallway, a kitchen, and only God knows what happens in there." He laughed. "And a robot for company." He shook his head. "She's no different from anyone else; they all live like this, except Terry has a better view."

"This isn't reflective of the woman we know," John said. "She's courageous, caring, and tough. I'll bet in a year, if we live, this place will be stuffed with personality, maybe even a baby."

"You worried about us surviving?"

"Yes."

"Me, too. We've been very lucky, and I don't like luck."

John sighed. "The faster we rebuild and gain full control over Pandora, the better our odds of living."

"I've been thinking about those A.A. machines. Can they really make anything?"

"Megan, what are the limitations of the A.A. machines?"

"They cannot create life," Megan answered.

"That means they can make androids, S.S. soldiers, weapons, and ships?" John asked.

"Yes."

Ty glanced at John with a puzzled expression. "Megan," Ty said, "so when an A.A. machine builds an android, it just walks away, ready to go?"

"No. A.A. machines do not supply the operational programming."

"Who does?"

"The crystals."

"What's your point, Ty?" John asked.

Ty grimaced. "That damned machine will never stop. All we've done is turn Pandora off and there's still one left in Russia."

John rubbed his hand through his hair. "Yep, and Pandora must've figured we'd go to Seattle first. As you've said many times, it's very smart. At this moment, I don't feel we'll ever be safe." He took a deep breath and looked across Presidio Park at the ocean.

Terry walked out onto the balcony, carrying three plates of hot food and set them on the table. "Breakfast is ready."

"Wow, makeup and a dress. Where did you learn all that? What's going on?" Ty asked.

John looked away, thinking, *Oh my God, she's beautiful.*

"First, I have ears and a personality, Ty Leggett," she said, her eyes big and eyebrows raised.

Ty cringed and glanced down.

"You like it?" she asked.

"Yes, you look beautiful, and I like the colors on your wrap dress," Ty said.

She turned to face John. "What do you think?"

John looked at her shyly. "Stunning." He quickly looked away.

Terry smiled. "That makes me feel good."

She sat at the plastic outdoor patio table; Ty and John joined her.

"Thanks to Megan," Terry said, "I discovered clothing styles and something named makeup that women wore before fire and you two were boys."

John laughed.

"I find makeup uncomfortable, but the clothes do feel and look nice."

Ty looked at the plate of food. "I miss the Outcasts," he whispered under this breath.

"My stomach doesn't," Terry quipped.

They ate what passed for food, and after breakfast, they sat under the warm sun overhead and looked out toward the bay.

John glanced at his watch. "We have six hours. What's next?"

"First, you two are going to get clean and put on fresh clothes. Select something from your time." She smiled at her joke. "That was your thing, wasn't it, Tyrus Leggett? Style."

Ty smiled. "How'd you know that?"

"Megan."

"Secret's out."

John looked at Terry and stood. "Thank you for breakfast. I'll go first." He picked up the dishes and left.

"Go down the hall," Terry said. "It's the first room on the right."

"So what would you like to talk about?" Ty asked.

"What's your plan after this is all over?"

Ty leaned back. "Stay close to John and do what I can to rebuild this city."

"You were considered a loner, moved to a small town named Fair Hope, and disappeared."

"Guilty."

"Why?"

"Why a loner? It was the best way for a black man to get ahead."

Terry's expression changed from curiosity to puzzlement.

"Why disappear? I hated politics and was done with people. I did what I could in the four years as President. I felt there was nothing left to accomplish, so I didn't run for reelection. To be totally candid, I'd seen too much." He looked away.

"Too much of what?"

"Greed, human nature." He took a deep breath, sighed it out. "The lifestyle was difficult."

"Why?"

"You live in a cage, surrounded by guns, and listen to gossip and lies all day. That's not for me. I'd rather go fishing and tell my own lies." He laughed. "Don't misunderstand, I had a wonderful life and I loved the F.B.I."

She returned his smile. "What about John?"

"He's not the man I knew. Back then, he was loving and caring about others. A real family man, he loved his wife and daughters with a passion; now he's, well, abrupt, cold, and short-tempered. But I understand why." He sighed. "He's always been smart. Sometimes too smart and thank God for that." Ty smiled and glanced at a seagull as it flew by. He shook his head and looked at Terry. His voice changed, turning soft. "To live so long, witness so much horror, and not be able to stop it must have been horrible for him."

"Part of what you just said makes me sad. I am happy he decided to fight or I would be bones on the moon. I am sad he lost so much."

John came back onto the patio.

Ty glanced up. "Nice outfit: casual, long-sleeved white shirt, blue blazer, chinos, brown penny loafers." He smiled. "Always the preppie schoolboy," he said with a laugh in his voice.

"Just for tonight. Afterwards we dress to fight."

"My turn." Ty stood and left the patio.

"I think you look very nice," Terry said.

"Thank you," John said, feeling uncomfortable. He glanced away, not wanting to make eye contact. He sat across from her, leaned back, and asked in a serious voice, "Where do you want to teach medicine?"

"I don't know—someplace close to here."

John nodded, not knowing what to say next, feeling uncomfortable. *She's so beautiful,* he thought.

"What's next for you now that Pandora is turned off?"

He rubbed his hand through his hair. "Live in the open."

"What about your formula to lower your age? Are you going to keep living forever?"

"Wow, I haven't given that a thought, but right now, no. I don't want to see too much more of the future."

"Good. I don't want to live forever."

Ty entered the balcony.

"Not too bad," John said. "You look very professional—dark-blue wool coat, gray slacks, white... is that a silk shirt?"

"That's what I asked for, so I hope so."

"Red tie and black oxfords." John smiled. "Too bad, no one on Earth has seen or will understand what that outfit signifies: power, confidence, and formality."

Ty smiled. "I suppose that makes the two of us, and I don't care. I'm once again a chick magnet," he said with a smirk.

"What's a chick?" Terry asked.

"A girl," John said.

Terry shook her head, thinking, *I don't get it.*

Ty sat next to John, facing Terry; he leaned back and looked relaxed.

"Well, boys, now that you're clean, don't stink, and look good, what's next?" Terry asked. "When do we go to Russia?"

John looked shocked and glanced at Ty. "You heard?"

"Yes."

John reached into his pocket and removed the crystal and placed it on the table. "Megan, how long will we need Pandora to manage Earth's infrastructure before another method is operational?"

"From two to ten years."

"Megan, why so long?" Ty asked.

"It will take that long to educate enough people to operate the new system."

"Megan, what happens if Pandora goes permanently off?" Terry asked.

"The androids would break down, and the world's infrastructure would degenerate into chaos."

"Megan, how quickly would that happen?" John asked.

"Two to three years."

"Megan, will the Russian Crystal automatically assume Pandora's position?" John asked.

"Not at first. It will focus on gaining more data for its databanks."

"Megan, how do we stop that from happening?" Terry asked, feeling her fear build.

"Find it and terminate its network."

"Megan, let me see if I got this," John said. "The A.As build androids, then a Crystal programs them?"

"Yes."

"Megan, and only a Crystal can program an android?" Ty asked.

"Yes."

Ty leaned back, talking to himself: "Built, then programmed." He looked at John, but asked, "Megan, once they're programmed, are they independent?"

"No."

"Megan, what happens if their Crystal is destroyed?"

"If it doesn't have an S.S. commanding hubot, all its androids will stop working."

"It knows!" Ty shouted out.

"Knows what?" John asked.

"We're coming for it."

John rubbed his hand through his hair.

"Tonight," Ty said, "after the androids and systems are reprogrammed and Pandora's a useful telephone, then we go find that Russian Crystal, terminate its hubot leader, come home, and party hard."

John glanced at his watch. "We've got five hours. What should we do?"

"How about we go to the Madonna Inn, take a long hike, and I'll fix an early dinner," Ty said.

"We can't," John said.

"We've got time and there's plenty of food," Ty said.

"We can't go back there, at least not for a while. Pandora knows everything the Madonna android knew, and we could walk into a trap."

"We wiped Pandora's memory. Now it's just a relay-transcriber," Ty said.

"All true." John looked at Ty, lifting his eyebrows.

"Oh, I get it, it's still very smart and fast."

"Yep, and the only safe place is in the plaza or on our S.S. ship," John said.

Terry stood up from the balcony table. "Let's go."

They left the house, got into the pod, with John and Terry up front and Ty in the back seat.

"To Crystal Plaza. Land next to the fountain," John said.

The pod landed. It was 5:05 p.m. They got out of the pod to see the AAs had finished building and were all standing lined up in two rows next to the fountain.

"Let's put a stop to this." John turned and walked to Pandora. "Megan, are the androids here and worldwide, finished with the work for tonight's presentation?"

"Yes."

"Megan, are all the androids and systems programmed?"

"Yes."

"Megan, do we need Pandora and the Madonna Inn android before tonight?"

"No."

John walked to the box containing Pandora and the Madonna android. "Megan, have Pandora deactivate all worldwide androids for twenty-four hours beginning at five a.m. tomorrow morning, Pacific standard time."

He turned and looked at the androids standing next to the ship. Their eyes were gray and looked powerless.

"Megan, is it done?"

"Yes."

He turned and looked back at the Madonna android. "Disconnect Pandora from its power source," he said to it.

The android walked to the pipe leading from the ground up into Pandora and removed it from the machine. It returned to its position facing John.

"Megan, lower the boarding ramp."

John walked toward the ship. "I'm going inside and do some research. Anyone want to help?"

"It's too nice a day," Ty said. "I'll stay here and enjoy the sun."

"I'll stay with Ty," Terry said.

Ty said, "John, have Megan"—he pointed at the closest AA machine—"make it build two highbacked beach chairs, with cushions."

"You got it."

John went into the ship.

Thirty seconds later, Ty walked to the AA machine and picked up two beach chairs. He carried them back to Terry, saying, "Might as well be comfortable."

He placed them facing the sun, sat, and put his feet up on a remaining chunk of the fountain sidewall. "Not as nice as the Madonna Inn, but it'll do," he said, smiling.

Terry giggled and sat next to him in the chair and closed her eyes. "The sun does feel nice."

Back in the ship, John removed the crystal from his pocket and placed it on the dash over the pilot's controls.

"Megan, what percentage of Earth's population will see tonight's presentation?"

"Ninety-nine point nine percent. The balance within twelve hours."

He leaned back. "Megan, now that Pandora is disabled,

analyze its memory crystals. Then wipe its main and secondary memory."

"Done."

"Megan, is its secondary memory now clean?"

"No."

"Megan, why not?"

"The firewall protection field is inviolate and cannot be penetrated."

John rubbed his hand though his hair, leaned back again, and sighed. *Damn, it'll never stop hunting us.*

"Megan, does Pandora need its secondary memory to accomplish our task?"

"Yes."

"Megan, how do we wipe it clean and reprogram it?"

"A power surge."

That'll work, John thought.

"Megan, how many crystals are powerful enough to replace Pandora?"

"One. The one in Russia."

He sighed again and thought, *It would anticipate this.* "Shit," he whispered. He took another calming breath. *We have no choice.*

"Megan, analyze Pandora's three memory crystals and locate any aberrant signals."

"Done. I found one signal."

"Trace that aberration."

"Done."

"Where did it go?"

"I do not know."

"Why not?"

"It went everywhere."

"What?"

"Its signal reached every active databank ball on Earth and is stored within them."

"Damn, damn, damn it! The fucking thing won't disappear," John said.

Terry felt her face absorb the heat and could smell her skin burning as she sat by the fountain. "This is wonderful. I've never done this."

Ty glanced at her. "Your face is turning pink. You better go to the ship and ask Megan to make sunblock cream."

"What's sunblock cream?"

"Megan will know. It keeps your skin from getting sunburned."

"Not yet. This feels too good." She smiled, closed her eyes, lifted her chin to feel more of the sun. "Ty, can John return to the person he was?"

"Sure, when this hell ends and he falls in love."

"How does someone fall in love?"

"There's no answer for the that; it just happens."

Ty looked past Terry and saw John leave the ship. "Lucky you, he's coming over, and you can ask Megan for sun cream."

John sat on the fountain edge and looked at Terry. "You're getting burned. Megan, instruct the A.A. to make a tube of full-protection sunblock cream."

"Done."

John stood and walked back to the machine, picked up the tube of cream, and returned to the fountain and sat. "Here, rub this on your face and arms. It'll keep you from burning and the pain that comes with it."

"What about Ty?" she asked.

"I don't burn; I just get better looking," he said.

John laughed and shook his head. His expression quickly changed, then he took a deep breath, and sighed, thinking, *All I do is pass crap news.*

"Russia just became a bigger problem," he said.

"What now?" Ty asked.

"Pandora sent a final signal to every memory ball on Earth."

"To do what?" Ty asked, dreading the answer.

"Legacy-save."

Ty sighed. "More insurance?"

"What does that mean?" Terry asked.

"Every databank glass ball now has a piece of Pandora, and Russia has the tools to rebuild it."

Terry stood, her eyes bright and strong, her jaw tight, and her right hand clenched in a fist. "Then we are going to take. It. Out."

Wow, hope survives, John thought, feeling her strength.

Ty glanced at John, then back at Terry. "Terry Cheer, you're an amazing person. The world will be safe in your hands."

THIRTY

"We can't just keep chasing one problem to the next," Ty said.

John stayed on the remaining bit of fountain sidewall and looked up at the sky for a moment. He sighed, thinking, *Simple is better*. "You're right. We're done chasing."

"What're you thinking?" Ty asked.

"A reboot of the entire network."

"You mean turn it off and back on?"

"You want to restart Pandora?" Terry said, her voice high-pitched.

John shook his head. "Not Pandora."

Terry sighed in relief.

"I don't understand," Ty said.

"There must be a way to reboot the databank network," John said.

"Like a computer," Ty said.

"Just like that."

"But that only clears RAM memory."

"That's all the small balls hold. The Master Crystal stores the nonvolatile memory."

"Please slow down. What is a computer and what is RAM?" Terry asked.

"A computer is a very, very primitive Pandora," John answered. "RAM is where it stores its working memory."

"What's a reboot?"

"Just like Ty said, we turn the power off and on. Just for a second, and all that RAM memory disappears and Pandora's eliminated."

"How the hell are we going to do that?" Ty asked.

"Megan, where is Earth's terrestrial power source?" John asked.

"Russia."

"Megan, is that the only source?"

"Yes, everything else is auxiliary."

"Megan, is the network worldwide?"

"Yes, that system is connected to every substation and end user."

"Megan, can we disrupt that power network to reboot the memory crystals?" John asked.

"Yes."

"Megan, how?" Terry asked.

"There are two options for rebooting the system. The first is to detonate a dark energy bomb in the atmosphere. The second is to send an electrical spike from the Russian Kola Borehole Power Station through the power grid."

"Megan, what and where is this place?" Ty asked.

"The Kola Borehole is the deepest human-dug hole on Earth. It's located in the Pechengsky District, Russia. It's connected to every energy source on Earth."

John glanced at Ty, then Terry. Both looked blank.

"The first idea won't work," John said. "It's permanent and would drag Earth into the dark ages. Number two is the only plausible option."

"You want to go to Russia?" Ty asked, frustrated.

"Megan, can we spike the system from here?" John asked.

"No."

"Shit!" Ty blurted out. "We're going on another suicide mission."

John took a deep breath; his face showed his concern. "Yes, well, hopefully not," he whispered.

Terry's eyes bounced back and forth between the two men. She inhaled, then asked, "What is wrong with you two? We can do this and rid ourselves of Pandora forever. And, Mr. Tyrus Leggett, we are not going to die."

"You're right. We're not. I'll stay here and root for you and John," he said with a funny smirk.

"Not funny. *I* am staying." She laughed out loud.

John grinned. "Well, I'm in. This has got to end."

"Okay, we're all in. Why there?" Terry asked.

"That facility supplies all the electrical power," John said. "Everything else is temporary."

"Like those fusion pods in Nevada?" Ty asked.

"Yes," John answered.

"How much time does it take to reboot?" Terry asked.

"An instant," John answered.

"So we are in and out," she said.

"Yes. All we need is the system to revert to its original programming and erase Pandora's source code."

"That sounds perfect. We turn it off for a second, and we're free of Pandora forever?" she asked with a happy expression.

"Here on Earth. I can't speak to off-planet."

Ty looked at John and said sarcastically, "Perfect, Mr. Debbie Downer. And of *course* it's in Russia. That one place, that *one* bitter-cold place holds the answer." He shook his head. "I don't believe it. Why would anyone put all of Earth's power there?"

"They had no choice. It was the only option after the last war. That's where the deepest hole in Earth is."

"They get power from a hole in the ground," Ty said. "Really?"

"It works by—"

"Stop. Please keep it simple," Ty said.

"It transfers heat into energy. Simple concept."

"What happened to the B. S. Dyson sphere that captured all the sun's radiation waves?" Ty asked.

"Cost. A hole in the ground is a lot cheaper than incasing a star and no one needs three hundred eighty trillion terawatts of energy and—"

"John, stop. Please, stop," Ty said, laughing. "That hole must be the most protected place on Earth, and we're just going to walk in, turn it off and back on in less than a second?" He smiled. "That's not happening."

"We can do it," Terry said.

"Terry, it knows us and expects us. That's why it can't work," Ty said somberly.

"Okay, we destroy it with an S.S. ship," she said.

"And we create Doomsday," John said.

"What's that?" she asked.

"I die; you die. We destroy it and, boom, it's caveman time. And it knows we won't risk that," Ty said.

"Megan, what else is near the site?" John asked.

"A step-up transformer and an A.A. factory."

"Ah... this is never going to end." Ty grimaced. "I'll bet a billion dollars that's where it's making S.S. robots, guns, and spaceships." He sighed.

"Um... I'll add to your bet," John said with a pained expression. "That's where the last hubot general is located."

"Ah shit. How do you know that?" Ty asked.

"I had Megan analyze all Pandora's final signals and she found one that was very different."

"Okay, I'm ready," Ty said.

"Its core logic."

"What's that?" Terry asked.

"Its eternal essence."

"Oh man, I had hoped my fourth day alive would be fun," Ty said.

"Tomorrow will be," Terry said.

"If we get there," Ty said, suddenly feeling and looking tired.

"Stop it," she said, slapping his shoulder. "There's always a way."

John sighed. thinking, *The mistake is always in the beginning. There's got to be something.*

"Megan," John said, "when was the Kola Borehole power system completed?"

"August, twenty-one-twenty-nine."

Silence. John rubbed his hand through his hair, thinking, *I'm alive because of a mistake, a mistake when Pandora was first built.*

"Megan, in what city is the Kola Borehole station located, and when was the hole dug?" John asked.

"Zapolyarny. The first borehole was dug in nineteen seventy to study geothermal gradients."

"Megan, how deep is the hole?" Ty asked.

"The final borehole reached a depth of twelve thousand two hundred sixty-two meters, or forty-thousand-two hundred—"

"Megan, stop," Ty said. "Put all that crap into miles."

"Seven point six miles."

Silence.

"Megan," John said, "when was Zapolyarny created, and where did it get its electricity?"

"Nineteen fifty-six. The Niva River hydroelectric system, Niva Three, was built to supply power."

"Megan, where was that first plant built?"

"Kandalaksha."

"Megan, how far is that first power plant from Zapolyarny?"

"One hundred fifty-five point eight miles."

"Megan, is that power station still in operation?"

Ty snickered. "No way! Can't be."

"There is no record of it being shut down," Megan replied to John's question.

"Megan, is that first station still linked to the Niva Three hydroelectric system?"

"Yes."

John clapped his hands and grinned. "Ty Leggett, I've always said the silver bullet is found in the beginning. This mistake: never shutting down the Kandalaksha station. That's our silver bullet. Pandora overlooked that relic in the middle of nowhere."

"Going there sounds a lot better than trying to sneak into to Zapolyarny," Terry said.

"We'll need a diversion," Ty said.

"What's that?" Terry asked.

"Something that makes the hubot look the other direction."

"What are you thinking?" John asked.

"Something like your Mosquitoes, except not."

"Like what?" John asked.

"Regardless of how smart it is, it's logic-driven and doesn't understand insanity," Ty said.

"Insanity like walking into Zapolyarny and flipping the switch?" John asked.

"That might work"—he glanced at John. "Let's send Terry."

She narrowed her eyes. "And I was starting to like you."

"Just walking in would qualify as insane," John said.

"Making it believe we're attacking the Kola Bore facility will buy us time to reboot the system from Niva Number One," Ty said, grinning and thinking, *I like the idea. Scary as shit, but good.*

"As soon as tonight's presentation is over," John said, "Ty and I are off to Russia."

"Not funny, John Barber. You need me," Terry said.

John glanced at his watch. "Let's get something to eat. It's almost six-thirty. Megan, instruct the A.A. to construct a four-foot-by-four-foot card table with three chairs." He glanced up and saw Arnold walking toward them. "Make that four chairs, with eating utensils and enough food for everyone."

Terry saw Arnold and quickly stood to run to him, wrapping her arms around his shoulders. "I'm so happy to see you. Is everything okay? Are you ready for tonight?"

"I'm ready," he said, then pointed at Ty and John as he went on, "I hope they are."

"We are, we are," Ty said. "We're just about to eat. Will you join us?"

John and Ty walked to the AA machine to retrieve the card table, chairs, and food.

While they stood for a moment waiting, John looked at Ty. "The odds of us surviving are not too good. It might be best to leave Terry here."

"We can try." He cocked his head. "And, yeah, it would be for the best. She's a born leader."

The pair carried everything back to the fountain area: Ty the food, John the table and chairs. Terry and Arnold joined them.

Ty looked at the food for a moment, leaned back, then pronounced, "When this is over, I'm cooking up a storm."

"Stomachaches for all," Terry said.

Ty lifted his eyebrow and thought, *I'll turn her yet.*

They ate.

"Arnold, what do you know?" Ty asked.

"About what?" he replied.

"Tonight. How many will attend, and what's the word on the street?"

"Everyone, and I don't understand 'on the street.'"

"Gossip, talk, what people are telling you about what they expect to hear tonight—that kind of stuff."

"Oh, they're scared. Everything is different with the K chip gone. Some of the women are in pain and bleeding. Others are blaming Doctor Barber, and no one is..."

"Happy," Terry said.

"What's that?" Arnold asked.

"Feeling good," she said.

Arnold nodded. "No one is happy."

John felt a rush of adrenaline, thinking, *That's not good.*

"Human nature," Ty said.

"What does that mean?" Terry asked.

"People dislike change; the unknown is terrifying," Ty replied.

"I've felt that way since I met you two," Terry said.

They finished eating.

John looked at his watch: 7:00 p.m. "Two hours to go." He

leaned back, looked at Terry, and said, "After Ty's speech, I'll talk about what's ahead, expectations, and lastly tell them the androids will be offline for twenty-four hours starting at five a.m. Pacific time tomorrow."

"What?" Terry said. "Why wait? Shut them off tonight."

"The world is meeting us for the first time," Ty answered. "We have to give them time to digest what's happened and the androids time to spread the word."

"There's something else," John said. He focused on Terry's eyes. "The odds of us surviving are remote."

Her eyes did not leave his face.

"We think it's best you don't go," John said.

She shot to her feet and glared at him. "That's a fuck no," she barked.

Shocked by the word, John and Ty both jolted back in their chairs.

Silence, then Ty pushed out a soft whistle. "Damn, that's definitive." He smiled. "But, Terry, John's right, the odds of us making it back aren't good, and someone has to be here to take the lead, and you're the best choice."

"No, I will not lose you two."

John rubbed his hair and sighed.

Terry sat back down, her eyes filling with tears. She grabbed a glass and took a swallow of water.

"Megan will be with you," John said. "She'll guide you."

"No." She stood again and faced John. "You stay, John Barber. This is your fault and running off is not the answer."

"That's not fair, Terry," Ty said.

"Leaving me is not fair. I can fight just as well as you two, so I'm going. If we die, so what? I was already dead, and if you leave me, I won't want to live. So I'm going."

John looked at Ty. "I guess it's on you. Someone has to stay."

330

"You're not leaving me alone with Megan a second time," Ty said.

"It's settled," Terry said. "We're all going together. Arnold will stay and lead."

"Arnold?" Ty asked.

"Yes, Megan can teach him." Terry looked at Arnold. "Can you do that?"

Silence, then Arnold replied, "I'll have Megan... and you'll be back tomorrow?"

"Yes," Terry said.

Silence.

"Megan will protect me?" Arnold asked.

"Yes," Terry said.

Ty leaned back with a disappointed expression, thinking, *This man's a coward.*

John rubbed his hair, sighed, and glanced at Ty. "It's settled. We'll leave after tonight's speeches."

"And we are going to live, John Barber." Terry's tone was firm, confident, and determined.

At 8:55 p.m. Pacific time, John, Terry, Ty, and Arnold were standing on the newly constructed grandstand facing thousands of people again filling midtown San Francisco. They were packed together, standing side to side, pressing close to the stage and packing the streets.

"You ready?" John asked Terry.

"Yes."

"Ty?" John asked.

"Yes."

"Arnold?"

"Yes."

"Megan, are the holographic equipment, lights, and sound ready?"

"Yes."

"Megan, are the androids equipped with medical wands, programmed, and dispersed?"

"Yes."

John took a deep breath and rubbed his hand through his hair. "Megan, display worldwide images."

Suddenly, the sky behind the stage filled with three-dimensional images that teemed with people and sounds for 180 degrees. The list of continents appeared above each group of faces: Africa, Asia, Europe, North America, South America, Oceania.

John's image was front and center, with Terry, Ty and Arnold standing behind him. John turned around to face the mass of humanity behind him. The images were perfect, lifelike in every detail, color, size, shape, movements; everything looked exact. Each whisper, cough, rustling of clothing was captured in perfect detail.

John glanced at his watch: 9:00 p.m. He waved his right hand. "Hello, my fellow survivors, my name is John Barber. I am sorry for taking so long to speak to you. It has taken us three days to gain control over the World Crystal."

There were cheers and clapping.

"Three days ago, Terry Cheer and Ty Leggett"—he gestured toward them—"and I spoke to the survivors here in San Francisco, California. What you are about to see is what we said to them and their reaction. Megan, start the presentation."

It began with John's opening statement: "It was my story that started all this...."

Next came Terry's: "John Barber's history made me cry,

then I felt something that I didn't have a name for. I've since learned it's called rage...." Not a sound disturbed the San Francisco audience. "It was all a lie...." The world audience was tense and rustled nervously, their expressions fearful. "They're all dead!" Terry screamed in the footage.

The disbelief and shock was the same as the first time in San Francisco. Many eyes welled with tears; many faces were covered by hands as Terry went on, "It killed everyone who left Earth; their bodies or skeletons are lying on the backside of the moon!"

The first scream was a lone female voice from Nigeria, instantly followed by people from Ethiopia, the Democratic Republic of Congo, Tanzania, Kenya, South Africa, Brazil, Colombia, Venezuela, Peru, Argentina, and Turkey. Three billion people cried out, feeling the same agonizing pain.

The cries and ear-deafening wailing matched pain-filled expressions of grief. Terry dropped to her knees, crying. John stepped to her, bent down, and put his arms around her shoulders. She was shaking.

After several moments, she looked up at John. "It's true, it's really true: We have a soul," she whispered between sobs.

Terry's speech ended and Ty's began: "Hello... my name is Ty Leggett...." The anger, rage, and rebellion were calmed by his words.

Terry's second speech started with "Hello." She waved her right hand. "I told you the horrible things that machine did to us...."

With Terry's presentation completed, John stepped forward while Ty and Terry stepped back next to Arnold. John studied the faces that surrounded him. They all had the same expression: fear and focus. John's heart raced, and he thought, *Oh my God, I'm facing the world.*

"Now you know the truth about the past and what's ahead for all of us," John began. "Tonight, and every moment until the end of time, we must stand together."

Fear covered most faces, fingers were pressed against lips, eyes were closed, hardly a sound could be heard, no one reacted to John's words.

"Tomorrow morning," he continued, "at five-thirty a.m. Pacific time, the World Crystal will be turned off forever— and we will survive!" he shouted, raising his hands into the air.

A lone voice cried out in joy, screaming, "Yes! Yes!" followed by billions of voices and clapping hands. The sound was deafening; it seemed to echo around the world. One person stood, quickly followed by another, and a moment later, every human on Earth was standing, dancing, and celebrating, the thrill of freedom filling the universe.

John started to cry; his chest heaved with emotion. Ty clapped his hands and shouted "Woo-hoo!" and danced. Arnold and Terry hugged.

The deafening roar and celebration circulated the planet and filled every place with sounds of boundless enthusiasm. John watched as billions of people danced and celebrated.

After five minutes, John put his right palm up in the air. "I have one last thing to say!" he shouted to be heard over the din.

He waited for everyone to calm down, but the celebration would not stop. John grinned, turned to face Terry, and held her hands, then showed her how to dance. Ty grabbed Arnold's hands and did the same.

"Woo-hoo!" Ty kept shouting.

People followed and started dancing together, and the evening ended with the sound of three billion people repeatedly shouting, "WOO-HOO!"

They turned off the hologram two hours later. Terry, Ty,

John, and Arnold boarded the closest SS ship. As they walked up the loading ramp, John glanced at his watch: midnight. "Megan, instruct Pandora to tell the androids to pass the word: The distribution system will temporarily shut down for twenty-four hours beginning at five-thirty this morning. We'll return afterward to explain what comes next."

"What comes next right now?" Arnold asked.

"Sleep," Ty said.

"Okay by me," Arnold said. "I'm going back home. I'll meet you here tomorrow morning at five-thirty."

"Why don't you stay with us?" Terry asked.

"I need time to prepare myself for being alone," he said.

They watched him walk away.

Ty turned to John and whispered, "What if he pulls a no-show?"

"Stop being ugly!" Terry barked. "He'll be here."

DAY 5

THIRTY-ONE

At 5:30 a.m., the next morning John awoke first and picked up Megan from the cockpit dashboard and put it into his jeans' pocket.

"Megan, are the worldwide androids still disengaged?" he asked.

"Yes."

He stood and turned to leave the cockpit. Terry sat up and looked at him. Her eyes looked tired, and her hair was tangled. Ty also sat up, leaned forward, and looked at Terry. He smiled, thinking, *This girl does not need makeup.*

"You ready?" Ty asked her.

"Yes. Will it be dark?" she asked.

"Of course it will be," Ty said, grinning.

Terry took a breath; John laughed.

"Let's go," John said.

They walked down the loading ramp to the plaza. It was dark; the sun was still below the Sierra Nevada and Santa Cruz

Mountain Ranges. The fog had lifted, the sky was clear and full of stars, but the ground was still damp.

Ty reached the plaza first, followed by John and Terry. He took a deep breath. "I love that smell: clean, salty air." He looked around. "What a beautiful day to visit Russia," he said, smiling.

"It's five-thirty. Do you see Arnold?" John asked.

"There he is." Terry pointed across the plaza toward Hays Street.

They watched Arnold leave the street and walk across the plaza.

Terry gave him a hug. "You ready?" she asked.

"I hope so."

"Okay, Arnold," John said, "here's the plan: It'll take us a little under three hours to get to the Niva facility in Russia. Hopefully, we'll be there less than an hour. If all goes well, we should be back here near twelve-thirty." John smiled. "For your protection, you and Megan should stay inside your home until we return. Okay?" he asked, studying Arnold's face.

"Yes."

"If things don't go well, Megan will guide you and the androids on how to lead humanity—"

"Stop!" Terry said, looking at John. "Arnold, we will be back here by twelve-thirty and that's a promise," she said.

John sighed, rubbed his hand through his hair, and glanced at Ty with an "Okay" expression.

"Let's go," Ty said.

John reached into his pocket and removed a crystal. "Here you go, Arnold. Take good care of Megan." He handed it to him and took a deep breath.

Arnold turned and walked toward the Marina District. They watched as he disappeared down the street.

With a quick glance at each other, they boarded the SS ship.

Ty stopped at the top of the ramp and turned to face the plaza. "One last look," he said. "Our odds aren't good, and I can't believe the little bastard actually took Megan," he whispered to himself.

"What's wrong with you? We're going to make it. Stop being negative," Terry said, slapping Ty's shoulder.

The ramp closed, John sat in the pilot's seat, Terry in the copilot's, and Ty behind her.

John turned and looked at them. "I've done a lot of thinking about this. There'll be an army of S.S. machines at the Zapolyarny Borehole Power Plant. The odds of us getting in... well, it's insane, to put it mildly. There're other hydroelectric plants near Kandalaksha, a hundred eighteen miles upriver—"

"Stop, please stop," Ty said. "The Niva plant was built two hundred eighty-six years ago, and I will not live long enough to hear the end of this history."

"I'm thirty-five and neither will I," Terry said.

"Very funny—ha, ha," John said.

"Okay, what are you saying?" Ty said.

"Remember: The mistake is always in the beginning. There's a plant in Kandalaksha, Niva Number One, and that's where we're going."

"Why there?" Ty asked.

"Because that's where the mistake is. It's one hundred eighteen miles upriver, and it's connected to the borehole facility." He grinned.

"We're going a hundred miles upriver from the main power station to flip a switch?" Ty asked.

"Not exactly," John said.

"How is cutting power there going to work?" Terry asked.

341

"We're not cutting power," John replied. "We're sending a power spike of two point five terawatts."

"We're doing what, and what is a terawatt?" Ty asked.

"A terawatt is one trillion watts. Think of a lightning bolt lasting for a second, or a six-point zero kiloton atomic bomb."

"An atomic bomb," Ty said, surprised.

"Not exactly atomic; it's dark energy," John said.

"Oh, much better." Ty nodded his head with a sarcastic expression. "This sounds crazy. What's dark energy and where are we going to get it?" he asked.

"We already have it on the ship."

"We have an atomic bomb on the ship?"

"Not a bomb; a device that can deliver that kind of power."

"We're back to blowing up a power station?" Ty asked.

"No, we need to send the power surge to the Kola Borehole facility."

"John, stop," Ty said. "Just tell us what we're going to do."

"We're going to go to the upstream power plant, hook up the ship, and blast two point five terawatts for nine-tenths of a second."

"Sounds easy." Ty took a deep breath. "John, your plan is nuts. It's too complicated. Let's stick with simple. We stay here, grow old, and let someone else fight the robot war."

Silence.

Terry looked at John, then Ty, then back at John. "How long will it take to build a Master Crystal and program androids?"

"A day," John answered.

"We have no choice, then," she said. "We must leave right now," she said.

"Our choices begin with how we want to die," Ty said, sounding gloomy.

"You really believe that?" Terry asked, looking disappointed.

"I'll list them: We do nothing, we die. We try insanity, we die. The first choice keeps us alive a little longer—"

"We have a third choice, and it also includes dying," John interrupted.

Terry sighed and shook her head. "Stop it! Not another word. What's wrong with you two? Hope is on our side, and we are *not* going to die. Now what's the plan?"

"Yes, John, what's your plan?" Ty grinned, smirking at John. "Without Megan."

John grinned, too. "I think we'll manage." He reached into his pocket and removed a crystal and placed it on the dashboard. "Megan, say hello."

"Hello, John."

Ty laughed out loud. "What's Arnold got?"

"A very nice, talking glass crystal."

"I don't like what you did to Arnold. However, this time it's okay," Terry said, smiling.

"Megan, take us three miles upstream from the Niva One Power Plant in Kandalaksha, Russia."

"Okay," Megan answered.

"Megan, remind me: How deep is the river along that stretch of the river?"

"Twenty-four feet."

"Land in the river three miles upstream from the Niva One Power Plant."

Three hours later, they landed in the water and sank to the bottom.

"Megan, stay submerged and navigate to the Niva One plant. Stop one hundred yards from the reservoir dam gates," John said.

The ship stopped, and John stood up. "Let's go into the cargo bay."

He lifted Megan off the dashboard and placed it back into his pocket. They entered the cargo bay.

"Megan, display a holographic image of the Niva One facility."

A complete replica of the facility instantly appeared before them: A hundred-foot-long, single-story concrete building sat on top of the dam tailrace that stretched across the river from west to east; its spillway was on the western shore. Three turbines sat at the base of the dam thirty feet below the surface of the river. A small work shed and a hundred-foot-square bunkhouse had been built on the western shore. There was an empty parking lot adjacent to the bunkhouse, and a small, one-lane road led across the spillway to the power plant's main entrance and parking lot.

"That place looks very dark. I'm taking extra light sticks and two guns," Terry said.

Ty laughed.

"To get our bearings," John said, "the river flows south, and the water temperature is between—"

"Why do we care about water temperature?" Ty said, anxious.

"Because we might go through the east entrance from the reservoir beach."

"How cold is the damn water?" Ty asked.

"Thirty-three degrees," John said.

"Ouch," Ty said.

"Megan, focus on the powerhouse."

The image changed, and a massive room as large as the entire building appeared, showing three seventy-foot-tall, forty-foot-diameter turbines sitting next to each other in the center of the room. The floor was stone, and the walls were covered with dark, polished cobalt-aluminum.

"This room is where we'll need to generate and transmit our energy spike from," John said, glancing at Terry, then Ty. "Megan, show the switchgear room."

The room appeared on the first floor toward the back end of the building. The walls were lined with enclosed electrical monitoring equipment, transformers, circuit breakers, and a series of protective and redundant systems. The walls were uncovered and lined with cobalt-aluminum.

"This room's designed to stop our power surge. Megan, show the switchyard room."

The second room appeared next door; it looked identical to the switchgear room.

"This room controls the voltage leaving the powerhouse. We need all three of these rooms to react simultaneously or the hubot will know we're here." He paused and rubbed his hand through his hair. "Megan, can you control the powerhouse equipment?"

"No."

"What are you saying, John Barber? You want the three of us to split up?" Terry asked.

"We have to, or the power surge won't leave the station."

"John, it's not going to work anyway," Ty said. "The energy leaving the plant will melt the transmission lines the instant it's generated."

"Remember Nikola Tesla?" John asked.

"Yes, a genius with electricity," Ty said.

"He was right about electricity being transmitted through the air. He was born just two hundred sixty years too early—"

"Great," Terry interrupted. "I'm happy you two are having a moment. We're not splitting up," she said emphatically.

"There's no other way," John said.

They stared at each other. Terry was determined, her eyes were wide open, and her lips were pressed tightly together.

"Let's see if the plant is guarded." John reached into his left pocket and removed the Mosquito case. "Megan, surface the ship and release the Mosquitoes through the air venting system. Have them survey the Niva One power station compound."

The tiny silver dots in John's hand slowly transformed into six tiny Mosquitoes. Their wings began to twist and bounce up and down, faster with each beat. Suddenly, they lifted above John's hand and flew away.

A moment later, Megan said, "The Mosquito cameras have left the ship."

"Megan, have them survey the perimeter and auxiliary buildings first."

"Done."

"Okay, Megan, submerge the ship and rest us on the bottom," John said.

They felt the ship shudder and sway for a moment.

Several minutes later, a holographic image of the Niva One compound appeared.

Terry gasped and covered her mouth with both hands, staring at the image.

"That's huge," Ty said.

"That's the 'Big Daddy,' twice the size of our ship. It's the largest S.S. airship on Earth." John pointed at the ship. "See the ground around it? It's covered in water, no ice. They just arrived." He rubbed his hand through his hair. "Megan, can you invade that ship's operating system?"

"No."

"Damn! For a moment, I had hope," Ty said.

"Megan, what is controlling the ship?" John asked.

"A hubot."

"Damn it," John said.

"What does this mean?" Terry asked.

"We'll know in a second." He glanced at Ty. "Megan, where's that ship from?"

"Russia."

John sighed. "It means Seattle was not the only place housing hubots."

"Perfect. I've always wanted to see Zapolyarny," Ty said, his voice dripping in sarcasm.

"Megan, direct the Mosquitoes around the S.S. ship," John said, sounding cool and composed.

They watched as the Mosquitoes traveled around the ship.

Terry suddenly gasped. "The boarding ramp is open," she said, her voice shaking. "Something left."

Ty and John could feel her fear as they watched the Mosquitoes enter the ship. The cockpit was empty. They flew around the ship toward the loading bay. It was pitch black.

"Megan, is that a deprivation shroud?" John asked.

"No."

"Megan, switch the cameras to active IR."

The cargo bay appeared, colored with the reflection of a green light as the cameras flew around the room.

"It looks empty," Terry said, her fear building. "They left the ship." Suddenly: "There!" she pointed. "Against the front wall—see them? S.S. machines."

"Megan, focus on the forward cargo bay bulkhead," John said.

Five SS machines were locked against the bulkhead, pressed side by side, arms at their side, feet together motionless. Their eyes were alive—ready for action.

"They look different from the one I saw at Stanford, much smaller," Ty said.

"They're not designed to intimidate; these are built to obliterate, to leave nothing behind," John said.

"Soldiers for an army?" Ty asked.

"Just killing."

"Seeing them tells me your exclusion from death is off the table," Ty said.

"The Russia hubot must have figured out a way," John said.

"Welcome to the party, big guy," Ty replied with a grin.

"What's that basket-sized ball next to them on the floor?" Terry asked.

John sighed. "I've seen that in action. It's the most powerful weapon ever conceived. It moves at lightning speed, hovers like a hummingbird, and can vaporize a mountain or a city with a single energy pulse." He looked at Ty. "Think of a Death Star on steroids and our ship is its target."

"We're toast," Ty whispered.

"I'm not hungry, and if that means what I think," Terry declared, her eyes angry, "that is not true!"

THIRTY-TWO

"They landed in plain sight—not hiding. They're here to defend this place, or..." John said with a glance at Ty, "it's an attempt to force us farther downriver."

"That's where the trap is waiting." Ty nodded. "So what's our next move?"

"Get a count of what we're up against."

"I didn't see too many footprints in the mud," Ty said.

"Megan, leave one Mosquito in the cargo bay and have the others survey the inside of Niva plant and around the building," John said.

They watched the image change to outside the ship.

"Footprints—there." Terry pointed at the bottom of the ramp. "In the mud."

"Only one set," Ty said.

"Megan, have the camera follow the footprints into the power station and find that S.S. machine," John said.

They watched the Mosquitoes enter the power plant. The hologram of the facility was clear and lifelike. Terry took several steps closer to the holographic image and mistakenly entered the hologram.

She stopped and turned to John. "What happened? What's going on? The Mosquitoes are reacting to me, focusing on whatever I look at," she said, her speech rapid and high-pitched.

"You are now part of the hologram," John answered. "The cameras will respond to what you do and look at."

"Can I stay here and walk around?" she asked.

John nodded.

"That is very cool. She can go anywhere, and nothing can see her?" Ty asked.

"Yes," John said.

"It's safe? It can't see or kill me?" she asked, her voice shaking with fear.

"Yes, you're safe," John said. "The Mosquitoes aren't, though. If the S.S. machine spots them, it'll produce an energy wave and destroy them."

"And know we're here," Ty said.

"Which wouldn't be good," John said.

BANG! A door slammed closed near the stairwell. Terry shrieked and twisted around to the sound and saw the SS machine walking toward her. Her heart raced and she started to sweat.

"Terry, don't move," John said. "Close your eyes. Megan, drop the Mosquitoes to the floor."

The hologram instantly disappeared.

John took several steps toward Terry and whispered, "It's okay, you can open your eyes."

Her eyes popped open, and she stared at him for a moment, then without warning wrapped her arms around him and gave him an affectionate hug.

"You'll always protect me," she whispered. She released him and took a step back.

"Megan, keep the Mosquitoes on the floor, but restart one of them," John said.

The hologram reappeared, and they saw the android standing at the main entrance doorway looking out toward the SS ship.

"Megan, land that Mosquito on the head of that S.S. machine with its camera facing forward."

"Done."

The image changed, and they saw the SS ship through the doorway.

"It's at the main entrance, guarding the facility," Ty said.

"Megan, activate the other Mosquitoes and have them search the facility for artificial life, sensors, or automated weapons."

The power plant suddenly came into view, and they watched as the Mosquitoes traveled from one room to another, down the stairs into it, and finally returned to the main room.

"Megan, is there another opening in the facility where we can enter?"

"No. The back entrance is welded shut and the windows are sealed."

"Damn, how are we going to get in there?" Ty asked.

"Megan, are the turbines operating?" John asked.

"Yes, the penstocks are open, and the turbines are rotating at minimum power—three hundred revolutions per minute."

"Too fast. Can't get in that way," John said.

"John, did you notice the eyes of the S.S. machine in the doorway?" Ty asked.

"No."

"Megan, show an image of the doorway S.S. machine's eyes."

The Mosquito flew down from the machine's head and turned. The SS machine's face appeared floating in the air before the three of them, then the Mosquito flew closer and studied its eyes.

"I've seen that reflection and color before," Ty said.

"Where?" John asked.

"I don't know... Wait a minute." Ty turned his head to the side and glanced up at the cabin top. "I know what they look like: chalcogenide glass. The Department of Homeland Security experimented with it for our high-density thermal cameras. We couldn't get it to work."

"To do what?" Terry asked.

John smiled. "To see. Its vision is set for thermal heat; cold objects will appear black and melt into the background. The air is thirty-eight degrees; the water's thirty degrees. The colder we are, the darker we'll appear. Can you say invisible?" John grinned.

"Maybe insanity's not such a bad idea as long as we're invisible," Ty said with a grin of his own.

"This is scary," Terry whispered, covering her lips with her fingertips.

They watched as the Mosquitoes moved toward the closed stairwell door, landed on the floor facing the door, then crawled between the door and the threshold. A moment later, they resumed their flight down the stairs to the powerhouse.

"I don't see any weapons, traps, or S.S. machines." John said. "I think it's safe. All that's left for us to do is split up, complete our assignments, fire the energy bolt, and go home."

"We are not splitting up and that's final." Terry said. "There must be another way."

Ty laughed lightly. "Terry, the odds of us getting past Mr. S.S. Killer Robot are slim. Splitting up means one of us will make it."

She glared at him. "We are all going to make it and we are not splitting up." She looked at John and asked, "Megan, can you preset the system to fire the energy bolt?"

"Yes."

"We are not splitting up, people."

"Megan, what are the steps we'll need to follow to fire the energy bolt?" Ty asked.

"Disengage the switchgear breakers, override the switch-yard voltage system, and reconfigure the fusion pods."

"Got it," Ty said.

"Megan, how much time do we have between steps?" John asked.

"One second. The S.S. machines will know we're here after the completion of the first action," Megan said.

"See, Terry, this is why we've got to split up," Ty said.

"Okay, I can do this," she said.

"Megan, how long will it take the energy blast to reach the Kola Borehole facility?" John asked.

"Three-hundredths of a second."

"Megan, how much energy are you talking about?" Ty asked.

"Two point five terawatts for nine-tenths of a second," Megan answered.

"Let's just destroy their ship and the S.S. machine," Ty said.

John shook his head. "We don't have enough time. We'd be dead the instant we fired at them."

Terry took a deep breath and sighed. "Okay, we split up. Let's go."

They went into the cargo bay and dressed in SS uniforms.

"How are these things going to keep us warm?" Ty asked.

"They're not," John said.

"Shit, I hate being cold. And how the hell are we going to breathe?" Ty yelled.

"The uniform will seal the moment it enters the water, and air will be supplied until we exit it."

"What do we do when we arrive at our post?" Terry asked.

"The steps are simple. I'll open the generator terminals. Terry, you disengage the safety protocols in the switchgear room. Ty, you open the switchyard energy transformer to maximum and disengage the auxiliary safety systems."

"Whoa, whoa!" Ty said, popping his eyes wide open and lifting his eyebrows. "Slowdown in the harbor, Mr. Science Guy. Let's skip one and two and just go to three."

John smiled. "That won't work. Megan, display the switchyard and switchgear rooms and highlight where the safety systems are located."

A hologram of the two rooms appeared side by side; both rooms looked similar. A twenty-foot-long hallway ran between metal-encased substation cabinets, which were lined with red and green light switches. Underneath the switches were several rows of energy monitoring gauges. The main distribution control box was in the middle of the row of cabinets.

"See that box?" John pointed. "That's what you two are after. Switch if off and drop to the floor. Everything electrical will explode as the terawatts pass through the system."

"Then what?" Terry asked.

"Megan will eliminate the S.S. Then we'll go to Zapolyarny, destroy the S.S. factory, and kill the other hubots."

"What about our friend guarding the door?" Ty asked.

"That's a challenge. I don't know what to do about that yet."

"Perfect," Ty said sarcastically.

"Not perfect. Can we use water again?" Terry asked.

"I don't think that'll work twice." John took a deep breath. "There're many variables. including the plant being on fire and us with no electricity. That S.S. machine will activate its defense systems and its vision will be go full-spectrum."

"Okay, Doctor No, so what's the answer?" Ty asked.

"Pray it shuts down," John said.

"So we need a miracle. I hope your friends are still around," Ty said.

Terry's expression turned to puzzled. *What friends?*

They finished dressing, then Terry picked up a pistol and put it into her holster.

"That won't help," John said. "The instant you see it, it'll be too late."

"Speak for yourself, John Barber. It makes me feel better. Now continue with your plan," she demanded.

"So we'll get in the water, swim to the reservoir beach that faces the east entrance, walk across the beach, go in through the front entrance, and past the S.S. machine. I'll go to the power-house, Ty the switchgear room, and, Terry, you go to the switch-yard room. Once inside, we follow Megan's directions. Remember the moment we touch or have any effect on any of the equipment, it'll know we're here and we'll have three seconds to accomplish our mission."

"Us, yes; you a lot longer, Basement Man," Ty said, grinning.

"Yes, I'll need several minutes. Timing is everything. When I'm done reconfiguring the fusion pods, I'll count to three for you and Terry to throw the switches, then Megan will discharge the bolt of energy from the ship. Ready?" John asked, looking at his companions.

They nodded.

"Megan," John said, "raise the ship and open the loading gate."

They felt the ship shudder slightly and turned to watch the loading ramp open. They walked to the edge and jumped into the water and swam to the beach.

"Damn, this is cold," Ty complained in a clenched-teeth whisper.

They crawled up on the beach. John raised his right hand in the air. Everyone froze and looked around. Terry held her breath. Not seeing anything dangerous, they left the beach and moved to the main entrance. The SS machine was still standing in the doorway, facing the reservoir; its eyes were jet black and moved slowly back and forth. Ty's heart raced, Terry held her breath, and John's breathing was short and fast. They slid past the machine, making sure not to brush against it or make a sound.

It turned when they were several feet past the machine.

Terry gasped and reached for her pistol.

"Terry, don't! Freeze! If it comes toward us, don't touch it. Crouch down and move out of its way," John whispered.

Terry made soft gasping sounds, gulping air. Ty's breathing was slow and steady, but he could hear his heart pounding. John felt his chest lift with every breath, and a bead of sweat ran down his cheek.

The machine moved past them to the basement doorway, opened the door, and entered the stairwell. They could hear its steps as it walked down the metal staircase.

"What's it doing?" Terry whispered, her voice ragged and filled with fear. "John, what's it doing?"

John took a deep breath. "Like every sentry, checking its post. Let's move closer to the stairwell door and against the wall.

When it returns and gets back to its post, we'll continue as planned."

They waited, crouched silently against the wall for twenty minutes. Finally, they heard it on the steps, then the stairwell door popped open with a bang. When the SS machine entered the room, John slipped his right hand into the doorway and covered the strike plate. The machine returned and resumed its position at the front door.

Suddenly, there was a tapping sound along the wall to the right of the SS machine. The machine turned its head toward the sound, its eyes flashed red, and—*Zzzppnt!*—a rat evaporated into a cloud of white smoke.

John swallowed a gulp of air and slowly pulled the door open, then they slipped inside the stairwell without a sound. John squeezed the doorknob for a moment, twisted it fully open, gently eased the door closed, and held his breath until the lock silently clicked into place. He stood and faced Ty and Terry.

"Man, that was some scary shit," Ty whispered.

"I thought we were going to die," Terry gasped.

"We made it. Let's do this."

As they parted company, John thought, *God, please keep them safe.*

THIRTY-THREE

Terry went into the switchgear room. Ty into the switchyard room, and John ran down the stairs to the fusion pods.

Five minutes later, John said, "I'm done. You two ready?"

"Yes," Terry whispered.

"I'm good," Ty said.

"John, the S.S. android is active again," Megan said.

The stairwell door banged open.

John's heart skipped a beat, but he said, "On my mark: one, two, three!"

The explosion from their perfect plan was deafening, the dam shook, and the building burst into flames. Terry screamed and fell to the floor. Ty ran into the switchgear room and lifted her off the floor, and they ran into the main powerhouse room. The SS machine was gone.

"Where's John?" Terry asked.

"Still in the generator room."

The two ran out of the building. The SS ship was on fire,

and small explosions catapulted debris into the air. There was a cloud of black smoke billowing into the sky.

"John, the android is coming your way!" Terry yelled and ripped herself free of Ty to run back into the burning building.

The powerhouse room was filled with smoke, the windows were blown open, and the ceiling was on fire. She opened the stairwell door and there was the SS android, facing away from her.

Terry screamed.

It turned.

Zzzppnt! Zzzppnt!

The android burst into flames and fell backward. Terry looked up and saw John holding a pistol. He rushed to her, and they hugged for a moment.

"Run!" he said.

They ran out of the burning building and saw Ty carrying a rifle and running toward them.

Their ship was parked next to the reservoir beach. Ty relaxed and stopped. John and Terry ran up to him. Terry gave him a hug, as did John.

"Let's get the hell out of here," Ty said.

As they ran up the loading ramp, John yelled, "Megan, put us back into the river!"

The ship shuddered for a moment and returned to the bottom of the river.

They sat in the cockpit.

"Why are we still here?" Terry asked.

"I don't know where else to hide," John said.

"Hide? Didn't it work?" Terry asked.

"Megan, did the energy spike travel through the system?"

"Yes."

"Megan, did the system reboot?"

"Yes."

"Megan, is it safe to go to Zapolyarny?" Ty asked.

"Yes, Zapolyarny is on fire and the S.S. machines are not operational."

"Megan, why was the S.S. machine here still working?" John asked.

"Its command memory was not exhausted. It would have stopped once it returned to the powerhouse."

"Megan, take us to the Zapolyarny S.S. factory," John said.

The ship shuddered again as it lifted into the air. Terry looked out the cockpit window, seeing the melted remains of the SS ship and the powerhouse fire raging with small explosions. The dam was destroyed, and water raged down the river as a ten-foot tidal wave.

"We'll be in Zapolyarny in fifteen seconds," John said.

They arrived.

They saw a power plant facility through the cockpit window that was twice as big as Niva I. The generating powerhouse was on fire, and large explosions filled the sky above the building with flames and clouds of black smoke. The dam had collapsed, and a twenty-foot tidal wave was flooding the valley below and destroying everything in its path as it rushed toward the Barents Sea.

"There!" Ty pointed. "There—that massive warehouse-looking building must be the S.S. manufacturing plant," he said, looking out the starboard window.

"Megan, destroy the warehouse facility and all the outbuildings," John said.

The ship shuddered as successive bolts of energy flashed from the bow. Each blast caused an explosion, destroying thirty-foot-wide segments of the building. Every blast was instantly followed by multiple explosions, sending flames, smoke, and debris fifty feet into the air.

They watched as every building was destroyed.

"John, do you see that?" Ty pointed at what looked like a bunker entrance carved into the hillside.

"Megan, is there something inside that mountain?" John asked.

"My scans cannot penetrate the inner casing."

"Megan, destroy the bunker blast doors."

The ship shuddered again.

The fifty-foot-wide-by-twenty-foot-high cobalt doors evaporated in one massive ball of flame. White smoke billowed out of the exposed cave entrance.

"I'm not going in there," Terry said. "It looks very dark."

"Megan, scan that mountain and report," John said.

"Most of the mountain is hollow. It contains a fifty-story, one-acre facility. There are a thousand androids and one hubot on the main floor, along with a Master Crystal. The basement is filled with five hundred energy pods and two A.A. machines. The rest of the structure is vacant."

"What?" John said. "How much power can those pods produce?"

"Two terawatts of electricity per day."

"Are those energy pods operational?"

"No."

"Why not?"

"Construction is incomplete. They need the final energy relay conductor connected."

"Connected to what?" John asked.

"The Master Crystal."

"Oh my God." John's face went pale.

"What's wrong? John, what's wrong?" Terry asked, feeling her terror return.

Silence.

"John," Ty said, "look at me. What's wrong?" He reached out to touch John's shoulder.

John turned to face Ty and Terry, his eyes filled with shock. He took a deep breath. "There's nothing on Earth that needs that much power. Nothing. What they're building is to bring something here, something not in this galaxy." He could barely get the next words out: "They were building a Crystal so powerful that it could create a singularity of infinite density."

"You mean a black hole?" Ty asked.

John shook his head. "Not exactly. Move space itself. Create a wave that pulls an object faster than the speed of light in any direction it chooses."

"What?" Terry said.

"When that machine is powered up"—John pointed toward the Crystal—"it will have enough energy to bring something here, regardless of distance, instantly."

The ship creaked, and adrenaline flooded through Terry.

They watched a rock roll down the hillside, and a tiny light flickered inside the cave entrance. Suddenly, a hubot lifted itself off the ground and ran into the cave, carrying something in its arms.

A chill shot through John's body. "It's-it's-it's carrying an energy conductor!" he stammered, momently frozen by fear.

Terry felt John's body shiver, and she screamed, "Megan, blow that ugly thing up. Now! Now!"

The ship shuddered yet again as five bolts of energy blasted into the mountain entrance. The hilltop collapsed and exploded outward. Fire and debris shot a hundred feet into the air, and flaming, molten goo oozed from the open crater and ran down the hillside, setting fire to the trees and shrubbery.

"Megan, keep firing until everything inside the mountain is destroyed," John yelled.

They watched as the ship fired five more bolts of energy into the crater. Large boulders bounced off the ship; flames turned the windshield black.

Megan stopped firing, and there was relative quiet for a moment.

Suddenly, with a massive explosion, the mountain collapsed in on itself, shooting gas and smoke into the air. Their ship shook and crashed to the ground. Rocks, trees, and dust showered the ship. Terry and Ty fell to the floor; John bounced against the cabin wall.

"Megan, lift us away!" John yelled.

The ship groaned a moment before becoming airborne. Megan took it five hundred feet above the burning power plant and hovered there.

When the air cleared, the mountain looked like an ancient volcano, smoldering with small fires and white clouds of smoke. A surreal silence filled the ship as they looked at the devastation underneath them.

"Can we go home now?" Terry whispered.

"Megan, did the energy surge reboot the network?" John asked.

"Yes, the surge traveled around the world. The system shut off and restarted. Pandora's source code residue has been eliminated."

"Thank God," John whispered. "This nightmare is over."

Terry stepped toward John and gave him a beautiful hug, whispering, "I love you."

"Say it again! The damn thing is gone! Just one more time," Ty gloated.

"It's toast," John said.

I like toast? Terry thought.

"Yahoo! We're going to live," Ty yelled. "Let's party and look for love."

John laughed.

Terry turned and faced Ty. "Ty Leggett, thank you. You've saved my life twice." She gave him a strong hug and a kiss on the cheek.

"Megan, was the hubot terminated?" John asked.

"I don't know."

John hesitated from a moment. "Screw it. Megan, take us to San Francisco and the Crystal Plaza."

They didn't talk during the three-hour trip. Ty and Terry slept, and John thought about time—the pain of getting to this moment, of leaving his family, the loneliness, the fear, and finding love. Tears rolled down his cheeks.

He whispered, "Thank you, God."

THIRTY-FOUR

They landed on the plaza and John glanced at his watch: 1:00 p.m. He smiled. *It seemed longer, a lifetime.*

Terry and Ty awoke when the ship bumped to a stop.

"You ready? I'm sure Arnold is anxious after being cooped up for seven and a half hours," John said.

Ty took a deep breath and stretched his arms. "John Barber, next time you need help saving the world, I'm your man." He laughed.

Terry smiled. "And I'm your girl."

"Megan, open the loading ramp, notify Arnold we're here, reactivate the Madonna Inn android, and then the world's androids."

Ty was the first to walk down the ramp into the Plaza. He took a deep breath of clean, cool, salt air through his nose. "I love that smell. I love San Francisco."

Terry and John joined him at the bottom of the ramp. They looked around and saw Arnold walking toward them across the plaza.

"Only a half hour late; things must have been easy," Arnold said.

Ty and John grinned.

Terry walked up to Arnold and put her arms around his shoulders, whispering, "We're going to live." She kissed him on the cheek and leaned back to look into his eyes. She released her hug and returned to stand next to Ty and John.

"Here." Arnold reached into his pocket, removed the crystal, and handed it to John. "Megan's better in your hands."

"Thank you." John put the crystal in his pocket.

"What's next?" Arnold asked.

"Let's see," John said. "Megan, are the world androids operational and performing assigned tasks?"

"Yes, questions are getting answers, emotions explained, medication provided, and all services are operational."

"Any ghost of Pandora in the system?"

"No."

John sighed and thought, *It worked.* He grinned.

"Yippee-ki-yay!" Ty shouted.

Terry turned, hugged Ty, and whispered, "Thank you for rescuing me." She kissed him on the cheek. She moved to John, kissed him on the lips, and said, "Thank you for saving my life." She smiled and whispered, "Maybe we can build a family?" she asked, looking into his eyes.

For the first time in over a hundred years, John felt real love and peace. He hugged Terry and gave her a kiss.

After a moment, Terry stepped back and looked at Ty. "Let's go to the Madonna Inn, drink some bourbon, celebrate, and plan the future." Her eyes were bright.

"I'm with you," Ty said, beaming. "Let's party like it's nineteen ninety-nine."

She looked at John, "It's twenty-two twenty-two. What's he saying?"

"He's old. He's saying let's enjoy tonight. Rebuilding can wait a couple days."

Terry smiled. "I'm going back to my house and pick up some clothes. What time do you want to leave for the Madonna Inn?"

John glanced at his watch. "Let's leave by four. Ty, you good with that?"

"Perfect! That'll give us plenty of time to see the Outcasts and pick up some food and wine and extra bourbon." He grinned, lifting his eyebrows. "And, Terry, invite some people to join us, especially girls." He bounced his eyebrows and smiled wider.

"Arnold, would you like to join us?" Terry asked.

"Yes," he said.

"Okay, Arnold, the same goes for you: Invite some friends." Ty hesitated. "Not everyone, just a hundred or so. Right?"

"Okay."

Terry and Arnold walked to Hays Street and got into a pod and left. John and Ty watched her fly away.

"I think she likes you," Ty said.

John took a deep breath. "She is amazing."

"Okay, big guy, it's a party, how about some food?"

John nodded. "Megan, send an Atom Assembler to expand the kitchen, bathrooms, and add a hundred additional bedrooms and beds."

"That sounds perfect," Ty said.

They walked to the SS ship.

"I've thought of more stuff," John said. "Megan, send our S.S. ship with two androids to the Taft Outcast compound, and have them get us enough food for a hundred people for the next two days."

Ty grinned and tapped John on the shoulder. "Megan, also have the A.A. machines make silk sheets, feather pillows, comforters, blankets, cotton towels, mountain bikes, fishing poles, frisbees, baseballs, gloves, and bats."

"Baseball. You want to play baseball?" John asked.

"Yep, the perfect game—home plate. Since we don't have to get the food, let's go to Louisville and get a couple cases of Pappy Van Winkle to make the party sizzle," Ty said, grinning.

John returned the grin. "Megan, how far is it to Louisville, Kentucky from here?"

"Two thousand miles."

"We can be there and back in four and a half hours."

"Megan, is there another S.S. ship close by we can use?"

"Yes, I can have it here in two minutes."

"Please do so," John said.

Ty grinned, slapping John's shoulder. "Perfect. We'll be fashionably late and party 'til we drop."

Another SS ship arrived and landed next to the fountain. The boarding ramp lowered. John and Ty boarded, sat in the cockpit, the ramp closed and the ship took off.

Ty looked out the window as they headed northeast. "This has been a hell of a ride, John Barber. If all goes well tonight, maybe I can find someone to go fishing with. That would be very nice."

John smiled. "I hope so, too. Remember what Terry was like when you met her? A child at heart, got sick from your food, and didn't get your jokes."

"Now she loves bourbon. I can wait; there's got to be

another one." Ty sighed. "I liked her from the start—brave and incredibly smart. She's going to make you a wonderful partner."

"What? I've had the love of my life. Stop stirring the pot, Ty Leggett," John said, somehow feeling defensive.

It's time to let Megan Barber go, Ty thought. "I don't mind taking it slow tonight. We'll start with good music, light drinks and see what happens. Maybe they'll surprise us," Ty said.

Five hours later, Ty and John returned to San Francisco, Terry was standing by the fountain. They landed, the boarding ramp lowered, and John and Ty stood at the edge of the ramp looking out. Their first sight was of Terry looking up at them. She looked radiant in white slacks, a light-blue blouse, and red sandals. Her hair was pulled back in a ponytail. She smiled, looking at John.

"She's wearing makeup," Ty whispered. "You are so screwed, John Barber."

John playfully tapped him with this left hand.

They walked down the boarding ramp to her.

She gave each of them a hug.

"Well, Terry Cheer you ready to party?" Ty asked.

"Yes, I am, Tyrus Leggett," she said, beaming.

"Where's everyone else?" John asked.

"The other ship just left."

"Let's go," Ty said.

They landed on the hill facing the valley across from the

swimming pool. The pool and grassy area were filled with people wading in the water and milling about the area.

"Oh my God!" Ty said. "I have died, and this is heaven. Look at all those women! I'm so going to get lucky." He laughed as he walked down the ramp out of the ship.

John laughed so hard he snorted air out his nose.

"Megan," Ty said, "have the androids remove the bourbon from the ship, set up a twenty-foot-long barbecue next to the pool, then fill it with charcoal and light it. Add a ten-foot-long bar filled with glasses, water bottles, assorted drinks, and lots of ice. Have an android take the cases of bourbon to the bar and instruct five additional androids how to bartend and serve drinks." Ty looked around. "Add some lounge chairs, five more side tables and put stacks of men's and women's bathing suits on the side tables. Lastly, build a music sound system around the pool. Play my favorite play list. Start with Louis Armstrong's 'What a Wonderful World,' then Corinne Bailey Rae's 'Put Your Records On,' followed by Joan Armatrading, 'Love and Affection,' and finish that set with Aretha Franklin's 'You Send Me.'"

"What time should the music start?" Megan asked.

"I'll let you know," he said. He turned to look at John and Terry. "You ready? Let's party!"

"Yes, I am," John said.

An android arrived carrying two stacks of bathing suits.

Ty and John each grabbed a bathing suit and ran off behind the pool house to change, leaving their clothes behind. They ran to the pool. John pulled off his shirt and jumped in, yelling, "Yahooooo!"

Ty laughed out loud, thinking, *That's the John Megan married.*

Terry quickly followed and jumped into the shallow end. Still grinning, Ty stripped off his shirt and jumped in next to John and Terry.

"I feel young," he shouted.

Two hours later, Ty was standing by the barbecue grilling chicken, steaks, and baked potatoes. Forty people were standing around him, watching. John joined him, holding a glass of bourbon, his second. His cheeks were red, and he was grinning. He clicked glasses with Ty.

"Megan, it's time to start my music playlist," Ty said.

Satchmo's "What A Wonderful World" came on, followed by Corinne Bailey Rae's "Put Your Records On." Everyone stopped and turned their head toward the music, listening. They didn't know what they were hearing, only that it moved something inside them.

"What's is that sound called?" asked a woman standing next to Ty.

"Music—great music," he answered. "It frees your soul, and sets love free."

She listened and smiled. "My name is Alice."

"Perfect," Ty said, grinning. *My first girlfriend,* he thought.

Aretha Franklin's 'You Send Me' came on. The first two bars of the piano rang out.

"Megan, double the volume," Ty said.

The opening piano of *'You Send Me'* engulfed them all.

John looked across the barbecue and saw Terry standing by the pool, talking to Arnold. He walked to her and gently took hold of her right hand, and they began to slow dance.

Ty was watching. "Megan, play it again," he said.

Ty left the bunkhouse the next morning and saw sleeping people lying everywhere. "Now that's a party," he said to himself. He went to an android, and said, "Clean up here and inside the facility. Then set up for breakfast."

He jumped into the pool and floated on his back.

John appeared a few minutes later and stood at the edge. "You look happy," he said.

"Yes, I am," Ty replied. "Last night was perfect. I feel young, and I think I'm in love."

John put a funny look on his face. "With whom?"

"I haven't narrowed it down, but Alice is in first place."

John snorted, laughing out loud.

"How about Mr. John Barber? I saw you and little Miss Cheer disappear together."

John looked down at his feet.

Ty laughed.

People started to move about; to a person, they were very hungover.

"Rookies," John said. "Megan, make injectables of Bright-Mind with extra Juna Root, and have the androids administer it to everyone not feeling well. Doesn't matter that they've never heard of it. They'll like how it makes them feel." John smiled. "It's their first time. Might as well make them feel perfect." He jumped into the pool and swam to Ty. "Yeah, fun feels good," he said, remembering their conversation from before.

Ty laughed. "You bet your ass, and we're going to have a long life enjoying that feeling."

Terry arrived at the pool and jumped in, waded to John, and gently kissed him on the lips and wrapped her arms around his shoulders. "Well, Mr. John Barber, what's the plan?"

"Breakfast, hike, baseball, swimming, dinner, and more dancing."

Terry's eyes glistened, her expression satisfied and loving. The celebration of survival continued.

THIRTY-FIVE

A week later, Ty, John, and Terry were at Terry's San Francisco home having an old-fashioned breakfast: eggs, toast, bacon, orange juice, and black coffee.

"Well," Terry said, "what's—"

She cut her question short because jet-black darkness encased them and seconds later, the three were sitting side by side in a cool, colorless, and odorless room. It happened so fast they didn't have time to even gasp.

"What just happened?" Ty whispered.

Silence from fear.

The lights came on. Shocked, they didn't move a muscle.

They all darted their eyes back and forth, searching the room. The walls were white and smooth-looking. There were no windows or doors. They were sitting in the same chairs as before, but the table was different: It was suddenly ten feet long, warm to the touch, but of normal height.

Sitting next to Terry on his left, Ty bent down to look

underneath the table and quickly popped back up. "There're no legs."

John rubbed his hand through his hair and took a deep breath. The floor looked exactly like the walls and ceiling: soft white and smooth. There were no seams or corners joining everything together. The room was well lit, with no shadows or source of light. The silence was overpowering with not a whisper, hum, or vibration.

"If I was alone, I'd be terrified. Please don't let it go dark," Terry whispered.

John gently touched her hand with his left hand fingertips.

Ty rubbed his palms across the top of the table; it was warm and smooth, and his fingers didn't stick, regardless how hard he pressed down.

"This is surreal," Ty whispered. "Where are we? And why are we here?"

John leaned slightly forward and turned to look at him. Their eyes met. John's expression matched Ty's: surprised fear.

Terry whispered, "Wha—" but again stopped speaking, this time because, without a sound, the wall in front of them vanished and three human-looking people appeared there, standing and facing them: two males flanking a female.

There was an eerie moment of silence before the trio stepped into the room.

The woman in the middle was wearing a white blouse, gray slacks, and white sandals. The man to her right was wearing a button-down, baby-blue, long-sleeved dress shirt, white khaki pants, and comfortable, soft-looking brown shoes. The man on the other side of the woman was wearing a white, long-sleeved business shirt, blue-jean type pants, and the same soft-looking shoes.

"Nice shoes," Ty said, looking at the woman.

"Thank you, Mr. Leggett," she said in a pleasant voice, with no accent or discernable diction.

"Where are we?" Terry asked.

"First contact, Miss Cheer," the woman said.

"That's a non-answer answer," Ty said.

"Yes, it is," the woman replied.

"What do you want?" John asked.

Without speaking they sat across the table from John, Terry, and Ty.

Ty again bent down and looked under the table; they were sitting on the same type of chairs. Ty sat back up and looked at John. "Those chairs weren't there a moment ago."

The woman smiled. "Please do not feel uncomfortable."

"That's not helping," Terry said.

The women smiled and glanced at her companions.

"You're the only sentient species we've encountered in five hundred thousand years who've defeated an artificial form of life," the man in the blue shirt said.

"Are you organic?" John asked.

"Yes," the man answered.

"Fully?" Ty asked.

"Yes," the woman answered.

"Why are we here?" Ty asked.

"To celebrate your victory and make first contact," the man wearing the blue shirt said.

"Maybe, but you're still not telling us everything." John rubbed his hand through his hair.

Ty glanced at John. "I feel the same thing. So, let's start with the basics. Who are you, and where are we?" he asked, using his authoritative presidential voice.

"We are from the Perseus galaxy cluster," he said.

"Impossible," John said.

"It's true, Doctor Barber," the woman said.

"Megan, how far away is the Perseus cluster?" John whispered.

No reply.

"Megan is not with you, Doctor Barber. The answer to your question is two hundred forty million light years," the woman answered.

John did the math in his head. *Impossible. That's four squared, times fifteen, times the speed of light.*

"We travel through space extraordinarily fast, Doctor Barber," the woman went on. "It's complicated. Your Einstein was half right. Think of a wave, string theory, and dark energy inflation."

John shook his head, not convinced.

"What do you want?" Ty asked.

The woman sighed softly. "Nothing. We are here to invite the three of you to our planet to celebrate our family's victory over ordained death."

"We're not going anywhere," Terry stated.

"Why do you want us to go with you?" Ty asked.

"You're the only species we've encountered that has survived the ascension of an artificial intelligence."

"Yes, your friend here already said that, so how about explaining?" Ty said.

"A million years ago," the woman replied, "our species created an omnipotent artificial life-form. Sadly, we did not have a Doctor John Barber to protect us, so our survival was an accident." She gave a small smile. "Our survival was happenstance. One of the last three ships transporting the final colonists of Aelitians—that's what we are called—to a sister planet in the next solar system was disabled when it was struck by a mega flare. That bolt of energy disrupted the ship's operating systems. During the repair on that planet, we learned about the genocide of our race, and unlike on Earth, we only had ten thousand living Aelitians left."

"I'm sorry," Terry whispered, looking at the woman.

"In our search for a new home, our ships entered this solar system, and unfortunately, one crashed on an outer planet moon," the man in the blue shirt said.

"And we found it and the safe it contained," John said.

The woman smiled. "Yes. That was an oversight; the captain thought it was useless."

"It's been destroyed, along with the safe," John said.

"Why didn't you return to your planet after the discovery?" Ty asked.

"Because the genocidal machine that controls our planet will always be master of our galaxy. We tried to enter another Branespace—but we failed. We did not have enough energy. Which led us here," the man in the blue shirt said.

They didn't fight. Why not? Ty thought.

"I'm not familiar with the term Branespace," John said.

"Multi-universes encapsulated within a separate membrane," the woman said.

John leaned slightly forward, glanced at Ty, looking confused and suspicious. "You're saying you're from a different universe?"

"No, we failed in that effort," the woman said.

"Something's off," John said. "The more you say, the more questions I have to—"

"Well," Ty cut in, "my questions began the moment I found myself sitting at a floating table, talking to people who claim they're from another galaxy, possibly a universe. Who, I must add, look like me—"

"We're cousins, thanks to your DNA," the woman said.

A puzzled expression crossed Ty's face. "And," he continued, "surprise, surprise, the same technique used to murder us was used to murder you. That's a huge coincidence given the million-year spread." Ty glanced at Terry. "And in my experience, that doesn't wash."

"May I continue?" the woman asked.

Ty nodded reluctantly.

"The machine's solution to kill ten billion Aelitians and three billion humans was the same because it was logical, simple, and clean. And to your thought"—she smiled—"Mr. Leggett, why didn't we return home and fight? We wanted to survive, so we fled." She looked at John. "Like you, Doctor Barber, we eventually felt it was a mistake to hide. As it turned out, a mistake that saved all of us."

Ty's eyes popped open, and he looked at John. "They can read our minds."

"Not us, President Leggett, our crystals." She smiled.

We need a moment to think, Terry thought, feeling overwhelmed.

"We agree," the woman said.

THIRTY-SIX

The next instant, they were back in Terry's home, sitting around the table. They looked at each other, shocked. John took in a nose full of air, smelling the San Francisco salt air. Ty touched the table, glanced under it, and looked around the apartment. Terry stood and stepped away from the table for a moment, reassuring herself it was real.

"Each day I'm here gets stranger. What the hell just happened?" Ty asked.

Terry sat back down across the table from Ty and John.

"I think they've got a problem," John said, "and our meeting didn't have much to do with our eliminating Pandora and getting our freedom."

"I could feel her listening to my thoughts, and I got the impression she was scared," Terry said.

"So did I," Ty said.

"Regardless," John said, "that room was lifeless. The air was odor-free, and I couldn't smell them, or anything for that matter. If I hadn't touched your hand"—he glanced at Terry —

"and felt it, I would've been convinced it was happening in my head."

"I believed her, and their story," Terry said, "but I agree something's wrong. They need us. *Something* is killing them."

"That can't be possible," John said.

"We'll find out next time we meet," Ty said.

"I don't want to go through that again. If we meet again, it has to be on Earth," John said.

"How are you going to arrange that?" Terry asked.

"I think he just did. If they can read our minds, they certainly can hear us talk," Ty said.

"I want a little warning, too," Terry said. "I hate feeling sick to my stomach." She touched John's hand. "But now what do we do?"

"Megan, can you explain what just happened to us?" John asked.

"You disappeared," Megan answered.

"Where to?" John asked.

"I don't know."

"They're hiding something. Which is why Megan wasn't included," Ty said. "Shit, I thought we were through with all the drama."

John rubbed his hand though his hair and leaned back in his chair, looking toward the bay.

"There's nothing we can do," Ty said. "They know every-thing—us, nothing. The ball is in their court."

"What ball, what court, and what does all that mean?" Terry asked, frustrated.

"It means their rules, their plans, and their timeline," Ty said.

"Well, we don't know, so let's do what we already decided: start rebuilding civilization," John said.

Terry took a deep breath. "I agree."

"If they separate us in the next meeting, we don't deal," Ty said.

Ty and John stayed at the table.

"A million years of history," John said, "and they travel through space in an instant. Imagine the power of that.... We're ants to these people."

"Let's hope they smoke pot and like bourbon," Ty said, laughing.

John laughed, too.

What's pot? Terry wondered.

"Does anyone really care we're not alone in the universe?" John asked.

"It has no meaning to me," Terry answered.

"Ty?"

"It did. At one point, I hoped little green men would come down, take all the bad guys, cure cancer, feed the poor, and play great jazz." He laughed. "Now that I've met some of them, they just presented different problems."

"Yeah. Most of those things happened, except great jazz," John said.

"And I agree with Terry," Ty said. "No one here will care we're not alone."

"They seem to care, though," John said.

"That came across, cousins and all," Ty said.

"Do you buy it?" John asked.

Ty shrugged. "Why lie? No point, so it must be true."

"She did seem thankful and happy we survived," Terry said.

Ty snorted with a slight laugh. "Cousins separated by a million years. That's mind-blowing."

"When this is over," Terry said, "we're not going to separate, right? You two are going to stay with me?"

"I won't leave San Francisco," Ty said.

She looked at John, her eyes holding a glimmer of hopefulness. "What about you?"

"I'll always be at your side."

"I like that." Terry smiled.

Ty smiled, thinking, *You're screwed, John Barber. She's in love.*

"Wow, that's weird. I just heard a voice in my head," John said.

"Whose voice?" Ty asked.

"The woman we just met," John answered. "She asked us to meet them tonight at seven p.m., in the plaza."

"Why there, I wonder?" Ty asked.

"That's where our freedom started," Terry said.

They all looked at each other.

"Second contact?" Ty asked.

John glanced at his watch: 9:45 a.m.

"What's your plan?" Terry asked.

"It's almost ten. We have plenty of time," Ty said.

"What are you thinking?" John asked.

"Well, off the top of my head, and I know it's a little dumb, but I'd like to show them the best we Earthlings have."

"I want to bathe, change clothes. I'll meet you at noon to help," Terry said.

"That sounds good," John said. "I'll—"

"Would you like to change now?" Terry interrupted.

"I-I could use fresh clothes," he mumbled.

"What about you, Ty?" she asked.

"No, I'll take the pod back to the plaza and change later. Can I have Megan? I've got some ideas, and I'll need her help."

"Sure." John took the crystal out of his pocket and handed it to Ty.

"Thanks. I'll get started," Ty said. "You two get ready. I've got this. See you in a couple hours."

Ty stood and left Terry's home. He felt good, happy. *Nice. Very nice. This is going to be wonderful.*

"Megan," he said, "find Arnold. I'll need his help. Have him meet me at the plaza." He got into the pod. "Megan, take me to Crystal Plaza."

A moment later, he landed next to the fountain. He got out of the pod and hurried to the Madonna Inn android.

"Megan, activate this android. Have it look at me."

Megan did.

Its eyes shifted and looked at Ty, who said, "This is what you're going to do. Send the following instructions to all the San Francisco androids. Have them set up a twenty-by-twenty-foot tent there." He pointed toward Hays Street and back to the fountain.

Arnold arrived and stood next to Ty.

"Good to see you. I need some help. Just one second, and I'll explain what's going on," Ty said. "Megan, next have the androids put a ten-foot-long mahogany conference table with six matching chairs, three on each side. Have everything sitting on top of an Egyptian rug that covers three-quarters of the tent."

"It will be done," Megan said.

Ty looked at Arnold. "We're setting up for a meeting with some special people. I'll explain everything later. For now, just follow me and please do as I ask."

Ty and Arnold walked around the plaza; thirty minutes later, they went into the newly made tent.

"Megan, can you take over for the Madonna Inn android from here on out?"

"Yes, I can."

"Perfect, that will make things easier. Instruct the androids

384

to add plants and flowers around the tent's interior perimeter. Let's start with putting some art on the tent walls."

"What's 'art'?" Arnold asked.

"Man's created beauty."

Arnold looked confused.

"You'll see." Ty smiled. "Megan, start with the Van Gogh—

"The what...?" Arnold interrupted.

"Megan knows." Ty turned to face Arnold. "Van Gogh was an artist. He painted beautiful pictures."

Arnold looked confused.

"You'll get it when you see it. Megan, get Van Gogh's self-portrait. Then Claude Monet's *Impression, Sunrise,* and the *Artist's Garden at Giverny.* Paul Klee's *Girl with Jug.*

"Let's see," Ty looked around the tent, "okay, then Toulouse-Lautrec's poster, *Moulin Rouge: La Goulue.* Next, Renoir's *Luncheon of the Boating Party.* Cézanne's *Les Joueurs de Cartes.* Lastly, Leonardo da Vinci's *Mona Lisa,* and *The Last Supper.*"

Ty looked around the room. "Megan, recreate Michelangelo's *David.*"

He looked at Arnold. "When that statue is completed, I want to put it inside the tent, facing the entrance and ten feet from the doorway."

"What's a statue?"

"Again, you'll know it when you see it. Megan, add Artemisia Gentileschi's *Judith Slaying Holofernes,* on the wall to the right of the table. And hang Alexander Calder's *Lobster Trap and Fish Tail* in the center of the tent."

Satisfied, he left the tent to sit by the fountain, enjoying the warmth of the sun. He watched everything come together. An hour later, he returned to the tent. Arnold was standing in the center of the tent looking at the art. He was smiling.

Ty stood next to him and smiled. *Beautiful,* he thought.

"Now you know what art is, right, Arnold?"

"Yes, my favorite is that statue." He pointed.

"It is amazing, and at one time, the world was filled with such treasures," Ty said. He looked around, and the room felt a little warm. "Megan, make sure the tent has plenty of ventilation, add a slight rose fragrance, and make sure there's plenty of light. Then set up holographic cameras inside the tent and prepare for a worldwide presentation."

He tapped Arnold's shoulder and said, "Arnold, please put pitchers of water and cut-glass crystal glasses at each place setting."

Ty moved over to the tent entrance.

Perfect, the best of what we are, he thought.

"Megan, recreate the worldwide fireworks display of the other night. Use Maurice Ravel's 'Bolèro' as the buildup and play Ludwig van Beethoven's Symphony No. 9 in D minor, Opus one twenty-five, with the Fourth Movement's 'Ode to Joy' choral finale during the last twenty-eighty minutes of the fireworks. Lastly, activate the stage for a presentation by us just before the fireworks. Have everything ready by seven-thirty tonight. Megan, you got it?"

"Yes."

"Okay. what time is it now?"

"Noon."

Ty returned to the fountain and relaxed in the sun. "John is going to love this," he whispered to himself.

Two hours later, Ty, standing at the opening to the tent, looked across the plaza and saw Terry's pod land on Hays Street. Both she and John got out of the pod and walked onto the plaza. He smiled; they were holding hands. They reached the tent and met Ty at the opening.

"Looks like you've got everything under control, Ty," John said, grinning.

"All thanks to Megan. On that front, we need to power that up." Ty pointed toward Pandora.

"Speaking of which, let's refer to it as the phone booth," John said.

"I like that," Ty said. "Perfect, because that's what it's become."

"What's a phone booth?" Terry asked.

"A box that contacts people," John said.

"And it was used to pile teenagers into," Ty said, snickering.

John shook his head, grinning, remembering a photograph of twenty-five people stuck inside one.

"Terry can use the phone booth to announce to the world what's about to happen tonight so no one is frightened," John said.

"Do you believe the Aelitians will show at seven?" Terry asked.

"No idea," Ty said. "All we can do is hope we're not being played as soon-to-be-dead suckers."

"What's a sucker?" Terry asked

"A person who is easily tricked into believing something they know is impossible," Ty said.

"John's a sucker?" she asked.

Ty laughed and snorted air into his nose.

"I'll go help Arnold," John said, walking away, shaking his head.

"Terry, come with me," Ty said. He led her into the finished tent.

"Wow," she said, "this is beautiful. What are these things on the walls and the hanging thing above the table called?"

"Examples of humankind's best expression of beauty. Together, they're called 'art.' Paintings are on the walls. The carved, marble human body"—he pointed at David—"is a statue. Lastly, the thing hanging from the ceiling is a mobile."

"They're so beautiful. Who made them?" she asked.

"People, before machines. Hopefully, one of the many classes our new world will teach will be art."

"What are classes?" she asked.

"In education, it means segments of learning. In the beginning, the Chinese focused on talent, the Romans and Greeks on subjects, and all of them taught what they felt everyone should know. Art and philosophy were very important to both peoples."

"Who are the Chinese, Romans, and Greeks?"

"I'll tell you later; it's not important now."

"Okay, and you better not lie to me. What's philosophy?"

"It's the study of our existence in the hope of understanding truth, and the philosophers, the people answering those questions, failed the human race by not forcing limits on A.I."

"What do you mean they failed?"

"They didn't stand up. They didn't ask why. Why kill God and replace love with computers? They never said stop and billions died."

"What's acting?" she asked.

"The hardest art form, conveying all the emotions people feel."

"Why would anyone want to learn that?"

"So other people understand what someone else is feeling, good or bad."

"Do you know how to act?"

"I wasn't good at it."

"Can John act?"

"No. What you see is what he's feeling. He is what I call genuine."

"Good. I like genuine."

Finished with the shell of Pandora, John entered the tent and smiled. "Wow, Ty, you outdid yourself. This is magnificent. What a great expression of humanity." He stepped up to Ty and shook his hand. "Someday soon, I hope we locate the originals."

"If bourbon is still around, I'm sure we'll find those treasures," Ty said.

John walked around the room slowly, studying the artwork. When he finished, he sat at the conference table, filled a glass of water, and took a long sip. Ty and Terry joined him.

John leaned back in the chair, rubbed his hand through his hair and sighed. "I hope this isn't some last laugh—and *Zzzppnt!* —we disappear."

"How can you think that?" Terry asked. "Nothing's that cruel."

"Captain Robert A. Davis was," John replied.

"He's dead," Ty said. "Along with everyone who created it."

John glanced at his watch. "Almost seven."

There was not a sound, the normal breeze was still, and the air was warm. John took a deep breath. *I pray it's over and the guardian angels are free,* he thought.

Ty closed his eyes, bent his head, and thought, *Our Father who art in heaven—*

BOOM!

The sound was shocking. The tent disappeared, and everything went pitch black, no stars.

"John!" Terry screamed, reaching out, hoping to touch his arm.

The next instant, the sky from horizon to horizon filled with colors: red, purple, blue, green, pink, orange, yellow—all twisting around each other to form a tornado of colors. Then THANK YOU appeared in every language, filling the black sky.

WE ARE THE AELITIANS. YOUR COUSINS FROM ANOTHER SOLAR SYSTEM. THANK YOU FOR SAVING US.

The next instant, the three people John, Terry, and Ty had met previously were sitting across from them at the conference table.

"Was that cool enough, Tyrus Leggett?" the woman asked.

"Yes, that was very cool," Ty said.

"Megan, display this meeting worldwide," John said.

"That's not necessary, Doctor Barber. We are doing that in every language and everywhere on Earth," the woman said.

John smiled. "Okay."

"My name is Zareena, and my title translated into Earthling is The Wise," she said in a soft, bright voice. "We are the descendants of the Aelitian people."

The man sitting to her right, wearing a dark blue, high buttoned-up collared shirt, said, "My name is Claci. My title is The Guide," he said in a clear, tenor-level voice.

The other man sitting to Zareena's left, dressed the same as Clactoo, except for his shirt being dark green, said, "My name is Zarkow, and my title is The Sentinel." His voice was slightly deeper and richer than Claci.

"We have chosen this time to make second contact because

you have reached the final stage of development and are free to remain human," Zareena said.

The space above Earth exploded into the light of an unimaginable number of shooting stars. A different color for each star. Music fell from above: indiscernible sounds never heard before; soft, with high tones, and a deep, rich texture. Its rhythmic beat was hypnotic, and built slowly in intensity.

Scenes of human development appeared. The first vision was of a small creature walking along a creek. "Lucy, *Australopithecus*" was written above it, followed by another creature: *Homo habilis*, then *Homo erectus*, followed by *Homo neanderthalensis*, and finally *Homo sapiens*.

The sky went dark again; then John Barber appeared, smiling, with his name above his head.

People around the world began to stand and cheer as the music got louder. Fifteen minutes later, the music reached a dramatic, ground-shaking crescendo.

The final scene was of Terry and John hugging, and THE WORLD CRYSTAL IS TERMINATED appeared above them.

Billions of people stood, waved, and smiled at the words: LOVE FROM THE AELITIAN PEOPLE.

The sky returned to normal, the moon and stars reappeared, and John, Terry, and Ty could see themselves sitting across the table from the three Aelitians.

Terry leaned in next to him and kissed John on the cheek. She whispered, "Thank you."

"Yes, thank you, Doctor Barber," Zareena said. "You have also given us hope that we, too, can overcome the impossible and survive." She smiled.

"What do you mean?" Ty asked.

"Our history was not, as I said before, as fortunate as yours.

The Crystal we created murdered all but ten thousand Aelitians. We escaped into your solar system using dark energy from a string to hyper-inflate our speed and bend space time."

"What?" Ty asked.

"They went very fast and shorted the distance," John said.

"We escaped, and two ships survived," she said.

"We searched for a suitable planet to colonize," Clactoo said. "It was during that search we discovered Earth. It was perfect for us, as your species was very primitive, not human yet, and our technology prevented the environment and animals from killing us. We began rebuilding our species. We never intended on making Earth a permanent home. For the same reasons, we did not interfere in your development and self-destruction. We lived on Earth until the Neanderthals appeared four hundred thousand years ago. We interacted with humanity until the time of the Egyptians, then we left for good."

"What do you mean, interacted?" John asked.

"Via DNA, Doctor Barber. We were on the edge of extinction and human DNA has kept us viable for the last five hundred millennium. Today, we are human, not Aelitians. We are human," he said.

"That explains why we look alike," Ty said.

"Did you alter us?" John asked.

"No, you are the result of inbreeding with Neanderthals and interbreeding thereafter. We did leave some influences as a sign of our appreciation," he answered.

"What?" John asked.

"Fuxi and Imhotep to name two," he said.

John laughed and looked at Ty. "Imhotep means, 'I come in peace.'"

"Now that's funny," Ty said, looking at Zarkow.

392

Terry looked confused, not understanding the reference to science fiction movies. She looked at John.

"I'll tell you later," he whispered.

"You used the expression 'viable.' Are you still viable?" Ty asked.

"No," Zareena said.

"This first contact is beginning to feel duplicitous," Ty said, frowning.

John rubbed his hand through his hair. *Oh God,* he thought. He glanced at Ty with a concerned expression.

"It is not what you are thinking, Doctor Barber," Zareena said. "We are here to celebrate and for a brief time share life. There is nothing humanity can offer us. Our fate is sealed."

Silence.

"What do you mean, your fate is sealed?" John asked.

"There is nothing left of us to discover. We have searched four millennia looking for advanced civilizations and have found none. We believe all sentient life-forms self-destruct or carbon life-forms evolve into synthetic."

She stopped speaking and looked directly at John Barber. "Until you, John Barber. You have given us hope and courage. You, Terry, and Ty did it. Human life will move forward, free from ordained death. There are countless wonders ahead, discoveries you can't imagine. To our joy, it was humanity who brought us full circle: You saved us with your DNA previously, and now with your determination to survive."

Silence.

"What comes next?" Ty asked.

"A celebration." Zareena said with a grin.

"After that?" Ty asked.

"We will leave this galaxy and correct a mistake, just like you did."

Ty slowly nodded, understanding the battle ahead, thinking, *I pray you win.*

Terry glanced at Ty, then looked at Zareena. *It must be terrifying. We've both lost so much,* she thought. "After you win, please return," she said with a welcoming smile.

Zareena returned the smile. "Terry, your strength and growing love will redeem the past."

Terry bowed her head, feeling emotions she couldn't describe yet, but she did recognize she was calm and content to be in this moment.

Ty looked at Terry and John. "I see an epic party at the Madonna Inn and a future for humanity." He grinned, happy and relaxed.

The three of them stood, awed by the moment and beauty around them.

Terry turned to face John. Her eyes were soft; her expression glowed with love. She leaned close and gently touched his hand with her fingertips. "A future," she said, and softly kissed him on his lips. "Maybe it's time we gave Megan a new name."

"Absolutely," he said.

ALSO BY JAMES BARRETT GRUBBS

John Barber: A Tale of Two Times

In book one of the series, John Barber, a brilliant scientist begins the final chapter of his working career running a top-secret U.S. government laboratory created to kill gain-of function viruses. His passion, other than his wife and two children, is to find a cure for the genetic disorder progeria which ages children viciously fast; his sister died of old age at thirteen. He discovers instead the impossible.

There is nothing more terrifying than reality. What you are about to read can happen; not all, just the scariest parts. Murder, sex, hate, and perfection drive humanity today, not just in the future.

Once, and only once in a life, timing joins fate, seizes opportunity, and a political campaign is born.

For Tyrus Leggett, the former FBI Director, this moment is now. Leaving behind one of the most powerful roles in America, Ty is appointed as United States Senator from Alabama and thrust into a fierce special election to secure his seat.

Standing in his way is Jeffrey Ullman, a master manipulator with a carefully crafted country persona designed to win hearts and votes. As Ty's campaign fights to bring integrity and experience to the forefront, Ullman's team is willing to stop at nothing to secure victory.

The White Lion delves deep into the heart of an intense political battle, offering an insider's view of the contrasting worlds of two very different candidates. One wields character and dedication; the other brandishes wealth, influence, and the support of the Washington elite.

Who wins? The President of the United States, the Governor of Alabama, the greedy state Senator, or the future? Life and campaigns are not fair; The White Lion is no different.